They spanned the heavens above— and dominated the earth below...

THE FATHER

Herman Gold. He wasn't meant to till the earth. He was meant to soar like an eagle. He built an empire of the air. And it shone with the name Gold Aviation.

THE SON

Steven Gold. A fighting flyer ace who amassed kill after kill against the Japanese as one of the legendary Flying Tigers. He was his father's true heir—and bitterest rival.

THE DAUGHTER

Susan Gold. Passionate, rebellious, she felt the bloodline of a dynasty in her veins. She defiantly fell in love with a flying man—and, in the fires of war, made the ultimate sacrifice.

THE PARTNER

Tim Campbell. As a young banker, his early faith in Herman Gold lcd to a pact that madc his fortune. Then came the decisive showdown with Gold that only cunning could win.

THE PILOT

Blaize Green. The dashing aristocrat feared only one thing—the intimate touch of the woman he loved. When a new war came, he racked up an ace's score —until his luck gave out.

WINGS

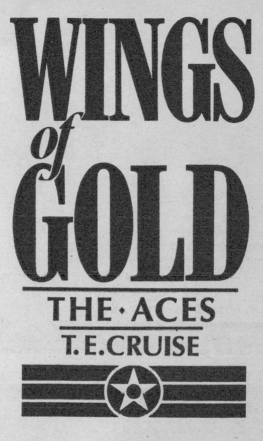

WINGS
of
GOLD

THE · ACES

T. E. CRUISE

POPULAR LIBRARY

An Imprint of Warner Books, Inc.

A Warner Communications Company

POPULAR LIBRARY EDITION

Copyright © 1988 by Warner Books, Inc.
All rights reserved.

Popular Library® and the fanciful P design are registered trademarks of
Warner Books, Inc.

Cover design by Mike Stromberg
Cover illustration by Mark Skolsky

Popular Library books are published by
Warner Books, Inc.
666 Fifth Avenue
New York, N.Y. 10103

Ⓦ A Warner Communications Company

Printed in the United States of America

First Printing: June, 1988

10 9 8 7 6 5 4 3 2 1

WINGS *of* GOLD

THE · ACES

BOOK I:
1918–1920

GRAND GERMAN LIGHTNING OFFENSIVE
PROPHECIES VICTORY FOR THE FATHERLAND

31 March 1918—
Sieg Heil! Sieg Heil! Courageous German soldiers, your comrades have driven deep into Allied territory!

The Imperial Second, Seventh, Seventeenth, and Eighteenth Armies, led by the Kaiser's Hammer General Ludendorff, have made spectacular gains against the British between Arras and the Oise River, along the Somme.

Operation Michael began on 21 March, when over six thousand artillery cannons devastated the British trenches with gas and explosives. The heroic Prussian Fist of our advancing infantry met little resistance as it confronted and crushed the paralyzed British Third and Fifth Armies, thanks, in part, to lightning advance strafing and bombing runs executed by the Infantreiflieger Schlastas.

Top cover for the operation was supplied by Jagdgeschwader 1, led by the national hero, Der röte Kampfflieger, Rettmeister Manfred von Richthofen. High above the noise and smoke-filled valley of the Somme the majestic, scarlet-tinged Jastas of J.G. 1 cleared the skies of Allied fighters in grand, cartwheeling dogfights.

Germans rejoice! Victory is within sight!

Der Soldaten Freund

Chapter 1

(One)
Jagdgeschwader 1, Imperial Air Service
Cappy, France
12 April 1918

Sergeant Hermann Goldstein scanned the lead article of the tattered issue of *The Soldier's Friend* as he waited in the ready room for an orderly to bring him his flight gear. When his gear arrived, Goldstein set the newspaper aside and pulled his tan, fur-lined flight coverall over his field uniform. The other pilots had strapped on sidearms, but Goldstein didn't wear one. He was a terrible pistol shot. His airplane was his weapon.

He put on his fur-lined flying boots, gloves, and his well-worn, cordovan leather helmet. He shrugged into his leather safety harness and grabbed his flight goggles. At the moment he was sweating, but at 6,000 meters the frigid wind would cut like a wire whip through the layers of protective clothing. He tore the front page off the Ministry of Propaganda rag he'd been reading, crumpled it, and used the "Grand Prophecies of Victories" to polish the lenses of his goggles as he left the ready room. At least he was putting the scrap to a far more honorable end than its mates would find in the latrine.

Outside, the sky was blue, broken by banks of puffy gray cumulus clouds. It was cool enough to dry the sweat on Goldstein's face. He let the balled newspaper scrap flutter away in the brisk April wind that buffeted the fourteen-color-splashed Fokker Dr. I triplanes on the muddy ready line.

Each pilot had his airplane painted according to his own taste. The Herr Rittmeister Richthofen's solid red triplane was glorious, but Goldstein thought his own gaudy Fokker "tripe" was the prettiest of all the scouts in Herr Cavalry Captain Richthofen's Hunting Echelon. Like all the fighters that belonged to Richthofen's J.G. 1, Goldstein's machine bore Herr Rittmeister's trademark scarlet hue everywhere but on the sides of its fuselage and its wings, where it was painted sky blue. On both rear side quarters were large, bright yellow ovals, each showing a centaur—a mythological creature, half man and half horse—rearing up to do battle. Just forward of the centaurs, and on her wings and tail, she wore black Iron Crosses, edged in white.

Goldstein swung himself up and into his Fokker's worn bucket seat, buckled himself in, and then signaled to his ground crew that he was ready to start his engine. All around Goldstein was the sputter and roar of the other Fokkers as their engines caught.

Goldstein checked that his machine's gas and air valves were full open and that its ignition switch was off; then he watched as his chief mechanic, Corporal Heiner Froehlig, began to swing his machine's propeller. Normally it took two men to turn the prop. But Froehlig, a stout, balding, middle-aged man with a walrus moustache, prided himself on having the strength to do it by himself.

As the mechanic cranked the prop, Goldstein gradually cut off his Fokker's air valve until the engine had sucked in enough gas.

"Contact!" the mechanic shouted, peering at Goldstein from around the side of the Fokker's nose.

"Contact!" Goldstein yelled back, and flicked on the ignition with his gloved finger.

The mechanic gave one final heave on the prop and quickly retreated. The engine coughed to life in a smelly blue cloud of burnt castor oil. The Fokker's mahogany prop picked up speed and whirled itself into a blur.

Goldstein scanned his four instruments: gas and oil gauges; a tachometer and a compass. He settled his left hand on the throttle and his right on the control stick, and waited. It would be a few minutes before it was his turn to taxi off the ready line.

He killed time by wiggling the stick and kicking the rudder bar to make sure his ailerons and rudder were working. He knew they were. Every morning he performed a maintenance check on his machine. Goldstein knew that it irked the mechanics to have him double-checking their work, but he liked to spend time tinkering with his machine. Sometimes when he was done working, he would just sit in the plane for the sheer enjoyment of it.

The Fokker was so graceful and powerful. It was everything that he was not.

Goldstein was nineteen and a half years old. He had freckles, light blue eyes, not much of a beard (he had to shave only twice a week), and close-cropped rust-colored hair that had already begun to recede from his high forehead. He was tall to be a flier, almost too tall to fold himself into the cramped cockpit of his fighter scout, but he was also very thin, and that was good. The lighter the sum total of man and flying machine, the higher the ceiling the partnership could achieve. Greater altitude translated into tactical advantage in battle flying.

To stay skin and bones, Goldstein dieted and abstained from alcohol. The Fokker Dr. I had a fast rate of climb and excellent maneuverability, but a mediocre top speed and service ceiling. By keeping his own weight down, and making a few modifications to his machine's 110-horsepower, Oberursel nine-cylinder rotary engine, Goldstein was able to both increase his speed and coax extra altitude out of his Fokker.

He was elated to be among those chosen for today's patrol. For the past week fog and wind-driven rain had grounded all flights, making everyone restless and edgy. "Pilot's Sunshine" they liked to call the bad weather at other aerodromes, because when flying conditions were impossible a pilot could drink too much and then sleep late the next morning. That was not the way it was at J.G. 1, where the pilots were always eager for a scrape to increase their scores. If a pilot wasn't that way, the Herr Rittmeister shipped him right out.

This afternoon at lunch it was announced that the Weather Service had forecast clearing skies by late afternoon. "If there is enough blue to make a shirt, we fly," Herr Rittmeister had proclaimed from his place at the head of the main table, and had gone on to say that he would lead the hunt.

Goldstein and the other fliers had cheered. It was good to see their leader smiling. The Herr Rittmeister had recently been depressed. The Herr Cavalry captain was being forced to fly less due to his administrative duties and the demands of his extensive propaganda tours back home. In addition, Operation Michael—and its follow-up, assault Operation Georgette, begun on April 7—had not been as successful as the Ministry of Propaganda's newsrags wanted the rank and file to believe. Despite the facts that the Russians had disposed of their Czar and there was no longer an eastern front, there was still the inclement weather to contend with and the fact that the Allies were putting up a stiff land and air resistance. The German advance, meanwhile, had bogged down as it outran its own artillery and supply support, and as the Fatherland's soldiers, pushed too far and stretched too thin, were defeated by their own exhaustion.

When Michael began, J.G. 1 had been stationed at Léchelle, a comfortable, permanent aerodrome the British had only recently vacated. That first week J.G. 1's four Jastas flew constantly. It had been the most intense period of fighting in Goldstein's ten months at the front, and the hunting had been good. Herr Rittmeister Richthofen's circus was then ordered farther west to keep pace with Herr General Ludendorff's advancing infantry. J.G. 1 had packed itself up onto its horse-drawn lorries and hurried to this muddy, barren field a few miles north of Cappy, a small, bombed-out village on the Somme. The weather had immediately turned bad, preventing flying and making daily life a muddy, cold misery that sapped the men's strength.

But today, true to predictions, by sixteen hundred hours the rain had stopped. The ground crews in their greasy overalls had fueled the planes and rolled them out to the ready line. The pilots had clustered around Richthofen as he went over the map. The Air Warning Service's observers had telephoned from the front that ten British Sopwith Camels and five Bristol F.2b two-seaters were headed toward J.G. 1's patrol sector. With around three hours of daylight left the Herr Rittmeister and his cubs could have themselves a good hunt and be home by dark.

At last it was Goldstein's turn to take off. He signaled to his ground crew to pull the chocks from the Fokker's hard rubber wheels. At once the plane lurched forward, and Goldstein turned it into the wind as he opened his throttle. As his Fokker gathered speed Goldstein adjusted his goggles against the roaring wind that blew his engine's putrid exhaust fumes into his face. He pulled back on the stick and felt his usual thrill as the ground dropped away.

He maneuvered to take his place in the stacked Vee formation of Fokkers circling the field. Herr Rittmeister Richthofen in his scarlet machine was in the lead —the point of the Vee—with the least experienced pilots just behind and above him. The most experienced fliers formed the two widened legs of the Vee, highest up in the formation. Goldstein's place was high up in the widest part. He was proud that the Rittmeister had assigned him this place of honor. It meant that Richthofen considered him to be good enough to take care of himself, if need be.

The formation of fourteen airplanes gradually gained altitude. Goldstein could see the drab, smoke-filled valley of the Somme below. He had sharp eyesight or else he wouldn't be where he was, so he could make out figures wandering in that desolate, chocolate-hued mudscape broken by straw-colored patches of dead grass. He could see the twisted trunks of leafless blackened trees, and, scattered everywhere, the glinting wreckage of killed tanks and who knew what other kinds of ruined machinery—

Goldstein glanced at his reflection in the rearview mirror attached to the wing. The wind was tugging back his cheeks to form a grimace, but his eyes behind the lenses of his goggles were sparkling with anticipation. Today could be very special. His score stood at fourteen enemy planes. At the ten mark he became an ace, and that had been an important milestone, but now he was within range of the magic number: sixteen kills were needed to join the elite group of fliers who wore the *Pour le Mérite*, the Blue Max.

It was regulation in the German Air Service for an N.C.O. to get his commission upon becoming an ace, but the Adjutant Herr Oberleutnant Bodenschatz had cautioned Goldstein that there was a paperwork backlog in Berlin and that it might take a long time for his promotion to come through. The thought that he was eventually to be a lieutenant was exciting, but not half as exciting as the thought of having the Blue Max around his throat!

The formation had reached patrol altitude and was flying toward where Richthofen had guessed they could most likely intercept the British patrol behind German lincs. The Allied fighters always came to them, which meant the German pilots used less fuel getting to the dogfight, and that allowed for more combat time in the air. If they were shot down and managed to reach the ground uninjured, German fliers could be back at their units and flying again within hours. For the Allied pilots, fighting over German territory meant they had to think about saving fuel for the ride home, and if they went down, and lived, it meant ending up a prisoner for the war's duration.

For that reason there were far more experienced pilots flying for the Germans than for the Allies. That gave further advantage to the Germans, because experience counted for a lot in battle flying. If a man could survive his first few weeks in order to learn the important tricks and techniques, the odds increased that he might survive indefinitely.

Nobody dared to guess if a battle flier, Richthofen excepted, of course, might possibly be able to survive the entire war.

Goldstein never thought about that. Lots of pilots did and got nightmares and nervous conditions for their trouble. Others flew with lucky charms, or else conducted elaborate pre-patrol rituals like shaving on only one side of their face in order to ward off misfortune.

Not Goldstein. His only ritual was to sensibly spend his time maintaining his own plane, although for that he was considered an eccentric. The other pilots, all of whom were commissioned officers from aristocratic families, felt it was beneath them to get their hands dirty. The others seemed to take an inordinate pride in their ignorance of how their machines functioned.

The formation flew on, a wedge of rainbow-colored machines high up in the sky. Herr Rittmeister's scarlet machine was still flying point, flying at the lowest altitude, weaving from side to side like a fretful sheepdog in order to keep all of the planes tightly grouped.

They were passing through fleecy clouds as gray as gunsmoke. Goldstein liked clouds. Flying though them gave a thrilling sensation of speed, and banks of cloud could be useful when staging an ambush, or escaping from one. Now and then the clouds would thin, and Goldstein could view the world below. At this altitude, the savage details had vanished. The wartorn landscape was a seemingly serene patchwork quilt of gold and brown.

Goldstein was happy. He was in his environment. There was the engine's vibration and its comforting drone to keep him company, the gleam of sunlight on the varnished wood of his cockpit, and the instant response of his machine to his slightest touch. There was, of course, the bitter windchill to contend with, and the ear pops and inevitable altitude headache, but those minor plagues aside, he was not the least bit uncomfortable being in the air.

Goldstein had never been afraid of flying. Not even during his very first training flight. He had not been a natural. Far from it. He'd cracked up several trainers, and had almost washed out, but he'd managed to pass the initial examinations, and then, one day, it all seemed to click into place for him. The rest of flight school was easy.

Learning to fly had changed his life. On the ground he was still the same gangling, carrot-topped introvert, but in the air he became something exceptional: a battle flier. He didn't think he was as good as his idol Herr Cavalrycaptain Richthofen, who had close to eighty confirmed kills in his two and a half years as a flier in the war, but Goldstein considered himself to be the equal of any *mortal* . . .

The formation climbed to 16,000 feet and leveled off as it entered the sector where the British planes were supposed to be. At this altitude the clouds had thinned out to wispy cirrus layers, making visibility reasonably good. Like all the others, Goldstein was trying to be the first to spot the enemy. Seeing them before they saw you was crucial for a successful attack.

As usual, it was the Herr Rittmeister who first spotted the enemy. He waggled his wings to signal the rest of the formation, dipping his Fokker's nose to indicate the enemy's position below. Once Goldstein knew where to look, the rows of black dots flying in the opposite direction against the cloud-swept, variegated groundscape leapt out at him. The formation of ten speedy Sopwiths was flying forward of the five more cumbersome Bristol F. 2b two-seaters.

As was prearranged, the German formation wheeled around and broke up into two ketten of ten and four. The flight of ten, led by Herr Rittmeister Richthofen, would go after the ten fast and vicious Sopwith Camels. Goldstein's flight of four, led by Herr Lieutenant Dorn in his yellow and black bumblebee-striped Fokker, would concentrate on chewing up the five Bristol F. 2b two-seaters.

Neither group would be an easy target. The Camels were single-seat biplanes, as fast and maneuverable as the Fokker "tripes." The Bristols, while not nearly as agile, were fierce battle machines in their own right. Its pilot had a machine gun fixed forward to fire through the prop, but it was the rear gunner's twin Lewis machine guns that gave the Bristol its real sting.

The Rittmeister commenced the attack, diving down with his nine followers arrayed in a mini Vee. The Bristols' rear gunners spotted the attack and began firing, more in the hopes of alerting the Camels' formation rather than hitting anything, but they were too late. The attacking German formation slid by the Bristols and closed on the Camels. At what looked like point blank range, Richthofen and his flight began firing. Members of the Camel formation scattered like a flock of frightened pigeons—some right into the Germans' concentrated field of tracer fire. Goldstein saw three Sopwiths fall, and then he had no more time to watch because his flight leader was signaling to commence their own attack.

Goldstein saw that the Bristols, all painted a mottled green and tan, had formed a closed circle, flying nose to tail around and around so that their rear gunners could ward off the diving German attack. It was a standard defense tactic for two-seater machines, and reasonably effective, but it took experience on the part of the British pilots to have the nerve not to cut and run when the shooting started. It was time to find out just what sorts were crewing these Bristols.

As flight leader, Herr Lieutenant Dorn would be the first to dive through the hoop formed by the circling Bristols in an attempt to break them up. If that didn't work, he would attack from behind and below, where the Bristols' guns couldn't reach, and then rise up to take his place at the end of the line formed by his three wingmates. Goldstein would attack second, following Dorn's pattern, and so on. If, or when, the Bristols finally did scatter, the Fokkers would split into pairs, with one flier watching the other's back as they went after their targets.

Goldstein watched the Lieutenant make his dive: the bumblebee plane flew unscathed through the crisscrossing streams of tracers coming from the Bristols' rear guns, and right through the hoop, but the Bristols held fast.

Goldstein, high above the enemy, his concentration focused, signaled his two wingmates, and went to work.

He rolled the Fokker upside down and pulled the stick into his belly to execute a split-S power dive toward the Bristols. He felt the giddy thrill in the pit of his stomach as he was rocked by the centrifugal force. Immediately the Bristols' five sets of twin Lewis guns swiveled toward him and began winking orange, but his angle of attack was too steep for him to be an easy target. The enemy gunners' tracers arced wildly as they tried to zero in.

The Fokker's engine roared and the wind screamed through its wing struts as the blue, white, and red bull's-eye roundels on the Bristols' wings loomed larger. Now the British gunners were finding their aim, and Goldstein was diving into a fiery orange-red tunnel formed by the whizzing tracers, but he held his own fire until he was close enough to almost touch his targets—

Forty meters above the circling planes Goldstein aligned his fixed gunsight on a Bristol's engine and pressed the firing button mounted on his control stick. He couldn't hear his gun above his own engine's racket, but he felt the plane shuttering with the recoil and tasted the bitter gunsmoke blowing back into his face as the orange tracers raced ahead of him like a stream of water coming out of a hose. He fired a three-second burst; approximately twenty-seven rounds; the LMG .08/15 Spandau gun spitting 7.92-millimeter bullets at the rate of 550 a minute; and glimpsed the smoking holes he'd punched in his target's engine cowling.

He knew what he was *supposed* to do next, but he had an idea. He decided to try it, even if it meant that he would later catch hell from Dorn for breaking the formation.

As he pulled up into what he *hoped* his British adversaries would think was the beginning of a loop, Goldstein glimpsed Dorn and the others hanging in the air above him, likely wondering what was going on. As Goldstein reached a vertical position above and forward of the circling Bristols he kicked his rudder hard, causing his plane to sideslip to the left on its tail, and then he dropped its nose, into another attack dive at his previous target. This time he encountered no answering fire. As he'd hoped, the Bristols' rear gunners had anticipated firing at him while he was upside down, above and a little behind them, finishing his loop. By the time the rear gunners had wrestled their twin mounted guns around to face him, Goldstein was firing another burst into his adversary's engine.

He saw the Bristol's prop waver, then stop, as its engine began leaking smoke. The crippled plane drifted out of its place in the battle circle and glided toward the ground. Now that the circle had been broken the four other Bristols lost their nerve and scattered like leaves caught in a gust of wind. Dorn and the other two pilots were on them at once, but weren't having much luck. The Bristols were heading home, and their rear gunners were doing a good job of holding the Fokkers off.

Goldstein knew it was high time for him to rejoin the formation, but he followed his own kill down, watching as it pancaked on a stretch of pasture bordered by forest. The pilot and gunner seemed unharmed as they quit their plane. They didn't try to run for the trees, but merely stood with their hands upraised as German troops rushed toward them.

Fifteen kills. Just one more . . .

By the time that Goldstein had gotten back up to battle ceiling the Bristols were long gone. Herr Lieutenant Dorn and the other two Fokkers were distant specks headed back. The Herr Rittmeister's flight and the Sopwith Camels were nowhere about. Probably homeward bound, as well.

Goldstein was all alone in the sky, but he wasn't concerned. There was no need to maintain formation once an attack was over. Many pilots chose to, in order to guard against an ambush on their way home, but the decision was personal preference. Goldstein had confidence in his own ability to get himself out of any situation. He liked to proceed home at his own pace.

Now he reluctantly put his Fokker into a gentle, banking turn toward Cappy. He was resigned to the fact that he was not going to further increase his score, and that his Blue Max would have to wait for another day, but he was still emotionally keyed up. His engagement with the enemy had lasted less than a minute. Dogfights rarely lasted longer before ending in someone's victory or inconclusively breaking off—

Goldstein saw the dot when it was about a quarter of a meter away, coming at him head on, an instant before it began firing at him. The attacking machine was small and fast. It had to be one of the Camels, Goldstein decided as he banked to the right, out of the path of the lazily oncoming tracers.

The plane flashed past him on the left. It was a Sopwith Camel, all right. Its distinctive humped engine cowling was red. Its fuselage was painted tan with white vertical stripings. Its rudder was British-striped red, white, and blue.

The Camel had escaped the Herr Rittmeister's attentions and was now running for home. The pilot was definitely a neophyte. No experienced battle flier would waste ammunition firing at a target a quarter of a mile away. His lack of experience would also explain why he had survived the dogfight. Flight leaders on both sides often ordered their green fliers to hang back and merely watch and learn during their first couple of engagements . . .

The Camel was well past Goldstein as he zoomed upward,

banked sharply left, and kicked his tail around to the rear to give pursuit.

Goldstein knew that the Camel was faster than the Fokker, even a lean, mean "tripe" like his own. The Camel had about a half kilometer lead, and the British lines were now only a couple of kilometers away, so it was clear to Goldstein that he wasn't going to get his all-important sixteenth kill by letting the British pilot turn this into a horse race. Once again, everything would hinge on experience, but Goldstein already had indications that his opponent was new at this game.

The Fokker's hard-pressed rotary engine screamed in protest as Goldstein pushed his throttle full-open. He checked his fuel gauge. He was low, but that was good. The less fuel in the tank, the lighter the weight and the faster he could go.

He'd not very much closed the gap between himself and the Camel when Goldstein played his trump card: without even aiming he pressed his firing button. His gun made the Fokker shudder, and the recoil actually slowed his forward speed, but his ploy worked: the Camel's pilot, seeing those chasing tracers in his rearview mirror, had begun evasive maneuvers, not realizing that Goldstein didn't have a prayer of hitting him. Every zigzag meant to throw off Goldstein's nonexistent aim cost the Camel's pilot forward speed. Goldstein, sporadically firing short bursts while flying true as an arrow, was gradually closing on his quarry.

They were now close to the German front lines, but Goldstein had cut the Camel's lead by a quarter of a kilometer. The Camel's evasive maneuvers had also cost it altitude: it was now less than a hundred meters above the ground. Goldstein had ignored the lunatic howl of his own engine as he'd power-dived in pursuit, and that had further increased his own speed, helping to close the gap.

The terrain rushed past in a blur, as Goldstein followed the Camel down to what would have been treetop level, if the war had seen fit to leave trees standing in this part of the world. He could imagine the troops in their trenches on both sides of the line stopping what they were doing in order to crane their necks, shield their eyes from the sun, and watch the show. It made him feel good to be the center of attention. It made him feel like he belonged; it made him feel alive.

The Camel had passed over the German front lines and was just entering into no-man's-land when Goldstein, about seventy meters behind, decided that it was now or never. He centered his sight on the Camel's tail and fired. He kept up a steady stream of bullets—he might as well empty his magazine—while delicately adjusting the angle of his Fokker's nose to try to put the orange tracers on target.

He managed to zero in by sheer dumb luck. For an instant the Camel's tail and the Fokker's chattering Spandau were linked by an amber strand of gunfire.

Then the Camel abruptly dived.

Goldstein guessed that his bullets had either chewed up the Camel's rudder or cut a control wire. Whatever, at the Camel's low altitude it was only an instant before it was leapfrogging along the uneven ground. It bounced out of control amidst the shell-torn craters of no-man's-land for about two hundred meters before its prop caught in a tangle of barbed wire, stopping it dead. The Camel's forward momentum caused its ruined tail to flip up and over. The plane came to rest, wings crumpled, belly up toward the sky.

Goldstein made a pass over the downed Camel, anxious to spot the pilot. The Camel had not caught fire, which was promising, but no-man's-land was a bad spot in which to crash. If the pilot was hurt a local truce would have to be worked out to allow a medical party to get to him. It could be done, but it took time, and time was something injured men didn't always have—

There he was! Goldstein was elated as he watched the pilot scurry from the wreckage and run for all he was worth toward his own lines. This British pilot would fly again. He'd crashed well out of German rifle range.

Goldstein banked toward his own lines, watching the first explosions blossom around the Camel as the German mortars lobbed shells at the downed plane. It was just for fun. The Camel's flying days were over, mortar-hit or not.

He put the Fokker into a slow climb, nursing it upward while gingerly working the throttle and fuel-tank air pressure pump. He was pretty much flying on fumes now. He needed to nurse the last bit of time out of the engine.

The sun was beginning to set, a ball of molten fire, as he headed for home.

Goldstein was at three thousand meters and about three kilometers from Cappy aerodrome, when his fuel ran out. The engine coughed and died, but that was fine. He'd learned long ago that his machine could glide about a kilometer per three hundred meters of altitude, provided there was no headwind, and tonight the breeze was at his tail. He often cut his engine on the way home in order to enjoy a glide. It was wonderful to fly with no engine noise to punish one's ears; with no sound at all but the rush of wind making the wing struts sing.

It was wonderful to be alive—

In full view of the German lines he had made his fifteenth and sixteenth kills! He would be getting his Blue Max!

Goldstein wondered if life could get any better than this. There was sex, of course . . . He'd overheard some of the other pilots boasting about their sexual exploits . . .

Goldstein had never been with a woman, so he couldn't know for sure, but he doubted that even sex could compare with how it felt to own the sky.

(Two)

As Cappy airfield came into view Goldstein felt the depression that always came with the end of a flight. Below was nothing but mud and mildew and loneliness.

He still had enough altitude to make several circles of the field. He did so, like a bird reluctant to return to its cage. As he spiraled down, the drab features of the place loomed up at him. The buildings and tents were all clustered at one end of the field. There was the ready-room hut, beside the big tents that sheltered the planes, and next to the tents, the rows of fuel tank lorries. Next came the operations hut; the long, single story wooden barracks; and the mess for the support personnel. Behind that was the stables tent, and the parked transport lorries. Next was the pilots' mess hall and administrative offices, and, finally, the rows of pilots' huts.

Goldstein could see that things had been happening here while he was gone. There were the smoking wrecks of two airplanes smack in the middle of the field, and a bomb crater nearby the hangar tent. Work crews were busy disposing of the debris and repairing the damage to the field.

Goldstein also noticed an unfamiliar-looking airplane parked near the hangar tents. It didn't seem to have a triplane's shape, and its colors were wrong for J.G. 1: gleaming white all over, with the exception of its tail fin, which was raven black. It couldn't be a captured Allied machine, because it carried Iron Crosses on its top wings and fuselage.

It was getting too dark to fly, so Goldstein landed, knowing from experience just where to touch down in order for his machine to lose enough momentum to come to a stop in front of the hangar tents. His ground crew was waiting.

"Your fifteenth and sixteenth, Herr Sergeant. Congratulations!" Corporal Froehlig exclaimed as he helped Goldstein extricate himself from the cockpit.

"You've already heard, Herr Corporal?" Goldstein asked as he pulled off his goggles and helmet.

"The Air Warning Service boys telephoned in both confirmations fifteen minutes ago." Froehlig's smile was wide beneath his walrus moustache. He almost bodily lifted Goldstein to the ground in his exuberance.

"That's a relief," Goldstein said. The last obstacle in his path to the Blue Max had been removed. A kill had to be officially confirmed to count in a pilot's record. He gestured toward the wrecks and the bomb craters. "What happened here?"

Froehlig shrugged. "A couple of Frenchies came in at us low, from the southwest. They carried the markings of the No. 30 Spad Squadron, based at Matigny. They dropped a bomb and strafed the field, but nobody was hurt and nothing was really damaged. Some of the fellows in Jasta 6 were about to take off and chase them away when that pale beauty popped out of nowhere to come to the rescue." He indicated the gleaming white airplane parked nearby. "Her pilot is no slouch, either. He shot both those Spads down before they knew what was happening. Both Frenchie pilots were killed."

The white machine was a biplane, of a sort that Goldstein had never seen. It carried the markings of Jasta 27, a squad based to the northeast of Cappy, at Erchin.

Froehlig saw him looking. "A beauty, isn't she, Sir?" Froehlig said.

Goldstein nodded. "What is she, Herr Corporal?"

"That's one of the first of the Fokker D VII series."

"I heard about them!" Goldstein nodded. "But if they've been built, then why don't we have any?"

"We will, Herr Sergeant. That one's a prototype," Froehlig replied. "They're still gearing up for quantity production, and I heard that J.G. 1 is first on the list to get them. Go have yourself a look at her, why don't you."

Goldstein hurried over to the airplane. It was magnificent. Much longer and leaner than his own "tripe," the D VII's low profile looked fast just sitting on the ground. This new machine made his own triplane look as outmoded as a horse and buggy.

"Word has it that she can do one hundred twenty-five kilometers per hour," Froehlig said, coming up behind him.

"That's faster than anything else in the air!" Goldstein exclaimed.

The mechanic chuckled knowingly. "She's got a one hundred sixty horsepower Mercedes engine—"

"You don't say! Christ! I'm in love! What I wouldn't give to take her up." He smiled. "Or take her apart, to see what makes her tick . . ."

"You'll have to wait for your own to do that, Herr Sergeant."

"Why is she here?"

"She belongs to the C.O. of Jasta 27. He flew in to meet with Herr Rittmeister, why, I couldn't say, and ended up arriving in time to score himself two kills. Two *more* kills than he already has, I should say. He's got to have at least sixteen. He was wearing the Blue Max." Froehlig paused. "Herr Sergeant? A question, if I may?"

"Um? . . ." Goldstein was engrossed with the D VII.

"Will *you* be getting the medal, Sir?" Froehlig asked.

Goldstein turned to regard his mechanic. "The Blue Max? Well, yes . . . I certainly expect to."

"And the Herr Sergeant not even twenty years old!" Froehlig beamed. "You may turn out to be the youngest to ever wear it."

"Well, we'll see . . ." Goldstein muttered. Talk of the Blue Max reminded him that he still had to change out of his flight clothes and report in. "Well, please see to my airplane, Herr Corporal." He walked quickly away toward the ready room.

Behind him, Goldstein could hear Froehlig barking orders to the others on his ground crew. From the corporal's tone Goldstein sensed that he'd hurt the man's feelings by not prolonging their chat. He wished that he weren't so awkward with people . . .

In the ready room an orderly was waiting to take away his flying gear and return with Goldstein's black leather boots and field cap. Goldstein put them on and checked himself in the mirror.

He frowned.

Commissoned officers had their uniforms custom tailored, but N.C.O.s had to make due with government issued. They'd had trouble fitting Goldstein because he was so much taller and thinner than average. His gray tunic with its black and scarlet piping hung in ungainly folds. As he tugged and tucked the garment, he tried not to soil the linen embroidery on both collar and sleeves that showed his rank. His matching gray trousers with scarlet piping down the side seams ended too far above his ankles, but there was nothing he could do about that. Only his field cap, with its black band piped with scarlet around the crown, fit him correctly.

Goldstein took his handkerchief from his back trouser pocket and polished his metal flier's breast badge. It showed in relief a Taube monoplane, flying over a landscape contained in a laurel and oak leaf wreath, with the Prussian royal crown at the top.

He had no other decorations or medals. Others who had become aces had received the Iron Cross in recognition of their achievement, but for some reason Goldstein's Cross had not come through. When he had asked the adjutant about it the officer had said that he would look into it, but so gruffly that Goldstein had not wanted to pursue the matter. What was the point of an honor if you had to grovel and plead in order to receive it?

Anyway, an Iron Cross was nothing compared to the Blue Max ... Goldstein, gazing at his reflection, let his fingers rise up to his throat, where the blue and gold Maltese Cross would hang from its black ribbon. By then he would almost certainly be wearing a custom-tailored lieutenant's uniform with *lace* braid.

He left the ready room, breathing lightly through his mouth as he hurried along the lantern-lit path, past the stink of the stables tents, to the offices, where he reported in.

"How will I file to receive my Blue Max?" Goldstein asked the bored lieutenant on duty when he was done giving his account of his successful pursuit of the Camel.

"You'd better see the adjutant about that," the officer said as he finished scribbling down the last of what Goldstein had said.

"Is the Herr Oberleutnant in his office, now?"

The lieutenant shook his head. "Tomorrow, Herr Sergeant."

Goldstein nodded, and left the office. He walked slowly down the long hall that connected to the pilots' mess, feeling his nervousness grow. The murmur of talk and laughter was audible even before Goldstein pushed through the double doors.

Inside the brightly lit hall the air was stifling; thick with swirling cigarette smoke and the sweet smell of spilled wine. The place was crowded with pilots and ground officers lounging in deck chairs as they ate and drank, or standing in groups, conversing.

Being a flier, Goldstein had every right to be here, even if it was a de facto commissioned officers' club, but having the right to do something, and feeling comfortable doing it, were two very different things.

Goldstein, uncertain, stood just inside the door. So far,

nobody had noticed him. Goldstein didn't expect much in the way of acknowledgment, but he usually did receive a few congratulations for a kill, and today he had shot down *two* planes, and his tally had finally reached the magic number. Surely all of that would buy him some comradeship . . .

Beside him along the wall was a sideboard loaded with bread, cheese, and sausage and bowls of tinned fruit. Goldstein helped himself and found a chair off in a corner. He was settled and had begun to eat when his eyes locked with one of the pilots. The man pointed Goldstein out to his friends, and began to applaud. Quickly the other pilots and officers took note, stopped what they were doing, and began to applaud Goldstein, who felt his face turn bright red with surprised pleasure. He put aside his plate and self-consciously got to his feet.

"Speech! Speech!" Lieutenant Dorn began. The others took up the cry.

Goldstein, his mouth suddenly gone bone-dry, struggled to swallow. He saw the Herr Rittmeister across the room. Richthofen was twenty-five years old. He was of average height, but his square, muscular body gave him an imposing air. He had pale blue eyes, cropped blond hair, and a solid jaw.

Richthofen was standing with a young Oberleutnant whom Goldstein had never seen before. The Herr Rittmeister wasn't drinking, but then he rarely did. The newcomer first lieutenant was sipping at a glass of champagne. He had to be the C.O. of Jasta 27, the fortunate owner of that exquisite, all-white D VII. He was wearing the Iron Cross on his tunic, and the Blue Max at his throat. Despite the decorations, this officer didn't look like much. He was plump, with a broad, fleshy nose and wide, red lips. He had the impish, glinting eyes of a prankster. Those eyes seemed both amused and scornful as they looked Goldstein's way. Goldstein thought there was something unwholesome, even effeminate, in the manner in which the mysterious stranger took Richthofen's arm in order to draw him close to whisper something in his ear—

Goldstein instinctively knew that whatever this mysterious officer was whispering concerned him. He tensed, blushing again, this time in humiliation. What the newcomer had whispered was making the Herr Rittmeister laugh. This was not the way Goldstein had intended to be noticed!

"Speech, Herr Sergeant," Richthofen abruptly commanded, and smiled at Goldstein, who forgot his discomfort as his knees went weak.

It was the same wry half-smile that the Herr Rittmeister Baron Manfred von Richthofen wore in his photograph, the one that had become the best-selling postcard in Germany. Back home everyone knew of Richthofen's exploits. They could watch films about him in the movie houses or read his best-selling book of memoirs. The book was even popular in England. The British had put a five-thousand-pound price on Richthofen's head and formed a crack squad of aces to hunt him. It was said that Herr General Ludendorff regularly telephoned to ask Richthofen's advice, and that the Kaiser invited him to lunch.

For Goldstein, just to be near the Herr Rittmeister was intoxicating. Richthofen gave off such heat and energy that it was like turning his face up to the sun.

"Speech!" Richthofen repeated.

For a moment Goldstein was totally at a loss. Public speaking was one of his worst nightmares. His stomach was lurching as if he'd just executed a tailspin in his Fokker. He'd much rather face tracer fire than this.

It was the glimmer of lamplight on the Blue Max around the Herr Rittmeister's throat that inspired Goldstein.

"I, I made these kills, all sixteen of them, to b-bring victory to my c-country," Goldstein began. His voice wavered, he couldn't catch his breath, but he forced himself to continue. "A-and to win the Blue Max—"

There was a scattering of laughter, but a sharp look from Richthofen silenced it.

"I sincerely hope my successes will bring further honor to my fellow fliers, a-and to my unit—" Goldstein hesitated. He looked across the room, into Richthofen's steady pale blue gaze, even as the passionate tears welled in his own eyes. "And to my Herr Rittmeister and Geschwaderkommandeur..."

There was silence in the mess. Goldstein was embarrassed to find himself trembling. The others were all either steadfastly staring at him or making it a point to look away, but nobody was laughing. Goldstein's gaze dropped to the floor.

"Well said, Herr Sergeant," Richthofen softly commented. He began to applaud, and the others quickly followed his lead.

Goldstein, weak with love, realizing how ludicrous it would be for a pilot who had mastered advanced combat aerobatics to faint in a mess hall, blindly made his way to his chair and sat down, waiting for the dizziness to pass. The applause died away, and the conversation level in the room again began to rise. The Herr Rittmeister disappeared from view as he and his mysterious companion were surrounded by a group of pilots.

Well, that's that, Goldstein thought, feeling both relief and sadness.

He looked at his food, but he was no longer hungry. There was a pot of coffee keeping warm on the sideboard. He went and poured himself a cup, and took it with him back to his corner, where he sat quietly.

Nobody talked to him. Now and then he heard snatches of conversations concerning hunting, and travel, and society gossip, but he knew nothing about any of that, so how could he intelligently join in, assuming he found the nerve to try?

He wished that he smoked, or liked to get drunk. It would be something to do with his hands. To kill time. To look like he belonged.

To have to be alone right now seemed bitterly unfair. Well, maybe things would be different when he wore a lieutenant's uniform...

He finished his coffee, and left the mess. The clouds were moving back in, masking the stars. He hoped that the weather wouldn't interfere with flying tomorrow.

He walked along the dimly lit path that led to the pilots' huts. The huts were all small, and one room; built out of planks that let the weather in through the chinks. They were a far cry from the luxurious accommodations at Léchelle, but they were a hell of a lot better than the tents the pilots had lived in when they'd first arrived at Cappy.

Goldstein's hut had a window by the door, curtained with oilcloth. As he approached he saw light coming from inside, which meant that an orderly had been by to light a lantern.

Inside his hut the floor was bare. One wall was taken up with a wrought-iron peat stove. Its smokestack vented through the tar paper roof. On one side of the stove was a small pile of peat, and on the other a straight-back chair. Against the opposite wall was his bed, his footlocker, and a crate piled high with books and a lantern. Another lantern hung down from the hut's rafters. Beneath it in the middle of the room was a long wooden table.

Goldstein looked at his Fokker's machine gun laid out on an oily blanket on the table. Beside the table was a metal ammo crate filled with cartridges, and on top of that was a small case containing an assortment of gunsmith tools.

Goldstein had issued standing orders to Herr Corporal Froehlig to deliver the gun to his hut after every engagement. Goldstein had also ordered the armorer to deliver his replacement ammunition to the hut. It was the armorer's responsibility to maintain all guns and ammunition, but Goldstein preferred to look after his own armament. The Spandau machine gun was reliable, but careless cleaning, or a misadjustment of the head space between the firing chamber and the face of the lock could cause jamming, or misfires. A defective cartridge could also stop the gun.

So Goldstein cleaned his own weapon and checked every round of his own ammunition. It was his ass up there in the thin air. Anyway, working on the gun relaxed him.

He took off his tunic and cap and hung them on a wall hook. He got a fire going in the stove, then brought the straight-back chair over to the table, rolled up his shirtsleeves, and set to work.

He was finished fieldstripping the gun into its components, and was going over the feed-block mechanism with a small brush and lead solvent, when he heard a knock at his door. The only visitor he'd ever had was Herr Corporal Froehlig, who would sometimes come by at night to report on some maintenance problem concerning the Fokker.

"Come!" Goldstein called out. He heard the door open, but he did not raise his eyes from his work as he said, "Yes, Herr Corporal? What is it?"

"Forgive me for disturbing you, Herr Sergeant," Richthofen said.

Goldstein's head sprang up. The Herr Rittmeister was standing in the doorway with his walking stick in one hand and his cap in the other.

Goldstein slammed back his chair and bolted to his feet, almost putting out his eye as he snapped out a salute. He could not have been more shocked. Goldstein worshiped Richthofen, but tonight in the mess hall was the first time he had ever actually summoned up the courage to speak to the Herr Rittmeister, if you could call his tribute speaking to the man. Now, here Richthofen was, come calling on a private visit!

"May I come in?" Richthofen asked.

Goldstein stared blankly.

"Herr Sergeant?" Richthofen coaxed gently. "May I come in?—"

Goldstein shook himself awake. "Of course, Sir!"

"Thank you," Richthofen said as he entered, closing the door behind him. "You may stand at ease, Herr Sergeant."

"Please, Herr Rittmeister, sit down on the bed, Sir," Goldstein said. "It's softer than the chair."

"Thank you, the Herr Sergeant may sit down, as well." Richthofen sat down on the edge of the bed, setting his cap and stick beside him. He gestured toward the machine gun on the table. "Do you do that after every flight, Herr Sergeant?"

"Yes, Sir, I do . . . that is, if the gun has been fired."

"You don't trust the armorer to know his job, is that it?"

"No, it's not that, at least, not totally that . . . It's just . . . It's a pleasure for me to do it, Sir."

"Ah! Now I understand." Richthofen smiled. "I always enjoyed cleaning my own shotguns after a day spent hunting boar on my family's estate."

"Yes, Sir." Goldstein had never seen a boar, nor an estate. He'd spent his life on the streets of Berlin.

"But you are cleaning just one gun, isn't that so, Herr Sergeant? Your airplane was issued twin guns, but you choose to use only one. Why do you put yourself at such a disadvantage?"

"With all due respect, I don't see it as a disadvantage, Sir," Goldstein explained. "Flying with only one gun decreases my flight weight. By leaving one forty-pound gun behind I increase my top speed and ceiling by that much more—"

"But that's not the real reason, is it, my boy?" Richthofen interrupted.

Goldstein couldn't look Richthofen in the eye. "No, Sir."

"What *is* the real reason, my boy?"

Goldstein thought that it seemed very natural for the Herr Rittmeister to address him so paternally. Richthofen, despite his youth, commanded a father's respect from all his pilots, and now that Goldstein had the chance to really study his leader's face, to see the deeply etched worry lines and the dark shadows under Richthofen's pale blue eyes, he thought that the Herr Rittmeister looked far older than his true age.

"Well, Sir, the real reason is that with just one gun I can fire more accurately..." Goldstein swallowed hard. "... And more *carefully.*"

"Today's report from the front says that you didn't try to strafe the pilot of the Camel you downed when he began running for his lines."

"No, Sir." Goldstein looked down at his boots.

"Before coming here, I read your file, Herr Sergeant," Richthofen said. "I noticed something very curious about the fates of the British personnel who have fallen to your guns —Excuse my error," the Rittmeister dryly added. "Your *gun.*"

Goldstein's heart was pounding. He was sweating, even though he was only in his shirt-sleeves. *Oh God! He was in his shirt-sleeves.* He shot a despairing glance at his tunic hanging on the wall. His first private conversation with the

Herr Rittmeister was turning into an argument, and he had to be caught out of uniform!

"All but two of the men you shot down were captured and made prisoners of war," Richthofen continued. "Those two exceptions escaped back to their own lines." Richthofen paused. "Don't you think it unusual that with sixteen kills to your credit you have yet to spill a drop of blood?"

"May I speak frankly to the Herr Rittmeister?" Goldstein asked.

"You may."

"Sir, by using only one machine gun, I can carefully place my shots to bring down the enemy plane without harming the pilot or gunner."

"So! My suspicions were correct." Richthofen nodded. "You *do* go out of your way to spare the enemy—"

"Sir, with all due respect, I don't *spare* the enemy," Goldstein said carefully. "I always shoot them down, which is, after all, what's most important. I just don't see the point of harming another human being when I'm good enough at my job to put the other fellow out of the game for the rest of the war by dropping him and his machine into the hands of German troops."

"Is that what you think? That battle flying is some kind of game?" Richthofen demanded, sounding angry.

"No, Sir," Goldstein replied. "It's my life."

"But you needlessly risk your life with your sharpshooting—"

He doesn't understand what I meant, Goldstein thought, but he was too in awe of the man sitting across from him to interrupt.

"And when you put yourself at risk you put your fellows at risk." Richthofen was frowning. "Don't think that Herr Lieutenant Dorn didn't file a report on how you broke formation during your attack on those Bristols." Richthofen shook his head. "I believe in safe, conservative battle tactics, Sergeant. A flier keeps in formation and he shoots to kill."

Goldstein felt sick to have to be reprimanded by the Herr

Rittmeister. "I'm very sorry about everything," he said plaintively.

Richthofen stared at him a long moment, and then he smiled. "Don't be too sorry. You're a strange one, Goldstein, but you do seem to have the knack for shooting down the enemy. I don't have many experienced pilots like you left, you know," he sighed. "Sooner or later, I'm afraid, the odds catch up with all of us."

"Except the Herr Rittmeister, of course," Goldstein said in hushed and respectful tones.

"Do you really think so, Herr Sergeant?" Richthofen asked. "Shall I tell you something I've never told anyone? That I couldn't tell any of the others?"

I have to be dreaming this, Goldstein thought. "I would be honored to hear such a thing, Sir—"

Richthofen cut him off with a wave of his hand. "My time is coming," he said.

"No, never!" Goldstein said, horrified.

"If you can't understand this now, you may, someday," Richthofen said, shaking his head. "Skill and experience count only up to a point, against the odds. It may be an ace who brings me down. It may be a fledgling pilot firing his guns for the first time. It may be my own machine that betrays me. It's the ever-mounting odds that will get me, my boy. In our business, sooner or later, everyone's luck does run out."

Goldstein didn't know what to say. It had never occurred to him that this handsome and accomplished idol of an entire nation could have a dark side to his shining existence. Richthofen seemed to sense Goldstein's total bewilderment. He tried to smile, but his weary grin only made Goldstein more aware of just how heavy the Herr Rittmeister's burdens had become.

"I bring up such morbid topics only because I'm concerned about you, my boy," Richthofen soothed. "For instance, what if the odds decree that your single gun should jam?"

Goldstein pointed a thumb over his shoulder at the disassembled weapon. "Sir, I see to it that it doesn't jam."

"As you see to your airplane? I'm told you spend as much

time working on your Fokker as you do flying it." Richthofen picked up some of the books on the crate to scan their
titles. "*Principles of Aeronautics*," he read out loud. "*Flying
Machine Design*; *The Theory and Maintenance of the Rotary
Engine*—"

"Sir, your own book is there," Goldstein quickly said.

"No doubt," Richthofen murmured wryly. "Do you really
understand these technical subjects, Herr Sergeant?"

"Yes, Sir. As a boy I received a mechanic's training."

"Yes, in Berlin. At that orphanage." Richthofen nodded as
he set the books aside. "I did read in your file that your
parents died early on."

"My mother during my birth," Goldstein replied, wondering where all of this was leading. "My father, a few years
later, of consumption, or so I've been told. I really don't
know very much about my parents, Sir."

"Except, of course, that they were Jews," Richthofen declared.

"Yes, Sir. They were— I am—a Jew." Goldstein nodded,
and then shrugged. "But I don't know very much about that,
either. The orphanage in which I was raised was a Christian
institution, and, um, well, I guess I'm not very well versed
in any sort of religion . . ." He trailed off.

"But you were born a Jew," Richthofen said softly, almost
to himself. "That's the beginning and end of it, you see . . ."

"See what, Sir?"

Richthofen looked uneasy. "Herr Sergeant, I came here to
discuss a matter of some delicacy with you. It's a difficult
matter, and because of that, I have been procrastinating. It
concerns your application for the Iron Cross, and your application for promotion, and, of course, now that you have
sixteen confirmed kills, your intended application for the
Blue Max . . ."

Goldstein, sitting very still, and feeling absolutely quiet
inside, nodded slowly. "These honors will be coming to me,
won't they, Sir?"

"No."

Goldstein winced. "Is it because of my record, Sir?
Because I sometimes break formation? I promise to do better—"

"Herr Sergeant," Richthofen looked him in the eye. "It's because you're a Jew."

"I don't understand, Herr Rittmeister," Goldstein said slowly. "I know that the other fliers ostracize me because of my background. I accept that. I don't expect anything better. I mean, I wish for their friendship, but I don't really ever expect it. But we're not talking about the men's behavior. We're talking about decorations and promotions that are rightfully due me . . . Sir, with all due respect, there are rules concerning anti-Semitism. Proclamations from the Herr Kaiser himself. There is to be no anti-Semitism in the military."

"Officially, there is none," Richthofen nodded. "Officially, all the papers for all the honors due you will be processed, but I tell you now, Herr Sergeant; I tell you frankly; those papers will never *finish* being processed. Signatures will be missing. Records will be misplaced. Finally, the completed forms will be lost in transit, so that the entire laborious process will have to begin again." Richthofen studied him carefully. "*Now* do you understand?"

Goldstein struggled to hide his broken heart. "I do, Sir," he made himself say calmly.

"It's simply not up to me," Richthofen was saying. "If it were, things might be different, but as things stand, I've been told by my superiors that there can be no Jewish officers in the Air Service. For the same reason you haven't received the Iron Cross due you, and from that we can assume that the Blue Max will be out of the question. I debated letting things drag on, and letting you build false hopes, but I decided you deserved to know the truth."

"I appreciate the Herr Rittmeister coming to speak with me concerning this matter," Goldstein said evenly. "The other pilots have always felt that they have valid reason to shun me because of my social and religious background. Tonight they must think I'm such a fool for spouting off about receiving the Blue Max . . ."

"No one thinks you're a fool, Herr Sergeant," Richthofen said as he stood up.

Goldstein quickly jumped up from his chair and stood at attention.

Richthofen put on his cap and picked up his walking stick. "Your abilities as a flier are respected," he continued. "You must not forget that you really *are* a hero, an ace, and a gentleman, at least, in my eyes."

Goldstein smiled. "That means a lot to me, Sir," he earnestly replied. He meant it. If his achievements couldn't bring him official honors, he could at least continue to add to the Herr Rittmeister's stature, and add to his own, in Richthofen's eyes. "Thank you for saying that."

Richthofen nodded. "You've made our chat relatively easy for me, Herr Sergeant. For that, *I* thank *you*. Perhaps I can use my influence to at least get you your Iron Cross," he added as he walked toward the door.

"The Herr Rittmeister mustn't trouble himself." Goldstein meant that, as well. He'd coveted the Iron Cross as a military honor. He would not have it as a bribe.

"We'll keep this little chat our secret, yes, Herr Sergeant?" Richthofen was reaching for the door.

"As the Herr Rittmeister wishes." Goldstein saluted.

Richthofen absently returned the salute. His thoughts had already moved on to other concerns, Goldstein realized. In a moment the Herr Rittmeister would be gone and Goldstein would once again be alone, except for his dashed hopes, and the ugly reality of his lowly status.

"I'm relieved to get this unpleasantness out of the way," Richthofen said as he opened the door. "I've been called to the rear for staff meetings, you see. My senior officers will be coming with me."

"Who will lead J.G. 1?" Goldstein asked.

"A very good flier," Richthofen said, stepping outside. "An Oberleutnant, the C.O. of Jasta 27. He flew in this afternoon."

"The Herr Firstlieutenant who was with you this evening, Sir?" Goldstein thought about the plump, effeminate young officer he'd seen with the Herr Rittmeister in the mess hall.

"I've known him a while, and I'm quite impressed." Richthofen nodded. "His name is Hermann Goering."

Never heard of him, Goldstein thought. He stood at attention as the Rittmeister left.

Chapter 2

The weather had turned overcast, matching Goldstein's gray mood. Despite what he'd told the Herr Rittmeister, Goldstein had grown increasingly bitter as the realization sunk in that he was to be deprived of his promotion and decorations.

He avoided the pilots' mess as much as possible; being around the other fliers only made him feel worse. He was lonely when they ignored him, yet he felt if they spoke to him he wouldn't be able to rid himself of the feeling that their polite countenances were a sham, that he was being mocked.

From now on, he'd decided, he would respond to the other fliers' aloofness with an indifferent, cool contempt of his own.

The continuing poor weather grounded all flights. Since there was no need to ready the airplanes, Goldstein knew that the hangar tents would be pretty much deserted. The solitude and the opportunity to relax and forget his troubles by tinkering with machinery appealed. Goldstein got up early and grabbed some breakfast before any of the other pilots were awake. By midmorning he was in the hangar tent, wearing a pair of mechanic's overalls over his field uniform, engrossed in overhauling his Fokker's throttle mechanism.

"I am at the Herr Sergeant's service—"

Goldstein looked up. It was Corporal Froehlig. "You needn't be. I know you're not on duty this morning . . ."

Froehlig nodded. "I just thought the Herr Sergeant might like some help, and some company."

Goldstein nodded, noncommittal. "Then grab a wrench. Some of these nuts are rusted in place . . ."

Froehlig went to the locker for a pair of overalls. He put them on, and then moved to the toolbox. "Begging the Herr Sergeant's pardon, but I heard about it," he said as he knelt to rummage through the tools for an appropriate wrench.

"About what?" Goldstein muttered, struggling with a cross-threaded bolt.

"About the Herr Sergeant's talk with the Herr Rittmeister," Froehlig replied. "About the Herr Sergeant being denied his promotion and medals."

"It was supposed to be confidential!" Goldstein's wrench slipped off the frozen nut, skinning his knuckles. "Dammit!" He threw the wrench against an empty oil drum. It clanged musically, and made a satisfying dent.

"The whole story has traveled the grapevine," Froehlig said. "Some of the men, myself included, feel it's wrong for the Herr Sergeant to be slighted."

"That's a comfort." Goldstein scowled.

"Most of the men, however," Froehlig continued, ignoring Goldstein's sarcasm, "think the Herr Cavalrycaptain was correct to put you in your place."

Goldstein nodded wearily. "Because I'm a Jew, yes, Herr Corporal?"

"What did you expect, Sir?" Froehlig asked philosophically.

"I'm no stranger to bigotry," Goldstein muttered. "There were bullies in the orphanage who made my life hell over the fact that I was a Jew."

Froehlig cocked his head. "The Herr Sergeant was an orphan?"

"Yes. In Berlin," Goldstein said.

"But brought up as a Jew?"

"That's the irony of it!" Goldstein exploded. "Despite the Jewish blood in my veins, I'm totally uninitiated into the mysteries of that faith. I've met Jews on several occasions, and I tell you that I am as uncomfortable with them and their strange ways as any Christian . . ."

"A changeling," Froehlig said.

"What?"

"The Herr Sergeant seems to me to be like those unfortunate changelings in the fairy stories my mother used to read to me," Froehlig elaborated. "You became lost to your own world early on through no fault of your own, and now there is no world in which you truly belong."

"Hand me another wrench," Goldstein replied. He busied himself attacking the cross-threaded bolt, disturbed and frightened by the truth in what Froehlig had said. "You know, Herr Corporal, I never really counted on friendship and acceptance around here, but I really believed in the military's assurances of fair and equal treatment."

"Why?" Froehlig shrugged. When Goldstein looked up, puzzled, the Corporal continued. "What is the Luftstreitkrafte, or the Reichstag, or any branch of the service, or ministry, or bureaucracy, but a bunch of old men more bigoted and set in their ways than these young gentlemen with whom the Herr Sergeant has been granted the honor of flying?"

"You know, I never thought of it like that," Goldstein admitted. "But I'll never be so naive again," he vowed. "My loyalty to the Herr Rittmeister remains unshaken, but I no longer feel any allegiance to my country——"

"Now the Herr Sergeant *is* being naive. And foolish too; a foolish young pup to speak in such a manner!" Froehlig scolded.

"Excuse me——Herr *Corporal*," Goldstein coldly emphasized.

Froehlig looked around to make sure that they were alone. "Excuse *me* for saying so, but I think that now I'm not speaking to a superior, but to a hurting, lonely boy."

Goldstein tried to interrupt, but Froehlig waved him quiet. "I'm *at least* twice your age, Herr Sergeant. I've been around long enough to know how terribly stupid and cruel bigotry can be, but when you make such emotional, unpatriotic statements you play right into the hands of your worst detractors. The Herr Sergeant must know that of all the charges leveled against his venerable race, their tendency towards socialism, and disloyalty to the Fatherland, ranks among the most serious."

"What's your point, Herr Corporal?"

"My point is that here you are making rash statements that seem to prove your enemies correct. Why give the bigots that satisfaction?"

Goldstein had to smile. "How very clever is the Herr Corporal."

"Not really," Froehlig sighed. "I *am* older, and perhaps that makes me somewhat wiser than a certain young sergeant pilot of whom I am rather fond."

Goldstein looked at Froehlig. "I *have* been a fool," he said softly. "All this while I've been just as bigoted and snobbish as the other pilots. Being a flier, I felt ground personnel were my social inferiors. All these months I've been sulking over my lack of friends, and I've had a good one, and didn't even know it."

Froehlig winked. "It would be unbecoming of a corporal to contradict a sergeant."

Goldstein chuckled. "Well taken. Allow me to introduce myself." He stuck out his hand. "A friend should call me Hermann, and please forgive my greasy hand."

"Heiner Froehlig, pleased to make your acquaintance, Hermann," Froehlig joked. "And your hand is no dirtier than mine. Now let's get working on those bolts."

(Two)

By early afternoon Goldstein and Froehlig had managed to get the Fokker's throttle working properly. They were surprised when the hangar tent began to fill up with mechanics.

"Patrols are going to be sent up, despite the bad weather, Herr Sergeant," one of the newly arrived mechanics informed Goldstein. "Your Jasta is flying."

"That's odd," Goldstein replied, going to the hangar tent's entrance and peering at the sky. "That soup is still pretty thick up there. How are we supposed to see where we're going, never mind fight?"

The mechanic shrugged. "The acting C.O. will give a briefing in the operations hut at thirteen hundred hours."

"That's just fine. The *acting* C.O.—" Goldstein muttered, returning to his partially disassembled Fokker. "The Herr Oberleutnant can't know very much if he wants to send us up into the soup."

"Calm down, Hermann," Froehlig warned him. "Don't go getting yourself grounded for insubordination."

"I'm an experienced and talented pilot," Goldstein bragged, remembering what the Rittmeister had told him. "I can't be grounded. I'm indispensable."

"What you are, is exceedingly young, if you believe that *anyone* is indispensable," Froehlig said firmly.

Goldstein shrugged. It was almost time for the briefing. He wiped his hands on a greasy rag and stepped out of his mechanics overalls. He patted the Fokker's cowling. "Get her ready for me, Heiner."

"She'll be ready, Herr Sergeant." Froehlig nodded, and began barking orders to his own newly arrived crew of mechanics.

Outside the sky was a mass of gray cotton wool. The air felt wet and heavy, threatening rain. Goldstein, hurrying to the operations hut, wondered what the Herr Oberleutnant was thinking, calling for a patrol in this soup.

Outside the hut there were many more pilots milling around the entrance than were going to be flying on patrol. Goldstein was not surprised. Everyone was curious about this mysterious Herr Firstlieutenant Goering.

As Goldstein took his place in the queue, waiting his turn to enter the hut, he noticed several pilots glancing at him, smiling and laughing as they nudged each other. It was as Froehlig had said: everyone knew about his conversation with Richthofen. Goldstein resolutely recalled what *else* the Herr Rittmeister had said: that Goldstein was a hero and a gentleman. If Richthofen believed that, Goldstein would not let his idol down. He would do his best to ignore the ridicule, and hold his head high.

It was just as crowded inside the hut as outside, but Herr Lieutenant Dorn waved to Goldstein and made a place for him at the end of one of the long backless benches.

Goldstein was both grateful and surprised, but then, of all the pilots, Dorn was the most friendly. At least he was on occasion.

Up front, on the raised platform, was Herr Oberleutnant Goering, dressed in a flight suit and wearing knee-high black boots, a double-breasted, black leather jacket trimmed in brown fur, and an ivory-gripped pistol peeking out of the flapped holster strapped around his waist. He was impatiently tapping a swagger stick against his leg as he waited for everyone to find a seat. Behind Goering, on an easel, was a large map of the Somme, with black arrows depicting the Allied and German infantry positions.

"Gentlemen," Goering began once everyone was settled. "The Weather Service has informed me that the cloud cover is expected to remain, and that there may be intermittent drizzle and fog. I have nevertheless scheduled a sortie for Jastas 11, and 6." He approached the map. "Air Warning Service has telephoned reports of Allied fighters harassing our Infantreiflieger Schlastas ground-attack bomber squadrons as they attempt to soften a dug-in pocket of British resistance to our advancing infantry."

As he spoke he pointed to a sector on the Somme about fifteen miles northwest of Cappy to indicate where the action was taking place.

Dorn nudged Goldstein. "We were talking about the situation over breakfast this morning," he whispered. "It's very bad."

Goldstein was amazed that Dorn was being so cordial to him. Maybe he had a friend in Dorn, after all. "But how can that be?" he whispered back. "Our troops are advancing, aren't they?"

Dorn shrugged. "The talk is that the Herr Rittmeister has been called to the rear to advise the Herr General."

Up on the stage Goering was rambling on. "German fighters are needed to neutralize this Allied air attack on our Schlastas. Only then can the Schlastas do their job of supplying air support to our soldiers. As J.G. 1 is closest to the action, the escort and protection sortie falls to us."

Goldstein looked around. None of the others seemed perturbed by Goering's use of the word "us," as if he'd been with the Jagdgeschwader a long while.

"We will be flying at a very low altitude to stay beneath the cloud cover," Goering said. "And, of course, to be of use to the low-flying Infantreiflieger Schlastas. There will be no room for pilot error, and, obviously, parachutes will be useless. We will also be flying past our own lines, so there is some chance of being shot down over enemy territory. Accordingly, all pilots will see to their sidearms, and be sure that their airplanes are equipped with flare guns. It is expected that any pilot downed in enemy territory will avoid capture long enough to use his flare gun to set fire to his machine. Any questions?" Goering looked around. "Very well. Pilots of Jastas 11 and 6 will be on the ready line with their airplanes for my inspection in thirty minutes. Dismissed."

In the ready room Goldstein shrugged on his flying gear. He hesitated, then called to the orderly to bring him his sidearm. When it was handed over to him Goldstein gingerly drew the nine-millimeter Parabellum from its flap holster. The Luger was dusty, and slightly sticky. He pressed the magazine release near the trigger on the lefthand side. The magazine popped out: there were no cartridges in it. He worked the gummy toggle slide to make sure that there was no cartridge in the breech. There wasn't. That was just as well, Goldstein thought as he peered down the Luger's grimy, four-inch barrel. If this fouled weapon were fired it would probably blow up in his hand.

Goldstein knew that he had no time to fieldstrip and clean the weapon. He slid the Luger back into its holster, buttoned down the flap, and strapped it around his waist. He would have to hope for the best during the inspection. The fact that the pistol was useless didn't personally bother Goldstein. He had every intention of immediately surrendering if he went down behind enemy lines. He was a flier, not an infantry soldier. If the Herr Oberleutnant had any problem with that he could just come visit Goldstein in the P.O.W. camp in order to reprimand him.

On the ready line Goldstein made sure that his flare pistol

was clipped in place in his Fokker's cockpit. He came to attention in front of his airplane as Goering appeared, swagger stick in hand, with Adjutant Bodenschatz, thirty years old and matinee-idol handsome, in tow.

Standing ramrod straight, staring straight ahead, Goldstein watched out of the corner of his eye as the Herr Oberleutnant walked the line, pausing here and there to look over an airplane, or nod to a pilot. The suspense mounted as Goering approached, but he seemed unconcerned with Goldstein; was passing him by; Goldstein was about to breathe a sigh of relief—

Goering glanced at Goldstein's Fokker, and then stopped. "Herr Sergeant, why is there only one machine gun mounted on your airplane?" he asked ominously. "How can you expect to perform your duty of shooting down enemy machines with only one machine gun?"

"Sir, using only one gun I have shot down sixteen airplanes up to now with no great problem—"

"Quiet!" Goering snapped. He looked at the adjutant. "This man's name?" he demanded.

"Hermann Goldstein," Bodenschatz replied.

"Ah, yes." Goering nodded jovially. "I thought he looked familiar. This is the young fellow who made that touching speech about winning his Blue Max." He smiled at Goldstein. "I presume the Herr Sergeant has been set straight concerning that ludicrous notion?" When Goldstein didn't reply, Goering's smile faded. "I asked you a question, Herr Sergeant."

"Yes, Sir, I have been set straight concerning that, Sir."

Goering gestured toward Goldstein's single Spandau gun with his swagger stick. "Your airplane's armament is totally against regulations. All the other pilots see fit to fly with standard-issue, twin machine guns." He stepped in close to Goldstein, and used his swagger stick to tilt up Goldstein's chin. "What's good enough for *decent*, *Christian*, *gentlemen*," Goering took his time, spitting the words into Goldstein's face as he used the stick to lever Goldstein's chin ever higher, "ought to be good enough for the *likes of you*, Herr Sergeant."

Goldstein heard snickers of laughter up and down the line.

His rage, so long bottled up, bubbled over inside of him. "Begging the Herr Firstlieutenant's pardon," Goldstein heard himself say, "your decent Christian gentlemen are content to fly guns. *I* fly airplanes."

"Not today will you fly airplanes!" Goering exploded. "I won't have your insolence! You're grounded! Herr Adjutant! Make note in the official record that Herr Sergeant Hermann Goldstein had been officially reprimanded and grounded by the acting C.O. of J.G. 1. —"

"Sir, the Herr Rittmeister knows about the Herr Sergeant's single gun," Bodenschatz tried to protest. "The Herr Rittmeister—"

"Isn't here!" Goering snapped. "But I am here!" He stepped back to address the entire line. "All of you better realize that I will brook no insolence! No nonsense! Things will be done exactly as I order them! Exactly by the book! Understood?"

The line was deathly silent. Goering shifted his attention back to Goldstein. "You, Herr Sergeant, are to consider yourself confined to quarters until further notice!" He waved his swagger stick as if he were flicking away an insect. "Dismissed!"

Goldstein stood where he was, too dumbfounded to move. Goering, staring at him, turned red. "I said that you were dismissed—"

Goldstein saluted, and stepped back, out of the line. He felt everyone's eyes upon him as he briskly walked to the ready room to turn in his gear.

(Three)

Goldstein was stretched out on his cot, trying to read about the principles of aircraft design, without much success. He was still too angry concerning the way that Goering had ripped into him two hours earlier to see the words on the page.

He set his book aside, and surrendered to an elaborate fantasy dogfight in which he, with his single Spandau gun, managed to punch enough holes into Goering's white D VII to blow the machine right out from under the screaming Herr Oberleutnant's fat ass—

And then, Goering's wails in Goldstein's daydream turned into the air raid siren's mournful howl.

Goldstein sat up, skeptical, expecting it to be a false alarm. Then he heard the roar of airplanes overhead, and the flat, kettle-drum boom of a bomb exploding. He ran to the door, but then hesitated. The Herr Oberleutnant had restricted him to quarters.

The window-rattling explosion of a second bomb decided it for him. At any moment the enemy might begin strafing the pilots' huts. He had no intention of dying in this flimsy wooden hovel.

Outside everything was noise, smoke, and confusion. Panicked pilots and ground crews were dashing about, shouting conflicting orders at each other. Overhead, three bright orange Spads, wearing the coiled serpent insignia of the French Squadron 30, had command of the sky. Goldstein heard the distinctive chatter of the Spads' Vickers machine guns as they strafed the field and the answering racket put out by the sleigh-mounted, water-cooled Maxim machine guns manned by the ground air-defense crews assigned to Cappy.

As Goldstein approached the hangar tents he saw one of the Spads dive toward the nearby rows of parked fuel-tank lorries. A half-dozen sandbag emplacements of Maxim guns bordering the lorries put up crisscrossing lines of defensive fire. The fast-diving Spad shot back, tearing up a Maxim gun and its three-man crew. As the Spad roared past, it came out of its dive to release a bomb which whistled down toward the lorries.

Goldstein, like everyone else, threw himself to the ground and waited for the bomb to detonate—and then the huge fireball as the fuel-laden lorries ignited. The image of the Spad and the number painted on its tail was emblazoned in his mind: *The airplane that's killed me is number 17.*

Nothing happened. The Spad's bomb was evidently a dud.

Goldstein got to his feet, dripping mud. He saw Corporal Froehlig standing at the entranceway to one of the hangar tents and ran toward him. Froehlig was screaming orders to mechanics and ground crew to get the closest Fokkers fueled and rolled out to the ready line.

As Goldstein reached Froehlig he saw the adjutant, Herr Oberleutnant Bodenschatz, approaching. The adjutant was riding as the passenger in a motorcycle sidecar on which was mounted a shoulder-stock, drum-fed, Parabellum light machine gun. Bodenschatz was hopping out of the car almost before the cycle driver had skidded to a halt, spraying mud.

"What's going on?" Goldstein yelled over the noise of the Spads, shouting men, and ground defense machine gun fire.

Froehlig looked furious. "The Herr Oberleutnant Goering neglected to issue orders for a squad to be prepared for air-defense of the field."

"An understandable oversight," Bodenschatz cut in, loyally attempting to defend a fellow officer. "With the weather so poor the Herr Oberleutnant didn't believe Allied fighters would attempt the venture."

"As the Herr Adjutant wishes," Froehlig murmured. "But now it'll be at least ten minutes before we can get anything in the air."

"But my Fokker's still on the ready line—" Goldstein exclaimed. He stared at his airplane. "My God, the propeller's turning! Who started the engine?"

"I did," Corporal Froehlig said. "I ordered the crew to start her up as soon as the siren sounded."

"Then why isn't she in the air?" Goldstein asked, exasperated.

Corporal Froehlig looked away. "The Herr Adjutant will explain."

"Explain what?" Goldstein demanded impatiently.

"No one will fly your machine," Bodenschatz said, looking embarrassed.

"Because it has only one gun?" Goldstein asked in disbelief.

Bodenschatz shook his head. "Because the others consider it unlucky . . . and unclean." His voice trailed off. "—because you're a Jew."

Goldstein shuddered, disgusted. *These fools can no longer humiliate me*, he thought. *They can only humiliate themselves.* "Then I'll fly it," he said, turning away.

Bodenschatz stopped him. "You've been grounded."

Goldstein saw that Spad No. 17 was coming around for another try at the fuel lorries, while the other two flew top cover to protect their companion against an ambush from a returning German patrol. "Begging the Herr Adjutant's pardon," Goldstein replied. "But we'll all be *dead* if we don't get a plane in the air to at least *distract* the enemy."

"But those Spads will be on you as soon as they see you rolling," Froehlig objected. "You'll be shot up before you leave the ground."

Goldstein looked at Bodenschatz. "Sir, will you help?"

"But how can I?"

"Your motorcycle sidecar, Sir. It has a machine gun. If you were to ride alongside my Fokker, affording me covering fire until I was airborne?..."

Bodenschatz's dark eyes lit up. He grinned and quickly nodded. "Herr Sergeant, I'll be beside you when you need me."

Goldstein ran toward his airplane, with Froehlig keeping up beside him. "Your helmet and goggles—" the corporal began.

"No time for them," Goldstein muttered.

"The windchill," Froehlig protested.

"Heiner, look on the bright side. It's going to be three against one, assuming I can even take off. I'll probably be *dead* before I feel any discomfort."

As they reached the idling airplane Froehlig reached out to grasp Goldstein's arm. "Good luck, Hermann."

"Thanks, my friend," Goldstein smiled, and then he was hoisting himself into the cockpit. He quickly buckled himself into his seat as Froehlig pulled the chocks from the wheels. As the Fokker began to roll Goldstein slapped open the throttle and steered for open ground.

Goldstein, squinting against the engine exhaust smoke, looked up over his shoulder. The Fokker was bouncing and jolting its way along the rutted field. The Spads would spot him any second now.

He saw Spad No. 17 break off strafing the fuel lorries, luckily, before any of the Spad's bullets could ignite the petro. The Spad came around onto Goldstein's tail, with the other two stacked above it, still acting as lookouts as they patiently waited their turn to shoot German fish in a barrel.

Goldstein smiled grimly. At least he'd succeeded in drawing the enemy away from the vulnerable fuel deposit and the hangar tents. He didn't think the Frenchies could resist his decoy maneuver. Blowing up fuel lorries or parked airplanes was important work, but destroying a *piloted* airplane, even if it was still on the ground, would count as a kill on a pilot's record.

Goldstein waited for the last possible moment before turning his Fokker into the wind, so abruptly that his triplane's wing skid scraped the ground. The Spads overshot him. He heard their Vickers guns, and saw their rounds kicking up mud, but no bullets hit his airplane. Goldstein had his throttle wide open, the Fokker was rattling along fit to jar the teeth out of his head, but it would still be another minute before he would be going fast enough to get airborne.

The Spad pilots would know that as well, just as they'd know that now he *had* to remain on a straight course if he wanted to reach takeoff velocity. All the Spads had to do was get behind him and use their machine guns to nail him down.

Goldstein again peered over his shoulder. The Spads were closing in. He saw orange fire licking out from the barrels of No. 17's twin Vickers. The mud was erupting in molten spurts all around his Fokker. He hunched down in his seat and waited to get shot. Where the hell was Bodenschatz?—

Thanks to his own engine making such a racket, Goldstein didn't hear the motorcycle until it had pulled up alongside his airplane. Bodenschatz jauntily waved and then hunched over his sidecar's Parabellum and began firing short bursts up at the offending Spad.

Goldstein never expected Bodenschatz to do any damage; all he'd wanted was for the adjutant's gun to buy him a little breathing space. Goldstein watched what was happening in his rearview mirror and couldn't have been more shocked when Spad 17 began spewing black smoke, the thick oily clouds effectively shrouding his Fokker, preventing the other Spads from accurately returning fire.

Goldstein heard Bodenschatz bellow, "Good God, I've

got a kill!" He watched in his mirror as Spad 17 banked steeply onto its side and then nosedived, its prop biting into the mud. The Spad erupted in thunder and flames as its momentum cartwheeled it end over end across the field. There was no way the Spad's pilot could have survived that, Goldstein thought as Bodenschatz's driver, panicked by the shooting flames, veered off.

He pulled back on his stick, and the Fokker responded. He glimpsed Bodenschatz behind his smoking machine gun, his fists held aloft in triumph, and then the motorcycle and sidecar dropped away. Goldstein was airborne.

As soon as he had enough altitude not to scrape his tail, Goldstein hauled up the Fokker's nose, putting his machine through a severely tight Immelman loop. He heard his Fokker's struts groan in protest and knew that he was risking tearing the fragile, three-tiered, wood and canvas wings right off his machine, but he held to the aerobatic maneuver, up and over and right into the surprised faces of the two Spads. Like jousting knights, the three planes converged upon each other. Goldstein fired a burst from his Spandau gun point-blank into the prop of the nearest Spad, even as his opponents' Vickers tore holes in his own engine cowling. Then he was past the two Spads, and fighting for altitude.

Goldstein knew that the Spads were equipped with Hispano-Suiza in-line engines that put out 220 horsepower as compared to his engine's puny 110. It was a given that the Spads could fly rings around any Fokker triplane, but Goldstein's Fokker was a stripped-down machine, carrying only one gun, and he himself was a pilot who, like a jockey, had disciplined his body to go without so as to be as light as possible.

The Spads at the field's far end would climb higher and faster than his Fokker, but all three airplanes would have to stop climbing prematurely to avoid entering the heavy cloud cover that canopied the sky. Goldstein hoped the Spads' pilots would overestimate their altitude advantage when they began their attack dive. If they did so, their superior speed, relatively low altitude, and proximity would not allow the French pilots the time to correct their misjudgment.

The wind tore at Goldstein, almost blinding his unprotected eyes as he came around in a steeply banking turn toward his two adversaries. The Spads had come around as well. They were hurtling toward him head on at top speed. As he'd hoped, the French pilots had underestimated his modified Fokker's climbing ability. They'd figured he'd be lower than he was, so their angle of descent was too steep for them to use their own guns.

As they crossed Goldstein's path, well forward of him, he put a burst into the nearest Spad, plowing a 7.92-millimeter furrow along its fuselage from nose to tail.

The Spad he'd shot up went into a tailspin, just pulling out in time. Goldstein watched the bullet-pocked airplane skirt Cappy field in a wide bank and then head for home. The other Spad was turning tail and running off as well. Goldstein didn't understand what was going on until he saw Jastas 11 and 6, in stacked Vee formation, coming home.

It was over, and he was alive.

Goering's all-white D VII buzzed Goldstein as he came in for his landing, swooping past the still burning wreckage of the Spad that Bodenschatz had shot down. Goldstein wondered what that was all about as he touched down, cutting his engine and rolling to a stop before his Fokker's hangar tent, where a number of pilots were congregated. Froehlig and Bodenschatz were hurrying toward him. Glancing into his rearview mirror, Goldstein saw Goering's airplane touch down a couple of hundred feet behind him.

"Congratulations, Herr Sergeant!" Froehlig exclaimed as Goldstein climbed out of his Fokker. "That was a magnificent performance."

Bodenschatz was dancing about madly, overcome with excitement. "Did you see it, Herr Sergeant?" He laughed. "I shot down an airplane! I must be the first ground officer to get himself a confirmed kill!"

"I saw, Herr Adjutant." Goldstein grinned. "My congratulations. You can fly with me anytime." He noticed the other pilots standing some distance away. They were scowling at him. "What's the problem with them?"

"They're angry because you had all the fun, I suppose," Froehlig replied. "Those fine young gentlemen weren't prepared to do the job, and I suppose they just can't accept the notion that *you*, of all people, saved their aristocratic asses."

Goldstein shrugged wearily. "The important thing is that J.G. 1 has been saved."

Goering's white airplane had come to a halt beside his own. "You!" Goering screamed, hopping out of his cockpit. "You disobeyed my orders!" He tore off his goggles and helmet and hurled them to the ground as he raced toward an appalled Goldstein.

"Sir, begging the Herr Oberleutnant's pardon," Goldstein stuttered. "I-I thought you'd be pleased. I saved the aerodrome—"

"What you did was disobey my orders!" Goering roared, stopping short just inches from where Goldstein was standing. The Firstlieutenant's face was red, and spittle was flying from the corners of his mouth. "I specifically confined you to quarters! I specifically grounded you! But you took it upon yourself to fly—"

"Sir, we were under attack, and my Fokker was the only machine that was flight ready—"

"I don't care!" Goering looked around, his eyes wild. "My orderly! Where's my orderly? Where's my stick?"

The orderly, looking deathly pale, seemed to appear out of nowhere. He quickly ran over with the Oberleutnant's swagger stick. Goering grabbed it away and began to rhythmically slap it against his boots.

"Herr Oberleutnant," Bodenschatz began. "You may not understand the situation—"

"I don't need to understand anything but that this man disobeyed my orders!" Goering shouted. His breath thudded into Goldstein's face. "Must I have insubordination from you, as well, Adjutant?"

"May I remind the Herr Firstlieutenant that we hold the same rank," Bodenschatz quietly replied.

"Yes, and may *I* remind the Herr Adjutant that he is a ground officer," Goering sneered. "And may I *also* remind him that the Herr Rittmeister left *me* in charge. I am acting C.O. of J.G. 1." Goering's stick sounded like a whip as it slapped against his boot.

"That's all quite true, Herr Oberleutnant," Bodenschatz acknowledged.

"And as for you, Herr Sergeant," Goering began, "I will not have you disobeying my orders, no matter what." The tip of his swagger stick found Goldstein's chin, tipping it up, tipping back Goldstein's head. "Do you understand me, Herr Sergeant?"

"Yes, sir."

Goering grinned fiercely. "I don't think you do—"

Goldstein saw Goering's left hand flash up in a roundhouse arc, but with his head still tilted awkwardly back by Goering's stick, Goldstein had no time to dodge or deflect the blow. Goering's palm caught him on the side of his face, the noise of impact as sharp as a pistol crack.

Goldstein's head rocked as white-hot pain erupted all along his jawline. His knees sagged, but he kept himself from crumpling as he looked at Goering with dazed, shocked eyes.

All around him was quiet. Froehlig, Bodenschatz, and the other pilots and ground personnel who'd been watching were too shocked to do or say anything.

"*Now* I think you understand how it is, yes, Herr Sergeant?" Goering asked lightly.

Goldstein, still punch-drunk, shook himself. Never in his life had he intentionally harmed another human being, but right now he felt as if he could tear Goering apart with his bare hands.

"Herr Sergeant!" Goering shouted. "I asked you if you understood. Have you bitten off your tongue?—"

"You bastard!" Goldstein snarled at Goering.

Goering's smile instantly disappeared. "What? *What* did you call me?"

"Calm down, now, Herr Sergeant," Bodenschatz was saying.

"I called you a bastard!" Goldstein repeated. "Because that's exactly what you are."

"You swine!" Goering said thickly. "You insufferable Jewish swine!"

Goldstein charged forward, tackling Goering, and then they were falling; struggling and rolling in the mud. For one brief instant Goldstein was straddling Goering. His hands found Goering's throat— Then he felt hands pulling him up and away.

"How dare you!" Goering was on his feet, dripping mud; the sable trim on his leather jacket was matted with the stuff. "How dare you!"

Goldstein struggled to reach Goering, but found himself smothered in Corporal Froehlig's powerful bear hug. "No, Herr Sergeant!" Froehlig was desperately pleading in Goldstein's ear. "No! Stand still!"

Goldstein sagged, the fight gone out of him. He would be court-martialed for this, he realized. Court-martialed for attacking a superior officer.

"Look there!" Bodenschatz called out. "A motorcar is coming."

Goldstein turned, as did everyone else, to watch a mud-splattered, gray Mercedes touring car approach. The car gave the still smouldering, wrecked Spad a wide berth as it bounced its way across the field.

"Thank God," Bodenschatz said. "It is the Herr Rittmeister returning." He looked at Goering. "Herr Oberleutnant, I trust you will agree that you are no longer C.O.? Herr Corporal Froehlig!" Bodenschatz continued before Goering could reply. "You will escort Herr Sergeant Goldstein to the infirmary to see if he needs medical attention. Then you will escort him to his quarters, where he will remain until further orders. Dismissed!"

(Four)

At the infirmary an attendant examined Goldstein's jaw and told him that nothing was broken. His jaw would ache for a few days, and the long, purple bruise running along the side of his face would fade in about a week.

Froehlig accompanied Goldstein back to his quarters. Once they were inside the hut the corporal pulled a small silver flask from the back hip pocket of his mechanic's overalls and offered it to Goldstein. "For the pain, my young friend."

"I'm tempted, but I can't," Goldstein sighed. "The Herr Rittmeister will soon be summoning me. I can't report to him with schnapps on my breath."

"Hermann," Froehlig said sourly. "Considering your circumstances at present, I really wouldn't worry about taking a little drink."

Goldstein nodded sadly as he took the flask and had himself a long swallow of schnapps. The stuff burned his throat going down and made his eyes water.

"Have another," Froehlig coaxed as Goldstein tried to hand back the flask.

Goldstein shook his head. "I'm not used to it, Heiner." He returned the flask and flopped down on his cot. "Although I suppose I should get drunk now. They don't allow schnapps in prison, right?"

"A court-martial and prison are hardly a certainty," Froehlig reasoned. He turned the straight-back chair around and straddled it, resting his forearms and chin on its back rail. "The Herr Rittmeister is the one who will decide. If he tells Goering not to pursue the matter the Herr Oberleutnant would not dare try to go over the Herr Rittmeister's head."

"But the Herr Cavalrycaptain is himself a stickler for discipline," Goldstein said sadly.

"But he's also fair," Froehlig pointed out between sips from his flask. "Mind if I smoke?" When Goldstein shook his head, Froehlig put away his flask and took out a short-stemmed, black briar pipe and a leather tobacco pouch. "The other pilots who witnessed the incident have it in for you, and will probably back whatever story Goering chooses to tell." He filled his pipe, then found a wooden match in his pocket and flicked it against his thumbnail. "But Bodenschatz will tell the truth." He puffed his pipe alight in a cloud of blue smoke.

"Well, whatever happens, I hope it's soon," Goldstein said. "It's getting dark out. I don't want to spend the night worrying about what's going to happen." He paused, to smile at Froehlig. "And whatever happens, I want to thank you, Heiner. When you grabbed me, and stopped me from attacking Goering a second time, you probably saved me from having to face a firing squad."

Froehlig, scowling, waved away his pipe smoke, along with Goldstein's thanks. "The way I see it, you saved my life, and the lives of everyone else, thanks to your defense of the aerodrome. You deserve a medal for what you did today, not a court-martial."

"I feel like I'm in a dream," Goldstein muttered. "A few days ago I thought I *was* in line for honors: a promotion and the Blue Max. Now my neck seems to be on the chopping block for insubordination, and assaulting an officer . . ."

There was a knock at the door. "Come!" Goldstein called.

Two infantry privates carrying Mauser rifles stood in the doorway. "Herr Sergeant," one of them began. "The Herr Rittmeister will see you now." The private eyed Froehlig. "Our orders are that you come alone."

Goldstein, feeling sick, stood up. He smoothed his rumpled uniform and took his cap from its wall hook. "Heiner, if I don't get the chance to see you again—"

"You'll see me again," Froehlig cut him off gruffly. "One way or the other, you will. Friends stick together."

The soldiers silently escorted Goldstein to the Herr Rittmeister's office, located in the administrative section and attached to the pilots' mess. One of the privates knocked once on Richthofen's door and opened it for Goldstein. He stepped inside and heard the door click shut behind him.

The office was lit by a narrow, golden funnel of light cast by a polished brass lantern hanging from the ceiling. The walls were covered with canvas serial numbers cut from the fuselages of the Herr Rittmeister's kills. Off to one side, bracketed by file cabinets, was a mahogany and glass case which housed Richthofen's legendary collection of almost eighty diminutive silver cups, each one engraved with the particulars of a confirmed kill. Leaning in a corner were several propellers taken from fallen enemy airplanes, and on a sideboard was a collection of pistols taken from vanquished Allied pilots.

Richthofen was seated behind his desk. "Herr Sergeant Goldstein." He looked at Goldstein with interest, gesturing for him to stand beneath the lantern.

Goldstein took his place beneath the light and came to attention.

"Tell me, Herr Sergeant. The enemy has never managed to cause you to lose your temper and resort to violence to the extent reported to me today. How did the Herr Oberleutnant manage it?"

Goldstein told his story. When he was done, the Herr Rittmeister nodded.

"Your version of the events matches the Herr Adjutant's," Richthofen said, and then smiled. "Tell me, did Herr Oberleutnant Bodenschatz really shoot down that Spad?"

"Yes, Sir."

"My God, I would have liked to have seen that," Richthofen sighed. "But let's return to the matter at hand. Herr Oberleutnant Goering is at this moment on his way back to his own squadron. I have persuaded him not to press charges against you."

"Thank you, Sir!" Goldstein said, hugely relieved.

Richthofen nodded. "You may stand at ease, Herr Sergeant. I'd like to get a few things straight between us. We both know that what the Herr Oberleutnant did was inexcusable," Richthofen continued. "As a matter of fact, you would technically be within your rights to file charges against him. I assume you understand that you cannot do so, that you would hurt only yourself?"

"Yes, Sir," Goldstein said evenly. "I understand perfectly, Sir. What happened isn't important. The reality is that the Herr Oberleutnant wears the Blue Max; he is an officer and a gentleman. And I am—" Goldstein smiled thinly. "Well, Sir, we've already discussed what I am . . ."

Richthofen frowned. "I'm very sorry, Herr Sergeant."

"Yes, Sir," Goldstein deadpanned. "Thank you, Sir."

Richthofen looked uncomfortable. "Well, then, if we understand each other," he shrugged. "I suppose that you're dismissed."

Goldstein came to attention and saluted. He turned on his heel and went to the door.

"Herr Sergeant," Richthofen called softly.

"Sir?" Goldstein turned.

Richthofen stood up. His smile was almost shy. "Hermann, thank you for saving my Circus."

Goldstein felt the anger and hostility drain out. He grinned. "My pleasure, Sir."

Chapter 3

(One)
Jadgeschwader 1
Cappy
21 April 1918

Goldstein was in the hangar tent, overhauling his Fokker's machine gun synchronizer mechanism, when he heard that Richthofen had been shot down over enemy lines.

Goldstein's initial reaction was an illogical one: that the tragedy was his fault. If only his armament hadn't malfunctioned, if only he could have gone along with his Jasta on its patrol, then the Herr Rittmeister wouldn't have gone down.

J.G. 1 waited, along with the rest of the military and the German people back home, for word from the British concerning Richthofen. There was no question that the nation's hero had fallen, but perhaps he was a prisoner, alive and well.

On the evening of the twenty-second a British airplane buzzed Cappy Field to drop a tersely worded note of condolence from the R.A.F.—along with a photograph purported to be of Richthofen's grave. On April 23 the British officially announced that the Red Battle Flier Richthofen had been buried with full military honors in the cemetery at Bertangles.

That evening, as the pilots of J.G. 1 somberly drank memorial toasts, Adjutant Bodenschatz announced that Lieutenant Wilhelm Reinhard would be the new Geschwaderkommandeur. Goldstein couldn't shake the feeling that all of this was an awful dream, and that tomorrow he would wake up to find the Herr Rittmeister alive and well and ready to lead his cubs into battle in the heavens.

A few days later the order came down to change the Circus's official standard, from Richthofen's red to Reinhard's favored royal blue. It was only when Goldstein watched the painter's brush eradicating his Fokker's proud scarlet that his heart finally acknowledged that Richthofen was gone.

J.G. 1 spent the rest of April and the month of May traveling along the front lines, trying its best to shore up the exhausted German Army. General Ludendorff's second offensive at Lys, and his third, across the Aisne and Vesle Rivers, had stalled. Now the Allies, bolstered by the influx of fresh American troops, were on the offensive.

Goldstein spent his days flying double patrols, and his nights trying to grab a few fitful hours of sleep in tents or in the backs of jolting lorries traveling ruined roads. Each day J.G. 1 took its share of kills—Goldstein's count reached twenty—but each day there seemed to be more Allied planes to confront. There were swarms of them, and while most of their pilots were green, the Allies' sheer numbers bought them victory.

Goldstein knew that Germany had lost this war. He discussed it in private with Corporal Froehlig, who agreed with him. Now Goldstein only wondered if he would live to witness his country's surrender.

In June the Jadgeschwader received its allotment of Fokker D VIIs. Goldstein did not object when the armorer equipped his machine with twin Spandau guns. He didn't dare; the mood of the Circus was far too grimly vengeful. He still took his time and chose his shots. Goldstein was fighting hard now; fighting not only to avenge Richthofen's death, but to survive, and still he was determined to remain true to himself. To maintain the quality of mercy in a world gone rabid with cruelty.

But Richthofen had been right that night in Goldstein's hut: this was no game. It had taken the Herr Rittmeister's death for Goldstein to realize that.

(Two)
J.G. 1
Coincy Field, near Château-Thierry, France
3 July 1918

The day started out badly. Coincy was a mud-bog. Goldstein had spent the night in a sodden tent that stank of mildew. He'd been plagued by gnats so small that they moved freely through the mesh of the mosquito nets. He would never get used to tents: the insects, the filth, and the dark, dank atmosphere. It was like living in a cave.

At breakfast he was greeted with news that the Germans, still reeling from their defeat at Belleau Wood, had just been chased out of the strategically located village of Vaux by American Marines.

Later, while flying morning patrol with Jasta 11, Goldstein and the others encountered American pilots over Château-Thierry. The Yanks were flying superb Spad 13s. There were eight of them, jauntily daubed with the red, white, and blue of the American flag.

It was the first time that Goldstein had run into Yanks. Others of J.G. 1 had encountered them, and they'd had discouraging stories to tell about the Americans' prowess and bravado. Lieutenant Reinhard had said not to worry about the Americans: that they would be inexperienced, and would fall before J.G. 1's guns.

Reinhard was wrong.

The Yanks Goldstein encountered that morning were not inexperienced, or, if they were, they were incredibly swift learners. The dogfight started out even, eight against eight. When the tangle broke apart, the Yanks remained unscathed, but three of Jasta 11, including Lieutenant Dorn, had spun earthward in flames. Goldstein had spiraled down like an anxious mother bird around Dorn's burning Fokker, but there was nothing he could do for the lieutenant. Nobody could have survived Dorn's fiery crash.

Flying as low as he could, Goldstein ran for home, following what remained of his once proud squadron. High above, the Yanks were flying victory loops, rejoicing in the wide expanse of blue that had become their domain.

That afternoon Goldstein was in the umbrella tent that served as the pilots' mess. He was sitting apart from the other fliers, and, as usual, his nose was in a book. He'd borrowed the shop manual on the D VII's Mercedes engine from Corporal Froehlig and was studying it, doing his best not to think about the early evening patrol he was scheduled to fly.

"Gentlemen—"

Goldstein glanced up. It was the adjutant.

"Gentlemen, your attention," Bodenschatz repeated. "It is my sad duty to inform you that Herr Lieutenant Reinhard has been killed."

Goldstein put aside his book out of respect, and pretended to listen as Bodenschatz recounted the details of Reinhard's death. The truth was that while Goldstein felt sorry for Reinhard, who'd been a good man and an able leader, he couldn't find it within himself to mourn. So many acquaintances were dying that Goldstein had become numb to further loss.

It's the odds, Goldstein remembered Richthofen had said. *Sooner or later, the odds get everyone.*

Through luck, or destiny, Goldstein had managed to become one of the senior members of J.G. 1. This made him a figure of awe to the green pilots newly assigned to the ragtag caravan of lorries and airplanes roaming the faltering front lines.

That these boisterous and enthusiastic inexperienced fliers looked up to him the way that he had looked up to Richthofen appalled Goldstein. He went out of his way to discourage the friendship of these new pilots. He didn't want to get to know them. What was the point? Tomorrow they would be dead, and strange new faces would appear to take their place. The fact that these new fliers were blithely oblivious to the fact that they had a mayfly's life expectancy enraged many of the veteran pilots. One day there appeared a gruesome addition to the ridgepole of the tent that housed the new recruits. It was a carved wooden buzzard, winking as it contemplated the new pilots. The buzzard's claws held a carved scroll on which was engraved the question, *Wet or Dry?*

Every pilot knew that "Wet" meant bloodied in a crash. "Dry" meant burned to a crisp when one's airplane caught fire in the air.

The worst about the new pilots was that they knew Richthofen only as legend. The realization that the Herr Rittmeister—who had been so vital—had been relegated to myth profoundly shook Goldstein. It made him realize just how real death was; how it wiped you from the face of the earth, not caring one bit about your prior accomplishments in life.

It made him realize how fragile was his mortal existence. It made him, at long last, afraid to die.

Goldstein spent his off-duty hours with Corporal Froehlig, in the hangar tent, where the two of them explored the mechanical intricacies of the D VII beneath the hissing, flickering lanterns. While they worked they would quietly chat. Gradually Goldstein and Froehlig began to talk, at first shyly, but then with increasing enthusiasm, about a partnership in a motorcar garage in Berlin come the war's end...

"Gentlemen, a moment of silence," Bodenschatz commanded, shaking Goldstein from his dark thoughts. "Silence for all our fallen comrades, and, as always, for the Herr Rittmeister..."

It was nonsense, Goldstein thought. Those men didn't want silence; they wanted another chance at being alive.

After a decent interval Goldstein asked, "Herr Oberleutnant, who will be the new Geschwaderkommandeur?"

Bodenschatz looked away. "I'm sorry to say that your old friend Goering has been given command."

Goldstein, shocked, followed the adjutant out of the tent. "Sir, I respectfully request a transfer—"

Bodenschatz shook his head. "Not possible. You know as well as I do how understaffed we are."

"But the other Jagdgeschwadern must be understaffed, as well," Goldstein argued. "You could trade me for one of their pilots. I don't care where I'm transferred, or what I'm asked to do—"

"I'm sorry, Herr Sergeant."

Bodenschatz began to turn away. Goldstein pulled him around by his shoulders.

"You of all people should understand!" Goldstein pleaded. "You were there, you saw how Goering treated me—"

Bodenschatz frowned. "Herr Sergeant . . ." He trailed off. "Hermann," he said softly. "There's nothing I can do."

(Three)
J.G. 1
Near Soissons, France
17 July 1918

Goldstein, along with the rest of J.G. 1, stood at attention in the mess tent as Bodenschatz officially handed over command of the Jagdgeschwader to Herr Oberleutnant Hermann Goering.

"Thank you, Herr Oberleutnant Bodenschatz," Goering said. As the adjutant sat down, Goering, his arms folded across his chest, scanned the pilots who made up his new command.

Goldstein thought Goering had put on weight since he'd last seen the man. It came from piloting a desk rather than an airplane, Goldstein guessed. Rumor had it that Goering had been awarded command of J.G. 1 due to his administrative abilities rather than his flying skills.

Goldstein barely controlled himself from flinching when Goering's eyes flicked past, but the new Geschwaderkommandeur showed no expression at all as he looked at Goldstein. It was as if Goering didn't recognize him.

"Gentlemen," Goering began. "I needn't tell you that I take command of J.G. 1 at a desperate moment for the Fatherland. Our armies, intent upon a peace offensive, have been engaged in a desperate struggle, and I have personally informed Herr General Ludendorff that J.G. 1 stands ready to fight to the death to lend air support to our soldiers in their hour of need." Goering paused. "I don't wish to disparage the memory of Herr Lieutenant Reinhard, but I believe that your former C.O.'s lax adherence to the dicta handed down by the great German ace, and the founder of air battle tactics, Herr Hauptmann Oswald Boeleck, is what has led to the recent crippling losses suffered by J.G. 1.

"Accordingly, and because so many of you are inexperienced, new recruits, I will take total command of all of your actions in the air. Personal initiative in battle is hereby forbidden. The airplanes of J.G. 1 will operate together like the individual cogs of a single, finely honed machine. *I* will sit at the controls of that machine. During patrols there will be *no* breaking of information; *no* firing until I give the command; *no* free-for-alls, which means no chasing of targets, no matter how tempting.

"Any pilot who can report to me that another man has broken these rules will be rewarded. Any pilot caught breaking these rules will be punished. Is all of that clear?"

When no one spoke, Goering nodded. "Well, then, if you will all follow me outside, gentlemen . . ."

Goldstein glanced at Bodenschatz, but the adjutant seemed to be just as mystified as everyone else. Goldstein waited until it was his turn to join the throng filing out, and then followed Goering through the mud to the tent that housed the new recruits. The pilots all formed a half circle behind Goering as he drew his Luger and fired three shots at the ghoulish wooden buzzard, blasting the carving off the tent's ridgepole.

"Gentlemen, 'Wet or dry?' is not a question we ask ourselves," Goering said pleasantly as he holstered his smoking pistol. "It is a question we ask our enemy. You are dismissed."

Goldstein had to grin. At that moment he almost liked Goering.

* * *

"I'm glad to see you," Corporal Froehlig said when Goldstein came into the hangar tent. "When I heard those three shots I couldn't help picturing Goering shooting *you*—"

Goldstein smiled. "No, he didn't shoot me. Goering didn't take any special notice of me, at all." He hesitated. "Heiner, do you think he's forgotten about it?"

Froehlig looked uneasy. "I doubt that."

It rained hard all that night, drumming loudly, soaking through the threadbare tent canvas and making it impossible to sleep. Goldstein hoped it would keep raining. Every day spent grounded was a day closer to the war's imminent, inevitable end. In the three months since Richthofen's death Goldstein had come to feel very much older, and infinitely wiser. He'd become a confirmed devotee of "Pilot's Sunshine."

The rumble of artillery, like distant thunder, began around dawn. Those were German guns, located at Soissons, and they were rumbling at the advancing Frenchies, bolstered by those seemingly unstoppable American Marines.

Goldstein got dressed and went to the mess tent, the driest, warmest place in camp thanks to the big cook stoves. A number of pilots were already at the long tables, hunched over their coffee. It was quiet, except for the coughing spells of those suffering from the respiratory infections that were making constant rounds. Over everything was the patter of rain, and the rumble of the artillery battle for Soissons that they would sooner or later be asked to join.

Goldstein got himself some coffee and sat down at an unoccupied table, thinking that it was pitiful what had become of Richthofen's Circus, once the pride of the Luftstreitkrafte, now just a handful of tired and dirty men in tattered uniforms, coughing and sniffling like derelicts.

Goldstein smiled. It all would have been funny, if he weren't so tired and uncomfortable. And if the sounds of the battle weren't drawing closer.

At seven hundred hours the rain tapered off. Goldstein was about to leave the mess tent to go for a stroll when Goering, creaking in his black leather flying outfit, his medals jangling, appeared in the doorway. Goldstein announced the Geschwaderkommandeur, and the pilots came to attention.

"Gentlemen, we've been informed that the American Expeditionary Force, supported by French armor, have broken through our lines southeast of our position," Goering announced calmly. "Allied forces are also battling for control of Missy-aux-Bois, a few kilometers to our west. Accordingly, there is some danger of our position being overrun, so I have given orders for the Circus to break camp and fall back. Meanwhile, our soldiers need all the help they can get. Jastas 4 and 6, report to your flight leaders for briefing. Jasta 10 will remain with the Circus to fly air cover as it moves to its fallback position."

At least he learns from his mistakes, Goldstein thought cynically.

"Jasta 11, get into your gear and report to me at the ready line in fifteen minutes," Goering ordered. "All of you, dismissed."

On the ready line, Goldstein and the four other pilots who currently filled Jasta 11's roster stood at attention. Goering was pacing up and down, doing his best to be heard over the tumult of planes being rolled out.

"We have no bombs, but at least we can fly strafing runs against the enemy at the town of Missy," Goering shouted. "There is a possibility that we will encounter enemy fighters. Reports have it that the American 94th Pursuit Squadron has moved into Château-Thierry."

Shit, Goldstein thought. That was the American ace Rickenbacker's squadron. The 94th had developed a formidable reputation during its few months at the front.

"If *any* enemy fighters appear," Goering continued, "Jasta 11 will immediately break off its attack and retreat—*in formation*—to the Circus rendezvous point."

"Begging the Herr Oberleutnant's pardon," one of the newer pilots called out. "But we're not afraid to fight, Sir."

"Of course you're not afraid," Goering growled. "You're Germans! But most of you are inexperienced. It is better to live to fight another day. I repeat, at the first sign of enemy fighters you *will* retreat. Myself, and another experienced pilot—" Goering's eyes ranged across the small group, and stopped on Goldstein. "Myself and Herr Sergeant Goldstein will remain behind to prevent the enemy from pursuing."

Goldstein was not happy as Goering dismissed the line. These days, when the Allies flew they flew in force. Two airplanes would not stop them.

"Herr Sergeant, a word with you," Goering called as the other pilots ran to their planes.

"Sir." Goldstein came to attention.

"Herr Sergeant," Goering confided. "I didn't want to alarm the men, so I told them that it was only a possibility that we will confront fighters. Actually Air Warning has informed me that there are American fighters in the vicinity, and that a clash is definite."

Goldstein glumly nodded. "Will it be Rickenbacker, Sir?"

"That I don't know," Goering replied. "But in any event, when the enemy appears, you and I *must* delay their pursuit of the rest of the Jasta. It is imperative that the enemy does not discover the new location of the Circus."

Goldstein nodded. "Who watches whose back, Sir?"

"I'll watch yours," Goering said. "Recently I've been doing a lot more administrative work than flying," he gruffly added. "I'm probably a little rusty."

"Yes, Sir." Goldstein nodded. "Sir." he blurted out as Goering was turning away.

"Yes, Herr Sergeant?"

"Sir, is everything between us . . . I mean . . ."

Goering's face was expressionless. "I don't know what you're talking about."

"Sir, I mean concerning what happened last—"

"Get to your airplane," Goering interrupted, and walked away.

It'd been weeks since Goldstein had exchanged his old Fokker "tripe" for a D VII, but he still hadn't become jaded to the breathtaking surge of power when the D VII's wheel chocks were pulled, giving its magnificent Mercedes engine free rein.

Goldstein went down the field full throttle, feeling himself being pushed back in his seat as his ground speed built as quickly as the Mercedes' roar. The sleek D VII seemed to gather its strength like a predator as it leapt into the sky.

Goldstein banked sharply, gained altitude, and took his place in the staggered Vee formation. When all the Fokkers were up, the formation of six planes, with Goering flying point, headed east toward the battle that was raging for control of Missy-aux-Bois.

They were there within a couple of minutes. Off in the distance Goldstein could see the tall oaks of Retz Forest, looking invitingly serene as compared to the smoke-shrouded, rubble-strewn town below.

As Jasta 11 circled, Goering gave the signal to break up into three pairs. Four planes would make strafing runs while Goering and Goldstein stayed high to watch for fighters. At least that was something to be thankful for, Goldstein thought. He'd grown cynical and hard these past few months, but not so hard as to enjoy the idea of shooting helpless men running in terror from his machine guns.

Of course, that kind of strafing took place when an airplane happened to catch the enemy out in the open. Today, Jasta 11 was simply wasting ammo. With all the smoke, it was impossible to see what was going on down on the ground.

After a few minutes Goering seemed to recognize the futility of the mission. He signaled the planes to break off their runs. The six Fokkers were just coming around into the Herr Oberleutnant's cherished formation when the damnable enemy saw fit to make an appearance. There were ten of them, coming in fast from the southwest.

Goering dipped his wings to signal that he'd spotted them. The rest of Jasta 11—those lucky bastards—high-tailed it out of the vicinity at full throttle; dwindling into specks, and finally disappearing into the clouds to the east. Goldstein, meanwhile, was climbing fast, to gain the advantage of altitude in the dogfight that was imminent. He saw Goering's all-white plane take up position behind him, on his right, and breathed a sigh of relief. Anybody watching his back, even an anti-Semitic pencil pusher like Goering, was better than nobody.

When the enemy got close enough Goldstein saw that they were Spad 13s, and that by their markings, they were members of Rickenbacker's 94th.

Now that the fight was about to begin Goldstein felt cool and quiet inside.

Anticipation was always the worst part. He idly wondered if Rickenbacker himself was flying with his men. If he was, Goldstein was prepared to show the American ace that the German Air Service still had some teeth.

He glanced back at Goering, who was still on his right wing. Goering waved.

"So far, so good," Goldstein muttered to himself as he sighted in on the closest Spad rushing toward him. "We've had our differences, Herr Oberlieutnant, but surely we can put them aside while we deal with our common enemy."

The Spad's cowling filled his gun sight. Goldstein thumbed his firing button. His airplane shuddered, and glinting brass tumbled from the ejection ports of his guns as his orange tracers skittered forward, chewing bites out of the Spad's wings and fuselage.

The Spad slid away, its prop slowing. Goldstein glimpsed it leaving the battle.

One down. He grinned. *Nine to go*.

He put his own machine into a climb and was looking for another target when he saw tracer rounds streaking past him from the rear, tearing at his Fokker's wings, chipping away at his struts. He glanced in his rearview mirror. The glass was filled with a Spad on his tail, its twin guns winking fire at him.

"Get him off me, Goering," he muttered, as he twisted around in his seat to look over his shoulder.

Goering was nowhere.

"Bastard!"

Goldstein slammed the D VII's stick into the pit of his stomach, zooming quickly upward into a loop so that the enemy on his tail slid beneath him. He dropped down on the offending Spad's tail and let loose a burst, but now other

Spads were coming at him from every direction. His Fokker took more tracer fire. Rounds tore through his cockpit, shattering the compass near his foot. His engine began to cough and smoke. The needle on his petro gauge was sinking fast. A round must have cut his fuel line.

There was no longer any question of fighting. Goldstein was merely desperate to get away so that he could either glide to earth or parachute in relative safety. He kicked his rudder right, pushing his stick in the same direction, and the Fokker fell over, sliding sideways into a whirling, gut-wrenching spin.

The Spads backed off to see what would happen. Goldstein watched his altimeter, letting the Fokker plummet as long as he'd dared in order to buy himself some room. At five thousand feet he ran out of nerve. He didn't want to get any closer to the ground with a faltering engine. He struggled to pull out of the spin. The controls were sluggish, and for a second he'd thought he'd waited too long, but at last the D VII responded. Goldstein brought her around hard, and began to run for his own lines.

He was less than three minutes from safety, but he knew he wasn't going to make it. He was losing RPMs and altitude. He decided to use his parachute, but before he could the Spads were at him like angry bees.

He took a burst in his right wing. He slid his wounded Fokker sideways, but that just cost him more precious altitude and put him across the sights of another American pilot. Goldstein took more rounds into his engine, which died on him altogether.

And then Goldstein's guns were hit, and suddenly splinters were flying off the varnished wood trim of his cockpit, and he was screaming in pain as bullets leapfrogged across both thighs. His lap welled up with blood as his legs instantly, thankfully, went numb.

Goldstein was approaching German lines, but a succession of Spads were diving down on him. Their tracers were falling around his airplane like orange rain. Bullets hit his fuel tank, and what was left of his petrol ignited in a puff, setting on fire his tail section.

The Spads lifted off and veered toward their own lines. They knew he was finished.

He unbuckled his harness and tried to haul himself out of his cockpit in order to parachute to safety, but he couldn't make his legs function, and his arms were too thin and weak to hoist him over the cockpit's high sill. By the time he thought to roll the Fokker upside down and just fall out of the cockpit, he'd lost still more altitude. Now he was less than fifty meters above the ground; too low to parachute.

The wind was fanning the blazing tail section's flames away from him, but the heat was still blistering. His goggles were fogged with sweat, but he didn't dare remove them, not wanting to expose his eyes to the oily black smoke spewing from his killed engine. Sliding past beneath him in a blur were the men and machines of war, but Goldstein couldn't tell to what army they belonged. The ground was coming up at him fast. Directly ahead was a wooded knoll. He jerked the stick, and, miraculously, the ailerons sluggishly responded. He just managed to avoid the knoll, the trees' branches tearing at the Fokker's underbelly. He saw that the grassy pasture ahead of him had more trees, but now he no longer had a choice. He was just skimming the ground.

He belly-flopped hard. The impact collapsed the Fokker's tail skid, cracked the fuselage in half just aft the wings. Goldstein hoped the Fokker's broken spine would slow her down, but the flaming rear section of the fuselage dragged behind only a few yards before sheering off in a shower of sparks and twanging, snapped control wires. Goldstein cringed as what was left of the airplane careened on screeching wheels toward the trees. He threw up his hands as low branches stabbed into the cockpit. A tree trunk tore away the Fokker's left wing. Goldstein felt the Fokker slammed to a halt, spinning like a top. The whirling airplane hurled him from the cockpit, into darkness.

He woke up feeling blissfully comfortable. He was lying on his back, floating in warm sea. The sun was so bright! He had to squint, else the sun would make him sneeze.

He was at one of the resorts along Germany's northern coast. He was drifting on his back on the gentle waves, listening to the joyous cries of children frolicking in the surf. Far off, on shore, he could hear the bells and creak of the revolving carousel. He was thinking of going ashore to get himself an ice cream, when he fell back asleep.

When he woke up the second time, Goldstein's mind was clearer. He still felt comfortable, like he was floating, but he realized that he was lying on a cot, one of many cots, in a large, sunlit room. What he'd thought had been the laughter of children were the moans and cries of wounded men. The jingle and creak that had been his dreamy carousel was really the sound of traffic from the road that seemed to be just beyond the room's open windows.

He was alive. He'd survived the crash. He began to take stock of himself: he could think, see, and hear. His arms were all right, but he couldn't move his legs. His legs didn't hurt. They didn't anything. It was if they weren't there . . .

Weren't?—

Oh, Christ. Oh, Jesus—

"Help . . ." His throat was so dry. His lips seemed glued together. He raised his head to look down at himself, but he was covered with a blanket from his chest down. He was too weak to throw off the covering, and he just couldn't tell what remained and was missing under there.

"Help!" he croaked, adding his own voice to the cries of men in pain. "Someone, help!"

A boy suddenly appeared, leaning over him. "Easy, Herr Sergeant, rest easy."

"Easy? Fuck easy!" Goldstein shouted above the chorus of moans going on all around him. "Who the hell are you, boy?"

"I'm an orderly."

"My God, they're really robbing the cradle . . ." The boy looked about fifteen. He had blond curls tumbling over his forehead, and big, soulful brown eyes behind gold-rimmed spectacles. He reminded Goldstein of a boy he'd known at the orphanage. That boy had apprenticed himself to a butcher. On second thought, maybe it was this orderly's bloodstained white smock that reminded Goldstein of that other young meat cutter.

"Where am I?" Goldstein managed. "What's happened to me?"

"You're at a dressing station to the rear. You've been here since yesterday, when your flying machine crashed. You were thrown from the wreckage. Some infantrymen found you and you were transferred here by ambulance."

"I can't feel my legs," Goldstein murmured.

"You will, Herr Sergeant!" the young orderly said wearily. "You'll feel in spades! Right now you're full of morphine, but our medicine supply is running low. When your injection begins to wear off, you'll *wish* you were still numb."

"Why can't I move below the waist?"

"Your legs are in splints right now. The splints are intended to keep you immobile."

Goldstein's eyes widened. "What's happened? How seriously am I injured?"

"Your legs were fractured by machine gun bullets. Otherwise you just have some bumps and bruises. You're very lucky. It could have been your back, or your neck that was broken." The boy's puppy-dog eyes brightened behind his spectacles. "I almost forgot, your commanding officer has sent you a message."

"The Herr Oberleutnant?" Goldstein demanded. "What's that about my C.O.?" Goldstein remembered how that bastard Goering had left him to the American Spads.

"Your commanding officer was informed that you'd been brought here," the orderly said. "He telephoned a message for you." The boy took a scrap of paper from his smock, unfolded it, and handed it to Goldstein.

The Herr Geschwaderkommandeur of J.G. 1 offers his sincerest condolences to Herr Sergeant Hermann Goldstein. How fortunate for him that he survived. The C.O. regrets that he was forced to withdraw from the air battle due to his airplane's malfunctioning armament. The Herr Geschwaderkommandeur is certain that the Herr Sergeant will understand that the former could not remain in battle with just one functioning machine gun.

Goldstein let the scrap flutter to the floor.

The orderly quickly snatched it up. "You'll want to save it, of course. I'll see to it that it's put safely with your personal items."

Oh, that bastard Goering, Goldstein thought. He could just see Goering's eyes glinting with swinish malevolence as he'd dictated that note. How it must have aggravated Goering when he'd found out that Goldstein had survived!

Goldstein hoped the fact that Goering's cowardly strategy hadn't managed to kill him festered in the Oberleutnant's fat gut. Goldstein knew that was all the revenge he would ever have against Goering. As Richthofen had made plain long ago, an officer and a gentleman is not to be challenged by a Jew.

"I had hopes of being a flier, myself—" The orderly was blushing.

"What?" Goldstein muttered. "What did you say?"

"I wanted to fly, but I couldn't pass muster." The boy tapped his spectacles. "Weak eyes, you know. I hope there's an opportunity for you to tell me about some of your adventures before they ship you out."

"Ship me?..." For a moment Goldstein didn't understand. "You mean home?" he asked tentatively.

"Home to Germany," the orderly confirmed. "As soon as the doctors have set your fractures. Herr Sergeant, for you the war is over."

It was only when the orderly was gone that Goldstein thought to ask how the war was proceeding. Later he found out that the news was bad. The Allies had broken through all across the line and had crossed the Marne. Last night, while Goldstein slept, huge bonfires lit the sky as German soldiers burned everything they were unable to carry before pulling back.

The constant traffic outside the window was the sound of the German army running away.

Chapter 4

(One)
Berlin, Germany
12 June 1919

It was a cool night. The breeze blowing down the Unter Den Linden smelled of smoke. Goldstein zipped up his brown leather jacket and stuffed his hands into the pockets of his loden trousers as he walked slowly, minding his steps across the rain-slicked, iridescent cobblestones. The sidewalk was crowded, and now and then someone would grumble an insult as they pushed past Goldstein, which he ignored.

He'd been out of hospital a couple of months, but when the plaster casts came off Goldstein had to relearn the art of walking. The doctors assured him that he would eventually walk as well as he ever had, but for now using his legs delivered the same thrill, and required the same amount of concentration, as had flying.

Goldstein kept his head bowed as he passed the disposed Kaiser's palace and the sentries at the entrance who watched the street from behind their tripod-mounted machine gun. One man wore an army infantryman's uniform and helmet, the other was nattily attired in a velvet-collared, gray tweed suit and matching fedora. He had on pearl gray, calf-skin gloves that looked intended for handling a furled umbrella, not ammo belts. Both men wore the armbands of the Social Democratic Party, which had swept the January elections for a New National Assembly to replace the exiled Kaiser's Imperial Government. The newly elected Assembly had met in Weimar to elect as President of the Reich the Socialist Freidrich Ebert. The hope was that the Weimar Parliament would end the months of vicious street fighting in Berlin and other major cities between rival political factions on both the left and the right.

Peace born of political stability was the hope, but the new government was taking no chances. The harsh provisions of the Versailles Treaty had stirred up bitter resentment all over the country. Nationalist politicians were making defiant speeches threatening rebellion, as if they'd forgotten that Germany had lost the war. The Officer Corps was especially alarmed by the Allies' insistence that Germany disarm. The newspapers were filled with reports of bloody skirmishes: between soldiers and socialist or communist factions; between socialists and communists when the soldiers were not around. The machine gun emplacements and roadblocks infesting Berlin attested to the fact that the fledgling Weimar government was prepared to clamp down on this dissent using whatever means necessary.

Goldstein turned left onto the Friedrichstrasse, past the imposing State Library. He was on his way home to his room in a boardinghouse near the railroad tracks, on the far side of the Spree River, about a quarter mile from the Weidendammer Bridge. He'd been walking for quite a while, and he still had a couple of kilometers to go, but the doctors had said that the more walking Goldstein did, the faster his legs would mend.

He had the money to take a motorbus if he chose. He was getting by earning a living doing odd jobs. He'd put on his old uniform and go calling at shops and residences with his pack of tools on his back. With the terrible inflation, the mark was worth only a fraction of what it had been at the beginning of the war. Most everybody was broke, but people, seeing a young veteran at their door, seemed always able to find the money to pay him to fix something, and often invited him in to share a meal.

For the chance to eat, Goldstein was especially grateful. Food was scarce, like most everything else in Germany excepting bitter recriminations. With his injured legs it was difficult for him to stand in one place for very long, and the lines were long at the sporadically open bakeries and groceries.

In the evening, Goldstein went for long walks to exercise his legs, or read: either technical books on aviation and mechanics, borrowed from the library, or newspapers. He enjoyed current events. It was interesting, for instance, to follow what was going on in Palestine concerning the Jews, and to read about the American President Wilson, who especially fascinated Goldstein. In print, Wilson seemed an uncommonly just and kind man, considering the American President's Fourteen Points for what would have been a merciful settlement toward Germany, and his attempt to establish a so-called League of Nations to mediate all future international disputes, and thereby avoid another world war. The more Goldstein read, the more it seemed to him that only America had a leader wise enough to want to put aside vindictiveness towards vanquished Germany. The Americans had certainly seemed more willing to be fair at Versailles than the English, and especially those bastard French . . .

A crowd was backed up at a government sentry point on the Dorotheenstrasse, near the Winter Garden Theater. Goldstein was waiting his turn to pass when he saw Heiner Froehlig of all people, seated alone at a table for two in a sidewalk cafe across the street. Froehlig was wearing blue pinstripes and a derby, and had clipped back his once luxurious walrus moustache, but Goldstein was sure that it was his old comrade.

In November, after the Armistice, Froehlig had frequently visited Goldstein in the hospital. For a few months Froehlig showed up a couple of times a week, to pass Goldstein his silver flask when the nurses weren't about, and talk about their intended partnership in the motorcar garage.

Gradually, though, Froehlig's visits began to taper off. Finally, he no longer came at all. Goldstein was mystified, and deeply hurt. He concluded he'd been naive to have expected anything different. When would he ever learn? With the economy the way it was, the idea of starting a business was utter foolishness. Anyway, what did he have in common with Froehlig? Their friendship had been the result of a particular set of circumstances, a friendship of time and place.

Goldstein hadn't much thought about Froehlig since then. Now, seeing him again, Goldstein was filled with longing for his company. He was very lonely in Berlin. Perhaps his friendship with Froehlig could be resumed.

It was worth a try, Goldstein decided. He crossed the street to say hello.

Froehlig saw him coming, but did not look happy about it. "Hermann, such a surprise . . ."

Goldstein waited for an invitation to sit down. When it was not forthcoming he indicated the empty chair. "May I join you for a coffee? I have money," he quickly added, not wanting Froehlig to misunderstand. "Let me buy you a coffee," he said proudly.

"Well, I'm actually waiting for some people." Froehlig looked around nervously. "I'll be leaving at any moment . . ." Then he looked up at Goldstein and seemed to soften. "My young sergeant." He smiled.

"Not anymore," Goldstein said whimsically. "Just a civilian, like yourself."

"But your legs!" Froehlig exclaimed. "How could I have forgotten. And here I'm keeping you standing! Of course you may sit down. And allow me to buy the coffee."

A waiter appeared, and Froehlig ordered for both of them. "Would you care for a schnapps?" he asked Goldstein.

"It's so expensive!" Goldstein protested. He smiled. "Unless, of course, you're offering from the silver flask . . ."

"No. I lost that flask. I don't know what happened to it."

"Then just coffee is plenty," Goldstein said.

As the waiter left with their order, two young prostitutes leaning against a nearby lamppost strolled over, arm in arm. They paused at the table to raise their worn, faded skirts, showing off their high boots.

"Get away," Froehlig growled.

"Perhaps your balls were blown off in the war," one of the prostitutes taunted in oddly accented German. They sauntered off.

"Did you hear? A foreigner," Froehlig grumbled. "Berlin needs a good cleaning."

Goldstein nodded vaguely. There were lots of streetwalkers in his neighborhood, and he'd taken a girl up to his room on a few occasions. He saw nothing wrong with it. The girls were clean. Being with one once in a while eased his loneliness. "Tell me, Heiner, what have you been doing with yourself since we last met?"

"I've been involved in politics," Froehlig replied. "Organizing for the Deutsch Arbeiter-Partei."

"Heiner, you must excuse me, but I've never heard of it."

"Of *us*," Froehlig corrected. "We're all just decent, working stiffs, Hermann. Honest men who know that the government in power is to blame for our misfortunes."

"Heiner, I don't see how you can blame the Weimar Coalition for losing the war."

Froehlig shrugged. "Well, I don't see how President Ebert can claim it is the German military that failed us."

"I believe Ebert claimed it was the German military *leadership* that failed," Goldstein quietly pointed out, but Froehlig seemed not to hear him, and he decided not to press the point.

The waiter came with their coffees. Froehlig waited until they were served, and then said, "I don't know about you, Hermann, but I *resent* what Ebert is claiming." He scowled. "We soldiers fought hard, and risked our lives for our country. You yourself physically suffered on behalf of the Fatherland."

"I can't argue." Goldstein smiled.

"Of course you can't argue," Froehlig replied. "You shouldn't argue. Hermann, I go around every day. I talk to people. I *know*. Despite the fact the socialists won the election, every day more and more good Germans are coming to resent the way Ebert is stabbing our nation in the back. And then there are the shortages we're suffering—"

"But how can we blame the current government for shortages?" Goldstein interrupted. "There will continue to be a lack of everything while the Allied blockade is still in effect."

"And why is the blockade still in effect?" Froehlig asked rhetorically. "Because the French wished to kick us now that we are down. Those cowardly Frenchies would never dare presume to tread upon the German people if Ebert showed some guts, some nationalistic pride, the way the Kaiser would have."

"It's the Kaiser your German Workers Party wants back?" Goldstein asked, surprised.

"At least under the Kaiser there was food, and it was safe to walk down the street," Froehlig said. "But no, we don't want the Kaiser. He belongs to yesterday. Germany must change if it is to regain and maintain its superiority in the world. We want a leadership that understands that. Ebert's moderate Socialist party is too busy trying to placate the Allies in Paris to understand what is needed, and the left wing communists are too busy engaging in class warfare, and endorsing the dictatorship of the proletariat." Froehlig looked disgusted. "The German people don't want power handed over to them. They appreciate a wise and just leader telling them what to do."

"You're leaving out the military," Goldstein pointed out.

"Like the proletariat, the military desires a master," Froehlig said.

"Well, whatever the German Workers Party says is fine with me." Goldstein looked down at his coffee. "Heiner, I have to ask," he began timidly. "Why did you stop coming to see me in the hospital?"

Froehlig looked uncomfortable. "Hermann, we both know that there are many Jews in the socialist, and especially the communist, factions of the Weimar Coalition . . ."

"Yes, I suppose so."

Froehlig was frowning. "This is difficult for me to tell you. Have you ever read *The Protocols of the Elders of Zion?*"

Goldstein shook his head. "I've never even heard of it."

Froehlig nodded. "I believe you, my boy. I don't think you'd lie to me." He reached inside his suit coat and brought out a thin, tattered pamphlet, which he placed on the table. "It's a document that was smuggled out of Russia in 1905, by some unsung hero. It reveals the international Jewish conspiracy to control the world's industry."

"What are you talking about, Heiner?"

"I'm talking about Germany's future," Froehlig said forcefully. "And the future of the world! The Jews have seized control." His fist came down on the pamphlet. "It's all here in black and white. Read it with your own eyes. Thanks to the Zionists' grand designs, our country is to be surrendered to her enemies."

"But President Ebert—"

"Is merely a puppet, whether or not he knows it," Froehlig insisted. "Like the entire Weimar Coalition. Jews from all over the world are pulling the strings, whether or not the politicians know it." He paused, and smiled. "You know, Hermann, our running into each other might have been destiny...I have an idea... You once told me that while you were born a Jew you don't feel you have anything in common with those of your race. Do you still feel that way?"

"Yes, I suppose I do."

"Excellent." Froehlig sounded relieved.

"What are you getting at?"

"Do you understand the importance of propaganda?" Froehlig asked.

"What?" Goldstein was utterly confused.

"Never mind," Froehlig said. "You know, if I told my friends in the party about you they'd think that you were something very special. A Jew, there's no denying it," he mused, "but also a battle flier, and an ace who was wounded in action; a man who flew with Richthofen."

Froehlig reached across the table to grip Goldstein's arm. "Think of the publicity you'd get, and the good you'd be doing for Germany if you publicly renounced your heritage! If you admitted that the *Protocols* are true, and if you publicly endorsed the German Workers Party's efforts to expose the international Jewish conspiracy for what it is?"

Goldstein stared at his friend. "That's what this party of yours is all about?" He picked up the pamphlet. "To help them make Jews into some sort of scapegoat for Germany's failings?"

"We only want to expose the truth," Froehlig coolly replied.

"But how can I accuse innocent Jews of something I know nothing about?" he demanded.

"First off, they're not innocent."

"How do you know they're not?"

"Read the pamphlet, boy," Froehlig growled.

"The hell with your pamphlet." Goldstein tossed it into Froehlig's lap. "I'm a Jew, but *I'm* innocent. I never heard of any conspiracy—"

"But *you* were an orphan," Froehlig pointed out. "Your parents died before they could initiate you. And *anyway,* some innocent are always swept away with the guilty. Look at what happened in the war! It's the way of the modern world. It's God's way."

"Is this a joke?" Goldstein demanded, incredulous. "Are you mad? You spoke of the war. What about the thousands of Jews who served in the Kaiser's army? We didn't have many in the Air Service, it's true, but so *many* Jews were infantry soldiers. They fought and died for their country just like any other German."

Froehlig looked disgusted. "When did you become such a Jew lover?"

"When did you become such a Jew hater?"

"When I learned the truth," Froehlig said, exasperated. "Hermann, be reasonable. I don't hate all Jews, you *know* I don't. I hate only the bad ones; the ones that need to be punished."

"Goering thought that *I* needed to be punished," Goldstein said quietly.

"Dammit, Hermann! That was something totally different!" Froehlig turned red. "You're letting your emotions confuse the facts." His fist pounded down on the pamphlet. "But why are you so concerned in the first place?" he demanded. "You keep telling me that Jews mean nothing to you, and yet you keep defending them—"

"God help us all, Heiner," Goldstein said sadly. "Thanks to your pamphlet, and your new friends, you've turned into a bigger bastard than Goering ever was."

"Who are you to talk, you little piece of shit!"

"That's better," Goldstein said calmly. "Now, at least, you're being honest about how you feel. Now you and Goering are on equal footing . . ."

To his credit, Froehlig seemed suddenly to comprehend

Goldstein's point of view. "I've always been a gentle man, Hermann. You can remember that about me?..."

"I do remember it, and I wish I still knew that man."

Froehlig looked genuinely anguished. "But the world has been turned upside down. Everything now is so complicated. I don't understand what's happened to my country. We were winning the war, but then we lost. How could that have happened? My friends in the German Workers Party seem to understand what happened, and they've told me how I can help to put things right." He sighed. "When they tell me that I can do something, I feel good. It's hard to feel good these days—"

"This shit your friends are feeding you is not the answer," Goldstein said bluntly. "Hatred will not solve Germany's problems."

"—I want everything to work out all right for everyone," Froehlig said. "But first comes me, you understand? First come Germans. Germans before Jews."

"Jews *are* Germans!" Goldstein declared.

Froehlig shrugged. "I see that we can only agree to disagree. You asked me questions and I answered them. Now, if you'd be so kind as to go. My friends are expected."

"I wouldn't want to embarrass you in front of your friends," Goldstein said dryly. He stood up, and placed some money on the table. "I'll buy my own coffee, thanks."

"As you wish," Froehlig nodded. He opened up his pamphlet and began to read.

Goldstein stared at his lost friend another moment. "I would like to read that pamphlet, if you wouldn't mind."

"I can get another copy easily," Froehlig replied, handing it over.

That night, in his room, Goldstein read the damned *Protocols* through, three times. When he was finished he tore the pamphlet up into little pieces and burned it in the washbasin.

As he watched the smoke curl against the cracked ceiling plaster, the idea came to him that he should leave Germany. He had no family or friends here, and more and more it looked as if he had no future.

His eyes fell on a stack of old newspapers taking up one corner of the room. He thought about America. The American President Wilson had wanted to be merciful; it seemed that of all the world, America was the least vindictive toward Germany and its people . . .

Now that the idea had crystallized, he wondered why he hadn't thought of it before. Excited, he went through the entire newspaper stack, tearing out anything that had to do with America, arranging the articles in chronological order, trying to construct a mosaic of facts about America out of the brief clippings. He came upon a photograph of Wilson. The American president was clean-shaven and had short gray hair. He wore spectacles and had the look of a benevolent schoolmaster.

Goldstein tore the photograph out of the newspaper and propped it up beside his bed. He was not someone to go off half-cocked about something as important as immigrating to America. He would sleep on the idea.

He wished President Wilson good night, and slept soundly.

At dawn he woke, to tell the American president that he was sure. He would be coming to America.

(Two)
Munich, Germany
20 March 1920

Air Park No. 34 was really an airplane graveyard. Located on the outskirts of Munich, the Air Park was created in response to the Versailles Treaty, which stipulated that Germany disarm. All tanks, warships, and military aircraft not confiscated as desirable equipment by the Allies had to be destroyed. The Air Park, which had been a plumbing supply warehouse before the government had requisitioned it, was admirably suited to destroying airplanes. It fronted on a stretch of straight, paved road that could serve as a landing field, and it had plenty of space to stack the broken-winged carcasses once they were stripped of their engines.

Periodically, Goldstein, who'd been manager of the Air

Park since September, would have his work crews pile the fuselages in the yard and burn the war birds in great, towering bonfires.

The former warehouse's loading docks were exposed to the elements, and today the weather was raw, with a mixture of sleet and rain slanting down. Goldstein and the Russian, whose name he could never remember, stood stamping their feet against the dock floor's iron grating. A trash fire flaring and waning in an old petrol barrel afforded them some warmth as they watched the work crews wrestle aircraft engines into the back of the lorry.

Goldstein studied his clipboard as the last of the engines were loaded and the lorry pulled out of the loading dock. Another lorry, motor idling, was waiting to take its place. Now it began backing into the loading dock.

"It must please you that the German Air Service will survive," the Russian said. "Even if it is on foreign soil. Perhaps, someday, you too will come to my country. We could use your talents as a flier and mechanic."

Goldstein smiled politely. The only place he was going was America. He'd already begun studying the language and had worked more than halfway through an English primer, thanks to the help of a language tutor he'd found in Munich.

Goldstein waited until the last lorry was in position and the workers had begun loading it with engines. He then guided the Russian into the warehouse, out of the line of sight of the workers.

"My money, please," Goldstein murmured. The Russian handed over a sheaf of bills, which Goldstein quickly crammed into his pocket.

It had been easy for Goldstein to get the manager's job. The government bureaucrats in charge of the Air Park needed someone who could on occasion pilot an airplane as well as dismantle them, and most fliers, ex-officers all, were refusing to cooperate with the disarmament program, considering it another example of cowardly surrender on the part of the government. To disarm was simply beneath the dignity of officers and gentlemen.

Goldstein had hardly begun the job when he was discreetly approached by a group of high-ranking German officers who were willing to pay if he'd help them channel a certain number of the best aircraft engines to Russia. It seemed that aircraft fuselages, instruments, and machine guns that were to be matched up with the engines were moving to Russia from other German disarmament facilities, and that the same thing was happening with tanks, and so on. The Russians were allowing the Germans to reassemble and train with their illicit equipment, in exchange for the Germans teaching the Red Army how to soldier.

"See you in two weeks," the Russian said as the last engines were loaded in the lorry.

Goldstein nodded. It struck him as ironic that the Russians and the right wing German military were in bed together concerning this rearmament conspiracy, considering that it was the politically conservative Friekorps and Reichwehr which were so violently against Germany's current socialist left wing government. Goldstein had wondered if the officers had thought he'd be amenable to the scheme to benefit Russia as well as Germany because he was a Jew.

Finally, he didn't care what the officers thought. He would have been willing to send the engines to hell if it helped pay his way to America.

He'd already inquired into the cost of the steamship ticket. By summer, his bribes combined with his meager salary would total enough cash to allow him to set sail. He figured his English would be pretty swell by then as well.

(Three)
Port of Hamburg, Germany
9 August 1920

On the day Goldstein set sail for America the newspapers carried brief articles buried in the back pages concerning the meeting of the Deutsch Arbeiter-Partei in Salzburg. The newspaper coverage was sparse because D.A.P. was just a fringe organization, but Goldstein was interested because it was the political organization to which Heiner Froehlig had said he'd belonged when they'd met that night in Berlin, almost eighteen months ago.

Goldstein carefully read every article on the D.A.P. convention. He felt sentimental now that he was bidding Germany farewell, so, although he couldn't abide Froehlig's views, he was nevertheless happy for the man who had once been his friend. Since Froehlig's little organization had seemed so important to him that night, it was nice that the newspapers had him as a prominent figure in his party, along with someone named Adolph Hitler.

BOOK II:
1921

Chapter 5

(One)
Hillsboro Aviation Field, New Jersey
14 March 1921

"Please, if you'd tell me where I might find Captain Bob? I wish to apply for the position of stunt pilot advertised in *The New York Times*."

"You and every other squirt hereabouts." The gaunt, elderly watchman standing guard at the Hillsboro looked disgusted. He wore a shabby overcoat and a wool knit cap, and had a clipboard. It was a cool, damp spring morning, and the weather was making him suffer. His ears and nose were red, and his pale eyes were runny. He kept stamping his feet and blowing into his hands. "Well, what's your name, kid? Can't go in until I've got your name wrote down . . ."

"Herman Gold." He watched the guard write it down on his clipboard. His new name still sounded funny to him, although he liked the way it looked on paper: much more American than Hermann Goldstein. He wasn't sure just which immigration officer had cropped it for him as he was being processed. It wasn't until much later that he noticed his new name inked into permanence on his entry papers.

"What's a kid like you want to get mixed up with them fliers, anyhow?" the guard scolded. "I'm only telling you because I can see you're an immigrant, and maybe ignorant about such things."

Gold stiffened, feeling insulted. Look like an immigrant, indeed! He had on his brand new, brown wool suit and was wearing a white shirt and a green and red, striped four-in-hand—not knickers and a cap... "Sir, if you don't mind..."

"Take my advice, learn yourself an honest trade. You wouldn't catch me up in one of them flying contraptions. No sir. If the Lord wanted men to fly, he'd given them wings."

"May I go through the gate, now?" Gold asked politely.

"Don't say I didn't warn you," the watchman sniffled. "You go through here, and follow the crowd to hangar three."

"Thank you."

"Good luck with the captain," the guard called after him. "You'll need it. Lots of young men are here today looking to be stunt pilots. I can't figure why."

Gold hurried away, scowling as he tried to pick a path through the mud. He'd dressed up to make a good impression on his prospective new employer, but it was just as well he hadn't been able to afford new shoes, and so was forced to wear his high, lace-up work boots. Hillsboro Aviation Field was just a large expanse of mud and weeds, bordered with crude wooden buildings. The control tower was a rickety wooden scaffolding with two lamps on top. The white lamp stood for caution, Gold surmised; green for all clear to land. Hillsboro had been used by the Americans as a pilot training school during the war, but it was far more primitive than the training fields in Germany. In fact, Hillsboro reminded him of the temporary, wartime aerodromes he'd frequented in France.

The feeling of being back in Europe with J.G. 1 was intensified as Gold approached hangar three. It was a large, barnlike structure, painted a blistered, peeling yellow, with CAPTAIN BOB'S AIR EXTRAVAGANZA in fading black script on the hangar's side and above its door. Parked nearby were a number of motortrucks and trailers painted the same yellow with black lettering, and ten similarly painted biplanes, tethered down to keep them from being blown about by the wind. Gold recognized the large, ungainly, two-seater machines as Curtiss JN-4D war surplus military trainers, nicknamed "Jennys."

It had been a long time since Gold had been near a flying machine. He would have enjoyed poking around the Jennys, but he didn't want to get grease on his new suit, nor waste any time. There were at least twenty men queued up at the door to the hangar, and when Gold looked over his shoulder he saw that more would-be barnstormers were coming through the gate.

Gold quickly took his place in line, mentally rehearsing what he intended to say to Captain Bob in order to get the job. He was going to be sincere and honest; those qualities had so far served him well in America.

He'd had good luck since his arrival seven months ago. He'd already gone looking for work at the many motor garages and trucking companies in New York City. On his second day of looking, he was hired as a mechanic at Red Apple Trucking, a firm on the lower west side of Manhattan. The Russian Jew who owned the company was impressed by Gold's mastery of English and his mechanical skills, and for some reason the Russian thought it was humorously ironic that he was giving a newly arrived German Jew an opportunity to make a start in America.

The job went well. After six months Gold's boss had given him a raise and had promised to make him maintenance manager as soon as the position opened up.

Gold should have been happy, but he wasn't. Something was lacking in his life. In the beginning he thought it was just the inevitable disparity between his expectations and the reality of life in his new country.

Gold had imagined taking his place in an adventurous, energetic American society, a confident nation ready to lead the world, but he'd actually arrived just in time to witness the president he'd worshipped from afar leave office a rejected, broken man. The new president, Warren Harding, inaugurated just ten days ago, had won office by promising Americans a return to the serenity and normalcy of the past.

This new America being trumpeted about in the newspapers disturbed Gold. It was one thing for those already prosperous, who could sit fat and complacent, quite something else for those still anxious to raise their lot in life, and perhaps do some greater common good in the process.

He'd been spending his evenings reading American history as well as current events, eager to understand everything about his new country. He'd come to the conclusion that America's most successful pioneers had made their own opportunities. He'd decided that if America's past was any indication of its future, he would not achieve success working for someone like his current, kindly, but unimaginative employer, who believed, like President Harding, that hard work should be its own reward and that dullness was a virtue.

Somewhere in America there were still people who thought like Woodrow Wilson. Gold simply had to find them.

The line into the hangar had plodded along, and now Gold was inside. It was one big, barnlike room with a sawdust floor. Open sliding doors on all sides of the hangar let in lots of daylight. Electric lights hanging down from the roof rafters offered more illumination. The hangar was divided into two sections by rope-strung, canvas curtains, at present tied back. The rear three-quarters of the hangar was equipped as an airplane repair shop. A half dozen mechanics were back there working on several biplanes in various stages of disassembly. The front quarter was an office area. There were several desks, worn-out armchairs, and a number of file cabinets. The walls were taken up with gaudy posters from the barnstorming troupe's previous tours. Off to the side was a glass-partitioned office. Inside, a man seated behind an oak desk was dialing a candlestick telephone.

That had to be Captain Bob Brook, the owner and promoter of the troupe, Gold figured.

About a dozen young men in baggy trousers, sweaters, and brown leather flying jackets with "Captain Bob's Circus" emblazoned on the back were lounging about the office area. They were smoking cigarettes and laughing among themselves as they watched the new applicants file in. Each applicant had to pause at a table where a young woman in a tan wool dress and a bulky, dark blue, cardigan sweater sat behind a typing machine. There were now just three men ahead of Gold.

When Gold saw Captain Bob's newspaper solicitation he'd realized that what was missing in his life was the excitement and exuberance he'd experienced when he was flying. He had to somehow recapture that joy; otherwise, no matter how prosperous he became, his life would be meaningless.

The problem was that there were scarcely any civilian flying jobs to be had. Gold had confidence in aviation's future, but most Americans shared the elderly watchman's view that aviation had no practical applications in peacetime. Barnstorming was the only way for a pilot to get back into the air. Accordingly, Gold was not surprised to see so many applicants here at Hillsboro. There had to be thousands of eager young fliers in America, all of them grounded by peacetime and now trapped in mundane jobs.

Barnstorming was dangerous work, and Gold prided himself on not being foolhardy, but his instincts told him that any job he could get that had to do with flying was a step in his own, personal, right direction. If that job was risky, so be it. Nothing ventured, nothing gained.

The woman seated at the table was asking the applicant ahead of Gold the man's name and the particulars of his flight training. "Come back in an hour," the woman told the applicant after she'd typed the answers to her questions onto an index card and added it to the pile next to her typing machine. "By then the Captain will have reviewed your card and decided if he wants you to wait around this afternoon for a personal interview."

The applicant moved on. Gold took his place before the young woman. Despite her youth, he thought she looked very businesslike with her brown hair twisted up into a tight bun. She had very nice breasts. Gold had been to a couple of bordellos in New York, but the whores in America had not shown near the caliber of professionalism of the prostitutes he had known in Germany. Accordingly, he'd gone without . . . for what, by now, had turned out to be a very long time.

"Name?" the woman asked crisply, rolling a fresh card into her typewriter.

"Herman Gold."

The woman hesitated, glancing up at him. "You're a foreigner?"

"Yes." Gold nodded.

"I'm sorry, Mister Gold, but we're looking for fliers."

"Yes, I understand—"

"No, I guess you don't," the woman said lightly. She looked past Gold, scanning the number of applicants behind him on line. "We need people who already know how to fly an airplane—"

"Excuse me," Gold said. "But I flew in the war for the German Air Service—"

"Oh," the woman said, surprised. "I never thought of that. I'm sure you did." She paused, distracted, as a couple of Captain Bob's pilots approached. Both men had longish, blond hair slicked back from their foreheads, and brown eyes. One had a thick moustache. The two were both in their early twenties, and of average height. They looked fit beneath their open leather jackets.

"This Hun giving you trouble, Margie?" the pilot with the moustache asked the woman at the table.

"It's under control, Hull," the woman said, and turned back to Gold. "I'm sorry, but the advertisement is for *American* military veterans."

Gold took his folded-up copy of the advertisement out of his pocket, smoothed it out, and placed it on the table in front of the woman. "Where exactly does it say that?" he asked softly, trying hard to show the woman that he wished to be courteous.

"*I'm* saying it," the one named Hull cut in. "Look, we kicked your ass over *there*, and we got no use for you Huns over *here*, got that straight, Fritz?"

"Excuse me, but I'm having a conversation with the young woman," Gold quietly replied.

"I'm sorry, Mister Gold," the woman said. "But you see all the applicants we already have. There are too many Americans who want flying jobs."

"But that's not fair," Gold protested. "At least allow your employer Captain Bob to make the decision."

"He would agree with me," the woman said. "Now, if you don't mind, I have lots of people left to screen." She looked past Gold.

"You heard her, Fritz," Hull said. "You either walk out of here right now, or you'll be giving my brother and me the excuse we need to kick your Hun ass right back to the Fatherland."

Gold was angry, but he struggled to control his temper. He wasn't afraid. His legs were strong from all the exercise he'd done to build them up after his injuries, and he'd put on weight and upper-body strength from working in the trucking garage. He believed he could handle himself in a fight, but he'd come here for a job, not a brawl.

"Thanks for your time," he told the woman and left the hangar the way he'd come.

Outside, Gold quickly circled around to the side of the hangar where Captain Bob's glassed-in office was located. He intended to use one of the open sliding doors that led to the workshop area of the hangar to get inside and then plead his case directly to the captain. Gold hadn't taken the day off from work to travel at the crack of dawn across the Hudson River on the Forty-second Street ferry, then beg rides west, and finally walk the last five miles to Hillsboro, just to be stopped at Captain Bob's door by a couple of apes in leather jackets who thought the war was still on.

He watched and waited just outside the sliding door until the mechanics' backs were turned and then darted into the hangar, hugging the wall as he hurried directly to Captain Bob's glass-partitioned office. He heard shouts. He ignored them as he stood transfixed, his face up against the glass like a hungry street urchin gazing through a bakery window, looking in at Captain Bob Brooke talking on the telephone.

The Captain was in his fifties. He was bald on top, with a wreath of longish, honey-colored hair around his ears, and a goatee tufting his chin. He was dressed in a green tweed suit, and as he sprawled back in his swivel chair and swung his feet up onto his desk, Gold could see that the Captain wore his trousers tucked into the tops of his high, cordovan boots. A red satin waistcoat stretched across the Captain's expansive belly. From the waistcoat's fob pockets a glittering, golden watch chain curved, like Midas's grin.

Captain Bob had his candlestick telephone propped on his big paunch. He was murmuring at it like a papa crooning to an infant. Although Gold couldn't really hear the Captain, he instinctively understood what the man was saying, as clearly as if he were watching a silent movie crafted by a brilliant director. The Captain was making deals; charting a course into the future; sounding an economic charge: just like Woodrow Wilson.

The Captain, on his telephone, looked the way Gold felt when he was flying.

Gold pounded on the glass. The Captain, startled, said something into the telephone and then hung up as he stared back at Gold.

Angry hands were reaching toward Gold, but he twisted free, lunging for the office door. He found it unlocked, and he barged through.

"Please, Captain, I must talk to you!" Gold yelled as Hull and his brother came in, grabbing his arms.

"Sorry about this, Cap," Hull muttered. "We'll throw him out—"

"Wait, let me talk a minute!" Gold pleaded.

"Turn him loose, boys. He looks harmless enough," the Captain drawled, reaching for a cigar smoldering in the ash-tray on a corner of the desk. The pilots released Gold, but stayed close by. "Now then, son. What can I do for you?" the captain asked.

Gold took a deep breath. He now realized that honesty and sincerity were going to get him nowhere. He was going to have to act American. "It is what *I* can do for *you* that is what the matter becomes that I've arrived to talk about—" He cursed himself for allowing his nervousness to affect his English. "What I mean is—"

"I know what you mean, son." The Captain chuckled. He swung his boots off his desk and stood up. Gold was startled by how small the man was, except for his belly. He'd looked positively huge talking on the telephone. "I guess you're German, son?"

"I'm German."

"How long you been here, son?"

"Seven months."

"You got a job?"

"Yes, Captain, I'm a mechanic—"

"Son, we're not looking for mechanics right now," Captain Bob said, studying the end of his cigar. "We need fliers."

"I *am* a flier!"

"Sure you are," Captain Bob humored him. "Nice try, son. If I wasn't so short of planes, I'd hire you, just on your gumption. But I can't afford to let you wreck any of my birds teaching yourself the ropes."

"You must listen! I was in the Imperial Air Service."

The Captain laughed, and Gold heard chuckles coming from behind him.

"Bet he was an ace, Cap," Hull chuckled. "How about it, Fritz, were you an ace?" The man's breath was hot on Gold's neck. Gold kept reminding himself that he was looking for a job, not a fight.

"My brother asked you a question, Fritz." The other man was smiling. "In America, a Hun gets asked a question by an American, he'd best answer."

Gold turned slightly, to regard the two. "Very well, the answer to your question is yes, I was an ace. With twenty confirmed kills," he added proudly, enjoying the look of astonishment in the men's eyes.

"I think you're a liar, Fritz," Hull accused.

"I'm not concerned with what you think," Gold said. "I wish only to complete my interview with the captain—"

The smile vanished from Hull's face. "You uppity Hun sonofabitch."

Gold, ignoring the insult, turned back to Captain Bob. "What's important, Captain, is the fact that I flew with Richthofen."

The office abruptly went quiet. Captain Bob was staring at him.

"He's lying, Cap . . ." Hull declared.

Captain Bob grinned apologetically. "You'll have to excuse Hull Stiles, and his brother Lester. What's your name, son?"

"Gold, Herman Gold. And my rank was sergeant."

"Well, Mister Gold," Captain Bob continued. "As I was saying, you'll have to excuse the boys. They're a little sensitive about you Germans, and particularly the Red Baron. You see, during the war they were both shot down on the same day by a member of Richthofen's Circus. They spent the rest of the war in a German P.O.W. camp."

"I don't find that hard to believe," Gold couldn't resist saying.

"What's that supposed to mean?" Lester Stiles demanded, shoving him.

"Keep your hands off me," Gold warned. "It means that with equal airplanes, any German aviator could outfly any Yank. Plenty of Germans shot down two planes in one dogfight." Gold remembered with great satisfaction that April day in 1918 when he'd dropped the British Bristol two-seater, and then the Sopwith Camel, to give him his fifteenth and sixteenth kills— Then again, that really wasn't during one *single* dogfight . . .

He smiled. There *was* that winter afternoon in 1917 when he'd bagged a pair of Frenchies one right after the other, during the same tussle. "I remember when I managed to shoot down two—"

"Liar!" Hull shoved him. "Let's hear you admit it—"

The hell with it, Gold thought. *I'm not going to be hired, anyway.* He turned around to face Hull. "How's this for an admission?" he asked pleasantly. He snapped out a right uppercut intended for Hull's chin, but Hull saw it coming and moved away. Gold's knuckles just grazed the tip of the man's nose.

Hull's head rocked back, and blood began trickling out of his nose. His eyes turned murderous. "*You-little-Hun-son-ofa—*"

"Would you boys mind taking this fight out of my office?" the Captain suggested.

Gold put his shoulder into a right aimed at Hull's stomach. Hull sidestepped, grabbing Gold's extended arm and shoving him hard in the small of his back. Gold heard his jacket rip at the armhole as he was propelled, off balance, through the office doorway. Hull tripped him, at the same time letting go of Gold's arm. Gold belly-flopped in the middle of the hangar.

"For this I had to wear a new suit," Gold muttered into the sawdust. He pushed himself up to his knees, drew off the torn jacket sleeve, and stuffed it into his pocket. He noticed that all activity in the hangar had stopped, and that everybody was looking at him.

Hull was standing in the doorway of the Captain's office, wiping the blood from his moustache with the back of his hand. "I'm going to kick your ass, Fritz." Everyone in the hangar began to close in to watch the action. "And I'm going to keep kicking it until you admit that you're a liar."

Gold got to his feet. "I'm *not* a liar. I *did so* fly with Richthofen!"

Hull lunged at him. Gold crouched low, and used his powerful leg muscles to drive forward, jamming his shoulder into Hull's stomach. Hull grunted, doubling over. Gold tried to straighten his legs, intent upon throwing Hull up and over his shoulder, but Hull punched him in the ear, and the pain was blinding. As Gold's legs sagged, he slid his hands down to the backs of Hull's knees and pulled hard. Hull's legs folded and he hit the sawdust on his back.

Gold, exhausted, the side of his head throbbing from Hull's punch, and thinking that this brawling wasn't all it was cracked up to be, rolled away. He was at least gratified to see that Hull, the wind knocked out of him, lay sprawled, trying to catch his breath.

"If what you're saying is true . . ." Hull gasped, ". . . you were with the Red Baron's Circus . . . when my brother and I were shot down, back in 1917 . . ."

"Don't be ridiculous." Gold gingerly explored his ear. It felt swollen, and it was still ringing. "You Yanks didn't get into it until the spring of 1918."

"Nah." Hull propped himself up on his elbows. "My brother and I didn't want to wait for America to get involved. We volunteered for a French unit."

"Really? Where were you shot down?" Gold asked. He didn't really much care, but he'd rather converse than fight. He saw Captain Bob leaning in his office doorway, watching and listening.

"Near La Fère, on the Oise River," Hull said.

Gold forgot about his ear as he stared at Hull. "Near La Fère?— What were you flying? Nieuports or Spads?"

"Nieuports . . ." Hull muttered.

"Do you remember the airplane that shot you down?"

Hull spit blood. "Of course I do, you dumb—"

Gold was nodding, feeling more certain by the moment. "You and Lester were shot down by an Albatross D 5, weren't you?"

"We got shot down by an Albatross double-decker," Hull reluctantly admitted, pushing himself up on his elbows. "But just because you knew what kind of airplanes the Red Baron's Circus flew doesn't mean that you were there..." he added quickly. He brightened. "Or maybe you were a ground mechanic?..."

"Nieuports, Nieuports...Around La Fère..." Gold concentrated, trying to separate the images of that particular, unusual day from the jumble of memory. "Your squad number was N 111, yes?"

"Oh, shit," Lester Stiles sighed. Everybody looked at him, and then back at Gold.

"The Albatross that shot you down was painted sky blue with yellow ovals on the rear side quarters, isn't that so?" Gold persisted gleefully.

"Shit, shit, *shit!*" Lester was mourning.

"And painted on each yellow oval was a rearing centaur," Gold said in triumph.

"What's a centaur?" Hull asked fearfully.

"Half man, half horse," Captain Bob eagerly volunteered.

"Oh shit..." Hull groaned, lowering himself back down to the sawdust to stare up at the ceiling rafters. "That was you, in that airplane, Fritz?"

"That was me," Gold confirmed happily. "You and Lester were my numbers eleven and twelve." He paused and shrugged. "Or vice versa."

"Hallelujah!" Captain Bob rejoiced, clapping his hands. "The Lord has seen fit to deliver unto me a bona fide Imperial race!"

Gold got to his feet, brushing himself off. He extended his hand to help up Hull, but Hull pretended not to see it, and stood up on his own.

"So what if he really was a German flier, Cap," Lester Stiles argued. "Having him in the show would just piss ticket-buying Americans off. It'd cost us business—"

Gold knew that what Lester had said made mournful sense. He could see that the Captain was pondering it as well. Gold was desperate. Everything depended on what happened next. He needed an idea—

"May I tell you about my proposal for your show, Captain?" Gold asked.

"All ears, Fritz." Captain Bob nodded.

"First of all, my name is Herman," Gold firmly announced. "Now, as to my proposal . . ." He took a deep breath. *Herr Rittmeister*, he thought, *wherever you are, please forgive me*. "Captain Bob, are you familiar with William Cody?"

"Buffalo Bill?" the captain snorted. "Course I am! Buffalo Bill is the patron saint of traveling show promoters. But how would the likes of you know about Buffalo Bill?"

"I enjoy reading history," Gold replied. "Then you are familiar with William Cody—Buffalo Bill's—singlehanded duel and defeat of the Indian chief Yellow Hand during the Sioux War of 1876?"

Captain Bob's grin stretched from ear to ear. "Oh, the Lord has indeed delivered me a treasure! Buffalo Bill *included* a re-creation of his famous duel in his traveling Wild West show, didn't he, son?"

Gold nodded. "And *we* can put on an exhibition of the Red Baron's final flight. The dogfight that cost him his life."

"So what do we need you for?" Hull Stiles grumbled. "Anyone of us could play the Red Baron as well as you—"

"The fact that I was Richthofen's comrade-in-arms would lend to the tableau a certain authenticity, I believe," Gold added modestly. "Of course, if the captain doesn't agree, I could offer my expertise to some other barnstorming troupe—"

"Call me Cap, son," Captain Bob said heartily. "All my people call me Cap."

(Two)
Outside of Blue Field, Kentucky
24 April 1921

It was four o'clock in the sultry, partly cloudy afternoon. The barnstorming circus had been on the road for three and a half weeks.

"Ladies and gentlemen—" Captain Bob shouted through his tripod-mounted megaphone. "Boys and girls!"

The captain was standing in the center of a damp, clover-studded dairy cow pasture, separated from the deserted, two-lane macadamized road by barbed wire. Cow pies, as black and flat and round across as dinner plates, were everywhere. The fly population was astonishing.

"The time has come for our feature presentation," the captain barked through the ungainly, cardboard funnel. About two hundred and twenty-five people, most of them standing around the refreshments trailer, drinking lemonade and munching on candy apples or steamed red-hots, began to lazily applaud.

"Captain Bob presents—'The Demise of the Red Baron'!"

Gold, strapped into the cockpit of his airplane, peeked over the front cowling. "That's our cue," he told his mechanic.

The mechanic twirled the prop, Gold hit the ignition, and the Curtis JN-4D Jenny reluctantly rattled to life. The Jenny had a scarlet paint job, and German Crosses had been plastered onto her wings. A pair of fake machine guns, carved out of wood and painted black, had been mounted on her engine cowling. In case anybody didn't get the idea, "The Red Baron," painted in white block letters a foot tall, ran along both sides of the fuselage.

Gold adjusted his goggles, checked that his white silk scarf was securely wrapped around his neck, and buckled the chin piece of his red, patent-leather helmet. The mechanic pulled the chocks from the wheels, and the tricked-out Jenny began to taxi. Gold steered her once around the pasture so that the paying customers could get a good look at "the Red Baron, in his deadly Fokker."

The spectators gawked, fathers taking their sons in hand and pointing as Gold rolled by. He drove the Jenny past the trucks, trailers, and passenger motorcars that made up the Circus, and then past the entrance to the pasture, a spot in the fence where the barbed wire had been snipped away and where Captain Bob's big, lemon-yellow McFarlen touring car was parked. ("The very make and model the world heavyweight champ Jack Dempsey drives," the captain liked to proudly point out.)

Jimmy Cooper, the ex-newspaper reporter who acted as the troupe's advance man, stood guard by the McFarlen and winked at Gold as the Jenny sputtered by. Jimmy sold the admission tickets, slipping the cash receipts through a slot cut into the locked metal trunk of the McFarlen, as if the car were the world's largest child's bank.

As Gold finished his circuit he watched Captain Bob wildly gesticulating while yelling through the megaphone. One of the pilots, a snare drum suspended from his neck, was now standing next to the captain. The engine's throbbing roar was too loud for Gold to hear what the captain was saying, but they'd rehearsed the bit so many times that Gold knew the captain's spiel by heart.

"*Ladies and gentlemen, boys and girls,*" Captain Bob would repeat. "*Imagine, now, that you have been transported from this great land of ours to the war-torn trenches of France . . .*"

At the far end of the pasture, Gold saw three more Jennys firing up. These were striped red, white, and blue, but armed with the same mock machine guns. In this particular demise of the Red Baron, Richthofen was going to be shot down by a trio of Yank pilots—never mind the fact that he was really brought down by the combination of British fighter and Canadian infantry ground fire—about nine months before the American military even stepped foot in Europe.

Gold opened up the Jenny's throttle. A rusty spray from the radiator hit his goggles. Scowling, he checked his water temp, tapping the glass to make sure the gauge's needle was functioning. Radiator malfunction was one of the Jenny's many Achilles' heels. Satisfied that she wasn't going to blow up just yet, Gold began to taxi the Jenny down the pasture in order to take off.

"*Before you is an authentic facsimile of the Red Baron's infamous Fokker fighter plane,*" the Captain would be shouting right about now. Gold found that pretty funny.

The Curtiss JN-4D was almost ten feet longer, and had almost twice the wingspan of the Fokker Dr. 1 "tripe": the machine Richthofen was flying when he went down. The Fokker had a 20,000-foot ceiling, could do well over 100 miles per hour, and was highly maneuverable. Most Jennys could make 6,000 feet on a good day, and their 90-horsepower Ox 5 engines had a top speed of 75 miles per hour. As far as maneuvers, a Jenny could go right and left, and up and down, as long as her pilot wasn't too impatient.

The Jenny's saving grace was that there were a hell of a lot of them. The United States had manufactured more than 10,000 by the time the war had ended. Besides being cheap to own and maintain, they were two-seaters, which meant that you could use them to take folks for rides. Airplane rides formed a large part of the troupe's gross.

You could also modify a Jenny. The one Gold was flying had a 150-horsepower Hispano-Suiza engine stuck in her nose. This Hisso-equipped Jenny was the only one the troupe had; the Hisso engine was rare and expensive, but the captain had gone to the expense so that the "Red Baron" would have the power to do a loop and roll for the audience. The fact that the standard-engine Jennys lacked that kind of performance would also help to make the "Scarlet Ace of Aces" look even better in the air. Never mind that Richthofen disdained stunt flying in favor of the battle tactics of surprise and superior marksmanship.

Right about now, the Captain would be introducing him, Gold thought.

"The scarlet bird of prey you see before you now is being piloted by none other than Baron von Richthofen's flying instructor; the Red Baron's closest friend and comrade-in-arms during the war; the man who himself is an authentic Imperial ace: the noble Count Fritz von Strohgruber!"

Gold waved to the crowd one last time and made sure that his white silk scarf was dramatically streaming, like a flag in the breeze, as he steered into the wind in order to build enough lift for takeoff.

Gold, alias the noble Count Fritz, was amused by the alias, and the tall tale the captain had fabricated, but then, as Captain Bob liked to say, the Good Lord had seen fit to bless him with a tremendous imagination. The Captain had apologized to Gold about the phony name and story, explaining that the truth just didn't have enough pizzazz.

Gold also guessed that Captain Bob wanted to protect himself. All the pilots in the troupe went under phony names such as "Wings Cuddy" or "Smoking Joe Falcon." The names were featured on posters and in newspaper ads; "Count Fritz von Strohgruber: Richthofen's Flying Master" was currently getting top billing. Captain Bob made up the phony monikers, and the employment contract every pilot signed made it clear that the Captain retained all rights to the "house name." That way, if, say, "Wings Cuddy" suffered an injury or death in a crash, a new guy could be "Wings Cuddy," and Captain Bob wouldn't have to go to the expense of reprinting the posters.

Gold pulled back on the control stick, and the scarlet Jenny left the ground. With her grand, double-decker wingspan, trussed together with enough rigging to outfit a four-masted schooner, she didn't so much climb as waft into the air. A Fokker gained altitude like a cat clawing its way up the drapes. The Jenny rose as if lifted gently on the palm of a giant.

Gold leveled off at 3,000 feet. Any higher and he'd be just a speck to the audience below, and that wouldn't make for much of a show.

As Gold banked the scarlet Jenny in order to circle the field, he watched below as the trio of striped airplanes took off. As the last plane left the ground, Gold pressed the stud on the stopwatch fastened to the Jenny's control panel: the scene would end with the Red Baron's demise in exactly ten minutes.

Down below, Captain Bob would be setting up the scene: *"Just days after his eightieth kill, the Red Baron again took to the air, to strike fear into the hearts of Allied troops."*

Gold buzzed the field a few times, pretending to strafe the spectators. On each of Gold's passes the pilot standing beside Captain Bob would be rapping his snare drum in a rat-a-tat approximation of machine gun fire.

"Rising up to challenge the Red Baron were three valiant, young Yanks; brave Falcons of Freedom, every one!"

Gold watched in his rearview mirror as the trio of striped Jennys locked on his tail and began to laboriously weave like swallows. Down below, he knew, the fellow on the snare drum would be just now mimicking a firestorm of machine guns. Gold opened up the Hisso and got the Jenny to pull a few stunts, always coming back to a period of level flight, so that the standard-powered Jennys could relock on his tail. He watched the stopwatch. Exactly eight minutes into the routine, as the Captain delivered the line:

"The Yanks fire on the Red Baron, but the clever crimson Cur outfoxes them—"

Gold put the Hisso-powered scarlet Jenny into a steep Immelman loop, coming around on the tails of the three red, white, and blue Jennys. The drummer, watching, would now be rattling off a long string of gunfire. Gold watched as the pilot of the rear, striped Jenny pulled the string on a smoke bomb attached to his fuselage.

"Richthofen has scored again!" Captain Bob would be shrieking into his megaphone. *"But the wounded young lad will be able to nurse his bullet-riddled flying machine back to his own lines, and land safely."*

Gold watched as the "wounded young lad" dropped his Jenny in a credible imitation of a smoky fall. At 500 feet, he leveled off, to land in an out-of-the-way corner of the pasture. Gold checked his stopwatch. Nine and a half minutes had elapsed. It was time for his own demise.

"The Red Baron has been cheated of his kill. And now, his time has come!"

The two remaining Jennys were again on Gold's tail. He kept his eye on his stopwatch, imagined the drum roll of gunfire going on down below, and at precisely the ten-minute mark pulled the strings that lit the signal flares mounted to the undersides of his wings. Tin plating, armoring the wings, protected the Jenny from catching fire, but from the ground the blazing signal flares would seem to engulf the scarlet plane, impressing the hell out of the paying customers.

"Yes, those good American boys have done it!" the captain would be shouting. *"They've killed the Red Baron!"*

Gold popped a couple of smoke bombs and began to play

dead, swaying the Jenny like a falling leaf as he fell toward the ground. This part was dangerous. The falling-leaf maneuver could easily put the Jenny into a spin she might not be able to come out of. He wouldn't have tried it at all if he didn't have the Hisso to rely on. Captain Bob had told him that at this point the spectators went wild.

At 1,000 feet he put the Hisso-powered Jenny into a split-S power dive, pulling out to just skim above the ground. The Jenny groaned, but she held together; Gold had designed and supervised the reinforcement of her structure to see that she would, and he personally went over her before every performance.

By now the flares and smoke bombs had petered out. Gold slowed the Jenny down to her stall speed of 45 miles per hour and prodded her along low over the crowd, dipping his wings in salute. Now he could see for himself that the folks were applauding him. He could imagine their excited cheers.

This was what really made it worthwhile for Gold: that he was helping to introduce America to aviation; that he was making airplanes a reality for people, many of whom had never seen a flying machine before. Tonight, over the dinner table, folks would be talking about what they'd seen. Later that evening, when the children went to sleep, their dreams would be filled with the vivid images of star-spangled and scarlet-hued airplanes cutting across the sky. Gold liked to think that he was spawning tomorrow's aviators at every performance.

Gold even thought that the good he was doing for aviation's cause would have led Richthofen himself to forgive him. The idea of parodying his onetime idol had troubled Gold, but he'd decided that since the Herr Rittmeister had loved flying, he would not have wanted the advances in aviation to be lost in the postwar economic gloom that had gripped the world.

Gold circled the field a final time, and then brought the Jenny down. He could see the crowd already leaving the pasture. The show was over for today.

Captain Bob's Circus had been here two days; the troupe stayed in one place as long as the crowds kept coming. Tonight Jimmy Cooper and the roustabouts would move on to the next town on the Captain's itinerary, to nail up posters and prepare the field. The mechanics with their parts trailer would camp out here, to keep an eye on the planes, while the captain and the pilots would drive into town to put up at the hotel for the evening. Early the next morning the mechanics would do their maintenance work and gas up the planes. By then the pilots would be straggling back. The mechanics would move on, and the pilots would fly off, usually taking the time to perform a few antics over the towns neighboring the new show site, to drum up business.

The better part of each show was given over to those profitable airplane rides, intermingled with stunt-flying exhibitions to keep the crowds entertained. Captain Bob's grand finale was the Red Baron skit, and so it went.

Gold was enjoying himself. He was seeing the country, and the captain paid his hotel expenses as well as fifty dollars a week. Gold would have been supremely happy if he wasn't so lonely. He was as alone now as he'd been in the German Air Service, except that now he was ostracized not only as a Jew but also as a German. All of the captain's pilots were military trained, and old grudges forged during the war would not easily die.

Hull and Lester Stiles were the ringleaders in the crusade to give him the cold shoulder. Gold supposed that he understood the way that they felt: after all, he had been responsible for knocking them out of the sky and into a German P.O.W. camp . . .

(Three)
The Trent Hotel
Magnolia, Missouri
9 May 1921

The lobby of the Trent Hotel was plushly carpeted in crimson. Above the walnut-wainscoted walls was green-flocked wallpaper. Cattlemen lounged on brass-studded leather furniture, smoking cigars as they commiserated over the dismal price of beef on the hoof.

Herman Gold and Captain Bob Brooke were seated in leather armchairs beside a huge potted fern. The captain was wearing a gray wool suit; Herman a tan corduroy Norfolk jacket, a white shirt, a maroon four-in-hand, and olive twill trousers. He'd taken to tucking his trouser bottoms into the tops of his high boots, in emulation of the captain. On the captain's advice he'd also let his curly red hair grow longer and had the beginnings of a decent moustache. The captain said it made him look older, and more like a rake, which helped make him more credible in his role as Count Fritz, the man who had taught the Red Baron how to fly.

Gold and the Captain were passing the evening reading newspapers and enjoying the breeze set up by the softly whispering ceiling fans, when the telegram the captain had been waiting for finally arrived. Gold lowered his newspaper and watched as the captain tore open the wire, then read it.

"They went for it, son." The Captain grinned. "We've got our commitment from Americana Oil. They're notifying their dealers all across the country to provide us with gas for the rest of our tour."

"You did it, Cap." Gold shook his head in admiration. "I didn't think you'd pull it off, but you did. Free gas . . ."

"Not free," the captain admonished. "We're paying for it, in advertising. Tomorrow I'll have the mechanics paint the tail of every one of our airplanes with the Americana trademark." He laughed. "Except the Red Baron's, of course. That wouldn't look too good for Americana now, would it? To have their trademark on the tail, and Hun Crosses on the wings."

"I guess not," Gold said quietly, and buried his nose in his newspaper.

"Oh, hell." The Captain frowned. "Here I've gone and hurt your feelings."

"You know, Cap, when this tour is over, I'm going to look forward to just being an American." Gold sighed. "It's not easy playing the villain all the time."

The Captain nodded. "Well, son, to me, you are an American. The good Lord saw fit to grant you the gift of bona fide Yankee ingenuity."

Gold chuckled. "Thanks for saying so, Cap." He laid

aside his newspaper on the hotel's leather-inlaid coffee table. "So what's next?"

"Next I contact Stallion Motor Supply and Medallion Tire. I'll tell them that Americana has accepted my proposal and ask do they want to come aboard. If so, we'll paint their trademarks all over everything, and I'll have parts and rubber as well as gas and oil, without paying out a single greenback."

"Real canny of you, Cap." Gold smiled.

Captain Bob regarded him. "Tell me something, son. You spend your evenings with me because you're interested in business, or because the other boys give you the brush-off?"

"A little of both, I guess," Gold admitted. "I'm sorry the others hold what I am against me, but that's been happening to me all my life, more or less, so I suppose I've grown used to it." He paused. "At least, I've learned to tolerate it... Anyway, I do want to get ahead in life, so I want to learn about business. I no longer believe I can accomplish much by working for someone else, not even you; no offense meant, Cap."

"No offense taken, son. I think you're thinking right."

"I'd like to make my mark in some facet of aviation," Gold confided. "But I don't have your salesmanship abilities."

"The good Lord has seen fit to grant only a precious few the gift of profitable gab, starting with that greatest of all salesmen, Jesus Himself," the Captain intoned. "But as for you, son, don't you worry, one of these days you'll see your opportunity, whatever it may be, and you'll take it. I've no doubt of that."

Gold tapped his newspaper. "I've been reading about the air passenger transportation business in Europe, Cap," he said excitedly. "I think there could be a future for that here."

"I don't think so, son," Captain Bob said. "Europe's roads and bridges and railways got all torn up during the war, and they're always crossing this or that channel, or sea, or whatever, to get where they're going. Now consider America. We've got nothing torn up, and just a few itty-bitty rivers to cross, now and again. Anyway, over in Europe, life's cheap. You won't find God-fearing Americans risking their necks in uncomfortable flying machines to go visit grandma on Thanksgiving Day."

"They go for rides with us, Cap," Gold respectfully pointed out.

"Thrill seekers ain't going to keep an air transportation company in the green."

"I guess what's needed are better, safer planes. Maybe that's what I ought to concentrate on," Gold mused.

"That's right, you're a bit of a mechanic," the Captain said. He took a cigar out of his jacket breast pocket and nipped it with a golden cutter on the end of his watch chain. "I've heard that you've been tinkering on my airplanes; improving their performance." He struck a match and puffed on the cigar to get it going. "My mechanics tell me that you worked miracles on that Hisso-powered Jenny. That after you were done modifying her structure and engine she could pull stunts like no other Jenny, no matter how skilled the pilot." He ignored the stand ashtray beside his chair, flicking the spent match into the nearby potted fern.

"I'm good with machines, but I want to be more than a grease monkey," Gold said. "I'm reading up on aero-engineering and design. I have books sent to me from New York City."

"Yeah, well, whatever, son." The Captain nodded. "Me, I never liked to get my hands dirty. But if you ever should come up with a new thingamajig, don't you hesitate to bring it to your old pal, the Cap, you hear?"

"Sure, Cap," Gold murmured evasively. If there was one thing he'd learned from Captain Bob, it was never to give anything away.

"I don't know shit about inventing, son, but I can promote the hell out of anything," the Captain declared. "And promotion and advertising is ninety percent of it today, and will be ninety-nine percent in the future. You mark my words. This war we've just been through has rattled everyone's cage pretty good. What folks are going to want is for somebody to tuck them in and tell them a bedtime story about how everything's going to turn out all right. That's what salesmen do, they tell bedtime stories." He rattled his newspaper. "Just like President Harding."

(Four)
The Golden Hotel
Atowa, Kansas
2 June 1921

Gold was on his way upstairs to his room after dinner when he heard Hull Stiles call out, "Hey! Wait a minute! I want to ask you something."

Gold waited for him on the landing. "What's up?"

"I wanted to ask you . . ." Hull began, but hesitated, nervously fingering the ends of his moustache. "Back during the war, you know? When you shot down Lester and me, we'd both noticed something, and we've always been wondering about it. I was hoping I could ask you about it now . . ."

Gold nodded. "Go ahead."

"Your plane had only one machine gun. Isn't that so?"

Gold sighed. "Yes, only one."

"I mean, it wasn't like one of your guns jammed, right? You had only one."

"That's right, Hull. I carried only one gun."

Hull nodded. "How come?"

"It's a long story," Gold began. "Let's just say that with one gun I felt I could shoot down airplanes without harming the pilots."

"That's what my brother and I thought," Hull replied. "Back then as well as now, I mean. We talked about it a lot in that P.O.W. camp. It had seemed to us that you went out of your way to choose your shots, to not simply spray the cockpit."

Gold looked away. "Hull, I don't mean to be rude, but it seems like such a long time ago."

"That's what Les and I have been thinking recently," Hull replied softly. "We've talked to the others about it. Everyone thinks you're a good pilot, and all . . ." He blushed. "Hell, I guess what I'm trying to say is that maybe it's best to let sleeping dogs lie . . ." He trailed off.

"Yeah, I guess that is best," Gold said thickly. "Well..." He smiled hard.

Slowly, Hull extended his hand. Gold shook it.

"There." Hull smiled shyly. "A bunch of us are taking a drive out to some hog farm that Eddie claims he knows about. He says they got some kind of still or speakeasy going on out there. White lightning, and like that." Hull shrugged. "Maybe some girls, I dunno..."

"Gee." Gold shrugged, still smiling fit to bust. "Sounds good."

"Yeah, it does... Probably won't amount to shit, though. Eddie's a talker. Anyway." Hull looked down at the dusty toes of his scuffed boots. "Feel like coming for a ride?"

"Sure."

Outside the hotel, a bunch of pilots were piled into the circus's puke-green, beat-up Oldsmobile. It was a soft-top, and missing its windshield. Lester Stiles, wearing his flying goggles and leather helmet, was behind the wheel, gunning the engine to keep it from stalling.

"Achtung!" Lester called out as Gold and Hull approached.

Gold flinched, feeling unsure. If they expected him to laugh, forget it. He'd be friends with them as their equal, not their clown.

Lester grinned. "Sorry, Herman, I just had to get that last one out of my system. Squeeze in, pal. We've been waiting for you."

Chapter 6

(One)
Outside Doreen, Nebraska
9 July 1921

The show site was a yellow-tan expanse of hard-packed earth and cropped grass, bordered by tall cottonwoods and chokeberry. The field was up against a straight-edge gravel road, set like a tile beneath the faded blue sky, amidst the amber and green vastness of the plain.

It was late afternoon, and hot. The high temperature and low barometer had combined to make poor flying conditions. Added to that, all through the difficult show the Jennys' radiators had been boiling over. One pilot had been scalded by a blast of rusty steam and had needed to see a doctor. He'd been rushed back to Doreen, a prosperous farming and manufacturing town fifteen miles away, on the banks of the Blue River.

Gold had just finished his Red Baron stint, ending the show. The crowd—business had been good here the past few days—was gradually disbursing. The pilots, anxious to get out from beneath the broiling sun, were peeling out of their sweat-soaked flying gear and hurrying to the automobiles for the drive back to the hotel in Doreen.

Gold was sitting in the scant shade cast by the scarlet Jenny, waiting for her engine to cool down so that he could check it over. While he waited he thought longingly about a nice cool bath and some lemonade.

"You ready to leave, Herman?" Hull Stiles called to him.

Gold waved him off. "I'll catch a ride in later. My temperature gauge was in the red all through my performance. I want to make sure I haven't done in the Hisso."

Hull nodded and headed for the cars. One by one the automobiles set up dust clouds as they made their way off the field, kicking up a spray of gravel as they fish-tailed onto the road. The terrain was so flat that the cars were visible long after the sound of their engines had faded. Gold watched them go, feeling envious.

His thoughts turned back to the Hisso. The Jenny already had a custom-built, extra-large radiator. Maybe he could rig up some sort of supplementary, extra-capacity cooling system to give him an extra margin of safety...

He found a scrap of paper and a pencil in his trousers pocket and began a preliminary sketch of his idea for an improved radiator design. As he hunched over his drawing, drops of sweat running along his nose plopped onto the paper, blurring the pencil lines.

"*Entschuldigen Sie* . . ."

Gold glanced up, startled to hear German. The man standing before him was gray-haired and barrel-chested. He looked about sixty. He was wearing work shoes, a pair of faded denim overalls that were the same washed-out blue as the sky, and an old-fashioned white shirt, minus its detachable collar.

"*Guten Tag, Herr Strohgruber,*" the farmer greeted Gold. "*Ich heise Curl Schuler,*" he introduced himself, doffing his wide-brimmed, sweat-stained linen hat. He cocked his head, his brown eyes speculative as he regarded Gold. "*Sprechen Sie Deutsch?*" he asked politely.

Gold shook himself out of his surprised stupor. "*Ja! Et tut mir leid!*" Gold apologized. "*Sehr angenehm, Herr Schuler.* Yes, indeed, I'm very pleased to meet a fellow countryman," he repeated, enjoying the opportunity to speak German. "But I'm afraid my name isn't Strohgruber. It's Herman Gold."

"A name is a name," Schuler philosophized. "What matters is that you're a German, like myself." He thumped his chest. "I am pleased to meet a fellow countryman."

Gold, smiling, got to his feet to shake hands. "Did you see the show, Herr Schuler?" he asked in German.

Schuler nodded. "My daughter and I. My wife, she wouldn't come. She said it would make her dizzy just to watch. My daughter even took a ride."

"But not you, sir?" Gold smiled.

"Ah, no, Herr Gold!" Schuler laughed. "Never in a thousand years would you see me in such contraptions! I don't even like motorcars," he confided. "My daughter, however! That child is afraid of nothing."

"We pilots have found that it's the children who take to flying the best," Gold agreed.

"But you in your German airplane!" Schuler shook his head in admiration. "You were quite wonderful!"

"*Danke*," Gold said shyly.

"Herr Gold," Schuler began. "I understand that your show will remain here?"

"Through tomorrow."

"The ticket seller assured me that you really were German, but I wanted to find out for myself," Schuler continued. "It's been a long time since I have had this pleasure of speaking my native tongue with someone outside of my family. Would you care to come to my home for supper this evening?"

Gold hesitated. "I wouldn't want to put you to any trouble—"

"No trouble at all!" Schuler said heartily. "Please, Herr Gold. It would give me great pleasure. You know, when I came to this country with my father and mother I was a mere boy. Everything was so strange! How I longed for home! You must be homesick for Germany a little, yes?"

"Often, I am," Gold admitted. "Especially since we arrived here in Nebraska."

"Here is not like Germany," Schuler nodded solemnly. "So, you will come? You'll have a taste of home. My wife is from Alsace, but she nevertheless cooks true German style."

Gold looked down at himself. He was wearing dark brown, greasy moleskin trousers tucked into his high boots, and a threadbare, gray flannel work shirt that lay plastered to his sweat-soaked torso. "I'm afraid that I'm hardly dressed to come to supper. All of my good clothes are back at the hotel in town . . ."

"It means nothing to us!" Schuler firmly declared. "We're a farming family. After supper I will take you back to the hotel in Doreen."

"You're very kind. I accept your generous invitation, Herr Schuler." Gold smiled. "Give me just a few moments to see to my airplane."

"Of course," Schuler said. "My daughter and I will wait for you in our wagon at roadside."

So this poor fellow still drives a wagon, Gold thought as he quickly performed a cursory but thorough maintenance check on the Hisso. Gold considered using a horse-drawn wagon to get around in this day and age to be the height of hicksville, and typical of Nebraska. He thought about borrowing a circus jalopy so that he could drive himself back to town after supper, but decided against it. He didn't want to take the chance of insulting Herr Schuler by suggesting that he was above the farmer's modest means.

Gold knew from his reading that agriculture in the Midwest had been hit hard by the postwar economic downturn. All through the fighting, and for a couple of years after the Armistice, the United States government was buying all the crops and livestock these farmers could produce. A lot of these farmers mortgaged themselves to the hilt, paying too much for land in order to expand, thinking the government-inflated prices would last forever. They didn't, and a lot of farmers in these parts lost everything when the bubble burst. Captain Bob had said that the reason the people hereabouts had the cash in their pockets to patronize the circus was due to the fact that Doreen had a strong industrial economy... And there was some tree-farm operation that employed a lot of people.

The Hisso looked as if it had survived the radiator boil-over. Gold nevertheless asked the mechanics—who had to remind him to switch back to the English language—to pay special attention to the cooling system. Gold tried to get the worst of the grime off his hands with a kerosene-soaked rag. He dug out of his back pocket the battered, gray felt fedora he'd taken to wearing to keep the sun off his head and headed off toward where Schuler was waiting in his wagon.

The two horses hitched to the wagon were huge and brown, with massive, shaggy hooves. It had been a long time since Gold had been around any mode of transportation that didn't drink gasoline. He'd never liked horses anyway. He gave these beasts a wide berth. They stank to high heaven, but as he watched them constantly flicking their tails to shoo the flies from their backs, Gold decided he was grateful for their presence, and the open-air wagon. He didn't exactly smell like roses at the moment, either.

Herr Schuler's wagon was big and black. It had polished brass lamps glinting in the sunshine, and bright red, spoked wheels. There was one seat for the driver, beside him, a space for cargo, and behind him, three rows of tufted, brown leather benches. Schuler was seated up in the driver's seat, idly twirling the reins.

"Ah! There you are, Herr Gold," Schuler said in German. "My daughter is just over there." He pointed out a figure in a blue calico dress, her blonde hair plaited into two thick braids, looking over the airplanes. "She can't get enough of your flying machines. Erica!" he called out.

She came skipping towards them, braids flying, slender and long-legged, like a colt. Gold, watching her, felt his heart begin to pound. She was no child, she was a woman; perhaps eighteen, or maybe nineteen. She had large brown eyes set far apart, and a slightly crooked nose that somehow only added to her beauty.

"Herr Gold, allow me to introduce my daughter, Erica," Schuler continued in German.

"Pleased to meet you," she said in English. "I hope you don't mind, but I won't speak German, although I can, and very well," she declared. "I just happen to think it's old-fashioned. Don't you agree?" she demanded.

"Well . . . I—" He looked helplessly at Schuler, who was laughing. *Dammit*, Gold thought. *I'm almost twenty-two! Why am I the one feeling like a little kid?*

"So now you've met Erica," Schuler said . . . in English.

This girl gets her way, Gold thought. He noticed that she had no German accent when she spoke English. She must have been born in America.

"Climb aboard, the two of you," Schuler said. "Mother's waiting supper."

Gold took her arm to help her aboard. He found touching her to be electrifying. She slid across the bench. Gold took a seat on the springy leather beside her. Schuler released the brake on the wagon and snapped the reins. The horses moved off, settling into a steady canter once they were on the gravel road.

"How far is it to your farm?" Gold asked Schuler.

"You're already *on* my farm," Schuler replied, over his shoulder. "I have six hundred acres."

"Really!" Gold tried not to sound surprised. "What do you grow?"

"Trees," Schuler replied. "I own a tree nursery farm."

"*You* run the tree farm?"

"The Reinhold Schuler Nursery? Yes, Herr Gold." Schuler glanced back, an amused smile on his face. "Why do you seem so surprised?"

"Papa told me that you aren't really a count," Erica interrupted, saving Gold from having to come up with a reply to Schuler. "I was disappointed."

"Didn't you enjoy the show?"

"Very much, but don't you think it's dishonest to pretend to be someone you're not?"

"Sometimes a little dishonesty doesn't hurt. In this case it made for a better show, don't you think?"

"You probably didn't even know the Red Baron," Erica challenged.

He let it go. He glanced at Schuler's back. With the noise of the horses and the creak of the wagon the farmer didn't seem to be able to hear the subdued conversation going on behind him. He remembered what Schuler had said about his daughter being a daredevil. "When did you break your nose?" Gold asked.

"What?" She turned toward him, a startled look in her wide-set eyes. Gold realized he had her undivided attention. A man could get used to that, he decided.

"You don't like my nose?" she asked defiantly. She said it in a way that seemed to suggest that if that were the case, Gold was certainly in the minority among young men.

"No," Gold said quickly. "I mean, yes—I do like it," he blurted, wondering how Captain Bob would use the gift of gab to get himself out of a mess like this. He shot a glance toward Schuler, who still seemed oblivious. "I think it makes your beauty special," Gold said softly.

Her smile was like the sun breaking through clouds. *Thank you, Captain,* Gold thought.

"I bet I *know* when and how you broke it," he said.

"I bet you *don't* know," she said, amused, rewarding him with another smile. "And I want—an *airplane* ride if you're wrong."

"You had an airplane ride, today."

"I want another." She licked her lips. "In your *red* machine."

Gold nodded. "You were a little girl when you broke your nose," he said. "A tomboy. The other children dared you into some foolhardy stunt, and that's when it happened."

Her mouth opened and closed. She didn't say a word. She just faced straight forward, blushing a delicate shade of coral.

Gold settled back to enjoy the ride, very pleased with himself, and his guess. His intuition was also warning him that it was a rare thing to get the last word with Erica Schuler.

The Schulers' farmhouse was tall and stately, a white-painted extravaganza of gingerbread trim, capped with a slate gray, mansard roof. The house was set apart from the rest of the farm buildings, and surrounded by tall shade trees and a whitewashed picket fence. As the wagon pulled up in front of the house, a shaggy, black and white dog roused itself from its slumber on the front porch and began to bark, wagging its tail.

"Erica, tell your mother we'll be right in. Herr Gold, would you mind giving me a hand with the horses? I will show you around the farm."

"Not at all, and please call me Herman."

Schuler nodded as his daughter hopped down from out of the wagon and went toward the porch. The dog ran to Erica, who made a big deal out of greeting it with hugs and lots of petting. Gold wondered if she was showing off for him. He hoped so.

The horses seemed to know their way about the place as Schuler conducted a wagon tour of the nursery. "My family came here in 1875, when I was just a boy," Schuler explained as he showed Gold the cutting and grafting house and other propagation buildings. "In the beginning my father, Reinhold Schuler, bought a small tract of land. He applied scientific methods to develop a profitable, well-equipped nursery farm."

Finally they toured the tree beds themselves. The rows of waist-high evergreens, fruit, and shade trees seemed to stretch forever, like a full-grown forest as seen from the air.

"We have our main office and our storage and shipping rooms in town," Schuler said as they made their way back to the house.

"Do you run this all by yourself?" Gold asked.

"Many people from the area work here, and my sons manage the town facility and also help me manage this farm."

"Oh, you have other children besides Erica?"

Schuler nodded. "I had five fine boys, but my eldest was killed in the war."

"I'm very sorry," Gold said.

Schuler nodded, looking grim. "There is much to be sorry about all over the world, thanks to that dreadful and foolish war, yes, Herman? Anyway, of my remaining sons, all of whom live in town with wonderful families of their own, two are involved in the family business. Then I have one son who is a doctor, and the other a lawyer," he added proudly as the horses came to a stop before the barn.

Gold noticed a garage, its double doors swung open, near the barn. He wandered over to peek in while Schuler was unhitching the team. Inside, parked in neat rows, were three trucks, two tractors and other farm machines, a raven black, gleaming, hard-top Cadillac—

And a low-slung, Pierce-Arrow two-seater roadster, cherry red, with black flared fenders.

Gold, mesmerized, approached the roadster. He knew all

about the Pierce. He'd read the literature: she was custom built for every customer . . .

"Ah! There you are, Herman."

Gold, startled, turned around. Schuler was standing silhouetted in the daylight streaming in through the garage doorway.

"You like my Erica's toy, eh?" Schuler chuckled. "It was a gift for her eighteenth birthday."

A gift, Gold thought as he followed Schuler out of the garage. The Pierce-Arrow cost seven grand.

"I have to ask," Gold began when they were in the barn, where, in addition to the horse stalls, there was a buggy and other types of wagons Gold couldn't identify. "With your Cadillac. Why bother with these wagons?"

"You sound like my sons, and my daughter." Schuler laughed. "They insisted that a man of my position in the community have a motorcar." He shrugged. "But you know what, Herman? For me, my horses and wagons are my way of having fun. But don't worry." He patted Gold's shoulder. "I'll take you back to town in the Cadillac. Now, help me finish here, we'll wash up, and my wife will feed you a supper like you haven't had since sailing from the Fatherland."

Frau Schuler was gray haired and stout where her daughter was slender, but Gold could find traces of her mother in Erica's lovely face.

They ate supper in the big dining room lined with sideboards and hutches laden with Frau Schuler's large collection of china and glassware. It was refreshingly cool, thanks to the early-evening breeze that set the room's lace curtains billowing. The Schuler womenfolk served up platters of roast pork, sweet-and-sour cabbage, string beans, and corn. There was a bottomless basket of biscuits, and pitchers of lemonade to wash it all down. Gold tried hard not to make a glutton of himself, but after all the months of hotel food, a home-cooked meal was heaven.

"Eat more!" Frau Schuler insisted, pushing the platters towards him. "You need to put on a little weight."

"Careful, Mama! Or his friends will be forced to leave him behind," Erica teased. "If he eats anymore he won't fit into his airplane."

"I bet poor Herman hasn't had a decent meal since he left Germany," Frau Schuler admonished.

"Actually, I never ate this well back home," Gold said. He told them about the food shortages that were being suffered in postwar Germany.

"Yes, of course..." Schuler frowned. "We knew it was bad there, but here, in the midst of all this plenty," he spread his arms wide, "we tend to forget..."

"Oh, we had our troubles during the war," Frau Schuler said quietly. "Erica! Help me clear the table for dessert."

"Yes, Mama." Erica smiled at Gold. "I baked an apple pie this morning!"

"What trouble was your wife referring to, sir?" Gold asked Schuler.

"Ah." Schuler shrugged. "During the war, a certain element questioned my patriotism, since I was German. Never mind all my boys were fighting for this country."

"But Papa was smart," Erica called out from the kitchen. "He beat them at their own game. He built the town a new elementary school."

"It just seemed like the right thing to do at the time," Schuler demurred. "And I could afford to do it. They put my name on it."

"And now he's financing a new addition to the hospital in town," Erica boasted as she came into the dining room, proudly presenting her apple pie for Gold's approval. She then proceeded to cut him a huge slice. "They're going to name the hospital wing after my brother who got killed in the war."

"Why not?" Schuler shrugged. "It'll be good for my son the doctor, now, and good insurance for the future." He winked. "I figure, if I put 'Schuler' on enough public buildings, sooner or later, people will have to think of it as an American name."

Gold nodded. "This pie is delicious," he complimented Erica.

* * *

After supper, Carl Schuler told Gold that there was some paperwork he had to sort through before he could drop it off at his office in town. He asked his daughter to entertain their guest for the half-hour it would take him before he would be ready to drive Gold back to the hotel.

"We'll sit out on the porch," Erica said, taking Gold's hand to lead him outside.

Gold noticed Frau Schuler's dark stare, but if the woman disapproved, she didn't say anything. He let Erica lead him out to the porch, through the comfortably furnished front parlor, with its corner brick fireplace.

The dog was still out there, lying on its side. It rose, shaking itself and going into a joyous, squirming greeting for its mistress. Erica immediately acted as if she'd forgotten Gold was there. She knelt to romp with the dog, and Gold tried not to stare at the graceful curve of her back as she showered kisses and lots of baby talk on the damn mutt.

It was almost dusk. The breeze had increased, and the crickets were making a racket. "Come sit with me on the glider," Erica commanded. Gold obliged, settling himself at the opposite end of the long, softly padded porch glider.

"You've been everywhere, haven't you?" Erica sighed, as she set the glider rocking.

"No, not really..." But then Gold thought about it. "Well, now that you mention it, I suppose I have done a lot of traveling in my life. It's funny, I've never thought about it that way."

"That's because you take your life for granted," Erica said.

"That's funny, coming from you."

"What's that supposed to mean?" Erica demanded.

"Only that you're very lucky to have a wonderful family and a comfortable home life. Look at your beautiful car..."

"But I haven't been anywhere," she complained. "You have no idea what it's like here," she sighed melodramatically. "It's *so* provincial... Have you read *Main Street*, by Sinclair Lewis?"

"Uh, no, why don't you tell me about it?" Gold suggested, taking the opportunity to slide a little closer to her.

The dog hopped up onto the cushions beside Erica and growled at him.

"Isn't Willie a good doggie!" Erica cooed.

Gold forced himself to smile pleasantly.

It was dark now. The wind had picked up, setting the trees rustling. Gold saw a jagged fork of lightning slashing the night sky as it stabbed the earth. "I suppose it's going to rain."

"Oh, no," Erica murmured as muted, rolling thunder eventually reached them. "That's how it is on the plains," she said dreamily. "It may have looked close enough to touch, but it's really a million miles away."

(Two)

That night Erica Schuler waited until her father had returned from driving Herman into town and her parents were having their bedtime cup of tea in the parlor. Her father was dozing in his chair. The newspaper was across his belly, and Willie the dog, a white and black furry oval, was curled around his feet. Her mother was in her rocking chair, working at her needlepoint.

Willie's tail thumped against the Persian carpet as Jackie came in. "Papa, Mama, Herman invited me to the air show tomorrow," she told them.

"But you saw it today," her mother said, frowning.

"I know," Erica said quickly. "But Herman said he would take me for a ride in his scarlet airplane."

"What are you talking about, child?" Frau Schuler sighed.

"The boy flies a special airplane," Schuler sleepily mumbled, his eyes still closed. "Jackie, if you were invited and wish to go, it is all right."

"Thank you, Papa!" Erica ran to her father to give him a hug and a kiss. "And you, Mama." She kissed and embraced her mother, and then skipped out of the parlor.

"You give in to her too much, Carl," Emma Schuler scolded her husband once Erica was gone.

"Ah, what's the harm?" Schuler replied. "He's a nice boy, and, anyway, after tomorrow the show moves on."

Upstairs, in her room, Erica turned on the lamp on the nightstand and sat on the edge of her canopy bed. She felt uneasy. She'd never lied to her parents before.

She undressed, slipping on a light cotton nightgown, and then sat at her vanity to watch herself in the mirror as she undid her braids and brushed out her shoulder-length hair.

It wasn't *really* a lie. Herman definitely *wanted* to invite her, and *would* have invited her, if he'd happened to think of it.

She put down her hairbrush and stood up, to slip her nightgown from her shoulders and let it fall around her feet. She stared at her body, tawny in the lamplight, and at the blonde thatch between her legs. She weighed her small breasts in her hands, furtively touching her dark nipples until they swelled like the buds on her papa's young fruit trees.

Girls in the city probably had bigger breasts. Did Herman like them bigger, she wondered?

She twirled slowly, looking at herself over her shoulder, canting her hip to study the deep cleavage of her bottom, trying to judge its swell and curve. She tried to be objective about herself, tried to judge her physical charms against those of the racy young Shebas she'd read about in the magazines and seen in the movies.

She'd taken it for granted that boys hereabouts found her attractive: she was never lacking for partners at the dances in town, and one beau or another was usually making a nuisance of himself coming around. She'd never had any real interest in those boys. She'd known them all for ages, from back when she'd been a tomboy, and could outswim, outrun, and outride the best of them.

She still could, most likely, Erica thought.

She smiled.

Herman had known exactly how she'd broken her nose ... He'd surprised her. She'd have to turn the tables. She could not endure his having the upper hand ...

She blushed, abruptly embarrassed at her brazen pirouetting, and her brazen thoughts; and at the moistness, almost like a betrayal, between her thighs.

She clicked off the lamp. By the silvery starlight coming in through the curtained window she quickly put on her nightgown and crawled into the familiar safety of her bed.

She'd been on her way upstairs when she'd overheard her father's comment to her mother. She took comfort in his opinion that there was no harm in what she was planning, and even a peculiar comfort that soon the barnstormers would be gone.

She fell asleep smiling, thinking that tomorrow would be the beginning and the end of it. Her darling aviator with his funny hat, his curly red hair, and devilish moustache was like a forbidden novel, thrilling for the brief duration, but when it was over she could forget the unfamiliar and unsettling emotions stirred up deep inside her.

(Three)

That night in his hotel room, Gold tossed and turned. Every time he dozed off he was tormented by fleeting fantasy-dreams of Erica Schuler. He gave up on sleep at dawn; showered and shaved. The hotel dinning room wouldn't be open for hours, but by now Gold had been in enough American small towns to know how things worked. He left the hotel and walked along the quiet, tree-lined streets until he came to the muddy, slow-moving Blue River. He crossed a narrow footbridge to the poor side of town near the railroad yard and police headquarters. A few blocks from the station he found a cafe filled with cops and rail yard laborers having their breakfast before beginning their shift.

He sat at the counter and had bacon and eggs, and three cups of black coffee to banish last night's cobwebs. Yes, Erica was a beautiful girl. A very special kind of girl, but he might as well forget her, just as she had doubtless already forgotten him. Today was the troupe's last performance in Doreen. By tomorrow afternoon he'd be flying west to the next show site, and he would never see Erica Schuler again.

Back at the hotel Gold ran into Jimmy Cooper the advance man and caught a ride with him out to the show site. The morning wore on, and the first of the spectators began to filter in. Gold was up on a stepladder, leaning over the Hisso, when he heard shouting. He looked toward the entrance to the show site. Tearing up the road toward them, sending up a huge dust cloud in its wake, was a cherry red Pierce-Arrow roadster—

The Pierce-Arrow, Gold thought, grinning. How many seven-thousand-dollar, bright red roadsters could there be in staid Doreen, Nebraska?

Gold watched, amused, as Erica Schuler expertly downshifted to throw the roadster into a sharp turn and through the entrance to the show site. She stepped on the gas, ignoring Jimmy Cooper's outraged shouts, and headed straight for Gold, arrogantly blaring her horn to scatter pedestrians and expertly swerving with a minimum of effort to avoid the parked airplanes and trucks in her path. As she closed on Gold she threw the roadster into a controlled, sideways skid, coming to a stop parallel with his airplane, with just inches to spare in a shower of dirt and gray engine exhaust.

She killed the ignition, and hoisted herself out of the ticking roadster without opening its door. She was wearing a white, long-sleeved blouse, and tan, snug jodhpurs tucked into riding boots. Gold saw her breasts heave, and enjoyed the curve of her ass as she swung her agile legs up and over the roadster's low sill.

"I came for my airplane ride in your red machine," Erica announced. "A real ride! Not one of those old-lady rides I got yesterday."

Gold pretended to frown, shaking his head. "But you lost your bet."

She made a face. "I never lose, and if I do, I make people give in. Now, do I get my ride, or do I have to get tough with you, Herr Count?"

"You don't need an airplane to fly. You were almost off the ground in your own red machine," Gold said admiringly. "Lady, you can drive!"

"I bet I could fly your airplane, too," she bragged.

Gold laughed. "I bet you could, given half a chance, but

today I guess I'd better do the flying. It'll be a few minutes to get her ready." Gold came down off the ladder. "I'll fetch you some flying gear."

"I didn't need flying gear last time," Erica remarked.

"Last time you didn't fly with me."

At the parts trailer he nabbed a couple of mechanics and asked them to gas up the Jenny. Next he rummaged around in the trailer and came up with a spare set of goggles, and a light, leather jacket to protect Erica against the wind. As he was walking back to the Jenny with the gear, Captain Bob intercepted him.

The Captain pointed to Erica, who had already climbed up into the Jenny's front passenger cockpit. "What's going on, son?"

"Taking a customer for a ride," Gold remarked, trying to sound casual about it all.

Captain Bob chewed thoughtfully on his big brown stogie. "Thought you told me you didn't want the Hisso used for rides." He squinted at Erica. "Nice-looking girl."

"I didn't really notice, Cap . . . ," Gold said lamely.

The captain mournfully shook his head. "Don't try to kid a kidder, son. You got the look of an eagle about to have salt sprinkled on his tail."

"Remember now, I want a real barnstorming ride!" Erica shouted over the noise of the Hisso engine as Gold made sure she was securely strapped into the forward cockpit.

Gold winked at her. "Once we're up there, don't worry, you can scream all you want." He grinned at her.

"Bet I don't!" she replied. She held out her hand for him to shake on the bet, and, when he did, he thought she gave his fingers an extra, lingering squeeze.

He taxied into the wind for an easy takeoff, letting the Hisso warm up, and keeping an eye on his water temperature gauge. Then he lifted them off into the clear blue sky. He banked gently as he began to climb for altitude; for all of his teasing, he really didn't want to frighten Erica.

"Faster!" Erica shouted. Her voice carried back to him on the wind. It was no use trying to talk to her, she'd never hear him over the engine racket.

Action would have to speak for him, Gold decided. If she wanted a barnstormer's ride, then that was what she was going to get.

He put the Jenny into a severe right bank—the horizon tilted sharply—and he heard Erica cry out in surprise as he felt his own stomach do a backflip. Next came a series of rolls. Over and over the Jenny went, earth and sky pinwheeling before them.

Erica was shrieking now loudly, but laughing as well. Gold was laughing too. The scarlet Jenny slashed its presence across the sky.

He prolonged the flight for as long as possible, hugely enjoying himself, and Jackie's reaction. As they were flying upside down, Erica's hair came undone and began to whip around in the wind. He turned the airplane right side up and went into an Immelman loop that made her howl. Gold laughed and laughed. There were no other planes in the sky. Everyone was watching as Gold took Erica for their sky dance. It was the most passionately exciting moment of his life. For this precious instant, not only the sky, but this magnificent woman, was his.

Finally Gold brought the Jenny down. After all the airborne excitement, he wanted to further impress Erica by the smoothest possible landing. As he dropped the airplane he throttled down the engine and pulled back the nose, until he had the wings angled just at the threshold of a stall. A foot or so above the ground he coaxed the nose back a little more. The Jenny lost her lift, plopping down in a perfect three-point landing. He cut the Hisso to roll to a stop where Erica's roadster was parked, and, in the ensuing rush of silence, heard Erica sobbing.

She twisted around toward him, removing her goggles. Her eyes were wet; tears had streaked tracks down her dusty cheeks.

"I've frightened you too much!" Gold exclaimed, removing his own goggles, unbuckling his harness, and getting out of the cockpit.

"No." Her tousled blonde hair shimmered as she shook her head. "It was just so beautiful and wonderful!— Was that all the tricks you know?"

"Not really." Gold smiled as he unbuckled her harness. "But it's every stunt I'd risk in the Jenny, taking into account your extra weight on board. Every airplane is different. They're like cars. You can do things in your roadster that you couldn't do in your father's Cadillac."

Erica's arms went around his neck as he lifted her out of the plane. She held on to him even after he'd set her down, hugging him, murmuring into his chest. "It was so gloriously wonderful and beautiful it made me cry! It was like being with the angels."

"You're the angel," Gold told her softly.

She rose up on her toes to kiss him. Gold, trembling, held her gingerly, sheltering her in his arms as she pressed against him.

"I wish you weren't leaving," he thought he heard her whisper. Or maybe he only imagined it, because that was what he so desperately wanted to hear.

All during the rest of the air show Erica Schuler was in a daze. She didn't really care if she saw the rest of the performance, but something was keeping her from leaving this place where the airplanes flew; keeping her from leaving Herman. After all, after today, she would never see him again.

Now it was time for Herman's performance as the Red Baron. She would stay to see him fly the scarlet Jenny this final time. Then she would leave, quickly and quietly, to spare them both the pain of farewell.

As she watched Herman soar across the sky she kept replaying in her mind the magnificent sensations of her own flight. As they'd tumbled through the sky she'd felt free as a bird, like a goddess. As a child she'd been an excellent horseback rider, and she'd become an accomplished motorcar driver. Perfecting these skills had made her feel vibrantly alive, but neither horses nor cars could compare to the scary, giddy thrill of flight.

She thought about Herman as she watched his scarlet airplane slide and soar, pursued by the trio of flying machines wearing America's red, white, and blue. How masterfully was he handling the airplane! How masterful had he been with her in the air. She thought about how easy and how exciting it was to be with him.

And then she reminded herself that he was leaving. Herman Gold was bound for great adventures, and she was staying right here in good old Doreen, Nebraska.

She watched the closing moments of Herman's performance, wondering why she was torturing herself by sticking around. As he did yesterday, Herman outmaneuvered his attackers. The drummer standing next to Captain Bob beat his instrument, and one of the striped machines spilled smoke and fell toward the ground.

Erica watched as Herman allowed the remaining two planes to settle on his tail, heard the drum go *rat-a-tat*, and saw fire and smoke envelop the scarlet plane.

She'd seen it all before, knew that it was just pretend. Still, she couldn't help feeling afraid as she watched Herman's plane, spilling light and smoke, seemingly fall from the sky. The scarlet airplane was fluttering down like an autumn leaf from the highest bough of the big oak tree outside her bedroom window.

The smoke ended, and the flares mounted under the scarlet plane's wings sputtered out, but still the airplane fell. It seemed to Erica that the plane was falling for a long time, that yesterday it hadn't spiraled earthward for nearly so long.

One of the pilots standing nearby blurted, "Christ, something's wrong!"

Oh, God, Erica thought. *Oh, God—*

Gold had gotten the idea while he was running his preperformance maintenance check on the Hisso Jenny. He toyed with the notion while he was waiting for his cue to take off. Halfway through the performance he'd dismissed the idea, with relief, as just too crazy and dangerous.

As he went into his falling leaf/power dive finale he remembered Erica's kiss, and knew he was going to do it.

He stopped brooding. He was going to need all of his concentration and every bit of flying skill to purposely crash his plane without totally destroying it—

Or himself.

He let the wafting Jenny stall and go into a spin. As the airplane tumbled, Gold clenched his teeth, struggling against the stomach-churning vertigo. The last time he'd crashed an airplane he'd come out of it with broken legs. *"You were lucky...,"* the field hospital orderly had told him. *"...It could have been a broken back...Could have been a broken neck."*

He waited until the last possible second of the spin and then wrestled the Jenny's nose down to regain stability and control. The earth was hurtling up as he leveled out, barely skimming above the field. He cut the engine and let the Jenny down hard, in that instant thinking that he wasn't the first, and likely wouldn't be the last, damn fool to kill himself for love—

It all happened in seconds. Erica watched, breathless, as the scarlet airplane stopped its tumble and nosedived toward the ground, its engine roaring as if in torment.

"Everybody stay back!" Captain Bob was trumpeting through his megaphone. "He's going to hit *harrddd!*" The Captain's voice rose in hysterical alarm.

Horror-struck, Erica watched the scarlet plane's nose rise in the nick of time. She heard its engine die as it slammed the earth, plowing a furrow with its nose and cracking off its propeller. The plane, spewing smoke from its engine, rose up like a trout leaping from a stream. It came down again, blowing its right tire and splintering the wooden landing gear, sliding along on its right wing. There was a loud cracking as the wing broke. The plane whipped around and came to rest in a cloud of dust.

People began running toward the crashed plane. Erica couldn't move. She just stood and stared at the cockpit until she saw Herman, in that ridiculous, bright red, patent-leather helmet, wave to his would-be rescuers. He hopped out of the broken flying machine's cockpit and walked away.

Erica found herself sobbing with joy for the second time that day.

* * *

Herman stood in the shade cast by the parts trailer, listening as the chief mechanic reported to Captain Bob on the damage to the Hisso Jenny.

"The engine took a beating, Cap." The mechanic scowled. "Just how bad, I can't say. In addition, she needs a new prop, radiator, landing gear and a rebuilt right wing."

A grounded eagle, all right, Gold thought, but had the brains to keep his mouth shut.

"She's also tore up her belly," the mechanic continued. "Now, maybe we could fake the prop with one of the spares we carry—"

"Bad idea," Gold volunteered. "The OX5's RPM's don't match the Hisso's—"

Captain Bob glared at him. Gold shut up.

"It don't matter anyway, Cap." The mechanic shrugged. "We don't have the woodworking capability to mill the wing spars or the landing gear, and we sure as hell can't do a thing with that busted radiator."

"Thank you, son." Captain Bob nodded to the mechanic. "I'd like you to see if there's a way we can dismantle the Jenny and load her onto a truck."

The mechanic looked doubtful. "How we going to find the space to manage that?"

"Well, I'm sure as hell not going to leave that airplane here!" the Captain exploded. He took a deep breath. "Just see what you can do," he told the mechanic. "Now, if you'll excuse us, I'd like to talk to the Red Baron, here, in private."

The Captain waited until the mechanic was out of earshot, and then asked Gold, "Give me one good reason why I shouldn't fire you, right now."

Gold shrugged. "Accidents happen, Cap."

"You call that an accident? You know what happened!"

Is he on to me? Gold wondered. "What are you saying, Cap?"

"I think you tired yourself out taking that—" He paused, scowling. "That *farmer's daughter* for a joyride. Stunt flying takes concentration. You used all yours up, and you didn't have enough left to do your work."

"I guess you're right, Cap," Gold said, trying to sound

contrite, hugely relieved that the man didn't have the slightest inkling of what had actually happened.

The captain was nodding. "I warned you, didn't I? I said you were heading for trouble, and now here we are. I may not know how to fly an airplane, but I've been around them a long time. I know that a stunt pilot can't let himself get distracted by every pretty skirt he sees."

"I'm really sorry for the inconvenience, Cap."

"Son, you cost me money today," Captain Bob said bleakly.

"You could fire me if you want, Cap," Gold said. "On the other hand, what's done is done. Why not let me make it up to you by *saving* you some money."

"Now how might you do that, son?" Captain Bob demanded sharply.

"Simple, Cap. For starters, you don't try to lug the plane with you."

"I don't?"

Gold shook his head. "You leave her here."

"Why the fuck would I?—"

"Try this on for size, Cap," Gold suggested. "I stay behind with the Jenny and have her trucked into Doreen, where there are woodworking facilities and machine shops to supply the replacement parts she needs. I'll supervise the repairs and then fly the Jenny to meet up with the troupe farther west. With luck, the Red Baron will be back with his circus in a couple of weeks . . . more or less," Gold added as an afterthought.

"That's not bad," the Captain said. "Yeah, that's not a bad idea at all . . ." He turned on Gold. "But why should I leave *you* behind? Assuming I don't fire you, that is. You're my best pilot, goddamn your ass."

"Up to you, of course, Cap." Gold elaborately shrugged. "But you'll need to leave behind an experienced mechanic to dicker the cost of the repairs and supervise the work; otherwise, you're going to get fleeced by the locals. In addition, you'll need to leave behind a pilot to fly the Jenny out of here. That's two men staying behind, costing you salaries, and hotel room and board."

Captain Bob nodded thoughtfully. "Or I can leave just one man: you. You're a mechanic and a pilot."

Gold smiled.

Erica Schuler was waiting for Gold near the damaged Jenny. "When I saw you crash I thought for sure you were going to die!" She gasped, embracing him. "Oh, I'm so glad you're safe!"

"No big deal," Gold muttered bravely, holding her. The press of her body made him dizzy. He felt intoxicated inhaling her scent as he nuzzled her hair. He even considered telling her the truth, but he decided to leave well enough alone. Things couldn't be any better between them than just the way they were. "Erica, who runs the best motor garage in town?"

"Teddy Quinn," she said flatly. "He takes care of my roadster. I wouldn't let anyone else come near it."

Gold nodded. "Would you mind driving me into town to see him?"

"That's it," Erica said as she guided the roadster into a narrow alleyway behind some riverfront warehouses.

QUINN'S GARAGE, THEODORE X. QUINN, PROPRIETOR read the sign stretching the length of the low, flat-roofed, cinder block building. Parked next to the garage was a rusty, olive green, U.S. Army surplus tow truck, with "Quinn's" lettered on the side of the cab. A Bluebird brand gasoline pump and stacks of automobile tires bracketed the garage's double barn doors.

Gold saw a man dressed in dark-blue mechanic's overalls up on a ladder, repainting the "Emergency Road Service" sign above the garage's single window.

"That's Teddy," Erica said as she cut the roadster's engine.

"Afternoon, Miss Schuler." Teddy Quinn nodded from his ladder. "Trouble with the car?"

Gold thought Quinn looked about thirty. He was thin, had black, wavy hair and round tortoiseshell spectacles.

"No, the roadster's fine," Erica said as Quinn climbed

down the ladder. "But my friend here could use your help. Herman Gold, Teddy Quinn."

Teddy squinted at Gold as they shook hands. "You're one of those barnstormers, aren't you?"

"Yes, and I'm afraid I just racked up one of the troupe's airplanes. I thought maybe you could help me get it repaired."

"Airplane, huh?" Teddy grinned. "Sounds like a nice change from working on tractors. About the only fun I get around here comes when Miss Schuler brings me her Pierce-Arrow to work on. Come on in out of the sun, and we'll talk about your airplane." He invited Gold and went inside the garage.

"I've got to get home," Erica told Gold. "Or else Mama will have a fit."

"It looks like I'll be here for a couple of weeks . . ." Gold began.

"Ummm," Erica nervously ran her long, graceful fingers around the steering wheel's varnished curve.

"Do you think it'd be all right if I came to see you?" Gold asked.

Erica smiled shyly. "Sure."

"Like maybe tomorrow, after supper?"

Erica nodded quickly. She leaned across the narrow interior of the car to give him a quick kiss. "Now go! I've got to get home."

Gold got out of the car, thinking that she was worth crashing an airplane anytime. He watched her drive away, thinking that he liked everything about her, even the fact that she didn't look back and wave.

Inside the garage it was dim and cool. There were tool benches and parts bins; a partly disassembled tractor and a black Ford Model T up on jacks. Old license plates, automotive posters, and parts supply calendars lined the walls.

Gold was impressed by the garage's professional layout. He noticed that all of Teddy's tools and equipment looked well cared for and neatly put away. Teddy clearly took pride in his work, and that was important.

Gold thought briefly of the motor garage that he and

Heiner Froehlig had talked about opening back in Germany; that day seemed like a hundred years ago.

Teddy was seated behind a dented steel desk at the rear of the garage. Behind him was a tall filing cabinet, a small stove, and an electric icebox.

"Pull up a seat." Teddy indicated a wooden crate.

Gold set the crate beside the desk and straddled it. Teddy pushed back his chair, reached behind him to the icebox, and extracted a couple of orange soda pops. He angled the bottles against the edge of the desk, banged the caps off with his palm, and handed a soda pop to Gold.

"Now, what can I do for you, Herman?" Teddy asked.

Gold filled him in on the damage suffered by the Jenny. "You ever do work on anything like this before?" Gold asked.

"During the war. I went over in the Army motor pool. Now and again we'd overhaul a Spad. As I recall, those airplanes had Hispano Suiza V-8s . . ."

"Excellent!" Gold exclaimed. "This Jenny has a Hisso." He explained the overheating problems he'd encountered and showed Teddy the rough sketch he'd made of his idea for a radiator design. "I figure, as long as she needs a new radiator, why not try to improve on the original?"

"For a Hisso, huh?" Teddy nodded thoughtfully as he studied the drawing. He took off his spectacles, breathed on the lenses, and polished them on a rag. His green eyes looked weakly out from behind the glass. "I like it," he finally decided. "Yeah, I do . . . Did you think this up all by yourself?" Gold nodded. "I'm impressed," Teddy said. "You know machines."

Gold arranged for Teddy to haul the Jenny back to the garage. Quinn would introduce him to the best craftsmen in town to mill a new wooden prop, wing spars, and landing gear assembly and to build the extra-capacity cooling system. Meanwhile, Gold would use the garage's facilities—with Quinn lending a hand when he was available—to diagnose and repair the damage the Hisso had suffered in the crash.

"Where you staying?" Quinn asked.

"The Red Bull Manor," Gold said. "Say, there's one last

thing you might be able to help me with. I'm going to need transportation. You have any cars you might want to rent out?"

"No cars." Teddy shook his head. "I do have something you might be able to use. Come around out back."

Gold followed him around to the garage's small backyard, littered with rusted sections of automobiles and trucks. Off in one corner was a small lean-to, beneath which was something covered over with a dusty canvas tarp. Teddy removed the canvas to reveal a dove-gray, red- and black-trimmed Harley Davidson motorcycle.

"Ever drive one of these?" Teddy asked.

"Not really." Gold shrugged. "I can figure her out, though."

Teddy nodded. "Don't see why not. You can't do her any harm. She's about six years old, and has already taken a beating. The fellow that owned her gave her up after he'd put himself in a ditch a few times." He pointed to the Harley's black, copper-clad engine. "You can get her up to about forty-five miles per hour, no problem. After that, the engine will still have plenty left, but you'll find the frame wobbles."

"She'll do fine," Gold said. The cycle would get him from town to the Schuler farm in ten minutes. "Can I rent her?"

Quinn made a face. "Hell, use her. You'll be doing me a favor. I'm so busy I ain't got time to take her out the way I should."

Chapter 7

It was after supper. Erica Schuler had just finished cleaning up the kitchen for her mother and had come outside to the front porch to catch a bit of breeze while she waited for Herman. The summer sun, molten and all-pervading throughout the day, had begun to set, turning the big sky into a purple and orange dome over the world. Erica was sweltering, though. She had her hair pinned up, and damp tendrils stuck to the nape of her neck. As she settled back on the glider she looked around to make sure that her father and mother were nowhere about, and then kicked off her slippers and folded up the hem of her rose-colored, light cotton sundress, to expose her knees to the gentle breeze.

She heard Herman's motorcycle long before she saw it. The dog, panting as it lay on its side on the porch, began to thump its tail against the floorboards. Finally, Erica saw the motorcycle's single headlight, bouncing like a firefly, as Herman made his way along the rutted dirt turnoff that led from the main road to the Schuler farmhouse.

She remembered her dress just as Herman pulled up, and flushed hot with embarrassment as she quickly flipped down her hem to cover her knees. She didn't think he saw. He'd been occupied switching off the cycle's engine, putting it up on its kickstand. Now he was removing his flying goggles, letting them dangle around his neck.

The dog got to its feet, yawning and stretching, and lumbered down the front steps to lick Herman's hand. Herman gave the dog a cursory pat, just to be amenable, Erica thought. She could tell from his time spent at the farm this past month that Herman wasn't very fond of animals.

"Mama made a chicken pot pie for supper," Erica said. "I've kept some warm for you in the oven."

"Thanks." He shrugged listlessly. "I'm not very hungry."

Erica pressed her lips together. "You feeling poorly on account of your work?"

Herman nodded. "Sort off."

Herman and Teddy had been working hard on some new-fangled gadget for the Jenny. When the work went wrong Herman invariably became remote and introverted. Erica put up with it. That's how men were, she guessed, and so God gave women the ability to flirt and tease them out of their silly funks.

"Come sit beside me and tell me about it," Erica comforted.

He came up on the porch and settled beside her on the glider, reaching tentatively, almost furtively, for her fingers, as if after all this time he expected her to slap his hand away. He'd gotten more shy as their relationship progressed. She wished that he understood people half as well as he knew his airplanes.

"Now tell me just what that nasty machine has been doing to you two boys," she began to joke.

"It's done," Herman interrupted, turning toward her with a look of anguish. "The work's done. I've dragged it out this past month, but I can't stall the captain any longer."

She nodded, beginning to cry. She was quiet and stoic about it; she wasn't going to act like a silly sob-sister, goddammit, but she couldn't help the tears filling her eyes and running down her cheeks.

"I haven't told you, but the captain's been sending me telegrams these past couple of weeks, demanding to know when I'm going to link up with the troupe," Herman was explaining.

"When are you leaving?" Erica asked simply, hopelessly.

"Tomorrow . . . Erica, I love you."

She laughed lightly. "And I love you." Her tears were on

her lips. She kissed him, letting him taste the salt. "Just hold me for a moment," she asked him. "Just for a moment . . ."

"Oh, God," Herman sighed. "Erica, maybe I don't have to go. Your father came to talk to me at the garage last week. He's no fool, your father. He knows how we feel about each other. He took me aside and told me that there was room here in his business for a son-in-law."

"You're no farmer," Erica scoffed.

"And Teddy and I have become friends this past month," Herman continued. "I've helped him out on some of his jobs. He's got more work in his garage than he can handle, and we work well together. Maybe I could become a partner with him." He paused. "A long time ago, I almost went into business with a friend running a garage . . ."

Erica pulled away from him. "If you do anything like that, I'll never see you again."

Herman stared at her. "I don't understand. You said you love me?—"

"I do. Too much to have you throw away your life," she said fiercely. "You've told me countless times that you want to achieve great things in the field of aviation—"

"I know, but—"

"I believe you, Herman. I believe you can do it. I will *not* have you stay here, wasting your talents scratching in the dirt or fixing tractors. I want to help you *accomplish* your dreams, not be the cause of you *abandoning* them. Do you understand?"

"It means I'll have to go away, Erica."

"Yes."

"I'll find something having to do with flying to support us, and then I'll come back for you."

"If you don't you're a bigger fool than I thought you are, Herman Gold," she warned him, nestling close. "You'll come back, and you'll take me away with you."

"Come with me flying," Herman said.

"Now?" Erica asked, startled.

"Right now. The airplane's all ready," Herman said. "We trucked it out to the field and gassed it up this afternoon."

"But it's almost dark."

He shrugged. "It's a clear night, and a full moon. We'll

have plenty of light." He took her hand and squeezed it. "Please come. I want to show you something before I leave."

Erica hesitated. Herman smiled down at her. God, she loved him when he was like this! She gazed at him; at his unruly red curls and thick moustache; at his piercing blue eyes, usually filled with obtuse thoughts about his machines, but just now simply bright with adoration.

She would go with him. It would be worth all the trouble that would come down upon her from her parents to go with him now. To be able to have this memory of him, like a soaring eagle, to hold once he was gone.

She rode behind him on the motorcycle, clutching on to him, letting his back shelter her from the wind. She'd never been on a motorcycle before. She thought the sensation was something like flying, and she understood why Herman loved the cycle so much.

When they reached the field she was surprised to see Teddy Quinn's truck parked next to the tarp-shrouded Jenny. Teddy was just finishing lighting a number of widely spaced lanterns running parallel to each other, marking out a stretch of runway.

"You knew we were going to go flying all along, Herman Gold!" Erica admonished above the buzz of the motorcycle.

"I wanted it to be a surprise," Herman said as he pulled up beside the truck.

"He took me up this afternoon." Teddy laughed as he came over to them. "I figure your ride is going to be a bit more romantic—"

"Hey!" Herman scowled. He pressed his finger to his lips.

"What's going on here?" Erica demanded suspiciously, looking from one to the other.

"I've said too much already." Teddy shook his head. "Never could keep my mouth shut."

Erica watched as the two men pulled the tarp from the Jenny. "She's beautiful, again!" Erica cried out. The airplane's fresh scarlet paint, and her bright new metalwork protruding from the open cowling, glistened and gleamed in the moonlight. "Where are the German Crosses?" she asked.

"We left them off," Herman said. "I figure it'd be healthier for the count to travel incognito until I can hook up with the troupe."

He helped her into the front cockpit, where she found a light jacket and pair of goggles. Herman strapped her in and then got into the rear, pilot's cockpit. Erica waited anxiously as Herman and Teddy went through their preflight routine. She wondered if she was going to enjoy night flying as much as she had flying on that glorious afternoon when Herman had turned the heavens upside down for her.

Finally the Jenny's engine caught, setting its brand-new propeller spinning. They taxied along between the two strings of lanterns, which blended into a glowing blur as the airplane picked up speed. She adjusted her goggles against the delicious wind. She felt the wheels rumbling along the short grass, and then came that supreme moment when they lifted off. She laughed, exhilarated, knowing now that flying would always be magical for her and that she would always love airplanes. She even patted the Jenny's vibrating, taut, fabric flank, like she would a beloved and faithful horse.

Herman flew gently. Erica felt as if she were being magically levitated. For a while they followed the river, the fat, ivory-hued August moon's reflection in the water turning that river into an opalescent serpent slithering across the dark earth.

The airplane titled back, its nose rising as Herman gained altitude. Now Erica could only see the night, velvety black, and the infinite and brilliant lacework of ice-blue stars, seemingly close enough to touch.

He brought the plane around in a gentle banking turn. Suddenly the engine was quiet! Erica, alarmed, twisted against her harness to look back toward Herman.

"Don't worry, I've cut her on purpose. Everything's fine," Herman reassured her. His voice carried clearly in the relative silence, except for the low burble of the idled engine and the soft rustle of wind. "Look down," he called.

Erica cried out, delighted. Below was the town—*her* town—but from this perspective it looked neither provincial nor drab. It looked magnificently dusted with a webbing of light, like a starry constellation fallen intact to earth.

Herman whished her back and forth over the town, the quiet, gliding airplane riding the wind. It was their own flying carpet, Erica thought. It was like flying in a dream.

"This is what I wanted to show you," Herman told her. "I've no money to buy you jewelry. Those lights are the jewels I can give you now. If you'll agree to marry me, they'll symbolize our engagement until I can afford to buy you a ring."

"I'll wait for you, my love," Erica called out to him. "I'll wait for as long as it takes."

"Remember tonight," she heard him plead. "Remember tonight when I'm gone."

(Two)

Gold brought the Jenny down to land, guided by the beacons strung out along the field, gratified but not surprised that Teddy had stuck to his offer to make sure that all the lanterns remained lit. Gold had learned that his new friend was a man of his word.

Gold cut the engine and came to a stop by the truck. Teddy was beside the plane even before the prop had stopped turning.

"Well?" Teddy demanded. "What happened?"

"The Jenny flew fine," Gold said, deadpan, hopping out of the plane.

"That's not what I'm asking about!" Teddy exploded. He looked at Erica, who had unbuckled her own harness and was climbing down to the ground. "Did this oaf ask you to marry him, or not?"

"He did, and I said I would." Erica laughed, happily embracing Teddy.

Gold watched, amused, as Teddy awkwardly endured Erica's kiss on the cheek, muttering all the while about sentimental womenfolk. Then he and Teddy set out to collect the lanterns and load them into the back of the truck. "Want me to help you cover the Jenny with the tarp?" Teddy asked when they were done.

"I'll do it after she cools down a bit," Herman said.

"I guess I'll be going, then," Teddy said. He shook hands with Gold. "Congratulations on your engagement, friend. You still planning to be on your way west, first thing tomorrow?" When Herman nodded, Teddy said, "Then let's meet at the garage at dawn. I'll give you a lift out to the field and see you off."

Gold and Erica stood arm in arm, watching as Teddy got into his truck and drove away. "Well, I guess I'd better get you home," Gold said reluctantly once they were alone.

"Not yet," Erica said. She took him by the hand and led him over to the tarp, bunched on the ground beneath the Jenny's wing. She settled down onto the soft, billowed canvas and then pulled him down beside her.

"Erica—" he began, but she quieted him with a kiss, her mouth pressing against his, her tongue darting. He pulled away, his body throbbing, his mind in turmoil. Her taste, wet and sweet, was now indelible in him.

"I want you to make love to me," she said.

He could see her clearly in the moonlight. Her glistening lips were parted. Her dark eyes were intent, almost somber, as she gazed at him.

What was he to do? What was his responsibility here? He wanted her, desperately, but what should he do? She was too important to make a mistake.

She kicked off her slippers and began to unbutton her dress. He watched her rise up on her knees to shrug the dress off over her head. She wore no corset. She didn't need one. Her camisole and brief knickers of white satin laced with pink ribbon shimmered in the moonlight.

"I've never been with anyone," she whispered. "But I guess you know that." She laughed nervously. Her eyes searched his. "Have you?"

He thought about the prostitutes of Berlin, and the New York City whores he had infrequently visited. Those sexual encounters had nothing to do with this. "No, I've never made love," he said sincerely.

She began to unbutton his shirt. He tried to speak, to ask her again if she was sure that this was what she wanted, but she kissed him and kissed him and when she stopped he no longer had the will to question.

She slid his shirt off, running her hands across his back, making him shudder. She undid his belt, working the buttons along his fly—

Gold panicked. His passion had kept him from thinking clearly. He couldn't let her see him naked. He was circumcised—

He had never told her that he was a Jew, but now she would know. He should have told her before this, he realized in despair, but he hadn't been able to bring himself to reveal the truth to her, afraid her affection would turn to revulsion.

She had peeled down his trousers, and his undershorts. She was running her fingers along the length of his erection.

"So this is what a man looks like," she breathed. She lowered her head to kiss him there.

She doesn't know— At first Gold couldn't believe it, but then he remembered her innocence. She'd never been with a man, didn't know what men looked like, or about circumcision. She didn't know anything . . .

He pulled off his boots and kicked off his trousers, then turned to her. Erica shivered like a bird as he untied the bows of her camisole. Like a small child being undressed, she raised her arms to allow him to remove it. He stared at her breasts. When he touched them she flinched. He pulled back, newly uncertain. Erica, smiling, shook her head.

"I'm sorry, I can't help it, but I'm frightened. I'll try not to be, but . . ." Her voice faded as she took his hands and placed them on her swollen nipples.

He gathered her up in his arms and kissed her, then gently laid her back on the tarp. The whores in Berlin had taken a shine to him. They had taught him things that they said women found pleasurable. He did those things now. His own excitement increased in measure to Erica's initial bewilderment as he slid the silky, damp knickers from her supple hips and she finally surrendered, abandoning herself to his caresses.

When he entered her she clutched at him, then seemed to relax, her arms and legs wrapping around him. When she climaxed she cried out, a touch of shrill panic in her voice, but just as quickly she murmured, *"Oh my love,"* her breath scalding his cheek as she clung to him. When he exploded inside of her he had a fleeting vision of them as if seen from the starry sky: two feral, naked creatures in the silvery moonlight, twisting together in their canvas nest beneath the wing of the scarlet Jenny, a benevolent mother bird sheltering her progeny in the midst of this vast field.

After, she lay curled beside him, hushed and trembling. He felt droplets on his chest and realized she was crying. Gold was frightened. He had never been with a virgin— What if he had somehow hurt her inside?

"Are you all right?" She didn't answer. "Erica! Are you—"

"Shhh, yes," she whispered. "I didn't know how it would be. I'd imagined it, of course, but I had no idea..." She propped herself up on her elbows to look at him. Her eyes were shiny and soft in the moonlight. "What about you, are you disappointed?"

"No!" Gold exclaimed. "Are you?" he asked, concerned.

"No..." she sighed contentedly, resting her head on his chest. "I hope we did right," she murmured. "I thought before that this would make it easier to be apart, but now I think it's going to make it worse..."

"I love you very much, Erica."

"I know, my love." She laughed. "You can't have any secrets from me."

Secrets, Gold thought. He felt so dishonest, *so dirty*. He had to tell her he was a Jew. She had to know if they were going to be married...

Gold knew that Erica and her mother belonged to the Lutheran Church, but that her father had dropped out, his faith shaken by the loss of his son to the war. Carl Schuler was presently involved in a Unitarian congregation that believed in mankind coming together for social betterment and universal peace.

"Herman, you know, you've never discussed your religious beliefs with me," she said softly.

He flinched. It was amazing how often she seemed to pick up on his thoughts. "This is hard for me to tell you," he began. "Don't be angry with me, please... Try to understand..."

"What are you talking about?" she demanded.

Gold panicked. So often in his life had the truth cost him; people changed toward him after he'd revealed his origins. What if his being born a Jew caused Erica to reject him? He couldn't bear that.

"Herman? What's wrong?" She was beginning to sound alarmed.

He had no intentions of ever practicing Judaism. None of the barnstormers knew he was a Jew. Why did *she* have to know? Why did *anybody*? It was totally up to him, he abruptly realized. He could reveal his past, or right now put it behind him, forever.

"What I'm trying to say is, don't be angry with me, Erica, but I'm not very religious."

She nodded. "But you do believe in Jesus?"

"I guess I don't believe in anything very much," Gold evaded. "I mean, I think I believe in God, but..." He trailed off helplessly. "I just haven't given it that much thought."

"Does it bother you that I believe in Jesus?" Erica asked.

"No!" Herman blurted.

"Well, then," Erica said, kissing him. "That's all settled."

"It's all right?" Gold asked. "You don't mind? What about your mother and father?"

"Papa might understand," Erica said thoughtfully. "Between us, I don't think he believes much, since the war. But Mama would be upset..." She shrugged and smiled. "So we just won't tell them. It's none of their business anyway, Herman. I'm the one marrying you, not them."

Gold nodded, grateful the ordeal was over, thinking that it was right to keep this one harmless secret from her, to ensure their happiness.

Chapter 8

(One)
San Diego, California
10 September 1921

Gold stood out on the ferry's deck, inhaling the salty air as they approached the mainland. He was smiling. San Diego was his idea of paradise.

Captain Bob had his barnstormers performing at the military airfield at North Island, in San Diego Bay. After the show Gold and the rest of the pilots would come across the bay to the mainland.

The ferry bumped against the pilings, tying up near where the fishing boats were unloading their day's catch of tuna. Gold and the Stiles brothers left the boat and killed an hour wandering the twisty, adobe-lined streets of Spanish Old Town. They hailed a taxi and headed for the Mexican community along the southern shore, where they ate tamales and barbecue. After dinner, while they were cabbing it back to the downtown area, their driver told them about a speakeasy in the basement of an office building near the waterfront.

Gold and his friends had no trouble getting past the guard at the speak's peephole door. Inside it was dimly lit, crowded and smoky. They were shown to a small corner table near the bandstand, where a half dozen Negro musicians done up in gaudy striped serapes and floppy straw sombreros were performing serviceable jazz.

Hull ordered tequila for the table. The speak had everything —scotch, rye, even Irish whiskey and French champagne— but a double shot of tequila, served with salt and lime wedges, was the cheapest, most potent drink you could get in San Diego. The dusky, dark-eyed Spanish girl who served them their drinks ran her fingers through Gold's hair as she left.

"That's one horny *señorita*." Lester Stiles nudged Gold. "You going to do something about it?"

Gold blushed. He had no problem resisting the waitress's charms. Erica was the only one woman for him now. "You guys just don't get it," Gold replied. "I'm already in love—"

"Herm," Lester patiently replied. "Love is not the issue at the moment."

"You're wasting your time, Les." Hull chuckled. "Herm, you're the goddamndest monogamous sonofabitch I ever laid eyes on. I just hope that virgin of yours is ready for it when you finally do get her into the sack."

Gold took the ribbing good-naturedly. When he'd confided in his friends that he was engaged to a girl he'd met back in Nebraska, the brothers had grilled him for what they'd called "the juicy details" concerning his relationship with his fiancée. Not willing to compromise her honor, Gold had told them that his relationship with Erica had not gone beyond a chaste kiss. Hull and Lester had found that hilarious. They never missed the opportunity to kid him about it.

"The problem with you, Herman, is you worry too much," Lester said.

Gold shrugged. He *knew* what he wanted: to establish his own aviation business so that he could settle down and support a wife. The problem was, he had no money and no idea what that business should be. Gold's instincts told him that California, where the climate favored flying throughout the year, was where he'd find his opportunity, but when it came knocking he would have to move quickly to take advantage of it. He would need start-up capital.

"Oh, shit," Lester groaned. "Herman's got that faraway look of his."

Hull rolled his eyes. "We'd better order another round."

"I don't see the waitress," Lester said, standing up. "I'll go order at the bar."

Hull waited until they were alone. "Is it being away from your girl that's got you so down?" he asked softly.

"I miss her very much," Gold said. "It's been two months,

but it's funny. In a way I feel like I saw her yesterday, and in a way, like I haven't seen her for a hundred years."

"Do you write her?"

Gold frowned. "I try, but I can't seem to put down what it is I want to say on the paper."

He'd tried just last night, so desperately wanting to describe to Erica the magnificent blue of the Pacific, as constant and overwhelming a presence as the blue Nebraskan sky. He wanted to promise that someday he would take her to hear jazz; to eat tacos; to see the funny Japanese huts built on stilts over the water. He wanted to write about the smell of the sea, and the citrus; what the desert looked like, and cactus, and palm trees, and mountains. His thoughts, like his love, were vivid inside him, but the words just wouldn't come.

"The few lines I manage to scribble look so puny," he complained to Hull. "I think to myself that I can't send such a letter to Erica, it would be like an insult..." Gold sighed ruefully. "I get so frustrated and upset I end up tearing up the paper and sending nothing."

Lester was returning to the table. "Hey, see that Mexican guy over there by the bar?" he asked excitedly.

Gold looked. The Mexican was standing with his back to the bar. He was wearing a baggy linen suit, an off-white shirt, and a dark brown tie. His slicked-back hair was as shiny as black patent leather.

"Where's our drinks?" Hull demanded.

"Coming," Les said irritably. "While I was ordering them that Mex came up to me. He asked if I was one of the pilots from the air show. I said I was, and get this: he asked me if I wanted to make some money flying hooch across the border!"

"Bootlegging?" Gold asked, pausing. "What kind of money do you think the guy was talking about?"

"Don't even think about it, Herm," Hull said. "It's night flying, and these bootleggers can be tough customers—and there's the law to worry about."

Gold nodded. Prohibition was a federal law, and he'd been in America only fourteen months. If he got caught the authorities would probably deport him—after his jail sentence. He'd never see Erica again.

On the other hand, what were his chances of being with Erica as things stood? If he wanted to get married he would have to leave the troupe. Captain Bob was firm in his rule against married stunt pilots. Gold was saving all the money he could. In the two months since he'd rejoined the troupe he'd accumulated a little over three hundred dollars, stuffed into a sock, buried at the bottom of his valise. At that rate, building up a nest egg large enough to both capitalize a business and support a wife was going to take a long, long time. What if his opportunity came along sooner rather then later, and he wasn't ready? What if Erica met someone else?

What if he went to jail? he reminded himself. Or got shot dead? He decided that he would take the chance. What it boiled down to was big dreams required big risks.

Gold stood up. "Wish me luck."

"You're really going through with this?" Hull frowned.

"I'm going to go talk to that guy about it." Gold shrugged.

He walked over to where the Mexican was standing. "I understand you're looking for a pilot," he murmured.

The Mexican regarded him with interest. "Please come with me, *Señor.*"

Gold glanced back to where his friends were watching him and looking very concerned.

"Come!" the Mexican said, amused. "Are you afraid, *Señor?*"

Gold followed him around behind the bar, through a beaded curtain, and down a hallway lined with liquor crates to a substantial-looking metal door painted pale green. The Mexican knocked once, a peephole opened, and the Mexican said something in Spanish. The peephole closed. Gold heard a number of locks being clicked, and then the door swung inward.

"Go in, *Señor.*" The Mexican in the linen suit stepped back to let Gold pass.

Gold was met by another Mexican, also well dressed and wearing a tie, but this man had his suit jacket off. Gold tried not to stare at the automatic pistol in the man's shoulder holster. The Mexican closed and locked the metal door. As it clanged shut the sound made Gold think of jail cell doors.

He was inside what turned out to be a brightly lit, window-

less storeroom that smelled strongly of spilt liquor. The man
with the shoulder holster led Gold through a maze of stacked
liquor crates and tables loaded with chairs turned upside down.
At the far end of the storage room five men, all with their suit
jackets off and all wearing guns, were seated at a round table,
playing cards. Off in one corner, at a table covered over with
papers and ledgers, a man in a plaid shirt, corduroy trousers,
and straw cowboy hat sat working at an adding machine. As
Gold approached, the man in the cowboy hat stopped punch-
ing the keys of his machine and looked up. He was middle-
aged and heavyset, and had a pencil-thin moustache. The man
with the shoulder holster spoke rapid-fire Spanish.

The man seated at the table nodded. "You are a pilot?" he
asked Gold in thickly accented English. "You are with the
flying show?"

Gold nodded. "My name is Herman Gold." He could just
hear the speakeasy's jazz band playing. He wondered if his
friends were still out front. He hoped so; the thought of them
nearby made him feel much less alone.

"I am Hector Ramos," the man wearing the cowboy hat
said, pushing back his chair and standing up to shake hands
with Gold. Ramos was wearing high-heeled cowboy boots,
but even with them he was no more than five feet, seven inches
tall. "I saw the air show, *Señor*; would I have seen you
perform?"

"I play the part of the Red Baron—"

"*Si!*" Ramos exclaimed. He spoke Spanish to the men
playing cards, punctuating whatever it was he was saying to
them by grabbing his testicles. The card players nodded,
smiling at Gold.

"You are a very brave and excellent pilot, *Señor* Gold.
Please, sit down." Gold pulled over a chair from a nearby
table and sat. "Would you care for a drink?" Ramos asked,
settling back into his own chair.

Gold noticed that none of the men in the room were
drinking. "Perhaps after," he demurred. "When our business
is concluded."

"Very good," Ramos approved. "Let us talk business,
then. Quite simply, I am in need of a pilot to fly cases of
liquor across the border from Mexico."

"You have an airplane?" Gold asked.

"A Standard E-1." Ramos nodded. "And two well-hidden airstrips, one in the Chula Vista section, a few miles from here, and one in the desert, on the Tijuana side. I have been running this operation for quite a while, and it works smoothly. It is a ten-mile round-trip. At dark you take off, you fly into Mexico, and you land. My people there will load up the airplane. The bottles are specially packed in cushioned cardboard tubes to withstand the journey and fit most efficiently into the airplane's cargo hold.

"You've obviously got all the details worked out," Gold said. "But you mentioned that you've been running this operation for a while. What happened to the last pilot?"

"A fair enough question, *Señor*. There was a group here in San Diego who wished to become partners with me in my business. I refused their offer," Ramos smoothly explained. "Regrettably there was some violence, and my pilot, he was shot dead."

Gold felt sick to his stomach. "This other group still around? Would I be in that sort of danger? I mean, flying in the dark looking for a hidden airstrip in the middle of nowhere is dangerous enough—"

"This is not a coward's business, *Señor*," Ramos interrupted, sounding gruff.

"How many times a night would I be expected to make the trip?"

"I expect you will want to make it as many times as you can, *Señor*." Ramos smiled. "Because each time you do I will pay you three hundred dollars."

Gold stared at him. "Three hundred per trip? You mean, if I could manage, say, three trips, I could earn nine hundred dollars a night?"

"Or twelve hundred for four trips a night. And the next night, and the night after that, and so on, *Señor*," Ramos said. "I am a supplier of alcohol all up and down the California coast. I can use all you can bring me."

Gold thought about all the guns in this room. "The air show will be leaving San Diego in ten days," he began. Actually, Captain Bob was moving on to Los Angeles sooner than that, but Gold didn't want Ramos to know the true date he'd be leaving. The bootlegger might decide that it made more sense to kill him rather than pay him for his last night's work. "When the show leaves town, I'll be going with it."

"As you wish, *Señor*."

"How come you haven't recruited one of the military pilots based at North Island?"

"Soldiers must account for their whereabouts to their superiors, *Señor*. Civilians do not."

"When would I start?" Gold asked.

"Why not tomorrow night?"

Gold took a deep breath. "You've got yourself a pilot."

(Two)
Quinn's Garage
Doreen, Nebraska
14 September 1921

Erica Schuler stood quietly in the doorway of Teddy's garage, watching him work. He didn't know she was there. His back was toward her, and he couldn't have heard her arrive in her car, due to the noise he was making removing the wheels of a tan, jacked-up Winston coupe. Parked next to the Winston was a green tractor with its partly dismantled engine spilling over the fenders. Erica knew that one of her father's trucks was due into the garage tomorrow...

Teddy was up to his neck in work, Erica thought. Maybe Herman should have stayed and become a partner in the garage...

Teddy must have sensed her standing there. He turned suddenly, and smiled. "Hi, Erica! What brings you here?" he asked, setting down his lug wrench.

"I was at the library reading up on something," she said. "I thought I'd come say hello."

"Well, isn't that nice! I'll get us a couple of orange pops and we'll chat."

"Thanks, but I can't stay too long, Teddy. I've got chores at home."

Teddy nodded. "What were you reading up on at the library?" He winked. "Airplanes, I'll bet..."

Erica smiled, noncommittal. What she'd been reading up on were the facts of life; how babies get started, and how a girl could know if there was one taken root inside her. She knew a lot from growing up on the farm, but knowing how it worked with sows and mares didn't help much when it came to the specifics of figuring out what was going on inside herself.

She'd been feeling funny inside these last few weeks, and she'd always been as regular as clockwork when it was her time of the month. From the reading she'd done at the library (where she'd had to make up a humdinger of a yarn to get the texts without raising the suspicions of the librarian, who belonged to her mother's sewing club), she'd confirmed her fears that the way she was feeling and the fact that she'd missed her period were pretty good signs she was pregnant.

"Teddy, I was wondering if you'd heard from Herman."

"No, haven't you?" he asked, frowning.

"A postcard or two, nothing more. Nothing about his plans. Where he was going." She shrugged, trying to sound nonchalant. "Or when he was coming back..."

"Oh, so that's it." Teddy laughed. "Now don't you worry, he's coming back! From what I know of him, I'd stake my life on it! And don't fret because he hasn't written. Some men find letter writing easy, and some don't. Just be patient. He'll show up one of these days."

"Just be patient, huh?" She chuckled.

"That's what you've got to be, all right..."

Erica caught him glancing at his work. "I'll be going," she said listlessly. "I know you're busy..."

"Erica? You sure you're all right? That's there's nothing else bothering you?" Teddy asked, studying her. "You're acting strange-like..."

She thought briefly about confiding her predicament to him. No, she couldn't do that. She had too much pride. Anyway, what could he do about it? It wasn't his problem.

She looked up at Teddy fondly. "You've got axle grease smeared all over your specs."

"Huh? What?" Teddy took off his horn-rimmed spectacles

and peered at them. "You're right, I do, but I can still see what I have to . . ."

"You're right, you can," Erica said, smiling faintly. "But don't worry about me, Teddy. I'll be all right."

"All right, then, but you come see me anytime if you need to talk, you hear?"

"You're a good friend, Teddy." She went to him and kissed him on the cheek.

"Careful now! You'll get yourself greasy—" he protested, getting all flustered.

Erica could feel his worried eyes upon her as she left the garage. She got back into her roadster and drove slowly through town. It was a sunny day, and very warm for the middle of October. Indian Summer was lasting a long time this year, but the gold and crimson leaves on the trees lining Main Street were starting to fall, a harbinger of the brutal Midwest winter that was just around the corner.

Summer's over, Erica thought as she left the outskirts of town. Once she was out on the open road she began to push the roadster faster toward home.

Summer was over, and so was her childhood, she thought. She was a woman now. An adult, and curled deep within her belly was an adult's responsibility.

She wondered how long before the baby would begin to show. She thought about going to her brother, who was a physician, in order to make sure the baby was healthy, but it wouldn't be fair to involve him in her troubles, to ask him to betray the family by keeping her secret. She realized that there was no doctor in town who wouldn't instantly pick up the telephone and call her parents. For now, going to a doctor was out of the question.

She had one hope: that Herman would come back for her, to take her away from here before the pregnancy revealed itself to the world. If only that could happen, everything would be all right: she could be married and have her child away from her hometown, and nobody would know the truth, and her family wouldn't be disgraced, and she wouldn't have to break her parents' hearts—

The S-curve in the road loomed suddenly. She downshifted quickly, hitting the brake, almost losing control of the roadster as it swung around in a rear-end skid that sent gravel flying. She steered into the skid, managing to regain control of the car, and came out of the curve intact.

When it was safe to do so she pulled off the road and sat, listening to the burble of the Pierce-Arrow's idling engine and feeling her own heart pounding in her chest. She'd driven this damn road a thousand times. She knew that curve was there, but she'd been going much too fast; hadn't been paying attention to her driving. That wasn't like her. But then, it also wasn't like her to be so helpless, waiting for a man to come rescue her from her predicament. She didn't blame Herman for any of this. She'd wanted him to make love to her. It was just bad luck that this happened when it did. She was not used to bad luck, but she'd never backed down from a challenge, and she wouldn't back down from this one. If Herman came too late, or didn't come at all, she'd rescue herself. She'd borrow some money . . . maybe from Teddy . . . Then she'd get in her car and drive until she'd left her family's reputation behind, or her cash ran out. Then she'd sell the car, pay Teddy back what she owed him, and live on the rest until she could get some kind of job to support herself and her child. She could do something like that, if she had to: she'd had secretarial training in high school. Of course, she didn't personally know any girl who had ever actually gotten a job. In Doreen, proper girls became wives and mothers; but then, she wasn't very proper, not anymore.

So she would manage a different sort of life, one step at a time. Maybe it would even turn out a marvelous adventure—

But for now, she would trust in the rightness of her love. She would believe that Herman was coming. Maybe he was even on his way. She would drive on home and help her mother prepare dinner. Then she would eat a lot, because she was eating for two.

But before driving home, she'd just sit here and cry. Just for a little while, Erica decided. Get the tears behind her and then get on with it.

(Three)
The desert outside of Tijuana, five miles from the U.S.
    border
15 September 1921

Gold signaled with his flashlight as he circled the field.
He slipped the flashlight back into the big, bellows pocket
of the ankle-length canvas duster Ramos had given him,
and pushed his flight goggles up on the crown of his
leather helmet, the better to see the answering blip of light
from the ground that would tell him that it was okay to
land. This was his fifth night working for Ramos's gang
of bootleggers, and his second trip of the evening. Gold
was tired, but happy. He'd been making four round-trip
flights—twelve hundred dollars—a night.

The Standard J1 was a breeze to fly; a bigger, more stable
version of the Jenny. She had some interesting modifications. Her skin was plywood instead of fabric, and she had a
covered cargo hold where the front cockpit used to be. Gold
could have flown the Standard in his sleep, which was lucky,
because most of the time he *was* half-asleep. Flying in Captain Bob's show during the day, and for Ramos most of the
night, was exhausting him.

It took Gold about an hour to complete each round-trip. He
was in the air about twenty minutes, with the rest of the time
taken up with loading and unloading the airplane. The airstrip
on the U.S. side of the border was a hot-topped parking lot
behind a warehouse on the outskirts of a little town called
Chula Vista, a few miles south of San Diego. According to
Ramos, the Chula Vista sheriff was in his pocket. Nevertheless, Ramos had armed guards keep watch while his work
crews, the lights bobbing on their miner hats, swiftly unloaded
the booze from the airplane into the waiting trucks. While that
was going on Gold hung around and watched, drinking black
coffee, or dozing. After the plane was unloaded, Gold would
get paid his three hundred by Ramos himself, and then he'd
take off for the return flight to Mexico, where he'd land and
kill time until his plane was loaded up, and so on.

So far everything had gone smoothly. Ramos had proved to be a man of his word. Gold was almost sorry that he'd broken his promise to the bootlegger about keeping the whereabouts of both landing strips a secret. He'd told Hull Stiles where the strips were. He'd wanted somebody he trusted to know where to begin the search for him in case something went wrong.

But nothing had gone wrong, and tonight, although Ramos didn't know it, was Gold's last night as a bootlegger. Tomorrow Captain Bob's Circus was moving on to Los Angeles. Good-bye and good riddance to a profitable, but short, career in crime.

Somebody had finally gotten around to waving a light at him. Gold frowned. That wasn't the agreed-upon signal. They were supposed to blink the light on and off three times to signal an all clear, and show no light at all if there was some kind of trouble . . .

What the hell, he thought lazily, yawning. Whoever it was down there had probably been sampling the booze and was now too drunk to remember the proper signal. He'd seen the Mexican work crews passing bottles back and forth among themselves while they loaded the plane. The Mexican side was the weak half of Ramos's operation. Discipline here was lax as hell. The workers were peasants. There were no guards, no guns, and nobody worth a damn in charge.

Gold's instruments were illuminated by a red light installed in the Standard's cockpit. Now he checked his altimeter, taking deep breaths of the cool desert night air, trying to clear his sleepy brain. The landing strip was just a short stretch of hard-packed earth, bordered with barbed wire to hold back the chaparral and the coyotes. It was a hastily constructed fork off the twisty, rutted, burro path the trucks used to haul the booze out into the desert from Tijuana. If Gold were to misjudge his landing, he'd be up to his ass in sand and rattlesnakes before he knew it.

Gold cursed as he brought the Standard in for his final approach. The crew down there was supposed to stand along both sides of the runway, turning on the lights on their miner's hats to guide him in. Luckily it was a clear, moonlit night, and his eyes were used to the dark, so he could see well enough to make out the strip. The Mexican work crew was nowhere about. Gold figured they were napping. They did that a lot, curling up beneath the parked trucks clustered at the end of the runway that connected to the road, seemingly oblivious to the scorpions that scuttled through the sand under the cover of night.

Gold brought the Standard in over the trucks, cutting his airspeed and angling his wings just to the point of stall. He felt the jolt as his wheels kissed the desert floor, and immediately stalled out into a pretty decent three-point landing, considering the conditions.

He swung the rumbling Standard around and taxied back the length of the strip, to where the hooch-laden trucks were parked. Where the hell was everyone? Gold wondered as he pulled into the loading area.

Headlights flashed on, blinding Gold. Something—a pickup truck—coughed to life and rolled toward him. "Federal agent!" somebody shouted at him from the bed of the truck. "Shut down that airplane! You're under arrest!" The agent underlined his orders with a chattering burst from his tommy gun, which spit orange fire.

Gold didn't even think about it. He swung the Standard around to face in the opposite direction and opened up the throttle to try for a takeoff. As his airplane gathered speed he twisted around to look behind him. The pickup truck, headlights blazing, was pursuing him. Gold couldn't hear the gun blasts over the sound of his own engine, but he saw tiny licks of flame as the truck's occupants shot at him. He hunched his shoulders as bullets splintered holes in the Standard's plywood skin. He glanced at the long-barreled revolver clipped beneath the instrument panel. He didn't touch it. What kind of chance would he have in a shootout against a truck full of heavily armed G-men?

He was almost at liftoff speed when a blast of gunfire from the fast-approaching truck chewed up his rudder. He wasn't going anywhere.

He cut his engine, slowing his airplane, hoping the agents would understand that he meant to surrender. As the sound of his own engine faded, Gold heard the buzzings of other airplanes hidden in the night sky.

Gold saw a biplane diving at the truck. As the government men fired up at the airplane its pilot hurled down something that glinted in the moonlight as it trailed flame. The projectile hit the ground just in front of the pickup, erupting into a ball of flame.

Gold smelled burning gasoline as liquid fire splattered the hood and windshield of the truck. He glimpsed the driver losing control as the man instinctively threw up arms. The truck swerved off the narrow airstrip, spilling its passengers as it crashed through the barbed wire to dip, out of sight, into a steep arroyo. Gold saw the G-men running and then heard the truck's gas tank explode, sending up spirals of fire against the night. Thanks to the burning truck, and the puddles of flame across the airstrip, the scene was well-lit. Gold could now make out the bodies of the Mexican work crew sprawled along both sides of the runway. He wondered why the agents had found it necessary to kill unarmed men.

For that matter, what were United States government men doing in Mexico in the first place?

One of the biplanes set down on the airstrip and taxied toward Gold swerving around the splashes of flame dotting the strip. The other plane stayed in the air to keep the agents occupied, strafing them with more gasoline bombs. The agents who hadn't lost their guns in the crash fired back blindly as they scattered across the sand dunes.

As the plane that had set down taxied close, Gold saw that it was one of Captain Bob's yellow and black Jennys. "Get in!" the pilot's familiar voice shouted.

"Hull?" Gold shouted back. "Hull Stiles?"

"Who'd you expect, Billy Mitchell? Get in, you dumb ass-wipe of a Hun!" Stiles swung the Jenny around alongside the crippled Standard.

On impulse Gold pulled the revolver from the Standard's instrument panel and slid the weapon into the pocket of his duster. He jumped out of the cockpit and ran for the Jenny as it rolled by. He grabbed a wing strut, hopped up, and swung himself into the front passenger's cockpit. Gold expected the Jenny to pick up speed, but Hull kept her throttled down, rolling the brakeless airplane in a loose circle around the Standard. Above them the second biplane circled, keeping watch.

"That's Les up there," Hull explained over the low grumble of the throttled engine. "He'll keep them from ambushing us until some of that gasoline splattered across the airstrip burns out and we can take off."

Gold nodded to himself. They were going to need a straight run in order to build up enough speed to clear the trucks at the strip's far end.

Gold twisted around to face Hull. "Thank God you're here, but how did you know I was going to need help—?"

Before Hull could reply, one of the goverment agents appeared on the runway. He leveled his pistol at the Jenny and fired off a round. Lester Stiles buzzed the shooter, but didn't throw a gasoline bomb.

"The guy's too close to us for Les to risk throwing a fire bomb," Hull shouted, opening up the throttle to pick up speed as they rolled along the fiery runway. "We've got no choice but to take off, now! Keep your head down!"

"Out of the frying pan—" Gold muttered.

The G-man was still squeezing off shots at them. Gold remembered the revolver in his pocket. He drew it, and as the Jenny pulled abreast of the agent, Gold aimed and quickly fired off all six shots. The agent disappeared into the shadows.

"And into the fire—" Gold finished. The Jenny was splashing like a waddling duck through the puddles of flame. Gold prayed that the Jenny's fabric skin and wooden landing gear did not ignite.

Then they were out of the flames. Hull had the Jenny wide open. For a moment Gold thought she was going to run out of airstrip, but at the last possible moment Hull managed to lift off. The Jenny's wheels scuffed the canvas tops of the parked trucks, but they made it. They were airborne.

Gold noticed that he was still clutching the revolver. He thought about the government lawman he'd shot at and wondered if he'd just killed a man . . . Hopefully the agent had merely ducked out of sight, but Gold would never know. Disgusted, he held the gun over the side and let the wind snatch it away into the darkness. Lester's Jenny settled in beside them as Hull flew for home.

(Four)
San Diego

They landed at the North Island facility, where Hull had already slipped the night watchman a couple of bucks to look the other way while he and Les "borrowed" the airplanes. It was too late for the ferry to be running, but they managed to grab a ride back to the mainland on one of the military boats patrolling the bay.

Now they were in an all-night eatery near their hotel. At this hour they were the only customers in the place.

"But how did you know I was going to need help tonight?" Gold demanded while they waited for their bacon and eggs.

"Les and I were in a speak earlier tonight," Hull said as the counterman came around with their food. "We overheard a guy at the next table bragging about how Ramos's operation was going to get squashed tonight. Of course, we were interested. The guy was already three sheets to the wind, but we kept buying him drinks, and he kept talking. It turned out the guy was a government stoolie. He was the guy the government men had paid to discover the location of the airstrips."

"But how could United States G-men operate in Mexico?" Gold asked.

"They couldn't! Not legally!" Lester exclaimed around a mouthful of toast. "Those men were crooked! Worse crooks than Ramos! Remember you told Hull that Ramos had said his previous pilot had been killed by a rival gang? Well, these men were that gang. They wanted to shake down Ramos—"

"You mean, get Ramos to pay them to allow him to bootleg?" Gold asked.

"Right." Hull nodded. "But Ramos wouldn't go along, so they kidnapped his pilot and killed the guy as a warning. When they found out Ramos's airlift was back in business, they decided to get tougher, but they had to be careful. They couldn't disrupt the U.S. side of the operation. It would have meant alerting the local cops, and it would have meant either arresting or killing Ramos himself, and that would have been the same as killing the goose that laid the golden eggs."

"So they decided to hit his operation in Mexico," Lester added. "They killed Ramos's men—those poor bastards—because they couldn't afford to leave any witnesses. They intended to hijack the truckloads of booze, which they could sell for themselves."

"And they intended to kill Ramos's new pilot," Hull added meaningfully. "To make it clear to Ramos that he couldn't operate without cutting them in for a piece of the profits."

"Do you think we have to worry about them in the future?"

"Nope," Hull said firmly. "Not about them, and not about Ramos. That informer in the bar said that the men don't know the identity of Ramos's pilot. They didn't get a good look at you tonight, did they?"

Gold shook his head. "With all the military fliers based in San Diego, I guess I'm safe."

"Anyway, those guys can't afford to follow up on what happened tonight," Lester said. He signaled the yawning counterman for more coffee. "How could they explain what they were doing in Mexico in the first place?"

"But what about Ramos?" Gold asked.

Hull grinned. "Les and I flew past the Chula Vista airstrip on our way out to the desert, just to see what was going on. It was deserted. My guess is that Ramos heard about the move against him and decided that San Diego was no longer a healthy place for him to do business."

Gold looked at both men. "I owe you guys my life . . ."

Hull shrugged. "The way we see it, it's now all even. Don't forget, you saved *our* lives . . . back during the war. You could have killed us when you shot us down, but you didn't. You went out of your way to spare us. Let's just say that tonight we paid you back."

"Well." Gold smiled as the counterman came around with the coffeepot. "Let's have a drink on it." He pulled the slender green bottle from the pocket of his duster and put it on the table. "If it's all right with the proprietor, who is welcome to join us in a drink, of course . . ."

The counterman stared wide-eyed at the label. "It's real scotch . . . from Scotland! By all means open it up! I'll get us some clean glasses!" He hurried away.

"Where the fuck did you manage to lay your hands on that?" Hull asked, amazed.

"I found a case of it on one of the trucks during my first flight tonight," Gold explained. "Ramos sells this stuff to his rich customers for fifty bucks a bottle. I figured he wouldn't miss a fifth, and if he did, fuck him, we were going to be on our way to Los Angeles tomorrow."

The counterman came over with a tray of glasses. Gold poured everyone shots. "To good friends," he toasted, raising his glass.

The counterman drained his glass and sighed. "Thanks for the drink. I haven't tasted anything that smooth for a long time."

"Help yourself to another if you'd like," Gold said. The grateful counterman did, and took it with him into his kitchen.

A newsboy came into the cafe to ask if anybody wanted the night owl edition of the paper. Gold bought one, figuring he would enjoy having something to read back in his hotel room while he was trying to unwind from the night's excitement. He scanned the front page.

"Herman, you can also pay for the meal," Hull said. "How much did you make off of Ramos, all told?"

"Huh?" Herman looked up from the newspaper. "Let's see . . . Counting tonight, five thousand, one hundred dollars."

Lester whistled. "That's a nice piece of change."

"And just enough." Gold stared at his newspaper. "And just in time, too," he added excitedly. "I *knew* my opportunity would come around, and now it has!"

"What are you talking about?" Hull demanded, pouring himself another drink.

Gold held out the newspaper, tapping the boldface headlines in the lower lefthand section of the front page:

POST OFFICE AIR-MAIL ROUTES ANNOUNCED—
FEDS GIVE FRISCO THE NOD TO BE SOLE
WEST COAST TERMINUS—

Hull scowled. "Forget it, Herm. You can make more money flying for Captain Bob than you can flying for the post office."

"Not flying *for* the post office . . ." Gold began. Hull and Lester were staring at him, obviously bewildered. "Look, I'll explain everything to you later. Right now I need to know something. I've been so busy these past few days that I haven't talked much with the Captain. Is he still planning to throw that party in Los Angeles?"

"Yeah, sure," Hull replied. "He thinks he might be able to swing a movie deal. Some kind of aviation picture, with all of us in the troupe flying the stunts."

"He's pulling out all the stops, too," Lester said. "Spending a lot of money and inviting bankers, movie people, oil tycoons; everybody who's anybody. As the captain says, it takes money to make money."

"All the bigwigs, huh?" Gold nodded thoughtfully. "Look, guys, if things work out the way I hope they will, I may not be working for Captain Bob much longer. I'll be working for myself, and I'll need some pilots." He smiled. "Men I can trust. Would you consider coming to work for me? You'd earn less in the beginning, but your pay would grow with the business."

Hull and Les looked at each other. Les nodded.

"This is the best scotch we've ever had," Hull said. "Any man pours us drinks from a fifty-dollar bottle, we'll follow him anywhere."

(Five)
Hotel Darby
Los Angeles
17 September 1921

The Hotel Darby, its yellow domes and red-tiled, bulbous turrets rising majestically over the swaying palms, reminded Gold of an oriental potentate's castle out of some exotic fairy tale. It was early evening, a few hours after the troupe's first show at Mines Field. It had been an invitation-only performance, intended to charm the city's elite, as was this buffet reception being held in a first-floor lounge of the hotel. It was a large room, done in the Spanish adobe style, with stuccoed walls and a red-tiled floor with a splashing fountain in its center. A wall of glass revealed a lantern-lit garden. In one corner, almost hidden by luxurious floral arrangements, a string quartet played soft classical pieces. On the far side of the room a buffet was being served. The only thing missing was liquor, which was, of course, illegal.

The captain's engraved invitations, hand-delivered to a select list by messenger boys costumed as pilots, had made the right, flamboyant impression. The party was well attended. The men were in business suits, their ladies dressed in silky, sleeveless, slim-fitting dresses. Soon Erica would be wearing such clothes, Gold thought to himself, and she would put these women to shame. He noticed that most of the ladies had bobbed hair, and began to worry that Erica would want to cut her beautiful, long tresses . . .

The Captain, dressed in black tie, interrupted Gold's musings. "Herman, what the fuck do you think you're doing here dressed like that?" he growled softly.

"Gee, I'm sorry, Cap. I must have forgot." Gold lied through his teeth.

"None of the others forgot!" The captain's arm swept the room, taking in all the other pilots, including Hull and Les Stiles, standing around in their leather jackets and tight-fitting helmets, looking totally out of place amidst all this elegance. The Captain had ordered his pilots to wear their gear to the party in order to establish what he considered to be the right atmosphere: he was trying to pitch an aviation adventure film.

Gold was wearing a charcoal-gray linen suit, a light-blue silk shirt with socks to match, and a white and blue polka dot tie. His low-cut, slip-on shoes were of supple, nappy, oyster suede. He'd spent a lot on this outfit, and even more to have the alterations done in time for today's party, but he felt the investment was essential.

"I want you to go and change," the Captain said.

"I'm sorry, but I can't do that," Gold apologized. He wished the captain well, but he was here for his own purposes, which he couldn't achieve looking like a walking publicity stunt.

The captain was staring at him. "What's going on, son? What have you got planned?"

"That's my business."

"But *this* is *my* business!" the captain said through clenched teeth. "I'm paying for all this, and I have a right to call the tune."

"Don't worry, Cap. I won't upset your plans."

"You do what I tell you—"

"No," Gold said calmly.

"Then you're fired!" Captain Bob glared at him. "Get out of here, or I'll have you thrown out—"

"Your voice is rising," Gold warned quietly. "People are starting to stare . . ."

The captain immediately shut up, nervously looking around. "What are you trying to do to me?" he hissed through a hideously artificial smile.

"Nothing, Cap," Gold said. "Just something for myself. As long as I'm fired I might as well let you know that I was intending to quit. Now, you can have me thrown out if you want, but I won't go quietly, and that would disrupt your party a lot more than just letting me be."

"First thing tomorrow you come by the show site to collect your back pay," Captain Bob said, backing down. "After that, I don't want to see you around."

"I'll inform the hotel where we're staying that I'm responsible for my own bill," Gold said.

"Fine." Captain Bob started to turn away.

"Cap?" Gold held out his hand. "You taught me a lot. I'm grateful. I'd like there to be no hard feelings."

Captain Bob scowled suspiciously. "This con you got in mind, does it involve fishing my part of the pond?"

"A different pond entirely, sir," Gold vowed. "I know better than to compete with the master at his own game . . ."

The Captain sighed. "What the hell, then," he grumbled. "No hard feelings, son." He shook hands with Gold. "Hook yourself a big, fat one, if you can." He walked away.

Gold was relieved his relationship with the captain had ended harmoniously. He really was very fond of the old rogue.

But it had ended, Gold realized. He was out of the Captain's nest. It was time to spread his wings and take flight on his own.

He saw Jimmy Cooper, the advance man, and went over to talk to him. "What was going on between you and Cap?" Jimmy asked.

"Nothing." Gold shrugged. "He was just bawling me out because I forgot to wear my flying gear. Jimmy, you put together the invitation list for this party, right?"

Cooper looked proud. "I sure did, and we've got almost one hundred percent attendance. Do you have any idea how much money there is in this room?"

"For instance? . . ."

"Well . . ." Cooper looked around. "Take Lane Barker, over there." He pointed to an elderly-looking man with a thick shock of white hair, dressed in blue pinstripe. "Barker is the president of Pacific Coast Bank."

Perfect, Gold thought. "Jimmy, you know everybody," he said enviously. "Who are those two guys Barker is speaking with?"

"The guy in the tan suit is Collins Tisdale, the publisher of the *Los Angeles Gazette*. The guy in gray is Paul Petersiel. He owns a number of businesses, and he's involved in local politics."

"Were they all at the air show this afternoon?" Gold asked.

"Yes, they were."

"Thanks, Jimmy."

Gold went over to the three men and introduced himself. "Gentlemen, my name is Herman Gold. I believe you saw me fly this afternoon? I played the part of the Red Baron . . ."

"Yes, Mister Gold." Lane Barker smiled politely. "It was quite enjoyable." He had a wispy, paper-thin voice, feathery around the edges, like well-worn currency.

"I'm glad you came over, Mister Gold," Tisdale said. "I'm in the newspaper business. I'd like to have one of my reporters interview you. I understand that you really were a German ace during the war? . . ."

"I was, sir," Gold replied. "And I'd be glad to speak to your reporter, but right now I have a question to ask all of you. I was wondering how you gentlemen felt about living in a second-rate city."

"What?" Tisdale turned red.

"How dare you insult Los Angeles?" Petersiel demanded.

Gold noticed that Lane Barker, his most important target, had said nothing in response to his provocation. The banker merely seemed amused.

"I'm not insulting your wonderful city, Mister Petersiel," Gold said. "But the federal government certainly has."

"What are you talking about?" Tisdale asked.

"The news that the United States Post Office has chosen San Francisco to be the sole West Coast terminus for its transcontinental air-mail route," Gold explained.

"Oh, that . . ." Petersiel acknowledged wearily.

"You must admit that it's a slap in the face, gentlemen," Gold said sadly. "What can the world think, if none other than the United States government has decreed that the City of Angels must take second place to the City by the Bay?"

"We intend to petition the government about this slight," Petersiel said. "I'm in the process of putting together a committee of private businessmen and municipal officials to investigate and then challenge the selection process . . ."

"You should do that," Gold said reasonably. "Of course, you know how the bureaucratic procedure can drag endlessly, during which time Los Angeles will be deprived of the benefit of speedy mail deliveries. Commerce and finance will suffer. As we all know, in business, time is money."

"Mister Gold," Tisdale interrupted. "What would *you* have us do?"

"I believe Mister Gold has been waiting for *that* question." Lane Barker laughed. "Go on, young man—" His pale gray eyes were sparkling. "—Make your proposal. I think you'll find this sort of thing only slightly more treacherous than stunt flying."

"Gentlemen, what I propose is a private air express company to ferry this city's mail back and forth from San Francisco. Incoming correspondence could be in Los Angeles within hours of its arrival at the federal terminus. Outgoing mail could arrive in time to take advantage of the very next post office departure flight from Frisco. The express service

I propose would also be available on an around-the-clock, special-hire basis for important documents for which time is of the essence."

"It sounds expensive," Petersiel muttered.

"Priceless in value, but reasonable in cost," Gold heard himself say, and imagined that somewhere in the room Captain Bob was sending blessings with a wink and a nod. "Especially considering the beneficial publicity Los Angeles would receive," Gold pressed on. The city fathers could no more effectively demonstrate Los Angeles's hospitable business climate than by taking the bull by the horns concerning this matter."

Lane Barker held up his hand to silence Gold. "I suspect you want my bank to finance your prospective endeavor?"

"Actually, my first concern is that I receive a positive response from the business community."

"Well, I, for one, think it's a firecracker of an idea," Tisdale enthused.

"So do I." Petersiel nodded. "I think the chamber of commerce will also endorse it. It's just the thing to level the playing field with Frisco."

Gold smiled, relieved. "Secondly, the post office would have to cooperate with me on this . . ."

"Don't worry about that," Petersiel said. "I've got some influence over there."

"As for a loan," Gold turned to Lane Barker. "I have the personal expertise, and the seasoned pilots, to make the operation a success. I also have the financial capital to commit to prove that I intend to do just that."

Lane Barker smiled indulgently. "Come see me at the bank tomorrow morning. We'll talk about it."

(Six)
Schuler farm
Doreen, Nebraska
28 October 1921

It was after lunch when Erica tiptoed upstairs to her bedroom. She locked her door, pulled down the window shades, and then got undressed.

She stood sideways, scrutinizing her silhouette in the mirror. She ran her palm over her belly. Her skirts had begun to feel a little tight, and her breasts were feeling funny, but she hadn't yet begun to show. She still had time, and thank God the fall weather had turned brisk. She could buy herself a little more time by wearing bulky sweaters . . . She needed all the help she could get in keeping her secret, she thought to herself as she got dressed. It was getting harder every day to keep the truth from mama.

All her life she'd been polishing off massive breakfasts, so it was understandable that mama would become alarmed now that even the smell of food in the morning was making Erica ill. She'd panicked when mama had suggested going to see the doctor; wouldn't that have been just dandy! She'd managed to talk her way out of that, claiming that all she had was some sort of cold in her stomach, but now mama was keeping an eye on her.

Erica was surprised that mama hadn't yet guessed the truth, but upon thinking it through, she supposed it was because the truth was so disgracefully unimaginable. Erica knew that she would have to go away very soon now. For the sake of her parents and their position in this stuffy little town that they so dearly loved, she would have to go . . .

The buzzing coming from the window was faint. Erica cocked her head and listened. It sounded like the persistent buzz of a hornet that had survived first frost and was now trapped in the room, perhaps between the window and the shade. She went to the window and pulled up the shade, intending to release the bug. Lately, all life had become very sacred to her.

She found no hornet, but then she realized that what she was hearing was some kind of far-off motor. She opened the window. The noise was louder now. It was coming from the sky.

An airplane? She stuck her head out the window and looked up, but the house blocked her view—

She ran across the bedroom to the door, and unlocked it. Downstairs, the storm door slammed as mama stepped out onto the front porch.

"Erica!" mama called. "Come out and see. I think it's—"

"I know who it is." Erica laughed. She realized she was crying, but she didn't care. She skipped down the stairs, out into the front yard to see the biplane, glinting turquoise and scarlet, looping and soaring like some enormous butterfly against the crisp, clear, blue October sky.

Papa had come out of his office in the main nursery building, followed by some of his employees. The plane was coming down. It landed gracefully in the field fronting the house.

Erica ran to Herman as he hopped out of the cockpit. He saw her coming. She watched him toss aside his helmet and goggles and reach out for her. She was in his arms almost before his airplane's prop could stop turning.

"I knew you'd come!" She laughed triumphantly, kissing and hugging him.

"Of course I was coming," he said as he held her tight. "You're crying?" he asked, looking alarmed. "What's wrong?"

"Nothing's wrong!" Erica murmured. She pressed against him, closing her eyes, her cheek against the cold leather of his flying coat. He smelled like varnish, and sweat and engine exhaust. He smelled wonderful. "Everything's perfect ...*I knew you'd come...*"

She heard footsteps behind her and turned to see her parents approaching. She realized that mama would disapprove of her lewd behavior—especially in front of papa's employees!—and tried to step out of Herman's embrace, but he wouldn't let her. He gently kept her at his side by keeping his arm around her waist. She felt weak with love.

"Sir, it's good to see you and Frau Schuler again," Herman said. "As you can see, I'm here in my own airplane."

Erica looked at the airplane. It was a big two-seater. Its fuselage was painted turquoise, with scarlet for the wings, tail, and wheels. On the side of the biplane, just below the front cockpit, was a large yellow oval on which, in black silhouette, a centaur reared. In curving black letters, above and below the oval, read the words GOLD EXPRESS.

"I have two other airplanes like this one. They're part of

my new business, an aviation transport company, back in Los Angeles, California," Herman proudly announced. "I believe that I'm now in a position to support your daughter, Herr Schuler. I've come to marry her."

(Seven)

That night Gold was the guest of honor at a celebratory supper for the entire Schuler clan. While the grandchildren played, and the women washed the dishes, Carl Schuler poured drinks for his sons, and future son-in-law, from a jug of sour mash. Gold was entranced by the warm embrace of this magnificent family; to be made so welcome in this big farmhouse glowing with love, like a brick and clapboard jewel nestled against the dark velvet of the Nebraskan plain.

Later, Gold and Erica bundled up against the brisk October night and went for a walk. That was when she told him that she was pregnant.

He listened to her confess to him haltingly, almost fearfully, as if she'd expected him to be angry . . . Gold guessed that he would never truly understand women. He was, of course, ecstatic. A family of his own was what he'd always wanted, and the sooner the better. He only hoped that the child would be a son. The business could always use another pilot.

They walked back to the house arm in arm, hips awkwardly touching, giggling like children and very in love. It was torture for Gold to part from her, to go to bed alone in the guest room. All night he was plagued with tantalizing dreams. He seemed to hear her voice in the wind rattling the rafters.

The next morning, while Erica and her mother fussed with the details of the upcoming wedding, Gold borrowed the roadster and drove into town to see Teddy Quinn.

Thinking about it, Gold realized that Erica's pregnancy was, in a way, convenient. Now they both had their reasons for wanting to get the marriage ceremony over with quickly as possible, and get on their way to Los Angeles. Gold could almost hear his new business crying out for his presence.

He'd put up $5,000 cash against a $15,000 business loan

from Lane Barker's bank. When the money came through he'd paid a thousand each for the three military surplus, De Havilland D.H. 4 airplanes, along with an inventory of spare parts. He'd put down seven hundred and fifty dollars on a lease for a hangar at Mines Field, and had arranged to pay a monthly fee for the use of a turnaround facility in Frisco. For the past month, Gold, along with his two new employees, Hull and Les Stiles, had worked around the clock to get the airplanes into serviceable condition. It hadn't been easy. The Stiles brothers were great pilots, but only passable mechanics. Finally, though, the planes were ready.

True to his word, Petersiel had smoothed things for Gold with the post office, and Barker had used his influence in the financial community to get a lot of business thrown Gold's way. The banks were now using Gold Express instead of trains to transport financial instruments between the two cities. Hull and Les were now making twice-daily hops, carrying full loads of mail back and forth at the rate of two dollars a pound.

Gold drove slowly through Doreen. He'd been away a long time, and it took him a while to find the alley where Quinn's garage was tucked away. He parked around the corner from the garage, and walked the rest of the way, wanting to surprise Teddy. He peeked in through the doorway and saw Teddy lying on his back, working underneath a tractor.

"I hear you've got a motorcycle for sale," Gold said, stepping inside.

"Huh?" Teddy scuttled out from beneath the tractor. "Well, I'll be goddamned." He grinned, getting to his feet and extending his hand. "It's about time. I was going to marry her myself!"

"Speaking of which," Gold laughed, "I hope you've got something nicer to wear than those grimy mechanic's overalls, because you're going to be my best man at the wedding."

"I can handle that." Teddy grinned. "When?"

"Day after tomorrow."

"Really?" Teddy said, sounding startled. "What's the rush, friend?"

"I've got to get back to California. I've just begun my own business, and I need to be there to watch over things."

"Come sit down," Teddy said, and fetched two bottles of

orange pop while Gold filled him in on the details of what he'd been up to in Los Angeles.

"These D.H. 4 airplanes you bought," Teddy began when Gold was finished. "Are they anything like the machine we worked on?"

"I think the De Havillands are better, but it's really a matter of personal opinion. They were built as bombers during the war, so they're sturdy. They've got 400-horsepower Liberty engines, and eventually will be able to haul about five hundred pounds of mail . . ."

"What do you mean by 'eventually'?" Teddy asked.

"They need some work." Gold told Teddy about the modified Standard he'd flown while bootlegging. "I think that plane's plywood skin, and turning the front cockpit area into a cargo bin, were good ideas. I've got some others: bigger wheels, engine modifications, and so on."

Teddy nodded. "Sounds like you've got your work cut out for you."

"I do, and I could use somebody to help me do that work."

Teddy smiled. "You proposing to *me*, as well?"

Gold laughed. "I love Erica, but I *need* you, Teddy. Why don't you come in with me as chief engineer? That's a grandiose title for doing exactly what you're doing now, except with airplanes instead of tractors."

"Why me?" Teddy asked. "Must be plenty of good grease monkeys out there in California."

"There are," Gold agreed. "And as the business expands, you can hire as many as you need to work *for* you. But you're not just a grease monkey, Teddy. I know that, because we've worked together. We came up with some great gimmicks for that Jenny, and a lot of those modifications were your ideas. I know that you've got all kinds of interesting notions in your head. What I want to do is free up those ideas, turn them into reality. The air transport company is just a beginning, Teddy. What I *really* want to do is build new kinds of airplanes."

Teddy thought about it. "No offense, but I don't know if I could work for anyone. Not even you, Herm. I've been my own boss all my life."

"You'd still be your own boss in a lot of ways," Gold

said, but then he shrugged. "Look, you'd be working for me, there's no getting around that, but the work would be a hell of a lot more exciting than changing spark plugs. We'll negotiate an arrangement for splitting the profits on any new patents we come up with."

"Patents!" Teddy chuckled. "Hell, I don't know . . . Sure I can tinker around, but inventing things? . . ." He shook his head. "I don't think I can do it . . ."

"Yeah, you can," Gold said. "I know what you're capable of. Just wait until you read the books I've got back in Los Angeles. Aeronautics, aerodynamics, engineering. You'll see, Teddy. It'll be like a light will go on in your head."

"But what happens if it doesn't work out?" Teddy asked.

Gold shrugged impatiently. "We can work something out . . . Like a lump-sum payment for you if you decide you made the wrong choice. Hell, you could always open a garage just like this one in California. There's just as many cars, and no Nebraska blizzards."

"Speaking of the garage, it'd take me a while to liquidate this business," Teddy said.

"You own the property?"

"No, I lease the garage, but I own all the equipment."

"Then don't liquidate anything but your lease," Gold said. "We can use all these tools, and any vehicles you own." Gold winked at him. "You do still have the Harley?"

"Yep."

"Bring it!" he said heartily. "Motorcycles were invented for California!"

Teddy's green eyes got very serious behind his thick spectacles. "You've got that much faith in me?" he asked quietly.

"I've got that much faith in myself," Gold said. "I'm brimming over with it. Come with me, Teddy. Catch the overflow."

"You promise no tractors?"

"Not unless you can figure out a way to build 'em with wings."

In consideration of Carl Schuler, who had left the Lutheran faith, the minister conducted the wedding ceremony—attended only by family and a few close friends—at the farmhouse. Gold considered the location to be a lucky break. He felt duplicitous enough toward his bride by masquerading as a lapsed gentile. He didn't want to further compound the sham by entering a church.

He knew that he should have told Erica about himself right at the beginning of their relationship, but he hadn't, and as she came to mean more to him, it had gotten harder and harder to take the risk of losing her by confessing the truth. Then they'd made love. To tell her then had seemed impossible. Today they were getting married. Now it was too late; he could never tell her.

He didn't feel at all guilty toward his own race, or the religion that his people practiced. A man couldn't forsake what he'd never known.

He paid little attention to the minister's ceremony; religion in general was unimportant to him. God was another story . . . If there was a God, Gold couldn't imagine Him thinking that what Gold was perpetrating was a sin. Gold deeply and truly loved Erica, and she loved him. She was going to have his child. They would be happy together; a family. *That* was the *real* truth, not the dimly remembered origins of his birth.

That night, Gold made love to his new wife in her canopied bed. He told her how much he loved her, and that when they got to Los Angeles he would take some of the money he'd borrowed from the bank in order to buy her an engagement diamond.

Erica wouldn't hear of it. "I already know what I want for a wedding gift. I want you to teach me how to fly."

BOOK III:
1922–1927

GUNMEN FELLED IN BOOTLEGGING FRACAS—
Feds Say River of Hooch Flows across U.S. Borders—
Philadelphia Tattler

OUT OF THE ASHES: POSTWAR GERMANY'S
AIRLINES SERVE EUROPE—
Germans at Forefront of Efficient Commercial Aviation—
Fares to Rome, Paris, Moscow,
Cheaper Than French and British Competition—
New York Herald

UNITED STATES IMMIGRATION ACT PASSES—
Congressional Advocates Cite Need for Racial Purity—
Washington Gazette

NATIONALISTS GAIN IN CHINA—
Chiang Kai-shek unifies Kuomintang—

Boston Times

20,000 NATIONAL SOCIALISTS RALLY IN
NUREMBERG—
Vociferous Germans Hail Party Leaders
Adolph Hitler, Herman Goering, Heiner Froehlig
Speak—

Los Angeles Tribune

LINDY DOES IT!
Charles Lindbergh Spans the Ocean—
The Spirit of St. Louis Completes the First Transatlantic
Solo Flight—

Baltimore Globe

Chapter 9

(One)
Santa Monica, California
2 August 1925

Gold was in his office when he heard about the plane crash. The telephone call came from his flight operations supervisor at Mines Field, telling him that his Spatz F-5a passenger transport, incoming from Las Vegas, had turned itself into a fireball while attempting to land in L.A. The plane had been loaded to capacity. All eight passengers and the two-man crew had been killed.

Gold told the panicked supervisor that he was on his way to the airfield, broke the connection, then punched the intercom button to buzz his secretary, a no-nonsense, middle-aged woman who pretty much ran the administrative and bookkeeping sides of Gold's operations. "Put me through to Teddy."

"Yes, sir." A moment later she came back on the line. "I've rung his office, and paged the shop, but Mister Quinn isn't answering."

Gold thought that his secretary was sounding pretty frazzled. Well, why not? He was feeling pretty goddamned frazzled himself. "Find him," Gold ordered. "Then tell him to meet me out at the airport. And call my wife. Tell her what's happened, and not to say anything to the reporters if they should call the house."

"Yes, sir. And sir? We all feel terrible about what's happened—"

Gold thanked her, and hung up. He sat in his chair for a

moment, letting it sink in. In a way he'd been lucky: he'd not lost an airplane up until now. *Ten people dead, and a brand new twenty-thousand-dollar airplane utterly destroyed*. His luck had certainly changed with a vengeance.

Gold's stomach was doing flip-flops; his heartbeat seemed to echo, as if he'd become hollow. He wondered, calmly, if he were suffering from some sort of emotional shock . . . He guessed that if he were thinking clearly enough to ask himself that, he probably wasn't.

His office was on the top floor. Skylights let in lots of natural light. The office had white painted walls, a bare wooden floor, and a metal desk. Against one wall was a massive drafting table on which Gold did most of his work. The table was flanked by a pair of glass-fronted bookcases crammed with technical volumes. Above the bookcases was a framed commendation for speedy delivery of the mail from the postal service, newspaper clippings about his air transport business, and photographs of Gold with Adolphe Menjou, Bebe Daniels, Ronald Colman, Will Rogers, and other Hollywood stars, all the photos taken in front of his airplanes, just before the celebrity passengers boarded.

And there were photographs of his family: Erica in her helmet and goggles, smiling triumphantly from the cockpit of her Curtiss biplane racer after participating at an air race at Santa Monica's Clover Field; Erica horseback riding in Wyoming. There was a photo of his two kids at the beach, with the nanny.

It was funny how there were no pictures of the family together . . .

His office had a view of the bay. The windows were open, and the tangy wind blowing off the sea was fresh and clean. He shielded his eyes as he stared enviously out at the blue water flecked with golden light, dotted with fishing boats being escorted by blizzards of gulls. The fishing boats trailed white, foamy wakes as they placidly chugged along. Life out there looked very peaceful and simple . . .

He went into the washroom adjoining his office and rinsed his face with cold water. He was twenty-seven, but he looked much older, and very tired, as he stared into the mirror. He smoothed down his moustache and thinning hair, straightened the knot in his necktie, and then went back for his suit jacket. He left the office the back way, so that he wouldn't encounter any employees on his way out to the parking field, where he got into his Stutz Bulldog Tourer.

Gold had coveted a Bulldog ever since he'd first laid eyes on the roomy convertible built on the frame of a Stutz Bearcat. Nineteen eighteen was the last year in which Stutz had built them, so Gold had been forced to settle for used, even though he could afford most any new car. He'd bought this one last year, plunking down twenty-eight hundred for the trade-in, at the Stutz dealership on Wilshire Boulevard. With Teddy's help he'd lovingly refurbished it and then had the Stutz repainted his colors: lacquered turquoise, with scarlet fenders the velvety hue of fine Burgundy.

As Gold drove to the airfield he couldn't help thinking back on the last few years, on how hard he'd worked to build something good. Now it looked like it might all crumble away...

That first year he and Erica lived in a small bungalow apartment within walking distance of the trolley line to Mines Field. Gold had been in the cockpit of one of his De Havillands, somewhere in the air between Frisco and Los Angeles, when Erica went into labor. A message had been waiting for him when he landed in Los Angeles. His wife was at the hospital. By the time he got there, Erica had given birth to a daughter. They named her Susan Alice, after Erica's two grandmothers.

In those days, Gold, along with Hull and Les, took turns doing the flying on their single L.A./Frisco mail route, but as the business expanded to include mail and cargo delivery routes all along the West Coast, Gold found himself increasingly desk-bound. He put Hull and Lester Stiles behind desks as well, in charge of recruiting and supervising the pilots who flew the military surplus airplanes that Gold gradually added to his fleet.

Gold Express really began to prosper when it began to haul passengers. Most of them were Hollywood people, the movie stars whose inscribed photos were not on his office walls. The flight accommodations were spartan. Passengers would dress in fleece-lined overalls supplied to them at the hangar/terminal. Once aboard the modified surplus bombers, they would squeeze themselves in as best they could among the mail sacks, to peer out through the porthole-like windows that had been installed in the fuselage.

Fortunately, show business people were game to try anything new, especially when it might get their names in the newspapers. Gold got the idea to have the fleece-lined overalls dyed turquoise, to have "Gold Express" stitched over the breast pocket, and his trademark centaur embroidered across the back. He let the passengers keep the overalls as a souvenir. Quickly it became a status symbol in Hollywood to have a pair. The publicity garnered more business for Gold Express, allowing Gold to pay off the balance of his original fifteen-thousand-dollar business loan.

He also bought a house, a *real* house, not a junky little bungalow shoehorned in among its neighbors on some treeless, sunbaked tract. He put down ten thousand cash, taking out a twenty-five-thousand-dollar mortgage on a sparkling white Spanish Colonial on a quiet street, lush with jacaranda trees and desert palms, in small-town Pasadena, ten miles to the east of downtown Los Angeles. The day he and his family moved in was one of the most satisfying in Gold's life.

Keeping on top of his business had forced Gold to drastically curtail his own flying, but Erica was spending enough time in the air for both of them. She'd taken flying lessons at Santa Monica's Clover Air Field. She'd quickly won her license, in the process becoming good friends with another of her instructor's pupils, a young woman named Amelia Earhart, who was always looking for extra money to pay for her flying. Occasionally, once Amelia had her license, Gold let her fill in flying mail and cargo when he was short a pilot.

It was Amelia who encouraged Erica to take part in a few local air meets. Erica did well and was bitten by the racing bug. She badgered Gold into buying her a racer; Gold got a good deal on a state-of-the-art Curtiss Navy Racer that had been almost totaled in a crash. Once his people had the Curtiss back together, Gold assigned Erica a mechanic full-time to take care of the plane. A nanny was hired to care for Susan so that Erica could be free to haul her race-bird up and down the West Coast. She rarely won a competition, which was fine with Gold, since the pilots who won the most were also the pilots who suffered the most accidents, but Erica almost always placed well in the pack. That, in itself, was a notable achievement for a woman racing against men. Soon she had a sizable collection of plaques and trophies. The fact that Erica was involved in a terribly risky sport such as airplane racing upset Gold. On the other hand, he knew that he'd married a daredevil.

Meanwhile, Gold Express kept growing, especially the passenger side of the business. Gold needed bigger, more comfortable planes: paying customers couldn't be expected to perch on mail sacks forever. The Stout Company of Dearborn, Michigan, manufactured a suitable airplane, but its entire output had already been spoken for by Henry Ford, who was running a mail delivery and passenger service out of Michigan. Gold looked to Europe, where the commercial airline business was thriving, especially the German lines run by the huge Spatz aircraft manufacturing company. When the Versailles Treaty forbade the Germans from building warplanes, Spatz gave up its fighter line and concentrated on designing larger aircraft suited for commercial uses. Gold had not flown any Spatz-built fighters during the war; they were used mostly by the ground-attack squadrons, but he had total confidence in German engineering. He had his eye on the Spatz F-5, a four-passenger transport monoplane. It was a lovely bird, thirty-two feet long, with a fifty-eight-foot wingspan and a shiny skin of corrugated duralumin. It was powered by a silky B.M.W. engine, and cost fifteen thousand dollars.

Gold went to Lane Barker, argued that his company's newly expanded feeder routes to Catalina Island, and as far east as Salt Lake City, warranted renewed and expanded financial confidence, and came away with a seventy-five-thousand-dollar loan. He spent thirty thousand on two Spatz F-5s. He now owned twelve airplanes. He used the rest of the money to make good on an old promise he'd made to Teddy Quinn, and to himself, by establishing a design and manufacturing facility in a warehouse in Santa Monica and allowing his chief engineer a fat research and design budget.

Gold changed the name of his company to encompass the expanded potential symbolized by his new Santa Monica headquarters. Gold Express became Gold Aviation.

Someday, he vowed, he'd be selling airplanes to Europe, and not the other way around.

In 1924, a second child was born. It was a boy, whom they named Steven, after Erica's brother who was killed in the war. Soon after, Teddy and his engineering team gave birth to a creation that brought Gold almost as much pleasure as he was receiving from his new son: the initial design for a new monoplane, dubbed the G-1 (Gold 1) Yellowjacket.

The new plane was going to need an engine. Gold talked to a number of established firms, but was intrigued by a small but promising San Diego company, Rodgers and Simpson. He liked their ideas, and the fact that they were young and anxious to do great things, like himself. He gave them the job, pumping cash into their endeavor to build a suitable power plant for the G-1.

About that time Spatz came out with a new, structurally strengthened version of the F-5— the F-5a—capable of taking a larger engine, which meant increased cargo and passenger capabilities. The F-5a cost twenty thousand dollars. Gold bought three, by selling off six of his older, smaller, military surplus airplanes to free up ten thousand in cash, and going back to Lane Barker to borrow another fifty thousand. His turquoise and scarlet fleet was now shrunk to nine airplanes, but five of them were large, modern aircraft that could more efficiently move an increased number of passengers and larger shipments of mail and freight. Gold came up with cabin and engine modification ideas that would allow him to further increase the F-5a's capabilities. He put Teddy in charge of carrying out the modifications ASAP; Gold couldn't afford to allow sixty grand worth of airplanes to lie idle for long.

It seemed to Gold that the bigger he got, the thinner were his operating margins. The money was flowing out as fast as it came in; faster, actually, considering the loans outstanding. Gold would periodically worry about it, but then put it all out of his mind. He was receiving all the credit he asked for, so he had to be doing something right. Anyway, his secretary was in charge of bookkeeping. Ledgers were boring, and pilots couldn't abide being bored.

He told himself that he had no worries because he had no competition. Whenever a Johnny-come-lately outfit tried to muscle in on his territory Gold would temporarily cut his rates on that particular line, letting his other routes take up the slack. Invariably the fledgling competition would shrivel up and die.

In February of 1925, with the full cooperation of the U.S. Post Office, Congress passed the Kelly Air Mail Act, which was intended to gradually take the government out of the air transport business by allowing private enterprise to take over the main transcontinental mail route. The Kelly Act turned out to be both less, and more, than Gold and the other private carriers had hoped. In July, the U.S. Post Office announced that it would temporarily keep control of the main transcontinental route, and, to Gold's dismay, that control of the feeder lines would now be officially assigned according to bids submitted through the local postmaster, with the process open to any interested party. The post office would pay a standardized rate for carrying the mail, but each contractor could charge what he wished for hauling passengers and private freight.

Gold quickly began preparing his bid to hold on to his routes. Meanwhile, he nervously waited for the other shoe to drop, and, a couple of weeks later, it did.

A pair of ex-postal service fliers, backed by an investment group, had formed an outfit they'd dubbed Southern California Air Transport to go after Gold's routes. SCAT's underwriting financiers were spreading the word in the business community—which, in turn, would most certainly influence the local postmaster's recommendation—that SCAT would fly cargo more cheaply than Gold Aviation. Gold had countered by promising to match the competition's low-ball bid to the private service sector. He had also reminded the business community of the post office's announcement that when the bids were opened on September 15, control of the Contract Air Mail routes—CAMs—would be awarded on the basis of financial stability, safety, and general moral fitness.

Gold, remembering the lesson taught to him by his father-in-law, had from the very beginning of his business career found the means to donate substantial sums to local charities and causes, establishing a solid reputation for himself as a philanthropist. He was confident that plenty of important people would attest to his moral fitness.

He also had been able to boast that dependability and safety were the hallmarks of Gold Aviation. At least they had been until today.

He turned right, onto the approach road to Mines Field. A couple of miles ahead an oily, black cloud was hanging like doom over his hangar/terminal facility. Even from this distance Gold could smell the stink of gasoline and burnt rubber. The opposite side of the road was clogged with fire-fighting vehicles leaving the scene. Several ambulances were also coming from the crash site. They seemed in no hurry, and their sirens were not howling.

Police were at the chain-link gate to his facility, holding back the reporters and the inevitable, morbid curiosity seekers. He beeped his horn and the cops cleared a path for him.

"Any comment, Mister Gold?" a reporter shouted as Gold drove through the gate. "What do you think caused the accident?" another reporter chimed in.

Gold ignored the questions, annoyed that the news photographers holding their cameras high over their heads were clicking his photograph like he was some sort of gangster. Once he was through the gate he stopped the car to summon over the uniformed sergeant in charge of the police detail. "See that those newshounds are kept out," he ordered.

"Yes, sir, Mister Gold." The cop nodded.

He drove up to the simple, corrugated steel building that was his hangar/terminal, and parked. As he got out of the Stutz, his flight operations supervisor, Bill Tolliver, came scurrying over.

"I don't know what happened, Mister Gold," Tolliver said quickly.

Gold noticed the other employees at the hangar watching him out of the corners of their eyes. They were giving him a wide berth as they went about their business, tending to his airplanes.

"She was coming in fine and all at once she exploded," Tolliver was saying.

"Before she even touched down?" Gold muttered, and then shook his head, perplexed. "Okay, Bill," he sighed, and then added sharply, "I don't want you making any statements to the press—"

"No, sir!" Tolliver said, sounding affronted. "I'd never do that, Mister Gold."

Gold smiled wearily. "I guess you wouldn't, Bill. I'm sorry. I don't mean to take this out on you. It's just that I . . ."

"Sure, Mister Gold, no problem," Tolliver said softly. "I understand. All them people, and Les . . ."

"What?" Gold felt dizzy. "What about Les?"

Tolliver paled. "You didn't know?"

Gold's eyes began to blur with tears. "Les was crewing on that plane?"

"I'm awful sorry," Tolliver whispered.

"But he wasn't on flight duty— He's been off it for years, goddammit!"

"He insisted," Tolliver said quickly. "The scheduled pilot took sick, Les couldn't find a replacement, so he took the flight. I'm awful sorry, Mister Gold, but I don't have rank over him. I couldn't do anything about it."

Gold felt numb. "Where's Hull?"

"He went to tell Les's wife."

Gold nodded. "I'm expecting Teddy," he managed, wiping his eyes. "When he gets here, please have—"

"He's here already, Mister Gold," Tolliver said. "He was out here running a routine check on another airplane when the accident happened."

"Where is he?"

"Out on the field." Tolliver shrugged. "Looking at what's left . . ."

Gold walked around the hangar/terminal and out onto the field. He saw Teddy Quinn, his fedora pulled low on his brow, his suit jacket and striped necktie snapping like flags in the breeze, wandering amidst the smoldering wreckage of the Spatz. Twisted chunks of metal were scattered all across the runway.

Gold paused to gaze at the crumpled tail assembly of the plane. His trademark was still recognizable on the vertical tail fin, but that scorched centaur against its field of blistered yellow no longer looked so proud now that it was lying in the oil-soaked mud.

Gold walked over to Teddy. "Enough here to tell us what happened?" he asked.

Teddy shook his head. "There isn't even enough left intact to tell us that this was an airplane."

Gold nodded. "Doesn't matter. We know what happened, don't we?" Teddy didn't reply. "We know what caused this." He paused, and then added bitterly, "Or should I say *who* caused it?"

"Come on, Herm," Teddy grumbled. "That isn't going to help anything."

"Bullshit!" Gold exploded. "Les was my friend! We went back a long ways together! Once he even saved my life! Did you know that I'd shot him down during the war? I didn't kill him then, but I sure as hell did today—"

"This is not your fault," Teddy said calmly.

"Yes it is, and you know it!" Gold replied. "This happened because I was in such a goddamned hurry to get these planes modified and into service! I wasn't thinking clearly, or responsibly. I was too anxious not to have to cancel our flights."

"With good reason. Canceling flights at a time like this, when our routes are up for grabs, would have looked very bad."

"Yeah," Gold sneered in disgust. "I wonder how my burning ten people to death, one of them one of my best friends, is going to look."

"*You* didn't burn anyone!" Teddy quickly said. "Don't forget, I triple-checked every modification made." Teddy took a crumbled pack of Luckies and a lighter out of his coat pockets. "I gave my approval."

"I bullied you into that—" Gold said fiercely.

"You're full of shit, Herm, if you think I would *ever* let

you bully me into something like that!" Teddy replied, angry now. With shaking fingers he extracted a smoke from the pack and cupped his hands against the wind to get it lit. "Why, you even piloted the modified prototype on its test flight, goddamn you!" Teddy continued, exhaling smoke. "You risked *your* life, because you didn't feel it would be appropriate to ask one of our pilots to do so. I stood down here, biting my fucking nails, thinking about how I was going to break the news of your death to Erica, while you put that fully loaded plane through every maneuver it was capable of, and some stunts it *wasn't* capable of, trying to get it to misbehave, but it didn't."

"Not then . . ." Gold said faintly.

"That's right, not then," Teddy sourly declared. "And not the next day, or the day after that, but it did, today. Or maybe a chance spark set off some stray gas fumes, in some sort of one-out-of-a-million freak accident." He glanced at his cigarette, and sighed. "Or maybe some asshole passenger set the cabin upholstery on fire while lighting a smoke . . ."

"Maybe this and maybe that," Gold said contemptuously.

"Maybes are all we've got," Teddy replied. "And probably all we'll ever have, Herm." He flicked away his cigarette. "There have been airplane crashes before, and there'll be crashes again. That's a big, mean sky up there, pal. It's just thrilled when it can dump one of our pretty birds right back into our cocky faces!"

Gold barely heard Teddy. He couldn't stop obsessing, worrying about the effect the accident would have on his chances of holding on to his CAM routes. He told himself that it was wrong to be so selfish at a time like this, when ten people had perished in one of his airplanes, but he couldn't help it, and was ashamed of himself. What if Teddy were wrong, and he really was to blame for pushing to get the modified F-5 as into service?

The horrid, unanswerable questions whirled in his brain. He wondered if there might ever be a time when the questions would not haunt him . . .

"It was an act of God," Teddy was insisting. "I was here. I saw it. One second she was in the air, and the next she was a fireball. The passengers and crew couldn't have known what hit them. It had to have been instant, painless . . ."

"For them maybe, but not for me," Gold said.

(Two)
Gold Household
Pasadena

Erica was in the living room, listening to the telephone ring. It had been ringing off the hook all afternoon, right into the evening. She'd heard nothing from Herman all day, beyond the call from his secretary informing her of the accident. Very soon after that the deluge of telephone calls from the print reporters and radio newsmen had begun.

The living room's walls were white stucco, the high ceiling was latticed with mahogany strips. There were tall, narrow, casement windows; a set of French doors opening onto the garden; and a large, gray slate fireplace which was never used, to spare the white wall-to-wall carpeting. Erica was wearing lounging pajamas of mauve crepe de chine. She was sitting on the fawn-colored, suede upholstered couch, idly flipping through magazines—*Time*, *American Mercury*, and that grand, swanky one they'd begun putting out in February, *The New Yorker*, without really seeing them. She listened as the live-in house girl picked up the telephone extension in the front hall to say that neither *Señor* nor *Señora* Gold was available. Then she heard Herman's car pull into the driveway.

She waited for her husband to put his car away in the garage and come into the house. She was worried about Herman. She'd been worried about him, and their marriage, for the longest while. Herman's desire for her seemed to have vanished. They'd been making love less and less frequently; the last time had been weeks ago. It seemed to her that the more successful Herman became, the more their relationship had suffered. He seemed to have neither time nor energy for herself or the children. Lately, she'd begun thinking about taking the kids and going back to Nebraska for a while, to think things through. She'd even begun to contemplate divorce. She was ready to face any obstacle *with* Herman, but somehow, she'd lost him. She'd taken her marriage vows very seriously; she would not allow them to exist as sham.

"Where have you been? I've been so worried," Erica asked as Herman came into the room.

"At the hospital."

"But I'd heard on the radio that there were no survivors?—"

"There weren't," Herman said. He loosened his tie and flopped down beside her on the couch. "Les's wife had sort of a breakdown upon hearing the news, so Hull took her to the hospital."

"Wait! Start from the beginning. What's Les's wife got to do with anything?"

She listened, shocked, as Herman explained it to her. "How terrible..." She pressed close against him and stroked his hair. "Why don't you go upstairs and have a long, hot soak in the bath? I'll wash your back for you. You'll feel better."

He nodded vaguely. She could tell that he hadn't really heard her. He did that a lot, and she was finding it increasingly annoying.

"Anyway, I was late because I sat with Les's wife for a while at the hospital," Herman said. "It turns out she's pregnant..."

"Oh, God..." Erica was appalled. "Did Les have insurance?"

"I'm his insurance," Herman said firmly.

"How is Hull taking it?"

"Like a guy who just lost his brother," Herman said sharply, pulling away from her.

Erica flinched. "You needn't take that tone with me," she began. The telephone began to ring. "There! You hear that? It's been going on all day!"

The house girl poked her head into the living room. "It is someone from the radio station, *Señor*," she said.

"Tell them I'm not home," Herman said.

"Herman, you can't hide forever..." Erica said.

"I can hide for tonight."

She nodded. "Do you want to talk about it?" When he shook his head again, she felt exasperated. "Don't shut me out! I'm your wife. Me! You married *me*, not Teddy Quinn, or Hull, or Les, or any of the others you prefer to share everything with!"

Herman glared at her. "Well, you sure as hell don't have to be jealous of Les, anymore."

"That's a terrible thing to say!"

"What do you expect?" he demanded.

"I expect us not to be strangers, at each other's throats—"

"I don't need you yelling at me, right now, Erica. Please! Keep your voice down! You'll disturb the children."

"What disturbs the children is that they miss their father!"

"I really doubt that!" Herman replied. "*You're* the one who's been away at your races and air exhibitions."

"How would you know where I've been? You're never here!" she shot back. "Maybe you wouldn't be so jealous of me if you were still flying an airplane, instead of a desk!"

Herman was scowling at her. She paused, thinking about what she wanted to say, wanting to get it right so that he might understand. "Competition, and winning, and women's place in aviation, in general, are all important to me. Aviation is a masculine world, Herman. Women pilots face an uphill battle for acceptance. It seems that women have to do everything twice as well as their male counterparts in order to be considered equal. You know how the business demands most of your time? Well, racing makes demands on me."

"But you have other responsibilities," Herman interrupted.

"And I meet them, or at least, I'm ready to meet them, given half a chance. But Herman, we *both* have responsibilities and priorities."

"What's that supposed to mean?" Herman demanded.

"That you're putting so much time and energy into your business that there's nothing *left* for the children." She paused, feeling herself blushing. "Or for me," she added, her voice thick.

"I'm working so hard for you and the kids—" he argued.

"No, you're not!" she said in frustration. "You're doing it to prove something to yourself! Meanwhile, you don't want a wife, you want some sort of wife/mother to be there to pat you on the head and tell you what a good, hardworking son you are. Maybe to replace the mother you never had!"

Herman angrily pushed the magazines she'd been reading off the coffee table to the carpet. "You get that brilliant insight from those?" he asked sarcastically.

"I don't need magazines or books to be able to read *you*."

"If you can read me so well, why don't you read that maybe things between us would be better if you had a little compassion for how hard I'm working," Herman accused.

"Maybe I would, if you came home early enough to *be* with me once in a while, instead of working yourself into exhaustion with Teddy Quinn and those others!" Erica said, and then wearily laughed. "I hired a private detective to find out about you, you know."

He stared at her, looking shocked. "Why?" he finally managed to sputter in anger.

"I was worried that you were seeing some other woman," Erica explained. "But the detective said that when you weren't home you really were working, either in Santa Monica or at Mines Field. The detective thought I'd be pleased, but I wasn't." She smiled thinly. "You see, Herman, I'd have a chance competing for you against some other woman, but not against the business . . ."

"Erica, this is foolish. I love you," Herman pleaded.

"No," she said sadly. "I love you, and maybe you *used* to love me, but I don't believe you do now, regardless of how you think you feel."

"I don't understand. What you mean?—"

"Herman, you only know how to love one thing at a time."

He was staring at her. He looked stricken. *Maybe now*, Erica thought.

"I'm going upstairs to bed," she said softly. *Maybe now he'll stop me. Take me in his arms and prove to me that I'm wrong, and it'll be like it used to be.*

He didn't stop her.

She really had lost him, she guessed. As she left the room

she was grateful that her back was turned and that he could not see her face, see the hurt she was feeling.

The telephone began to ring.

The telephone rang as Gold watched his wife walk out of the room, her lithe body fluid beneath the silky pajamas. The two pregnancies had not altered her figure a bit, he thought. She looked exactly as she had on the day they'd met, except for her hair. She'd bobbed her hair some time ago; something about how short hair was a lot more comfortable beneath a flying helmet, she'd explained . . .

He thought about going upstairs and making love to her. In a way he wanted to, and in a way it seemed like yet one more chore in an infinite series of arduous, endless days. She'd thought he had a lover; it was almost funny in its irony. If anything could seem funny to him today.

He wondered what he would feel if she took a lover. Anger? Jealousy? Despair? Relief? Nothing?

The telephone was still ringing. Where the fuck was the damned house girl?

He went to the windows to look out at the flood-lit garden. The palms were gently swaying, the fronds rustling in the breeze. He inhaled the fragrant scents of bougainvillea, and roses, and freshly mowed grass. A gardener came twice a week to care for the grounds. Gold had imagined that he would do it when he bought the house, but it had turned out that he didn't have the time.

The house was L-shaped, wrapped around the garden. As Gold stood at the downstairs living room window, he could see a light go on in the upstairs, bedroom wing of the house. He stood and watched, his hand pressed against the glass, until the light went out.

The telephone rang and rang. In the front foyer Gold paused to lift the earpiece off the ringing telephone's hook, silencing it, and then letting the earpiece dangle. He continued on his way out to the garage. Working on the Stutz helped him to unwind.

Chapter 10

(One)
Gold Aviation
Santa Monica
25 August 1925

Gold was chairing a meeting of his design engineers in the second-floor conference room. For the past hour he'd been listening to reports on the possible causes of the Spatz F-5a crash, and what could be done to ensure it didn't happen again. The bottom line was the same as it had been almost three weeks ago, on the day of the accident. Nobody knew why it had happened, and nobody could say with any certainty that it could be prevented in the future.

Immediately after the accident Gold had pulled the remaining two Spatz F-5as out of service. The loss of three planes, one third of his fleet, was causing havoc to his financial situation. His passenger revenues had already disappeared, thanks to the crash. His reduced fleet capacity was forcing him to turn away private freight business. Federal mail deliveries had priority, but even they were being delayed due to his lack of airplanes. The post office was complaining, and levying hefty penalties. His bank accounts were shrinking, and he had fuel and spare parts to buy and a payroll to meet. He was afraid to lay off any people. The last thing he needed was a disgruntled ex-employee spilling his guts to the newspapers about the dismal state of affairs at Gold Aviation.

As worried as Gold was about his cash flow, he was determined to keep the F-5as grounded until he could be as certain as possible that the modified airplanes were safe. He would not risk more lives, no matter what the consequences to his business. Meanwhile, he had an appointment later this afternoon to see Lane Barker at Pacific Coast Bank. Gold wanted to suspend the interest payments on his present loans and borrow another twenty-five thousand to cover his fuel bills and operating costs until he could get back on his feet.

South California Air Transport, the outfit bidding against him for his CAM routes, was not hesitating to kick him heartily while he was down. Their attorney had been pestering him with telephone calls for the past week, trying to get him to sell SCAT what remained of Gold Aviation's fleet— at a rock bottom price, of course. They'd also hired themselves a press agent, a real Hollywood flack with years of experience at playing dirty. The press agent had already orchestrated a news conference during which the clean-cut, All-American ex–postal service fliers who were fronting for SCAT had called for Gold Aviation to do "the decent thing" and withdraw from the competition, "to honor the memory of the ten who had died."

The meeting Gold was chairing was stalled on an argument concerning the F-5as' electrical systems. "Let's move on," Gold interrupted. "But remember that it's imperative that we get those airplanes back into service as soon as possible. We need the revenues." He looked around the table. "Now, then, tell me about progress to date on the G-1."

"We're ready to build a prototype," Teddy said. "Rogers and Simpson is ready to build us an engine. I've got cost estimates, right here." He pulled some sheets out of a manila folder on the table.

"What about the performance specs?" Gold asked. "I'd wanted some improvements in the G-1's projected capability to make short landings."

"We've still got a ways to go on that," Teddy admitted.

"That won't do!" Gold pounded the table. "Listen to me, all of you. I know the way things are *usually* done in this business: you build a prototype, find out what's wrong with it, then build another, and so on. We can't do that. The

G-1's got to be right the first time, because we don't have the financial resources for a second chance."

He paused, thinking to himself that right now he didn't know where the resources were going to come from for a *first* chance. He'd have to talk to Lane Barker about that.

"The G-1 had got to be fast, able to haul a heavy load, *and* land on a dime if we're going to sell them to the post office," Gold continued. "And we've got competition. There's Douglas Aircraft, right here in Santa Monica. And Curtiss, and I hear Ford is getting into it, and there's plenty of others, all after the same plum. What the post office buys, every outfit flying feeder routes will want to buy. And maybe even the military. This is it, gentlemen," Gold warned. "We either grab the brass ring this time around, or the merry-go-round ride will be over."

Back in his office, Gold settled down behind his desk and began to scan the supply purchase orders from the Mines Field facility. Normally he let his secretary handle this sort of thing, but with money so tight, he'd decided to personally approve all expenditures for the time being.

He was at it only a few minutes when he gave up. He couldn't concentrate. He found himself brooding about his marital problems.

He leaned back in his chair and stared out at the bay. Since their argument on the night of the plane crash he and Erica had become even more like strangers to each other, if such a thing were possible. She'd begun talking about taking the children on a trip to see their grandparents for a while; a *long* while . . . Gold could read between the lines; he knew what she was hinting at. The thought of losing his family— of being alone, again—horrified him. But in reality, wasn't he alone now?

His attention was distracted by a squawking flurry of sea gulls, hovering and darting above the fishing boats that were coming into port. The fishermen were tossing overboard the trash fish. The gulls were conducting aerial combat over the free lunch . . .

Gold's thoughts lingered on the gulls. He stood and went

to the window, leaning out to get a better look at the birds as they wheeled and dived.

He kept a pair of binoculars in his desk drawer for airplane watching. He went to get them and then returned to the window to focus in on the gulls, watching as they pivoted in the air, swooping down in abrupt, accurate dives, often to pluck the trash fish right out of the fishermen's hands. He noticed that the gulls' trailing wing feathers curved down when the birds came in for a landing on the scow's rolling deck . . .

Smiling to himself, Gold hurried to his drafting table. He made several rough sketches of an oversized wing flap that could be lowered into the airflow to act as an aerodynamic brake for short landings. When he was done drawing, he pulled the paper off the table and ran downstairs with it to the design lab Teddy shared with his staff.

Teddy, seated behind his desk, looked up in surprise as Gold dashed in.

"Everybody gather around," Gold called out as he slammed the drawing on Teddy's desk. As the designers formed a huddle Gold explained his concept. When he was finished, he said, "I want you to get outside and start feeding those damned gulls. While you're doing that, watch those trailing wing feathers in operation."

One of the engineers was looking at Gold like he'd gone crazy. "Let me get this straight. You want us to feed birds? . . ."

Gold smiled. "You're all looking too pale, anyhow. That's the trouble with this organization. We've been spending too much time with our noses pressed against our drafting table. When was the last time any of us enjoyed ourselves? Maybe even wasted a little time daydreaming?"

"I didn't think you were paying us to daydream." Teddy was grinning.

"I pay you to come up with ideas!" Gold challenged him. "And I don't mind a little daydreaming. Without it, I couldn't have gotten this far—"

He stopped short, thinking that maybe this was what Erica had been trying to tell him, in her way. He wondered how he ever could have forgotten it. And when he'd changed from a dreamer into a worrier. Supposedly he was doing what he'd wanted to do. When had it stopped being fun?

"I'll leave you gentlemen to your work," Gold said. "Get outside. Feed those gulls. Sketch and photograph them. I expect you all to be sunburned, sonofabitch sea gull experts!"

Grinning, feeling like the world's weight had dropped from his shoulders, Gold went skipping up the stairs to his office. He wanted to thank Erica for being so clever, to promise her that things were going to be different from now on. Tonight he would leave work early. They would go somewhere nice for dinner and celebrate, maybe at the Coconut Grove, over at the Ambassador Hotel. They would drink champagne, and dance, and get to know each other again.

He wondered what Erica was doing right now. He felt horny as hell.

"Get my wife on the telephone," he told his secretary.

"I will, but Collins Tisdale called while you were downstairs."

"Really? . . ." Gold was startled. The publisher of the *Los Angeles Gazette* was notorious for avoiding the telephone.

"He said that it was urgent, and asked that you get back to him at the newspaper as soon as possible."

Gold nodded. "All right, telephone him first." He went into his office, wondering what this was all about. His secretary signaled that she'd put the call through, and he picked up the telephone. A few seconds later, Tisdale came on the line. "Collins, how are you?"

"I'm fine, Herman," Tisdale said. "Herman, this is difficult for me, but I felt I should call you personally, before my paper went with the story."

"What's going on?"

"Your rivals for your CAM routes have just held a news conference," Tisdale said. "They've announced that they've rented a facility at Clover Field and purchased four airplanes."

"Jumping the gun a bit, aren't they?" Gold asked sardonically. "If you're looking for a quote from me, you can say that as far as I'm concerned—"

"SCAT also announced that they've made you an offer for your airplanes," Tisdale cut him off. "An offer that you're seriously considering..."

"That's a lie," Gold said flatly. "I'm going to need my airplanes."

"SCAT also made some serious personal charges against you."

"Such as?"

"They brought up your war record," Tisdale said.

"Well, hell, Collins... Everybody knows that I'm German..."

"You're not a United States citizen, are you?"

"Well, I guess not... I mean, not technically..."

"They made that point at the press conference," Tisdale replied. "They asked why a foreigner should be awarded government business while bona fide American citizens go begging. And they said more. That you're unpatriotic. That you bought German airplanes, risking the public's safety, because your loyalties still lie with Germany—"

"Now that's bullshit!" Gold exclaimed in anger. "Those Spatz planes were the best available at the time!"

"It gets worse, Herman." Tisdale hesitated. "They claimed that your name was Goldstein before you came to this country. That you're a *Jew*..."

Erica, Gold thought. *He'd never told Erica the truth—* "When did this all happen?"

"About an hour ago. It's already on the radio," Tisdale replied. "So, what they've said is true?...Herman?... Hello?... Are you still there?"

"Yeah," Gold managed. "I'm here... It's true."

"I see," Tisdale said briskly. "Well, then! I wanted to give you the benefit of the doubt before my paper ran the story," Tisdale said brusquely. "Good-bye, Herman."

Gold listened to the dial tone's hum. It figured that Tisdale would cut him dead, Gold thought as he dialed his home. Gold knew all along that he'd been playing a dangerous game concerning his charade. The important Jews in town, like those in the film industry, kept pretty much to themselves. Gold knew a lot of people like Tisdale who would not appreciate the fact that they'd been tricked into unknowingly socializing with a Jew.

But right now he could care less what Tisdale or anybody thought, except for Erica. Gold listened as the ringing went on at the other end of the line. He willed Erica to answer, but nobody picked up, not even the house girl. But that was typical, he thought.

He hung up, deciding that he would go home; that way he would be there to talk to Erica as soon as she got back from wherever she was. He buzzed his secretary. "I'm going home for the rest of the day—"

"But you're due to see Lane Barker, Mister Gold," his secretary said.

"Oh, hell, you're right!" he groaned. "And I'd better not stand him up, not today..."

(Two)
Pacific Coast Bank
Los Angeles

The Pacific Coast Bank was an imposing, red granite building located downtown, on the corner of Broadway and Temple Streets, near the Hall of Justice. Gold entered through the bronzed revolving doors and into the bustling lobby, with its gray and white marble floor, pale green walls, and high, gilded, cathedral ceiling. He walked past the island of public writing desks and the long row of tellers' cages. Off to one side, separated from the cages and lobby by a wall of potted ferns and palms, were a dozen or so desks. There men in dark suits sat scribbling in ledgers and talking on the telephone, while young women in high-collared dresses sat clacking away at typewriters and adding machines. Beyond the desks, separated from them by a waist-high, varnished wood railing, was a carpeted area with chairs and smoking stands. A matronly-looking receptionist sitting behind a desk guarded a series of doors which led to the private rooms in which the bank officers conducted important business.

He approached the receptionist and told the woman who

he was, and that he had an appointment to see Mister Barker. The receptionist looked uneasy.

"Excuse me—"

Gold turned. A short, stocky guy in his twenties, in a cheaply tailored, blue gabardine, double-breasted suit, was offering him a winning smile. The guy had a round face, with wide-set, dark eyes. His auburn hair was parted in the middle and slicked down.

"My name's Tim Campbell. I'm a junior loan officer. Mister Barker regrets that something has come up which will keep him from seeing you today."

"All of a sudden, huh?" Gold asked suspiciously. "When can he see me?"

"I'm afraid his appointment calendar is full for the time being," Campbell said. "He's very busy, you know."

"Yeah, I know." Gold's face began to burn. He felt the receptionist's eyes upon him. "So what's next, Campbell?"

"Mister Barker has authorized me to discuss your application. I've been looking over your financial statement . . ." He pursed his lips. "If you'd care to follow me to my desk?—"

Desk? Gold thought. *This guy doesn't even rate an office?* As Campbell turned, Gold noticed that the seat of the guy's pants was shiny, and that the heels of his shoes were worn down. He guessed that Campbell didn't have the authority to approve the cashing of an out-of-state check, let alone what Gold needed. Lane Barker was clearly giving him the brush-off. Gold knew that he had to take it, but he didn't need to be a masochist about it.

"Nothing personal," Gold said, stopping Campbell. "But I don't see any point in wasting each other's time." He turned to go.

"Wait, Mister Gold!" Campbell called out. "I have some things to discuss with you—"

"Look," Gold interrupted. "I have only one question to ask you. Is the bank going to give me what I want?"

Campbell hesitated.

"That's what I thought. You don't need to cushion the rejection with an explanation, Mister Campbell." Gold smiled. "But I do appreciate your trying to be tactful. This is an awful job that Barker's given you; you've handled yourself well. I hope that the bank will reward you some day. Maybe even give you a set of walls and a door to go with your desk. Good-bye and good luck, Mister Campbell."

Good luck to both of us, Gold thought as he left the bank and walked to his car. He was in a daze as he drove home to Pasadena; consumed with money worries, and worries about how he was going to face Erica. She had to have heard the truth about him by now...

As he turned into his driveway he was relieved to see Erica's green Packard Runabout. Thank God, she was home! He was sure that she would understand why he'd kept the truth about himself from her, and how much he loved her ... He would *make* her understand.

"Erica!" he called out as he entered the house. "Where are you? We've got to talk!" It seemed strangely quiet to him as he stood in the front hallway. Where were the children? He wondered. Where was Erica if her car was parked outside?

The house girl came into the hallway from the living room. She looked anxious.

"Ramona, where is everyone?" Gold asked.

"*Señor,* the *Señora,* she has gone away with the children. She ask me to give you this..."

Gold took the sheet of paper folded in half and opened it. It was a sheet of their personal stationery. HERMAN AND ERICA was engraved across the top in script.

"We've gone east, to visit my parents," Erica had written. "Please don't try to follow or contact."

That was all, except for seven words slashed across the bottom of the sheet, written so forcibly that the pen point had made dagger marks in the paper: "HOW COULD YOU HAVE LIED TO ME???"

"The *Señora* had me help her pack," Ramona was fretting. "Then she called the taxi cab to come take her and the children to the train station. Please believe me, *Señor,* she told me not to call you, not to even answer the telephone. Please don't be angry with me..."

"I'm not," Gold murmured, staring at the note as if he expected something more to appear on the paper. "You did as you were told. I understand that."

"*Señor,* the *Señora* and the little ones, they will be gone a long time?"

"I don't know," he said vaguely. "I hope not . . ."

"*Señor,* please! I am a good Catholic girl," Ramona shyly insisted. "My parents, they do not wish me to remain alone in a house with a man. Until the *Señora* returns, my parents wish me to sleep at their home. My father will come to pick me up each afternoon," she added quickly. "He will bring me back first thing in the morning. Each day before I go I will leave you your dinner in the oven—"

Gold was hardly listening. "I'll give you a key so that you can come and go as you wish."

"*Gracias, Señor,*" Ramona said, hurrying away into the kitchen.

Around six, a rumpled, dusty pickup truck rattled its way up the driveway. Ramona left for the evening, promising to be back by six-thirty in the morning. Gold watched the truck drive away. He felt like crying, seeing her go; now he was all alone in the big house.

God, he was in bad shape if he was missing the maid . . .

A few minutes later the telephone rang. Gold answered it and was subjected to a vicious, anti-Semitic crank call. He hung up. It rang again. He listened to the beginning of another hissed stream of bigoted invective, and then cut the connection.

What did he expect, calls from well-wishers? He'd been denying his origins for so long that he himself had begun to believe his own fabrications. It had been easy to forget that America was a closed society, where Jews and communists were synonymous, just as they'd been in Germany. Henry Ford's newspaper, the *Dearborn Independent,* had for years been publishing anti-Semitic garbage about the supposed international Jewish conspiracy. Meanwhile, respected college professors and government scientists were issuing well-received warnings that American I.Q. scores were declining due to the influx of immigrants diluting the Anglo-Saxon stock. Politicians were winning campaigns based on calls for racial purity. Just last year Congress had passed an immigration bill that placed restrictive quotas on Eastern Europeans coming to America...

The telephone began ringing again. This time Gold let it, until it stopped. Then he decided to take the phone off its hook for a while.

He wasn't hungry, but he ate the casserole that Ramona had prepared for him anyway, just to give himself something to do. He ate in the green and white tiled kitchen, listening to the rumbling of the electric icebox, reading the newspaper—Collins Tisdale's *Los Angeles Gazette*—propped up on the kitchen table. The metropolitan section of the paper was full of stories about him, and SCAT's accusations that he had intentionally bought unsafe German airplanes because of some German/Jewish international conspiracy. *How absurd*, Gold thought. A boxed editorial carrying Collins Tisdale's byline was in the center of one page. The headline read, *"WHAT ELSE HAS GOLD(Stein) LIED ABOUT?"*

That killed his appetite once and for all. So both Collins Tisdale and Lane Barker had turned against him. So much for friends in high places, he decided as he put the newspaper and his half-eaten meal into the garbage.

It was now around eight, and beginning to get dark. He wandered around the big, still house, clicking on lamps, listening to the floorboards settle and the ticking of clocks. He stayed out of the children's rooms, and the bedroom he shared with Erica. He thought about Erica and the kids on the train, wondering how far they'd gotten, feeling like he was all alone in the world. Erica had warned him that this would happen, but he'd refused to listen. He wondered if there was any way he might be lucky enough to get a second chance...

The house was so fucking quiet! The silence was making him nervous, but he wasn't in the mood to listen to the phonograph, or the radio.

He thought about calling Teddy Quinn, or Hull Stiles, to see what they were up to, but he decided against it. Teddy was likely with his fiancée, and Hull, who'd gotten married a couple of years ago, had a fine set of twin boys, toddlers now, who deserved some time with their father.

He tried to crack that new book Erica had brought home

and had been after him to read, *The Great Gatsby*. As he settled down in the living room with the novel he realized that it had been a long time since he'd read anything that didn't have to do with aeronautics. It was funny, he used to read a lot.

He had a hard time concentrating and found himself reading the first few pages several times. Around nine-thirty he was ready to give up, and maybe try to go to bed, when the telephone in his study began to ring. He'd had the separate, unlisted extension installed a few weeks ago, after the plane crash, when his home's existing telephone line was being tied up with calls from reporters.

Gold happily tossed the book aside. Only a few close friends had the unlisted number; he was more than eager to talk with any of them. He hurried from the living room into the adjoining study. It had yellow walls above dark, chest-high wainscoting, and colorful Navajo rugs on the polished wood floor. Four brightly polished brass lamps with green glass shades hung suspended from the ceiling by lengths of chain. They cast golden pools of light on the rectangular dining table of red oak that Gold used as his desk.

Gold shoved aside the piles of technical journals and grabbed the candlestick telephone off the table. "Hello?"

"Mister Gold, this is Tim Campbell. From the bank?"

"Campbell? How'd you get this number?" Gold demanded.

"Sir, your personal file was supplied to me by Mister Barker..."

"Oh, yeah, right..." Gold came around the side of the desk and pulled out his beechwood armchair. The chair creaked comfortingly as he settled into the woven leather.

"I tried to get you at your other number," Campbell offered. "But it's been busy for the last hour or so. I guess your wife's on it?"

"What's this about, Campbell?" Gold asked gruffly. He was in no mood to chat with this guy.

"It's about your financial situation, Mister Gold. For the past few hours I've been going over your statements. If you'll pardon me for saying so, your business is in big trouble."

"I didn't need you to tell me that, pal . . ." Gold replied. "But since you called, I will tell you that I was surprised and disappointed by the bank's refusing my loan request after all the business we've done together—"

"What did you expect, Mister Gold?" Campbell asked. "Think about it. Today's embarrassing revelations about you aside, if you could be objective, would you consider yourself to be a good credit risk? Like I said, I've got all your numbers spread out on my desk. I have no idea what amateur has been keeping your books, but believe me, they are a mess. I mean total chaos! Anyway, as far as I can tell, you've left yourself absolutely no cash reserves. Nothing at all. The money's been flowing through your fingers like water."

"Tomorrow I'm going to apply for the loan at another bank—" Gold began.

"I respectfully suggest that you're going to receive the same treatment no matter what bank you go to," Campbell said. "Again, try to see the situation objectively. You're in a neck-and-neck horse race against South California Air Transport for those CAM routes, the heart and soul of your business. Actually, I'd say that right now, SCAT is out in front, due to that airplane crash, and today's revelations about your past."

"That's just a smear campaign against me," Gold angrily protested.

"Of course it is," Campbell agreed. "But it's turning out to be a very effective one. Let me be totally blunt: you're a foreigner, a Jew. You're the very sort of person the United States Congress was targeting when it passed last year's Immigration Act—"

"I don't need a lesson in current events from you."

"Then you don't need me to remind you that there was an extremely acrimonious public debate on that bill before it was overwhelmingly passed by both houses of Congress—"

"So what?"

"Mister Gold, this is the same Congress that votes appropriations for the postal service."

Damn, Gold thought. That nasty implication had not occurred to him.

"Anyway, I think other banks would turn you down no matter who you were," Campbell was saying. "You're already financially overextended. Your business assets are mortgaged to the hilt to Pacific Coast Bank. What are you going to offer as collateral to any other lender?"

"I—" Gold hesitated. "I have my house, and cars . . ."

"Fine," Campbell said. "I've got the numbers right here. Give me a second—"

Campbell put down the telephone. Gold listened to the sound of an adding machine clacking. He realized he was sweating. This was turning out to be the worst fucking day of his life.

Campbell was back on the line. "As I see it, you could pull maybe twenty grand out of your personal assets, using them as collateral. That would be enough to keep your Mines Field facility—I don't even want to discuss your Santa Monica money pit right now—going for about three months. But you won't have three months, because when word leaks out that you put your house up, that'll be the finishing blow to whatever reputation you have left. Come September fifteenth, a little over two weeks from now, the postmaster general is going to look at your bid, think about how your business is operating on a razor's edge, and forget about you. The government can't afford to take a chance awarding CAM routes to an organization in danger of bankruptcy. SCAT may be the new kid on the block, but at least it's financially secure."

"So what should I do, Campbell?" Gold asked dryly. "Hang myself?"

"You've got a lot of problems, Mister Gold, but you also have a lot of potential. You're a visionary, you need to be free to dream—"

Gold was startled at the coincidence. It was as if Campbell had been listening in when he'd been lecturing Teddy and his design team, earlier today.

"What you need is someone to keep the books while you're off doing great things in the field of aviation."

"Someone, huh?" Gold smiled. "Just what are you trying to peddle, Campbell?"

"It's what I wanted to talk to you about this afternoon, at

the bank. I believe I have the solution to get you out of the mess you're in now, and keep you out of financial trouble in the foreseeable future, but it's a little too complicated to go into on the telephone. I'd like to arrange a meeting with you . . ."

"All right, Campbell. I'm ready to listen."

"Great! Why don't you drop by the bank around—"

"No," Gold cut him off. "You don't have an office, so you come to me. If we're going to talk about my financial situation, we'll do it in private. I'll see you at my Santa Monica 'money pit' tomorrow morning. Say, ten o'clock?"

"Ten o'clock it is," Campbell enthused. "You won't regret this—"

Gold chuckled. "See you tomorrow, Campbell." He hung up.

(Three)
Pacific Coast Bank

Campbell hung up the telephone. He leaned back in his chair and put his stockinged feet up on the desk. His jacket and tie were off, as well as his shoes; his shirt collar was unbuttoned and his sleeves were rolled up. He didn't care about his appearance. At this hour of the night all the bigwigs had gone home. There were only three people in the huge bank: himself, the Mexican cleaning lady, and the uniformed night watchman at his post all the way over by the locked revolving doors.

Campbell took a pack of Camels from out of the breast pocket of his shirt, extracted a cigarette, and lit it with a match. He puffed blue smoke rings at the high ceiling, feeling totally relaxed now that his call to Gold had been successfully completed. He watched the Mexican cleaning lady wheeling her cart and emptying wastebaskets. She smiled at him. Campbell smiled back. They were old friends. Campbell worked late a lot.

He thought about the manila folders under his heels. The folders were filled with the neat columns of figures that summed up Herman Gold and his business. Campbell smiled. Life was good, and getting better.

Life had not started out so well. He was born in 1899, in Providence, Rhode Island. He was the youngest of seven children. His father spent his days slaving away in a textile mill, and his nights getting drunk, then coming home to rage and swear and beat his wife, while the children watched, cowering.

Campbell ran away when he was twelve. He rode the rails to Boston, where he joined a gang of older boys, who found his big, dark eyes and winning smile useful in panhandling. In return, the gang took care of him, teaching him how to survive on the streets. He became a con artist, a pickpocket, but he stayed away from the rough stuff: rolling drunks, purse-snatching, things like that. He couldn't abide violence. It reminded him of his father, and the pain he'd witnessed the man inflicting on his mother.

When he felt he'd learned all that the older boys could teach, he ran away from them. He preferred being on his own. He rode the rails, aimlessly, figuring that he could stay reasonably warm and dry, and almost always find something to eat on a freight train. He was little and fast, and the years spent in his alcoholic, rampaging bastard of a father's house had taught him how to hide when it suited his purposes. A railroad-yard bull could shine his flashlight around a boxcar, and right at Campbell, and not see him there, crouched still as a rat between the stacked crates and burlap sacks.

In Tulsa, Oklahoma, a yard bull finally did catch him. He was turned over to the police. Campbell refused to tell the authorities where he was from because he didn't want to be sent back to Providence. He spent a terrifying week in a jail cell, waiting for his hearing. God! Even now, he couldn't imagine how men survived incarceration. To this day, he was still afraid of police . . . Anyway, his hearing finally came around. The judge gave him a final opportunity to disclose where he'd come from, so he could be sent home. When Campbell refused to say, the judge put him into a nearby boy's work farm run by the Protestant Church—until he was sixteen.

Campbell expected the worst, and was determined to run

away at the first opportunity, but the work farm turned out to be a pretty good deal. They gave him a clean, warm bed, good food, and decent clothes, even if the chambray work shirts were stenciled, in big white letters front and back, TULSA YOUTH FARM. The people who ran the place were stern, but fair. Mornings were spent tilling the fields. Afternoons were spent in the classroom, learning the "three Rs." There were church services every evening until bedtime. Campbell could have done without the preaching, but all in all, the farm was a hell of a lot better than the life had been in Providence. The fact that the work farm offered him the opportunity for an education was the main thing. Back in Providence his folks had never bothered to send him to school.

It turned out he had a head for classroom work, especially when it came to arithmetic. The instructors at the work farm were gratified to have a good student and encouraged him to progress by giving him extra lessons. By fifteen he'd earned his high school diploma. His new knowledge fascinated and intrigued him. He asked if there weren't some work he could do on the farm that would allow him to use his education, as opposed to scratching in the Oklahoma dirt with a hoe, which he detested. They let him teach reading and numbers to the youngest boys. His students called him "Mister," and "Sir"—Campbell reveled in the status and respect his cleverness had won for him.

When he was sixteen, and had to leave the farm, the people there arranged a job for him as an office boy for the Tulsa Western Union office. The job paid enough for him to support himself and also take night school courses in bookkeeping and accounting. He worked and studied in Tulsa for a year. During that time he heard a lot about California and decided to go there to seek his fortune. He tried to arrange a transfer to the Western Union office in San Francisco, but there were no openings available, so he settled for the office in Los Angeles.

It was 1916. He was seventeen, but looked and acted much older in his somber suit and tie, and a boiled white shirt with a detachable celluloid collar. Within a month of his arrival he landed a job as a teller at Pacific Coast Bank.

He resumed taking night courses, intent upon receiving a college degree in accounting. He celebrated his eighteenth birthday by going to the Flower Street Cafe, which was around the corner from the Los Angeles State Normal School, where he was taking courses, and treating himself to a steak dinner before his accounting class.

He sat at the counter, where he was served by a slim, dark-haired waitress with big blue eyes and a shy smile. It was a slow night, so while he ate she chatted with him. He told her that it was his birthday. She told him her name was Agatha Wilcox.

She asked him if he wanted dessert. He said that he didn't have enough money, so he'd skip dessert and tip her instead, because she'd been sweet enough for him. She laughed, and gave him a slice of blueberry pie on the house to go with his coffee. While he ate the pie she sang "Happy Birthday" to him.

He began stopping into the cafe every night for coffee before class. After a couple of weeks like that, she invited him to come for Sunday dinner at her parents' house in east Los Angeles. He understood what she was getting at, and decided that was okay with him. He began spending every Sunday with her. He would stop by at her house and spend a quarter-hour with her parents, and then he and Aggie would take the trolley to Santa Monica Beach, where they'd stroll the boardwalk, holding hands, dreaming and laughing together about the future, serenaded by the crashing waves and squawking gulls. They were ready to get married, but decided to wait. Her parents' house was too small for Campbell to move in once they were married. Between their meager salaries they weren't earning enough to both rent a decent apartment of their own and pay for Campbell to continue his education.

When the United States entered the war, Campbell was drafted, but the army turned him down as physically unfit due to an irregular heartbeat. He was very relieved. When he was twenty, after three years at Pacific Coast Bank, he was promoted to head teller. The increase in salary made marriage possible, at long last. He formally proposed to Agatha at the beach, and she accepted. After they were married they took a small bungalow apartment near the campus so that she could be near her waitressing job and he could quickly and easily come home from night school after his day at the bank.

Money was tight, but it was a happy time. Campbell enjoyed being married. During lovemaking they were as careful as they could be, but, as it turned out, not careful enough. Before their first anniversary had come around, Aggie was pregnant.

The pregnancy was difficult for Agatha. Her ankles swelled up so that she couldn't stand for very long at one time, and that put the kibosh on her waitressing. Their first child was a boy, whom they named Timothy, Junior.

In order to make ends meet, in addition to his job at the bank, and night school, Campbell worked weekends selling brushes door-to-door. It turned out that he was good at selling. After the war, when automobiles resumed rolling off the assembly lines, he quit the brush job in order to work weekends selling Fords. The owner of the dealership tried to convince him to come into the business full-time. Campbell discussed the opportunity with Aggie, but she was against it. She felt that he could become an important officer at the bank, but that meant he had to push on with school.

He had a talk about his future with his supervisor at the bank. His supervisor took the matter up with his own supervisors. A few days later Campbell was told that if and when he received his bachelor's degree in accounting, he would be promoted to junior loan officer.

His son was almost two years old, and Agatha was again pregnant, when Campbell finally earned his college degree in 1923. The bank kept its word, moving him out of his teller's cage to behind this desk, among the desks of the other junior loan officers the bank employed. A couple of months later, Aggie presented him with another son, whom they named Donald.

That had been a little less than two years ago. During that time Campbell saved his pennies until he was able to put down a thousand on a two-bedroom bungalow. Money was tight as ever. Aggie was talking about taking a stenographer's evening course and going to work part-time as a secretary once the boys were old enough to go to school. Campbell knew that it would be another three years, at least, before he could even begin to think about the possibility of being promoted to senior loan officer at a major financial institution such as Pacific Coast Bank.

If he stayed . . .

Campbell stubbed out what was left of his cigarette in the ashtray on his desk, stood up, and stretched. He put on his shoes and suitcoat, packed up the files on Gold Aviation, and slipped them into his briefcase. He'd go over them at home, in bed, while Aggie slept, fine-tuning the presentation he'd make to Gold tomorrow.

The night watchman unlocked the side door for him. Campbell stepped out into the night and walked the block to where his tan Plymouth coupe was parked.

He looked at the car a moment before he got in. He'd bought it used. The backseat upholstery had a gash in it. God, he hated used stuff!

According to the files, Gold drove a Stutz and his wife had a brand-new Packard roadster—

A Packard would do just fine, Campbell thought, grinning. He worked the Plymouth's starter. After a few tries it caught, and he pulled away.

He intended to be a wealthy man. Up until today, he'd thought that a career in banking was the way to go about it. Now that he'd taken a look at Gold Aviation, he thought he'd found a better way.

(Four)
Gold Household

After his telephone conversation with Campbell, Gold decided to go to bed. He went through the house, shutting off lights and checking the doors. Upstairs, in the hallway outside the bedroom, he hesitated, realizing that he didn't want to face that big lonely bed all by himself . . .

He went back downstairs, trudging through the shadowy house into the living room, where he kicked off his loafers and stretched out on the couch. He glanced at his wristwatch's luminous dial: it was almost eleven. After an interminable while spent tossing and turning, he drifted off into a dream: He was back at his terminal facility at Mines Field on the day of the airplane crash. Teddy Quinn wasn't there, but Tim Campbell was, chattering away about something Gold couldn't quite comprehend as he walked amidst the wreckage of his crashed airplane. The scene of the crash had taken on the appearance and dimensions of a World War I battlefield. Burned bodies and drifting smoke were everywhere, stretching as far as Gold could see. It seemed to him that all of this carnage was his fault, and then he realized that Erica and his children had been on the airplane, flying to Nebraska.

The air was filled with the raw smell of spilled gasoline—

He woke up abruptly, tense and sweating. He blamed the dream, but then he realized that he was sure that he had heard something that had disturbed his sleep.

He checked the time: quarter of four in the morning. Far too early for Ramona to have returned. Could he have heard a prowler? The dream vanished from his mind as he lay quietly, ears straining, eyes staring into the darkness.

He heard the noise again. Soft sounds of thin metal warping, and liquid sloshing. Was he merely hearing the plumbing in his house? No, the sound was coming in through the open windows facing the garden.

He suddenly realized that he was still smelling gasoline. *Really* smelling it.

Then he recognized what he'd been hearing. He'd heard it only about a thousand times during his career as a pilot. It was the sound of gasoline being poured from a fuel can.

He sat up, stepped into his shoes, and moved quietly to the windows facing out onto the garden. It was a cloudy night, with just a sliver of bone-colored moon, but there was enough light for Gold to see that somebody was near the side of the house, up to something.

Gold went to the fireplace, gripped the poker, and then hurried to the French doors leading out into the garden. Beside the doors was the wall switch that controlled the garden lighting. He flicked the switch, wrenched open the glass door, and rushed out, wielding his poker.

The prowler had been in the process of sloshing gasoline against the side of the house from a red and yellow five-gallon can. He was tall and fat, dressed in gray, baggy pants, and a dark brown corduroy jacket. He had blond hair curling out from beneath his tweed, visored cap. He hurled his candy-colored gas can at Gold, who sidestepped it, but gasoline splashed onto him; his shirt was soaked. The gasoline felt cold evaporating against his skin as he moved toward the prowler.

The prowler took a wooden kitchen match from out of his pocket and flicked it alight with his thumbnail. Gold stopped, staring at the sputtering little flame, aware of the gasoline from his soaked shirt dripping on his shoes.

The prowler smiled. "Come on, Jewboy—" He had a broad, bulbous nose, colored an angry red and broken out with pimples. "Come on, Kike... I'll fry you, then do the house and the wife and kiddies."

He lunged forward, tossing the lighted match toward Gold, who cried out, stumbling back from the lethal spark of flame darting toward him. The match winked out in midair, but while Gold was distracted the prowler escaped. He was startlingly light on his feet for such a large man. He dashed for the high stockade fence, and then hoisted himself up and over. He was gone.

Gold dropped the poker. He stripped down to his underwear, ran to where the garden hose was connected to the outside spigot, and turned it on. He washed himself down and then took his time soaking down the wall of the house, the grassy area around it, and wherever the gas had spilled, making sure that he had washed it all away. He locked the prowler's gas can in the garage and then went back into the house, where he turned on all the lights. He took the fireplace poker with him to the upstairs bathroom and took a shower, shampooing his hair to wash away the last traces of gasoline. Still damp, he put on a terrycloth robe and slippers, took his poker, and went back downstairs, into his study. He unlocked a built-in wall cabinet, took out a bottle of the genuine scotch that he had regularly delivered by a local bootlegger, and poured himself a stiff drink. He swallowed it down, grimacing, and then poured himself another. He took it, and the poker, over to his desk. He sat down, and stared at the telephone.

Of course, the thing to do was call the police. His home had been invaded, with an intent to commit arson. He himself had been assaulted.

Gold stared at the telephone, but did not pick it up. He could certainly describe the prowler to the police, but what were the odds that the cops would catch the bastard?

He sipped at his scotch. The police probably wouldn't even look at that hard. Gold could hear them now—

This was regrettable, Mister Gold, but, surely you're aware that there's a great deal of this sort of thing going around . . . We'll keep our eyes open, but don't count on too much . . . The most important thing is that you've suffered no injury, and that your property was unharmed . . . By the way, Mister Gold, have you ever considered getting yourself a watchdog?

And with the police would come the reporters. Gold could hear them, as well.

Why did this happen, Mister Gold? Who are your enemies? There are lots of Jews, why did he pick on you? Do you think he had a motive, Mister Gold? Maybe he had a friend or relative who died on your German airplane when it blew up?

Inevitably, one of the newshounds would imply that tonight's incident *hadn't* happened; and that Gold had fabricated it in a desperate attempt to counter the bad publicity and drum up public sympathy for himself. It was not at all far-fetched to think that by tomorrow's editions, the newspapers would have turned the whole thing around to make it seem as if Gold had tried to torch his own home in a last-ditch effort to salvage his business . . .

And when it was all over and done, with the would-be arsonist free, and Gold himself further humiliated and discredited, how many more crazies would be given the idea to do exactly the same thing, either to him, or other Jews? . . .

He looked at his watch. It was five-thirty. He went and poured himself some more scotch. An hour later he was still in his study, drinking and brooding, the poker within reach, when he heard the sound of a motor in the driveway. Ramona had arrived for the day. When he heard her key in the front door, Gold went upstairs to get dressed. When he came down, Ramona was waiting for him.

"*Señor*," she began. "On the fence in front of your house, someone has written," she hesitated, frowning, "oh, they have written terrible things . . ."

He went outside to take a look. KIKES LIVE HERE/JEWS ALL DIE/CHRIST-KILLERS was scrawled across the stockade fence in ugly, black letters a foot tall. Gold stared, his fists clenched and his heart pounding in his chest. He wanted to strike back, to hurt somebody—anybody—to relieve all of the hurt and frustration he was feeling.

He went back inside. "Ramona, call the handyman and ask him to come and remove that."

"Yes, *Señor*."

"Have him paint the damn fence white if he has to, but I want it gone, as soon as possible, do you understand?"

"I will see to it, *Señor* Gold," Ramona said. "If the handyman cannot come, I will have my father and brothers do it, but it will be done."

Gold forced himself to try to relax. He made himself smile. "Thank you, Ramona."

"You are a good man, *Señor*," she said fierccly. "God smiles on *you*, not on the evil ones who did that. Now, please, sit down, you must eat."

He didn't have the strength of will left to argue, so he ate the breakfast and drank the coffee that she'd prepared for him. While he ate, she called the handyman, and then came back into the kitchen to tell him that the man was on his way. Gold nodded. Everywhere he looked in the green and white tiled kitchen he seemed to see the black obscenities scrawled.

When he was done eating, he left for Santa Monica. On his way out to the garage, he checked the garden. The gasoline had wilted many of the shrubs and flowers, and left ugly brown splotches on the lawn.

(Five)
Gold Aviation
Santa Monica

"There is a way out of the predicament you find yourself in, Herman," Tim Campbell was saying over coffee in Gold's office.

It was ten-fifteen. Campbell had arrived at ten o'clock on the dot, had spread out the bank's files on Gold Aviation on Gold's desk, and had quickly reiterated everything he'd said on the telephone last night. Gold had listened patiently, preparing himself for the pitch that he knew was coming.

"Are you okay?" Campbell was asking. "You look tired."

"I had a rough night," Gold replied.

Campbell nodded. "Anyway, getting back to what I was saying, we've got to put this company on a more business-like footing—"

"'We', meaning *you*. Is that it, Campbell?"

"I mean *us*," Campbell firmly repeated. "You know about airplanes. You and your staff have the ideas, but ideas need organization to turn them into reality. I can supply that organization. I can straighten out your books, control your expenditures, and keep track of your billing." He grinned. "I can supply you the firm foundation Gold Aviation needs to reach the heavens."

Gold stifled his own smile. He was starting to like this guy. "Go on, I'm listening."

"The first thing we do is restructure your organization. We set up a holding company for your airplane manufacturing division and air transport line. We could call it Gold Aviation and Transport—"

Gold smiled. "GAT, huh?"

"GAT." Campbell nodded. "I come to work for you as C.E.O. of the company, in charge of the overall financial aspects of the two divisions."

Gold thought about it. He knew that what Campbell had said was true. His ledgers were in a mess; his business had simply gotten too big for his secretary to keep the numbers straight, and he sure as hell wasn't interested in taking on the bookkeeping drudgery. "So far, so good," he told Campbell. "But if I lose my CAM routes there aren't going to be any books to keep . . . What do you suggest I do, to beat out South California Air Transport?"

Campbell was beaming. "Here's the beauty part, Herman. You appoint me in charge of your mail and passenger transport business. That way, you can concentrate on your first love, thinking up and tinkering with new airplane designs, here in Santa Monica. I'll personally manage the Mines Field operation."

"How's that going to solve my problems?" Gold asked skeptically.

"Number one, it gives you a whole new aggressive image. No longer are you on the defensive, reacting to things. Now, you're on the offensive, making bold changes in your company to confront the changes in the status quo. Number two, the local business community and the post office can't argue with the fact that I've got the business background to whip Gold Transport back into financial shape. My being in charge will renew your financial credibility. Finally, I could take over as the public spokesman for Gold Transport during the bidding process. It would be my picture and quotes in the newspapers, not yours. I was born in New England. I'm as Yankee as they come. The fact that I'm in charge will completely neutralize SCAT's personal attacks against you concerning your being a German-Jew."

Gold shook his head. "But it's still my company, Campbell. Everybody will know that you're only a figurehead."

"It's still your company, and I'll be working for you, but I won't be a figurehead," Campbell said seriously. "That much you'll have to accept if you want my help. Remember what I said before. You're putting me in charge of finances. I'll have the authority to approve or disapprove of any financial expenditure. Once that gets around, the business and financial community, and the public in general, will come to accept that I'm for real."

"And if I should *disagree* with your opinions?" Gold asked.

"If at some point you don't accept my advice, I'd be wasting your time, and you'd be paying me a salary I wasn't earning," Campbell replied. "Here's the deal: I'll supply you with my written resignation. You stick that envelope in your desk drawer. The first time you think I'm wrong, or we can't come to a compromise, or you just think you can do better without me than with me..." Campbell shrugged. "Just open that envelope."

Gold leaned back in his chair and regarded Campbell. He seemed earnest enough. "You're starting to impress me. Now answer this: it's no secret I'm broke, and you yourself have said that the name Gold Aviation is currently poison at the banks. How are we going to raise the money we need to survive?"

Campbell frowned. "You're broke all right. For the short-term, we're going to have to get your suppliers to cut you some slack. I think I can do that; get the extended credit we're going to need."

"What about long-term?"

"We take our show on the road, for the long-term," Campbell replied. "Banks are no longer the solution for your financing problems; the private sector is. We're going to take GAT public. You and I are going to be traveling salesmen, peddling stock. The two of us will deliver a one-two punch. You'll get up and paint a bright picture for aviation, then I'll get up and close the deal with a detailed financial outlook on invested returns." Campbell paused. "If we believe in ourselves, we can get others to believe in us."

Gold nodded. "I'm willing to do that, but let me make one thing clear. I want to maintain a controlling interest. This is my company, and I intend for it to stay my company."

"Fair enough," Campbell said. "Let me tell you up front that I intend to use my bank contacts to borrow the money to buy as much GAT stock as as possible."

"I think that's a wise investment." Gold smiled. "Speaking of money, we haven't discussed salary..."

"Right now I'm making five thousand dollars a year at the bank. For the meantime I'll take the same, until I've gotten you out of financial hardship. After that, whenever I feel I've helped you to afford it, you'll give me a raise."

"I see." Gold laughed. "In other words, your salary is just another money worry you're going to take care of for me?"

"There's no sense worrying about tomorrow, today," Campbell reasoned. "I'll never ask you for more than I'm worth. If you should come to think I have, well, you can always use that resignation I'm going to supply you with."

"I see."

"The first thing I can do is telephone around to see how much you can borrow on your house, and cars, and your wife's airplane."

"Is that really going to be necessary?" Gold asked glumly.

Campbell shrugged. "You tell me how important your G-1 development program is. The twenty—maybe twenty-five—thousand you could borrow on your personal assets would be the money that would keep the project going for the time being."

"Then it's necessary, all right." Gold sighed. "Thank God, it's at least possible for me to put my house up . . ."

"What's that mean?" Campbell asked.

Gold told him about the attempted arson. "Thank God I'd fallen asleep downstairs, and not up in the bedroom, or else I would never have heard the guy fiddling around out in the garden."

Campbell nodded. "So that's why you look so exhausted. Hell, I would be, too, after an ordeal like that. Too bad the bastard got away." He scowled. "Well, you'll never see him again."

"Wrong," Gold replied. "I've already seen him again."

"What are you talking about?"

"Yesterday SCAT announced that they'd purchased planes and taken a terminal facility at Clover Field, right here in Santa Monica."

"Right." Campbell nodded. "They announced that during the same conference in which they revealed your past."

"Well, this morning, on my way to work, I drove past their facility," Gold explained. "There was no reason, beyond that I just wanted to see what it looked like. That's where I saw him. That guy who tried to torch my house works for SCAT."

"Jesus," Campbell breathed, shaking his head. "I can't believe they'd do anything that outrageous—"

"I saw the guy with my own eyes, I tell you."

Campbell nodded. "And it makes for a kind of nasty logic. They know you're financially strapped. Burning down your house would certainly have precluded you borrowing against it. Also, the emotional distress of losing your house might have been enough to have made you throw in the towel concerning the bidding competition."

"Fuck the house. I could have died. And what about my wife and kids?" Gold said, and then told Campbell about the filth scrawled on the fence. "Everyone, including myself, assuming I survived, would have assumed that some crazy bigot had done the crime," he finished. "No one would have suspected SCAT was behind it."

"Well, all you can do is forget about it, Herman."

"Forget about it?" Gold repeated. "No way. I'm going back to the SCAT facility tonight to give them a big taste of their own medicine."

"You mean burn them out? That's crazy!" Campbell insisted. "I won't let you do it."

Gold smiled. "Not only will you let me. You're coming along to help."

"What? No way!"

"Tim, listen to me," Gold said very seriously. "It so happens I was the only one home last night, but SCAT couldn't have known that, so they just didn't care. They were willing to risk my life, and the lives of my wife and kids, to get what they wanted."

"Two wrongs don't make a right," Campbell protested.

"Fuck you!" Gold said angrily. "It wasn't your house and family put at risk. You weren't the one insulted, called foul obscenities! I'm telling you now, I'm through being dragged through the gutter. I'm going to fight back. If you want to be my partner, you'll help me. If not, walk out that door. It's up to you. I need to know if I can trust you. This is the way that I'm going to find out."

Campbell weakly shook his head. "I could go to the police and tell them what you're planning . . ."

"You could." Gold nodded. "But I think you're too smart

to do that. You turn me in, it would only be your word against mine. Regardless of that, the bad press your charges would generate would finish me in business, once and for all." Gold smiled. "But *that* would keep you at the bank, making five thousand bucks a year. Come on, Tim, you really expect me to believe that you're the kind of guy who would kill the goose that lays the golden eggs?"

Campbell sighed. "When are you doing this?"

"Tonight."

"What do you want me to do to help?"

"Meet here at ten o'clock," Gold said. "I'll have what we need to do the job."

Campbell nodded. Gold extended his hand across the desk. "Lots of people think Gold Aviation is a sinking ship, but welcome aboard, Tim."

Campbell eyed Gold warily. After a moment he shook hands.

"When can you start?" Gold asked. "How much notice do you have to give the bank?"

Campbell grinned. "I gave them my two weeks' notice two days ago, about an hour after your files reached my desk."

"You're shitting me!" Gold exclaimed. "Come on, did you really?"

"Consider this your first lesson in salesmanship, Herman," Campbell smiled, packing up his briefcase and standing up. "You've got to give yourself appropriate motivation before you deliver your pitch."

Gold watched him walk to the door. "Tim," he called out. "Tell me the truth— Did you really already give the bank your notice without knowing how I was going to respond to your pitch?"

Campbell winked. "Here's the second lesson in salesmanship: Never give anything away."

Once Campbell was gone, Gold buzzed his secretary and asked her to get him Hull Stiles. When Hull was on the line, Gold picked up his telephone and said, "I haven't talked to you since the news about me came out yesterday." He paused. "I don't know how you feel about me now. I don't know if we're still friends . . ."

"Christ almighty!" Hull exploded. "I'm sorry I've neglected you, darling. I'll have a heart-shaped box of chocolates and a dozen red roses sent over soonest. Will that make it okay for my snookums?"

"Fuck you." Gold laughed. "In that case, meet me here in Santa Monica around nine-thirty tonight."

"What's up?"

"I'll tell you when I see you. I need some help doing something about the competition. Something that's going to be kind of rough."

"How rough?" Hull asked.

"Remember Mexico? As rough as that."

"No shit?" Hull replied calmly. "Well, then, I guess I'll see you later."

That night Gold was waiting in his car in the parking field of the Santa Monica facility when he saw a pair of headlights come lancing through the gates. Gold was wearing low-cut oxford work shoes, a pair of those sturdy, dark-blue denim pants held together with metal cleats that were being manufactured in San Francisco, and a brown pullover crew-neck sweater. While he'd been rummaging around in his closet for suitable attire in which to burn down a rival's business, he'd come across that moth-eaten, old, gray flannel fedora he'd used to wear as a kid to keep the sun off his head, back when he was barnstorming. He was wearing the fedora tonight, hoping that it would bring him luck.

He got out of the Stutz as Hull's black Chevrolet sedan pulled up. Hull shut off the engine and got out of his car. He was wearing his old flying clothes: dark moleskin trousers, boots, a faded, plaid flannel shirt and a leather jacket.

Hull listened quietly as Gold told him what had happened last night, and what he wanted to do this evening in order to even the score. When Gold was done, Hull said, "I think we'd better take my car. If someone should see us my Chevy's a hell of a lot less recognizable than that turquoise and scarlet battleship you drive."

"Good idea," Gold said. "I'll get what we'll need out of the trunk."

Another pair of headlights turned into the parking field. "Who would that be?" Hull asked sharply.

"Someone else who will be helping out tonight." Gold told Hull about Campbell as the latter parked his car and came over.

"I guess you haven't changed your mind about this?..." Campbell asked dolefully. He was wearing dark gray, twill work clothes.

Gold shook his head. He introduced the two men to each other, and then went around to the back of the Stutz and opened up the trunk. Inside was the same red and yellow gas can, newly filled, that had been left at his house, and a long, blanket-wrapped bundle.

"Let's stow this stuff in Hull's car," Gold said.

"What's in the blanket?" Campbell asked as he carried the gas can to the black Chevrolet.

Gold laid the bundle in the Chevrolet's trunk and unwrapped it. The moonlight glinted on a pair of shotguns of dark-blue steel, with varnished walnut stocks.

"They're not loaded," Gold said as Hull picked one up. "There's a box of shells for them in the trunk."

"Jesus, guns," Campbell muttered, shaking his head. "This fucking escapade is getting worse by the minute."

"Where'd you get these?" Hull asked Gold.

"I bought them today," Gold said. "You know about these things, I don't. Are they any good?"

Hull worked the action on the gun. "This one sounds smooth enough. They're Marlin, twelve gauge, pump actions. I guess they'll do fine." He shrugged. "Unless they blow up when we fire 'em."

"Let's hope we don't have to fire them," Gold said. "I brought then along just in case."

"Then I'd better show you how to shoot them, just in case," Hull said.

"Show him, not me," Campbell muttered, backing away as Hull thumbed shells into the shotguns. "I hate guns. I *hate* violence."

The short ride to Clover Field passed silently. Gold sat up front, beside Hull, who was behind the wheel. Campbell sat in the back, chain-smoking. Clover was less developed than Los Angeles's Mines Field. There were no lights, and the few buildings bordering the field were spaced far apart. Hull killed his headlights as they slowly drove past the open gates that led to the SCAT facility. The deep, squat hangar was set in about thirty yards from the road, its big, double doors facing out at them. Parked to the rear, along the side of the hangar, was a Reo two-ton truck with canvas sides. Everything looked dark and quiet. There was nothing stirring but the tall weeds bending in the breeze, and no sound except that of the crickets. Hull pulled over once they were past the facility.

"I made some calls this afternoon," Gold said. "They're still overhauling their new planes, so everything they own is inside that hangar."

"What about night watchmen?" Campbell asked nervously.

"They don't have any private security," Gold replied. "They rely on the regular police patrols."

"Oh, shit," Campbell worried from the backseat. "What if the police catch us?"

"What *if*?" Gold replied irritably. "Let's just do it."

Keeping his lights off, Hull put the Chevrolet in gear and made a U-turn, driving back to the SCAT hangar. He drove in through the open gates and then swung around so that the nose of the Chevrolet was pointed out toward the road. He shut off the engine. All three men sat quietly for a moment, listening to the crickets and the tick of the car as it cooled in the night.

"It's funny," Hull said quietly. "I figured we'd have to crowbar a padlock, or something, to get in—"

"Me, too," Gold said. He felt tense, and wondered if he should just forget the whole thing while it wasn't too late; tell Hull to start the car and drive them back to Santa Monica. "Well, maybe we're getting lucky." He opened his car door. "Let's get it done."

Hull got out, opened the trunk, and took out the gas can. Gold grabbed one of the shotguns. He chambered a round and pushed off the safety.

"Could you really shoot somebody if you had to?" Campbell asked softly.

"It isn't going to come to that." Gold scowled, evading

the question that Campbell had asked, and that Gold was asking himself.

"I'll wait here by the car," Campbell pleaded. "You know, keep an eye on things. Watch out for the police."

Gold nodded, suddenly feeling sorry for Campbell. He'd dragged the poor guy here. This wasn't Campbell's fight. Campbell wasn't even an old friend, the way Hull was. This was one hell of an initiation to put a man through before giving him a job. "Okay, Tim," he said, and tried his best to smile reassuringly. "You keep lookout for us."

Gold and Hull walked to the hangar. Gold stood and watched, the shotgun pointed toward the ground, as Hull sloshed gasoline against the side of the building.

"All set," Hull said. "I've got a match here. You want to do the honors, or should I?" He turned toward Gold, and froze. "Oh, shit," he said.

"What's the matter?" Gold began.

"*I'm the matter—*"

Gold turned his head. Behind him, pointing a revolver at him, was the same fat bastard who'd tried to burn down his house the night before.

"I had a feeling you might try to even things up tonight, so I decided to stick around here." The fat man grinned. "By the way, drop the shotgun."

Gold ignored the order. "Who are you? What do you do for SCAT?" he asked, playing for time.

"I was hired to be freight manager, but I let it be known I was willing to do other sorts of work, and my employers took me up on it."

"You mean arson." Gold nodded.

"There's the pot calling the kettle black." The man laughed. "You've got nothing on me to prove what happened last night, and just look at what *I've* got . . . I've caught you red-handed, haven't I, Mister Gold? All I need do is wait for the cops to come rolling by, then turn you and your friend over to them, and wait for the reporters to come around."

He said "friend," not "friends," Gold thought. Did that mean he didn't know about Campbell? Gold resisted the urge to glance toward the car.

"It seems like I'm going to be a hero," the fat man was

saying. "And you'll be behind bars." He extended the revolver toward Gold. "Or you'll be dead, if you don't drop that shotgun. Capturing an arsonist alive, or killing one in self-defense," he shrugged philosophically, "it makes no difference to me . . ."

Where the fuck was Campbell? Had he run off to save himself?

"I'm not going to say it again," the fat man sneered. "Drop it, Jewboy—"

Fuck you, Gold thought, swinging around the shotgun and firing it one-handed in the general direction of the fat man, who was darting sideways. The shotgun made a dull, flat report, and kicked hard in Gold's hand, hurting his wrist.

Gold realized he'd missed. The fat man was raising up his pistol when Campbell appeared with the other shotgun. The fat man saw him. His revolver wavered, and began to dip toward the ground. "I give up," the man said. He dropped his revolver.

"Herman, we can't leave him to identify us," Hull said.

"I know that," Gold said. He chambered a fresh round into the shotgun.

"Jesus, don't!" The fat man turned and ran, heading toward the truck parked alongside the hangar.

Gold followed after the fat man, who had reached the Reo and was swinging up into its high cab. He noticed Campbell standing off to one side, his shotgun held loosely in the crook of his arm.

"What are you intending?" Campbell asked, looking frightened.

Gold ignored the question. Behind him, Hull was scooping up the fallen revolver. In front of him, the fat man was grinding the truck's starter. The engine caught. The Reo's headlights flashed on. The glare almost blinded Gold. The truck began to roll forward. It was about ten yards away when Gold braced the shotgun against his hip and fired. One headlight winked out in a tinkle of shattered glass. The truck kept on coming, gears clashing as it picked up speed. Gold worked the pump action on the shotgun and fired again. This time he must have hit one of the front tires. The truck suddenly veered left, smashing into the hangar. It stalled out with its front half buried within the splintered wall. Gold hurried toward the wreck, his shotgun ready. When he reached the truck he saw flames coming up from the Reo's hood, sending sparks spiraling into the night sky. He saw no movement within the cab. A second later, the flames flared up as the truck's canvas sides abruptly ignited. The Reo was now curtained from view by a wall of fire.

Gold backed up to where Hull was standing. "You think the guy's still alive?" Hull asked.

Gold, watching the flames, shook his head. In the distance he could hear sirens wailing; they were still faint, but growing louder.

Hull gripped Gold's shoulder. "Let's get out of here while we still can."

They moved quickly, throwing the gas can into the flames and dumping the shotguns and the revolver into the trunk of the Chevrolet. Hull threw several small objects into the trunk, as well. "The three shell casings you fired," he explained.

Gold nodded dumbly. They climbed into the car. Hull started the engine, spun his rear wheels jackrabbiting through the gate, and then swung around in a wrenching turn, down the road the way they'd come. They'd gone maybe a quarter mile when they heard a blast and saw a fireball rise into the night sky behind them.

"Lots of flammables in your average airplane hangar," Hull said conversationally. "Won't be much left of that truck, or the fellow in it."

"Are we clear of it?" Campbell asked frantically. "Think we'll get caught?"

A police car and several fire engines, sirens wailing, passed them racing in the opposite direction, toward the fire.

Hull shook his head. "Assuming anybody heard those shots, which I doubt, they'll be written off as car backfires. The rest of it turned out terrific, considering. It looks like our friend the fat man—"

"I never even knew his name," Gold muttered.

"Who cares?" Hull demanded. "He's dead now. Anyway, what I was saying is that the authorities will figure he started up the truck, lost control, plowed into the hangar and caused the fire. Nice and simple."

"Except that I killed someone," Gold said.

"Tough shit!" Hull snapped. "You're the one who wanted to do this, right? Once we were into it, you had no choice but to kill him! If you'd left him alive it would have been the end of us! Now it's done! It's too late to regret any of it! And you're damned lucky it came out the way it did!"

Gold nodded. He twisted around toward the backseat. "Tim, I want to thank you. You appearing when you did stopped him from firing back at me. You probably saved my life."

"I'm sorry I took as long as I did," Campbell said sheepishly. "I told you before, I'm not used to guns, and . . ." He hesitated. "What can I say? I was scared shitless. I almost couldn't move at all. I felt like my feet were rooted to the ground . . ."

"Well, you found your balls when you had to," Hull said. "Welcome to Gold Aviation—"

"Gold Aviation and Transport," Campbell mildly corrected him. "But thanks for the welcome. Let's hope things calm down from here on in."

"You said it," Hull muttered. He glanced at Gold. "Why so quiet, Herman?"

Gold, staring out the windshield, shrugged. "I was just wondering . . . Whatever happened to that kid?" He turned in his seat to look at at Hull. "The one who used to go out of his way to shoot down enemy planes without harming their pilots?"

"Isn't that funny?" Hull replied, his eyes on the road, his face hidden by shadow. "I was wondering the same."

Hull dropped Gold and Campbell off at their cars. Gold felt quiet and composed as he took his time driving home. He also felt vibrantly alive, and acutely aware of his surroundings. Everything—the cool night air against his face, the sound of the tires on the asphalt, the smell of the Stutz's leather upholstery, the feel of its varnished wooden steering wheel—was making its impression on him. He realized that what he was experiencing now was the same sort of feelings he'd had years ago, after flying a combat mission. There was nothing like being close to death to make you acutely aware and thankful that you were alive.

As he pulled into his driveway he noticed that the lights were on in the house. He'd stopped home earlier in the evening, to change his clothes. He must have turned the lights on then, and forgotten to shut them off.

He parked the Stutz, went inside the house, and knew instantly that Erica and the kids had returned. It was quiet inside. There was nothing to give it away—no coats or suitcases lying about—but as soon as he stepped into the front hall he knew that his family was back.

"Hello, Herman."

He turned. Erica was standing in the living room. She was wearing a green wool dress. It had a knee-length pleated skirt, a high collar, and long sleeves. She had on blonde stockings and dark-green leather pumps. She couldn't have been home very long, Gold thought. She still had on her jewelry. She was wearing gold hoop earrings, a gold wristwatch with an alligator strap, a gold-link bracelet, a gold and emerald clip on her dress, and the diamond engagement ring he'd given her on their third anniversary to go with her wedding band.

"Look at you," she said fondly. "You're wearing that old hat you used to wear. You look the way you did back in Doreen, when you used to come calling for me on that motorcycle Teddy lent you . . ."

Gold nodded. "Maybe that's not such a bad way for me to look, right now. Like, I was coming courting, I mean . . ."

She smiled at that. He realized that he was grinning like an idiot. He walked slowly into the living room, coming close to her, but not too close. He felt awkward. Like they really had just met. He wanted to embrace her, but didn't know if he should. He felt as if he needed permission to do something he'd done countless times in the past. It was strange to feel so uncomfortable in his wife's presence, but it was also arousing.

"So, you're back," he heard himself say.

"Yes." She laughed. "The kids are asleep, upstairs."

Gold nodded. The silence was awkward.

"I noticed you had the fence painted while we were gone," Erica said.

Gold shrugged. "I'll tell you about it later. I'm glad you're back," he abruptly blurted. "Thank you for coming back—"

She nodded, then she blushed. "When I saw the newspapers saying such awful things about you, I felt I had to come back, before the papers found out that I'd left. I thought that my place was beside you at a time like this."

"That's right. You belong beside me, and I belong beside you." Gold gazed at her. "I'd like to hold you," he murmured.

"Nothing's stopping you," Erica said quietly, looking away.

He went to her, enfolding her in his arms, burying his face in her hair. She leaned against him. He began to shudder. He couldn't catch his breath. He realized that he was crying. Erica held him tight.

"I'm sorry you found out about me the way you did," he managed. "I should have told you. Honest to God, I know that I should have, but I was afraid that you would be ashamed of me."

"No," Erica said. "You're my husband and I love you. The only one who's ever been ashamed of you is *you*."

"But then why did you leave?" Gold asked.

"I was angry that you lied to me," Erica replied. "I felt humiliated that I had to learn the truth from the radio. Do you understand? That affront, coming on top of our other difficulties . . . I was so hurt."

Gold gently moved her at arm's length to look into her eyes. "Is that true, Erica? Is that really true?"

"I don't care what religion you were born into. Oh, maybe it would have been important if you'd told me while we were courting," she admitted. "It certainly would have given me pause. After all, I was just a young girl who knew very little about the world." She smiled. "It's not like there were any Jews in Doreen . . ."

"If that's the case, then I'm glad I didn't tell you," Gold said.

She laughed lightly. "I'm glad, as well. I might have missed out on being the wife of a wonderful man."

"I'm sorry," Gold began. "I'm so sorry—"

Erica pressed her fingers to his lips. "I know," she said. "But it's all over now. Unless you have something *else* to tell me. You *don't*, do you?" Erica pretended to scold.

Gold sighed. "Only that we're broke. We could lose everything, including the house, the cars, probably even your jewelry..."

Erica shrugged serenely. She tugged off her earrings and dropped them to the carpet. "There's jewelry and there's jewelry." She removed her bracelet, watch, rings and let them fall; everything but her modest, unadorned wedding band. "The best jewels you ever gave me nobody can take away. I'd trade everything in my jewel box for that nighttime ride we took in that old Jenny. All the jewelry in the world isn't worth that view of the lights of the city, and what you said to me that night when you showed me those lights..."

"I love you very much," Gold whispered. He put his arms around her and kissed her. "It's going to be different between us from now on."

Erica pulled away. "Don't tell me that." She took his hand, to lead him up the stairs. "*Show* me."

Chapter 11

Gold Transport
Mines Field, Los Angeles
25 October 1926

Gold stood in the quiet hangar, appreciating the beauty of the G-1 Yellowjacket. Three weeks ago the prototype airplane had been completed in Santa Monica, and then transported by trailer truck to Mines Field, where she was stored in a specially built hangar. The hangar was guarded by uniformed private security guards. Gold had decreed that only a few people had access clearance. He could be alone with his creation as much as he liked.

There were only a couple of the hangar ceiling floodlights on, creating a dim, shadowy, almost cathedral-like atmosphere. The dramatic shafts of light burnished the smooth curves of the G-1's silver skin, turning her into sculpture; if the Yellowjacket was poetry in motion, she was, in response, the artistic evocation of flight.

The monoplane had a steel tube frame, covered over with a duralumin skin. The only other all-metal aircraft design was the Ford Tri-Motor, but Ford's "Tin Goose" was a much larger, more expensive airplane. The G-1 was twenty-five feet long, with a forty-foot wingspan. Her heart was a 450-horsepower, air cooled, radial engine, the Yellowjacket AAA, developed exclusively for the project by the San Diego firm of Rogers and Simpson. In designing the G-1, Gold and Teddy Quinn and his staff had gleaned the best from Spatz, Fokker, Lockheed, Boeing, and the other aircraft builders, and then incorporated their own innovations. They'd also taken into account the design suggestions of their veteran pilots, many of whom had been flying the mail in all kinds of airplanes for close to a decade.

The G-1 had a variable rate propeller and hydraulic wheel brakes. Her open, single-seat cockpit was set well back. Her wing, which incorporated Gold's "C-Gull" brake flaps, was raised up on stilts to afford the pilot a better forward view and further increased aerodynamic efficiency. A duralumin "speed cowling" for the engine and matching "speed pants" on the fixed landing gear streamlined the G-1, cutting down on air resistance and in the process giving the airplane an aggressive, bird-of-prey appearance.

Gold had dispensed with his usual paint scheme for the G-1: she was pure silver all over, except on her vertical tail fin, which had two slender, diagonal slashes of turquoise and scarlet, and a small rendition of his signature centaur against its oval yellow field.

Gold knew the G-1 Yellowjacket was beautiful, but more important, he knew that she was stable and forgiving in flight; that she had an admirable cruising speed of one hundred and sixty-two miles per hour; and could take off and land, fully loaded, on a dime—and leave a nickle's worth of change.

He knew all that because he'd personally test-flown her every day for the last three weeks. Next week, right here at Mines Field, the G-1 would strut her stuff for the purchasing agents of the United States Postal Office, which was looking for something new to add to its aging fleet. The future of Gold Aviation hinged on the postal service's decision. As Gold had told Teddy and the other designers fourteen months ago, *"We either grab the brass ring this time around, or the merry-go-round ride will be over . . ."*

Back in August, the fire that destroyed South California Air Transport's Clover Field facility was front-page news, distracting the media's attention away from Gold Aviation's troubles. It turned out that the SCAT employee who'd died in that fire had a lengthy criminal record and had been wanted in New Jersey on a rape charge. That was all Tim Campbell needed to go on the offensive, holding press conferences in which he charged that any organization that would hire such a man was "morally unfit" to fly the mail.

According to the plan, Gold let the undeniably American Campbell do all of the talking for Gold Aviation. Gold also hired an attorney who specialized in such matters to help him through the naturalization process to become a United States citizen.

As the date for the postal service's awarding of the CAM routes moved closer, the situation began to turn in Gold's favor. Partly this was due to Campbell's efforts, and partly because a coalition of important Hollywood Jewish movie executives and Los Angeles Christian religious leaders publicly denounced the news media for allowing coverage of the bidding competition to devolve into an "open season on Jews." What really tilted things Gold's way was his announcing a cut-to-the-bone, low-ball rate for private freight transport. The business community was thrilled. Gold Aviation was practically offering to pay them for the privilege of carrying their freight. Pressure began to be applied to the investment group that was underwriting SCAT.

On September 14, 1925, just hours before the route assignments were to be announced by the postal service,

SCAT's backers pulled their financial support. SCAT was forced to withdraw its bid, vanishing like a bad dream. Gold Aviation retained its CAM routes. The same newspapers that had vilified Gold now called him a winner.

At the time, Gold didn't feel much like a winner. The low-ball private rate he'd been forced to offer his customers meant that his routes were now just barely breaking even. His creditors were complaining, and he had a payroll to meet.

Gold believed the solution to his financial problems was the G-1. He believed that there was a fortune to be made in America selling planes as well as commercially flying them, but the G-1 was still just a gleam in his and Teddy Quinn's eyes. Campbell had managed to get twenty thousand dollars for the project by locking up as collateral all of Gold's personal assets, but Gold knew that amount would barely carry the project past the drawing boards.

In October of 1925, Gold and Campbell began peddling stock in the newly named Gold Aviation and Transport Corporation. They began with GAT's employees, announcing that anyone who wanted to stay on would have to take one half of their salary in stock. Teddy Quinn convinced the Santa Monica contingent. Over at the Mines Field facility the pilots and mechanics balked, threatening to walk out, until Hull Stiles talked them into going along.

With his payroll burden slashed, Gold was able to keep up payments on his various loans, thereby holding on to his business and his home. He'd bought himself some breathing room, but it was only temporary. The true test lay ahead. It was time to take their stock-peddling act on the road.

Gold and Campbell traveled up and down the West Coast, and as far east as Salt Lake City. It was territory that had been served for years by Gold Aviation, and before that by Gold Express, so the name Herman Gold was well known. No town was too small for them. Gold and Campbell spoke at church suppers and chamber of commerce meetings; they placed ads in local newspapers in advance of their arrival, and then sat around in rented hotel suites, waiting for potential investors to wander in.

For almost three months Gold worked harder than he ever had in his life, and Campbell sure as hell did his part. They were fortunate that the American economy was booming and that folks were anxious to make a financial killing by investing in business. By New Year's Day 1926, Gold and Campbell had managed to sell $122,000 worth of stock. Gold kept a thirty-five-percent controlling interest. Campbell used his bank contacts to borrow the money to buy three percent.

The cash infusion allowed Gold to get the G-1 prototype built and keep his business afloat, but now the money he and Campbell had raised was almost gone. GAT was a trembling house of cards, stuck together with jury-rigged financing, precariously perched on the sleek, slippery back of the G-1 Yellowjacket. If, next week, the post office turned thumbs down on Gold's creation, everything would come tumbling down—

The hangar's sliding door rattled, then slid open, startling Gold out of his reveries. He squinted his eyes against the bright daylight spilling into the hangar's dark interior.

"Herman! You promised you'd be ready to go!" Erica scolded. She was silhouetted by the light as she stepped into the hangar.

Gold glanced at his wristwatch. "Damn! I totally lost track of the time!" In less than an hour his four-year-old daughter was graduating from kindergarten. All the parents had been invited to the ceremony. Susan was going to sing a song—

He looked down at himself. He was wearing old clothes: chino trousers, a light blue cotton sweater, tan oxfords, and a camel-hair, belted polo coat. The suit and shirt and tie he intended to wear to the recital were hanging in Hull Stiles's office. Considering the time it would take to change, and then drive to the school, they were going to be late—

Erica was laughing. "You should see your face. Stop worrying!"

"But Susan's recital—"

"Isn't for another *two* hours." Erica grinned, coming over to him. "I knew you'd pull a stunt like this, so I purposely told you the recital was an hour earlier."

Gold relaxed, smiling. "I guess you know me pretty well."

She was wearing a slimly tailored, gray silk tweed suit, gray silk stockings, and black pumps. Her earrings were silver and black onyx. She wore a black felt cloche hat with a gray grosgrain ribbon and carried a black leather envelope bag. She looked fabulous. Like an elegant flapper. Like the million bucks he very soon hoped to have.

She came over to give him a kiss. She smelled familiarly of lavender and roses, and fragrances which Gold could never identify, but which nevertheless never failed to stir him. He put his arm around her, feeling that jolt he always felt when he touched her. Even when things had been bad between them, the electricity had always been there.

"I ran into Hull Stiles at the main hangar," Erica said. "He told me you've been spending lots of time in here. I almost didn't come in, it seemed so dark. What do you do in here, all by yourself?"

Gold leered. "I'll never tell."

"Then I'm sorry I asked," Erica said, smiling. "Seriously, the purchasing agents will be here to evaluate the G-1 next week. There's nothing left for you to do."

"I know." He shrugged shyly. "I guess I just like to look at her. She's not just an airplane, she's *my* airplane. The first ever to carry my name. She wouldn't exist if it weren't for GAT. Can you understand?"

Erica nodded, slipping her arm around his waist. "Hull did confide to me that he thinks you've been unduly worried about how the post office is going to react to the G-1 . . ."

"'Unduly worried', is it?" Gold frowned. "That's Hull's opinion, but he doesn't have quite as much invested in this baby as I do."

"Actually, Hull and the others who work for you have quite a lot invested," Erica said evenly.

Gold nodded. "You're right, of course," he sighed. "I know I never would have gotten this far if everyone hadn't accepted stock certificates in lieu of cash for their salaries."

"Hmm." Erica nuzzled his cheek. "I think I like it when you're humble."

"Yes, I do owe so much to so many." Gold slid his palm over the taut, silky fabric stretched across the curve of her bottom. "I shall never forget that I'm not all alone in this. I want to thank all the little people who've—"

Erica laughed. "Not *that* humble, darling." She gently took his hand from her rump. "And no handprints on the merchandise, at least not until this evening. Speaking of little people, we *do* have a kindergarten recital to go to, remember?"

Gold nodded. "I shall restrain myself."

"That's better."

"But I don't know how I'll manage it—"

"That's better still." She patted his fly.

Gold laughed. "Come on. I'll change my clothes in Hull's office, and we'll be on our way."

Erica held on to his arm. "Before we go, darling, do tell me why you think the post office might not buy the G-1?" Her large brown eyes searched his. "Hull says that it's a dream to fly and does everything it's supposed to do. Why would the government *ever* turn it down?"

"There's no question in my mind that it's a successful design," Gold began. "One that totally fulfills what we set out to achieve . . ."

"Then what's the problem?"

Gold frowned. "She doesn't look like any other airplane, inside or out. *That's* the problem. I believe that the G-1 is a superior design, but the men who buy airplanes for the government are cautious and conservative. I just hope that the G-1's more flashy innovations don't blind them to her other qualities."

Erica looked thoughtful. "What you need is something to capture public opinion."

"Huh?"

"You know, like when you were fighting for your CAM routes? Something to rally the public to your side. So that the postal service can't possibly refuse you."

"You have any ideas, I'm ready to listen."

"Well, I don't," Erica admitted. "I just know that what we need is something to capture the headlines. Really put the government on the spot . . ."

"The old razzle-dazzle," Gold mused. "Too bad Captain Bob isn't around."

"That fellow with the megaphone you used to fly for when you were barnstorming?" Erica smiled. "God, I haven't thought of him in years. What made you bring him up?"

"He was a master of publicity," Gold said. "He knew just

how to stage an event to capture the public's imagination . . ." He stopped abruptly, gazing at Erica.

"What?" She smiled tentatively. "You have an idea?"

Gold nodded, grinning. "Captain Bob just whispered it into my ear. I know exactly how to prove to the world just how superior the G-1 is to anything else in the air."

(Two)
Gold Aviation
Santa Monica
2 November 1926

Gold was in his office, perched on his high stool, working at his drafting table, when Tim Campbell came in. Campbell was in his shirt-sleeves. His collar was unbuttoned and his tie was loose. As usual, he had a cigarette tucked into the corner of his mouth.

Gold set down his compass. He arched his back, stretching his arms above his head. He was wearing the green, shawl-necked cardigan that he kept in the office to ward off chills. Erica and the kids had given it to him last Christmas. He liked to wear it when he was working on design problems. The sweater made him feel secure and relaxed. Helped him be creative. "Well?" he asked.

"Well, yourself," Campbell grumbled wearily. "What are you working on?"

"Come see. It's the design for something new."

"*Another* plane?" Campbell laughed. "Optimistic bugger, ain't we?"

"It's a variation on the G-1; a closed cockpit, six-passenger transport version that Teddy and I are thinking about. We're tentatively calling it the G-1a Dragonfly."

"Nice, I guess," Campbell said. "You know I can't make heads or tails out of those scribbles you engineering types call designs."

He moved away from the drafting table to slump into the swivel chair behind Gold's desk, the only other chair in the office. "I feel like I've got a telephone growing out of my ear. I've been at it all morning, calling every newspaper and radio station in town."

"And?"

"And about half promised me they'll be there tomorrow, at Mines Field, at noon, to witness the G-1's test flight. The rest said maybe they'd come."

"Good work." Gold smiled.

"You sure as hell didn't make it any easier for me," Campbell griped, squinting through the smoke curling up from his cigarette. "I had to do some pretty fancy talking to convince those newshounds to come around to watch a routine test flight, without being specific. Why couldn't I tell them what was going to happen?"

"Because then I would have had to tell *you* what was going to happen." Gold chuckled.

Campbell scowled. "And don't you think your C.E.O. ought to know?"

"If I told you, I'd be honor-bound to tell Teddy, and what about Hull?" Gold explained. "You all probably would have tried to talk me out of it."

"It's that bad, huh?" Campbell asked bleakly.

"Let me put it this way: if the postal service got hold of it, they'd probably cancel the test flight."

"Oh, God," Campbell moaned. "My ulcers."

"You don't have ulcers."

"I know, but I'm practicing. Working for you, I'm sure to develop some. *Please* tell me what you're planning?—"

"Razzle-dazzle is what I'm planning. You want to know anything more than that, you'll have to wait for tomorrow, along with the rest of the world. Believe me, those reporters who *do* come will be very grateful to you for tipping them off."

"I hope so," Campbell said irritably. "I had to use up a lot of favors on this one. Does Erica at least know what you've got planned?"

Gold winked. "Ask me no questions and I'll tell you no lies."

Campbell stood up. "Cute, real cute. You need me for anything else, I'll be in my office . . . Updating my resume."

(Three)
Gold Transport
Mines Field
3 November 1926

Gold got to the field at seven o'clock in the morning. Teddy Quinn was already there, haranguing the mechanics who were attired in freshly laundered turquoise overalls and scarlet caps. Teddy was wearing his "don't bother me" expression. Gold knew his old friend well enough to know that Teddy needed to stay busy in order to remain calm. He stayed out of his chief engineer's way as Teddy supervised the fueling, and the last-minute maintenance on the G-1, fretting like a mother hen as she was wheeled out of her hangar onto the airstrip, where she gleamed in the sun like a silver bird.

There was nothing for Gold to do but wait for events to unfold. He studied the cloudless sky, and the wind socks gently undulating in the breeze. It had been unusually warm for the past week. Today the weather report predicted a high of eighty degrees, with low humidity: perfect flying conditions.

About eleven-thirty a black Ford sedan turned into the gates and parked. Out of it stepped the trio of postal service purchasing agents who would pass judgment on the G-1. At quarter of twelve, the newspeople began to trickle in. Teddy Quinn, his snap-brim fedora pulled down low over his brow to hide his face, began flitting around the edges of the crowd, chain-smoking and muttering darkly to himself. Sometimes Teddy liked to act a little touched in the head; it kept people at bay.

Gold had arranged for a sun-shield awning to be erected on the grass bordering the airstrip. Campbell, dressed like the banker he used to be, was under the awning now, chatting with the Feds, who were wearing wide-brimmed hats and somber-colored suits. Campbell was good at making small talk. Gold left him to it until the last possible moment, and then he went over to greet the postal service representatives. Gold was wearing an uncharacteristically conservative, navy blue chalk-stripe double-breasted suit, a plain white shirt, and a dull, crimson and black striped tie. As he stepped beneath the awning, joining all the other serious-looking men in their dark suits, he felt as if he were at a funeral. He hoped he was mistaken.

Morton Brenner, the senior purchasing agent for the post office, was fanning himself with his hat, and frowning. "Mister Gold," he began. "I don't appreciate having all of these reporters and photographers around."

Brenner was in his sixties. He was medium height, and built portly. His thinning gray hair was cut short, waxed, brushed back, and somewhat parted on the side. He had a florid complexion, a neatly clipped white moustache, and hard, hazel eyes behind a gold-framed pince-nez. His jowls, spilling over his shirt collar, were shaved as smooth as a baby's bottom. Gold couldn't begin to imagine how a man could shave that closely—

"I must confess, if I'd known these reporters were going to be here, I would have postponed today's evaluation," Brenner was saying.

"Well, sir, I do apologize," Gold replied mildly. "But it is a free country, sir. If the media wishes to witness the test flight, I don't see how I could possibly forbid them . . ."

"Yes, well—" Brenner noisily cleared his throat. He removed his pince-nez and massaged the two angry red spots it had left on the bridge of his nose. "Just so you're aware that the reporters' presence does not help your cause. As a matter of fact, on the contrary . . ."

We'll see about that, you old goat, Gold thought. Tim Campbell was standing just behind Brenner, and had been eavesdropping as the senior government man was sounding off. Gold saw Campbell wince and roll his eyes.

"Mister Gold," Brenner said. "Your airplane is a very unusual design."

"Thank you."

"We at the post office don't like that," Brenner flatly declared. "We appreciate that which has withstood the test of time."

"The most venerable of designs have had to start somewhere," Gold replied. "All I ask is that you withhold judgment until after you see the G-1 fly."

"Well, let's get on with it." Brenner took a pocket watch from his waistcoat and studied it. "Our schedule is tight. We're due at Turner Aircraft Works in precisely ninety minutes." He smiled thinly at Gold. "Turner builds a fine airplane, don't you think? And has been building them the same way, *for years . . .*"

The sound of the G-1's engine turning over saved Gold from having to think up a reply. Everyone turned toward the airplane as the Rogers and Simpson radial caught, then settled down into a fluid growl.

The mechanic who'd started up the G-1 climbed down from the cockpit as the pilot, covered from head to toe in a leather helmet, goggles, white silk scarf, gloves, bulky shearling flight overalls and boots, appeared in the doorway of the hangar. The pilot waved toward the awning, but went directly to the airplane.

"My God, it's got to be close to eighty out here," Brenner remarked, watching as the pilot climbed up into the cockpit. "How cold does it get, flying?"

"You'd be amazed," Gold replied cheerfully. He sensed Campbell coming up behind him. "I thought Hull was going to do the flying?" Campbell whispered. "Whoever that is looks kind of short to be Hull—"

"Just keep your fingers crossed," Gold murmured.

"You don't need to tell me that," Campbell said. "Hey, where's Erica? I can't believe she'd miss this—"

Gold sighed worriedly. "She's around."

"Just remember, she'll give you plenty of notice before she stalls—"

Hull's voice echoed in the empty hangar as he watched Erica step into the flight overalls. "And just remember, be ready on the rudder pedals when you use the C-Gull flaps—"

"I'll remember, I hope," Erica muttered as she shrugged the supple, shearling suit up over her wool trousers and long-sleeved cotton blouse. "Help me zip this thing up."

"You know, it's still not too late to back out," Hull fretted.

"I know." Erica pulled on her boots and then tucked her hair into the close-fitting leather helmet, buckling it under her chin.

"I could take over for you," Hull said.

"Uh-huh." She adjusted her goggles and then wrapped a white silk scarf around her mouth and chin. "Well, how do I look?" she asked, her voice muffled.

"Like a short pilot," Hull said.

"But not like a woman?" Erica persisted as she put on her gloves.

"Nah." Hull shook his head. "The suit hides you fine. I'm sure Herman will think you're giving yourself away, because he knows it's you, but the others have no reason to suspect anything, so they won't. Just go right to the plane. At the distance the others are standing, they won't notice a thing."

Erica nodded. Both she and Hull were quiet as they listened to the sound of the G-1's engine starting up. "Well," she laughed uneasily, "I guess it's show-time."

"Erica—"

"Hull, if you tell me one more time that I don't have to go through with this, I'll scream."

"It's just that you've only had two chances to practice handling the G-1 since Herman came up with this hare-brained scheme."

"She flies like a dream," Erica said firmly. "The mechanics have checked her out, and today's flying conditions are perfect. There's no reason I can't do this. And I *want* to do it. Not only for Herman, but also for myself, and all the other women pilots struggling to take their places in aviation. In just a few moments I'm going to make history as the world's first woman test pilot."

Hull shrugged. "Just remember, watch your throttle when you—"

"No," Erica cut him off. "No more reminders. I know you mean well, Hull, but what *you* have to remember is that I'm a pilot, and the G-1's an airplane. If we can't fit together, then there's something wrong with both of us."

Hull nodded, grinning. "Then get your tail out there and fly her."

Erica walked out of the hangar. As she crossed the thirty feet of tarmac to where the G-1 stood, its prop spinning, she glanced nervously at the huddle of spectators under the distant awning. She felt as if everybody in the world were watching her. She felt as if she were on her way to a firing squad. At any moment she was going to hear outraged shouts. The men from the government would pull strings to have her pilot's license taken away. God only knew what they would do to poor Herman . . .

Nothing happened. Nobody said a word. She guessed that it really was exactly as Hull had suggested: nobody suspected anything, so nobody was going to notice that he was a *she*. If they were going to look at anything, it was the airplane. Growing more cocky by the instant, she offered those beneath the awning a jaunty wave.

The mechanics had been briefed about the "last minute" change in pilots and were ordered to show no surprise. They stood back, grinning, as she hoisted herself up into the cockpit and strapped herself down. She settled her toes on the brake pedals and her heels on the rudder pedals, just below the brakes. She took hold of the stick and opened up the throttle, heeling and toeing the double-tiered pedals to gracefully move the G-1 off the line. She felt as if she needed three hands and an extra brain to coordinate all the traditional controls, along with the brakes and the C-Gull flaps, but she managed it, showing off the G-1's capabilities by smoothly becoming airborne after using up less than one hundred feet of airstrip. As soon as her wheels left the earth, Erica hauled up the G-1's nose, climbing at the rate of three thousand feet per minute. She leveled off at seven thousand, then snap-rolled the G-1 to the right, going into a tumbling spin, just to get the old heart pumping. At two thousand feet she came out of it, in a wide, banking turn that took her over the awning. She waggled her wings in salute and then began climbing, feeling properly warmed up and ready to do some flying. At 5000 feet she began a series of darts and loops, transforming the G-1 Yellowjacket into a silver needle, laughing to herself, knowing that she was darning her presence in history as she darned the deep blue fabric of the sky.

Gold watched excitedly as Erica put the G-1 through its paces. From the moment she'd gracefully recovered from that first spin he'd known that she was going to be all right.

He listened to the gasps and murmured exclamations from

the reporters as the G-1 streaked through its ten-minute aerobatic display. He glanced at Brenner and his subordinates: the two junior men were smiling, but Brenner himself wore the sour expression of a man suffering from a bad case of indigestion.

Gold heard Campbell murmur, "Whoever that pilot is, he sure as hell knows how to fly."

Gold chuckled. "Remember what you just said a few minutes from now."

Erica was bringing the G-1 around for a landing. The mechanics were planting two white flags into the grass bordering the airstrip. "The G-1 will touch down at the first flag, and come to a stop by the time she reaches the second," Gold loudly announced. "Two technical innovations—her hydraulic wheel braking system and her exclusive C-Gull wing flaps—combine to make this short landing distance possible."

Gold overheard Brenner murmur to his associates, "I say it can't be done—"

Just watch, asshole, Gold thought. Nevertheless, he kept his fingers crossed as Erica came in for her final approach. Fully utilizing the G-1's potential wasn't difficult for an experienced pilot once he'd gotten the hang of it, but Erica had only a couple of chances to practice. He also hoped that Erica had remembered to cinch her safety harness tight. When the G-1 came in for a landing she dug in her claws, and could flip an unwary pilot out of the cockpit like a bucking bronco throwing a rider. . . .

Gold watched nervously as Erica stalled the airplane, flaps extended. The wheels touched down, tires squealing and smoking and leaving rubber patches on the tarmac as Erica stood on the brakes. The G-1 trembled and shuddered like a living creature as the airplane hugged the earth.

"She did it!" Gold shouted as the G-1 jerked to a stop with her nose at least a half foot inside the second flag.

The reporters—and Brenner's two associates—burst into spontaneous applause as the G-1's engine cut off, and her twirling prop slowly came to a halt. Teddy Quinn and Tim Campbell, arms linked, were dancing a jig, hooting and laughing.

Gold slapped Brenner on the back. "What do you think of my airplane now?" he elatedly demanded.

Brenner's smooth jowls had turned bright red. His eyes were fiery. "Quite a remarkable demonstration, Mister Gold," Brenner said, his voice shaking, "but one I must totally discount in my evaluation."

"What?" Gold angrily shouted. "What do you mean?"

"Easy, Herman," Campbell coaxed as he placed a restraining hand on Gold's shoulder.

"Easy, nothing!" Gold roared, aware that his emotional display had captured the attention of the reporters. "How *dare* you say you must discount this demonstration? What you really mean to say is that you just can't take the fact that you've been shown up!" Gold glanced over his shoulder. Erica, still in her flying gear, had climbed out of the airplane and was now approaching.

"It's quite simple, Mister Gold." Brenner smiled coldly. "I say that you've rigged this demonstration by placing a highly skilled stunt pilot in the cockpit! Answer me this: could the average postal service pilot get your newfangled G-1 to perform so well?"

Erica was at Gold's side. She shucked off her gloves. She was wearing bright red nail polish. A couple of reporters in the first row, noticing the polish, realized what was up and began to laugh. Erica unwound her scarf, removed her goggles and helmet, and shook out her bobbed curls. Grinning in triumph, she saluted the astounded reporters.

"What do you say now, Brenner?" one of the reporters called out.

"Are you claiming that the average postal service aviator can't pilot an airplane *as well as a woman*?" another reporter challenged.

Flashbulbs, rattling and flickering like a volley of small-arms fire, lit up the interior of the awning. Reporters' voices clashed in an unintelligible roar of questions.

Brenner had gone white. "I—I have no comment . . ." he sputtered weakly, hands flapping against the barrage of reporters' queries. He stared at Erica, then at the G-1 murderously at Gold, then back at Erica again. "No comment at all."

Gold moved close to Brenner. "There's only one way to get yourself out of this," Gold murmured. "You can do it now, and be a hero, or do it later, under orders from your superiors, and be the laughingstock . . ."

Gold stepped back as one of the junior purchasing agents nudged Brenner in the ribs, and whispered something in the senior buyer's ear. Brenner looked glum. He reluctantly nodded and then turned to the reporters. "No comment," he loudly began, "except to say that it seems the United States postal service has found its new airplane . . ."

(Four)
Gold Aviation
Santa Monica
22 May 1927

Gold leaned over Campbell's desk to study the cardboard pasteup of the full-page newspaper ad. Campbell sat quietly behind his desk as Gold read the copy.

Campbell's small office was down the corridor from Gold's. Campbell had a mahogany desk with a leather-inlaid top and a large, royal blue and rose oriental carpet on the wooden floor. Otherwise his office was as unfinished as Gold's was.

Gold looked up, frowning slightly. Most of the ad was an intricate illustration of a busy airfield terminal scene. In the foreground was Erica, dressed in pilot's gear. The ad's headline was in the form of a banner held aloft in the sky by a pair of Gold's trademark centaurs. The headline read:

GOLD AVIATION, THE PROUD BUILDERS OF THE G-1
YELLOWJACKET, CONGRATULATES CAPT. LINDBERGH
ON HIS MOMENTOUS NEW YORK/PARIS SOLO
TRANSATLANTIC FLIGHT

The copy beneath the drawing was laced with swooning prose concerning how GAT shared Lindbergh's pioneering spirit, and how everybody could share in the excitement by using Gold Transport for their freight and travel needs.

"Isn't it a great drawing of Erica?" Campbell enthused.

"She looks good, all right," Gold admitted.

Erica's exploit as the first-ever woman test pilot had remained front-page news for weeks after the G-1's successful flight demonstration back in November. In the months that followed she'd been the subject of a dozen magazine articles, had been on the cover of *Ladies' Home Companion,* and had even been featured in a newsreel that showed her competing in a local air race (the Curtiss was gone, hastily replaced by a specially modified G-1 Yellowjacket).

"Notice how the copy suggests, but doesn't quite come out and claim, that Lindbergh flew the Atlantic in one of our airplanes," Campbell enthused.

"Sneaky." Gold smiled.

"I prefer to think of it as genius," Campbell jauntily replied.

"Sometimes you are a genius." Gold nodded.

It was after the newsreel that Campbell got the idea of making Erica the advertising spokeswoman for the company. Gold was undecided, and Erica was doubtful and almost refused to do it, but the newspaper advertisement that debuted "the GAT girl" increased Gold Transport's business by twenty percent.

"But today I think you're just plain sneaky," Gold continued. "I understand what you want to do, and I appreciate the effort, but I think it's a mistake."

"How so?" Campbell demanded.

Gold fought off his urge to smile. Campbell always got sensitive and touchy when he was criticized. "Sure, you can imply to the public that Lindbergh made his crossing in a Gold G-1," Gold explained. "But the people in the air transport industry know full well that Lindy flew a modified Ryan mail plane. That airplane was a masterpiece of engineering. I wish we'd built it, but we didn't. I think most folks will consider it a sign of our newfound strength for us to give credit where the credit is due." Gold pointed to the headline. "Change that so it reads, '. . . Congratulates *the Ryan Aircraft Company* and Lindbergh . . .'"

"That's going to make the headline awfully long," Campbell moped.

"Then reduce the type," Gold said. "But do it, okay? I'll see you tomorrow."

Campbell looked up. "You'll be out for the rest of the day?"

Gold nodded.

"Herm, before you go, I do need an answer concerning the Mesa deal."

"Oh, yeah . . . The Mesa deal . . ." Gold thought about it. Mesa was a holding company for several small air express companies controlling CAM routes linking Albuquerque, Denver, and points in between. Mesa was interested in selling out, and Campbell had been pushing to buy, in order to establish Gold Transport east of the Rockies.

"The idea of controlling that much territory is appealing . . ." Gold began.

"That's just the beginning," Campbell declared. "Next stop, Kansas City. I've got Kurt Bradley, the president of K.C. Airways, running scared, and when a man is scared, he's willing to sell, *cheaply*."

"It sounds good, Tim." Gold smiled tenatively. "But I'm worried that you're spreading us too thin."

Campbell laughed. "No offense, old buddy, but you really ought to let me worry about that sort of thing. I mean, that's what you pay me for, right?"

Gold nodded reluctantly.

"Right," Campbell firmly said. "Number one, the Feds have ordered one hundred G-1s, at twenty thousand each. Number two, we've got back orders from private concerns totaling another fifty airplanes, at prices ranging from twenty to twenty-five thousand each. We've got a two-year backlog on those deliveries." Campbell spread his arms, shrugging. "The facts speak for themselves. Our cash flow to debt ratio is terrific. Believe me, Herman, we can afford to expand the transport side of the business. In fact, we can't afford *not* to."

"I guess you're right."

"I *know* I'm right," Campbell insisted. "The problem here is that you're so understandably eager to darken the skies with Gold airplanes that you've lost track of the big picture. You've forgotten that you made your start as an air express company. Maybe you've even forgotten how we fought tooth and nail for our CAM routes. You seemed to think that they were pretty important back then, important enough to cost a man's life—"

"I never forget anything," Gold said quietly, but firmly. "Maybe you'd better just make your point..."

Campbell looked defiant for a moment, but then he lowered his eyes. "Okay, maybe I did just hit a little bit below the belt," he admitted. "I apologize, but when I get worked up like this it's for *your* own good, Herm. It would be tragic if you let unfounded money worries slow us down at the very moment we're at the top of our game. Consider the reception the G-1a Dragonfly got."

Gold nodded. When he and Teddy had completed their design specs on the enclosed cockpit, six-passenger version of the Yellowjacket, he'd asked Campbell to make a few calls to test out the market for such a plane. As a result, the telephone had been ringing off the hook with interested air transport companies ready to place their orders sight unseen.

"Bright as they are over at the Ryan Company, they're just too small to be much of a threat to us," Campbell was saying. "Our only real competition is Ford, and the German Fokker Company, and both of them are building tri-motors, too big, too slow, and too expensive for anything but the busiest air routes. The G-1 Yellowjacket is just what the doctor ordered for the government. When you and Teddy are ready to put the G-1a Dragonfly into production we'll have the best midsized passenger airliner on the market. That will give us the kind of cash base we need to build an *empire*."

"I'm not telling you this expansion notion is out of the question," Gold remarked. "All I'm saying is that it has me worried. This is my company, after all."

"Yes, sir, *Mister Gold*—"

Gold chose to ignore Campbell's sarcastic tone. He wanted to keep the lid on this.

Campbell's fingers tapped impatiently on his desk. "Herman, can I speak frankly?"

"Of course."

"Gold Aviation—the whole business of designing airplanes—is your baby."

Gold nodded. "And it's your job to oversee the financial health of the company, and sell our airplanes."

"But that's not enough for me, Herman. I want to do more. I want to do for Gold Transport what you've done for Gold Aviation. I want our colors to dominate the skies."

"Big dream," Gold quietly remarked.

Campbell shrugged and smiled. "No bigger than the dream somebody had about building an airplane based on a goddamned sea gull's wing..."

"Point well taken." Gold chuckled.

"Give me this chance." Campbell said solemnly. "I can make it happen."

"Okay," Gold said. "You've got your chance."

"Thank you, Herman."

"Fuck that." Gold waved him quiet. "I owe you. I wouldn't have made it this far if you hadn't been backing me up."

"You won't regret this." Campbell grinned.

"Hope not." Gold nodded, heading for the office door. "Just remember one thing, Tim. This is still my company, and I believe that GAT's ace in the hole is its design talent. I intend to exploit that talent by increasing our manufacturing capability. As long as there's extra money in the till, you can play. But Gold *Aviation* will *always* come first."

Gold stopped off at his office to change out of his suit into corduroy pants, a faded blue work shirt, and a pair of old oxford brogues. He went downstairs, and out to his car. He left Santa Monica, driving northwest on Ventura; after about ten miles he left the city of Los Angeles behind, entering into the open country of Burbank.

The Stutz raised a cloud of dust as it traveled through the acrid, tawny landscape studded with patches of pale-green sage and shaggy desert palm. Gold saw hawks circling in the flawless azure sky. Now and again brown jackrabbits the size of dogs, their long ears folded back over their lean haunches, would dart across the macadam ahead of the Bull-dog Tourer's wire-spoked wheels. Gold turned off the main road, onto a dirt access road that led up to a barbed-wire fence. Erica's green Packard roadster, coated with dust, was parked on the shoulder. Erica was out of the car, standing near the gate, which sported large KEEP OUT: PRIVATE PROPERTY signs. She was wearing a pink cotton sundress, leather sandals, and a floppy-brimmed, white linen sombrero. She smiled and waved to him as he pulled up.

Gold set the brake on the Stutz and got out of the car. "You look so good, you must be a desert mirage," he said, taking her in his arms.

As she tilted back her head to receive his kiss the sombrero fell to the ground. She'd been spending a lot of time out-of-doors sunbathing. Her skin was tan, and her blond hair shimmered with highlights in the sunshine.

"I still don't know why you dragged me out here," Erica murmured, her arms sliding around his waist.

"I told you, it's a surprise. Now come on, get in the car."

Gold opened the gate. He drove the Stutz along the bumpy, packed-dirt trail. All around them as far as they could see there was nothing but sand and rocks and chaparral, the parched monotony occasionally, inexplicably, shattered by vibrantly colorful wildflowers: poppies the rich yellow of egg yolk; fire engine red scarlet gilia; bright baby blue-eyes.

Gold drove slowly, mindful of the Stutz's suspension. They crawled along for a bouncing, jolting quarter mile, and then he stopped the car. In the sudden silence they heard a faraway coyote's mournful yodel. "We're here," Gold said.

Erica looked around. "How can you tell?"

Gold pointed out several foot-high wooden stakes fluttering scraps of red cloth. "That's where the ground-breaking ceremony for the new plant is going to take place." He got out of the car and went around to open the trunk. "I thought we'd have a little picnic." He took out a blanket and spread it out on the ground. "Just the two of us. To celebrate."

"That's your surprise?" Erica demanded, amused.

He went back to the trunk to fetch a wicker basket and a red metal cooler. "I brought champagne. Dom Perignon. Had to special-order it from our buddy Freddie the bootlegger."

Erica smiled. "Darling, you know how I get when I'm tipsy."

"That's what I was hoping." Gold plopped the basket and cooler onto the blanket and settled down. Erica followed him over and sat down beside him. She began to rummage through the basket. "I see fruit, and cheese, and crackers, but no champagne glasses."

"Damn, I knew I forgot something," Gold said, opening up the cooler and removing the champagne. "Oh well, we'll just have to pass the bottle."

"How swank . . ." Erica shook her head, laughing.

Gold shrugged. "This is our land," he said proudly as he stripped the foil from the neck of the emerald champagne bottle. "We can do what we like on it. Our closest neighbor is a movie studio, and they're miles away. We've got one hundred and nine acres of pristine wilderness that is not long for this world. Where the bees are buzzing and the jackrabbits fuck is soon to be a mammoth airplane factory—"

"Darling, do leave that part about the bunnies out of your speech at the actual ceremony."

"—with hangars. And parts and fuel-storage facilities, and paved roads, and a pair of runways, and a big sign that tells the world it all belongs to Gold Aviation and Transport."

"In other words, to you."

Gold, struggling to pop the champagne cork, looked up and smiled.

"But right now, I think you'd better direct your attention to something *else* that belongs to you . . ." She untied the bows on her shoulder straps, letting the sundress slip down to her waist. Her breasts were startlingly white in the sun.

The cork finally popped. The champagne, jostled from the bumpy ride, overflowed the lip of the bottle. Gold sprayed her breasts with foaming wine. Erica laughed. Gold pinned her down on the blanket. He licked her pink nipples, glistening with droplets of champagne.

She drew his head up, to kiss him. "I love you very much, you know."

"And I love you, and this is only the beginning for us," Gold swore to her. "We're back on top, and this time we're going to stay there."

BOOK IV:
1927-1933

STOCK CRASH HAS MARKET IN UPROAR—
Congress Presses for Investigation into Wall Street—
Hoover Reassures the Nation that Business Is
Fundamentally Sound—
New York Business Journal

**AIR INDUSTRY FLIES HIGH DURING NATION'S
HARD TIMES—**
Local Congressman Charges Defense Projects Bolster
Aviation Stocks And Asks: "If Aviation's on the Dole,
Why Not Auto Industry?"—
Detroit Telegraph

WATRES ACT PASSES CONGRESS—
New Law Aimed at Corruption and Waste in Air
Transport Industry—
Act Nixes All but Largest, Most Experienced Air
Carriers—
Washington Star Reporter

**KNUTE ROCKNE AMONG THOSE KILLED IN FIERY
KANSAS PLANE CRASH—**
Investigators Point to Wood Rot in TWA Fokker
Tri-motor—
All Fokkers Grounded for Inspections—
Los Angeles Gazette

**CRISIS AS BANKS CLOSE THEIR DOORS TO THE
COUNTRY—**
President-Elect Roosevelt Blames Big Business for Woes

and Vows His "New Deal" Will Bring Sweeping
Changes—

Boston Times

JAPAN INVASION REACHES CHINA'S GREAT WALL—

Japan Quits League of Nations to Protest Vote
Condemning Invasion—

Milwaukee Sun

GERMANY ELECTS HITLER CHANCELLOR—

Receives Nazi Salute From Cheering Throngs—

Miami Daily Telegraph

Chapter 12

(One)
Gold Aviation and Transport
Burbank, California
1 April 1933

Gold stared at the two envelopes on his desk. In one was Tim Campbell's resignation: just a few, cursory, typed lines on a sheet of stationery tinged yellow, gone brittle with age. Campbell had hand-delivered the resignation seven years ago, when he'd come to work for what was then Gold's down-on-its-luck, seat-of-the-pants operation.

The other envelope had arrived in the morning's mail. Inside it was an anonymous, typed note claiming that Campbell was trying to take over Gold's company behind his back.

Gold swiveled in his leather chair to stare out his office windows. His top-floor view overlooked the complex's airfields, where planes were scattered like children's toys; the yellow shack of a security-guard outpost; the high, chain-link fence topped with barbed wire; and beyond all that, the immutable, tawny, California hills. Gold couldn't claim that he didn't miss his old view of Santa Monica Bay, but these hills had their own serene beauty.

As Gold gazed out the windows, the light changed. Suddenly he could make out his own ghostly reflection in the glass. He was wearing a new, double-breasted, gray shark-skin suit. His tailor had suggested the double-breasted suit style as a way to "slim" the paunch he'd seemed to have developed, and, in general, to look more "youthful and vigorous."

The tailor had seemed anxious when he'd made the comments, but Gold hadn't taken offense. He could look in a mirror as well as anyone. He was only thirty-six, but he'd lost most of his hair on top. He was just one of those people who happened to look a little older than they really were . . .

Gold forced his attention back to the envelopes. The thing to do was confront Campbell, hear what the man had to say. Gold buzzed his secretary. "Tell Mister Campbell I want to see him immediately."

"Yes, sir." A few moments later she was back on the line to say that Campbell was on his way.

Gold stared sadly at the envelopes, realizing that one way or the other, a precious, sustaining friendship was about to end. As he waited for Campbell to arrive he thought about how far he and Tim had come.

Back in 1927, GAT and its competition were ready and eager to capitalize on the growing public interest in air travel spurred by Charles Lindbergh's solo flight across the North Atlantic. Investors who were once reluctant and had to be coaxed to put their money behind airline ventures now flocked to make aviation stocks the toasts of Wall Street. GAT, American Airways, Eastern Air Transport, United Aircraft, Transcontinental Air Transport, and the other big aviation companies flourished in the economic boom times.

Thanks to Campbell's aggressive expansion policy, Gold Transport now controlled half the major CAM routes, as well as the large share of the private freight and passenger business as far east as Kansas City. The original GAT stock was split, and new issues were offered. Its value kept skyrocketing.

Early one morning in the fall of 1928, Gold, Tim Campbell, Hull Stiles, and Teddy Quinn gathered at the Burbank construction site, where phase one of the factory/office complex was nearing completion. All four men had owned sizable holdings in GAT ever since the stock had first been issued. As they watched the sun rise on the sprawling building, they passed a bottle of scotch between them, quietly joking and congratulating each other on becoming million-aires.

GAT's G-1a Dragonfly six-passenger airliner hit the market in the first quarter of 1929 and was a success. Campbell, with Gold's blessing, used the occasion to restructure GAT into two separate companies. GAT remained the airplane design and manufacturing concern, while Gold Transport changed its name to Skyworld Airline.

Skyworld now had its own annual stockholders' meeting and board of directors. Tim Campbell and Hull Stiles sold their GAT holdings back to Gold, giving up their seats on GAT's board, in order to invest heavily in Skyworld. Campbell became president and C.E.O. of the new airline. Hull Stiles, who knew the air transport business better than anyone in the industry, became executive vice president and chief operating officer. Gold, who held a majority of GAT, and a twenty percent controlling interest in Skyworld, remained chairman of both companies.

Due to Campbell's prodding, Gold had originally been enthusiastic about the restructuring, but as soon as it was a *fait accompli*, he began to regret what he'd been talked into. When it had all been one company, Gold's relationship with his partners had been straightforward: he was the king and they were his ministers. Now things were more complicated, and Gold often thought of himself as being like Shakespeare's King Lear: his realm was passing from his control. Take Hull Stiles, for instance. These days Hull was working out of Skyworld's new, luxurious airport terminal and office complex in Los Angeles. Hull had used to report to Gold on a daily basis, but since the restructuring, Gold rarely heard from his old flying buddy. Now Hull's reports were going directly to Campbell, who was juggling his time between the airport facility and Burbank. Gold toyed with the notion of reestablishing his direct control of Skyworld—after all, he was still chairman of the airline—but he hesitated, not wanting to further disrupt what had become a stressed relationship with Campbell.

From the beginning, Campbell's expertise had allowed Gold to devote more time to his first love, aeronautical design and engineering, and so Gold had been happy to delegate his authority to Campbell on financial, managerial, and administrative matters. Since the restructuring, Campbell had changed from being Gold's right-hand man into an advocate for his "own company." Gold often found himself arguing with an increasingly belligerent Campbell. Days would pass during which they would do their best to avoid each other in the halls. Gold was uncomfortable with the situation, but he didn't know how to address the problem. If he took the drastic step of acting to remove Campbell from his position, the move would deeply divide the airline's board and create concern on Wall Street. Gold wasn't even sure he could convince the rest of the Skyworld board to go along with him. Campbell was doing a terrific job, even if he *was* freezing Gold out of the day-to-day operation.

The difficulties Gold was experiencing with his business associates seemed suddenly very petty, and were shoved onto the back burner amidst the turmoil of the market crash in October of 1929. GAT and Skyworld, along with the nation's other big aviation concerns, emerged relatively unscathed. GAT was sustained by its government contract for G-1 Yellowjackets, and while private industry orders for Yellowjacket cargo planes and Dragonfly airliners lessened, they did not totally dry up. Tim Campbell did his part for Skyworld by coming up with an innovative air-travel discount rate plan for business passengers. Those businessmen who were surviving the hard times still had to travel, and for them, time was still money—which made air transport a necessity. Campbell's "Blue Skies Ahead Credit Plan" offered these corporate customers a twenty percent discount in exchange for their cash deposit committing them to a certain amount of travel with Skyworld within a six-month period.

Campbell started small, strong-arming all of GAT/Skyworld's suppliers into signing up on threat of losing their accounts. Once the money-saving feature of the plan proved itself, Campbell didn't have to twist arms. Skyworld's exclusive discount plan kept old customers loyal and attracted new ones away from the competition. Soon more than 100 companies were signed up, and Skyworld had traveling sales representatives pitching the plan all over the country.

GAT/Skyworld's balance sheets looked so good that Gold

and Campbell were constantly arguing about further expansion. Thinking back on it, Gold realized that considering the differences in their personalities, conflict was inevitable. Campbell was a gambler. Gold was conservative in money matters. Campbell was a supremely confident financial wizard. Most of the time Gold had only the faintest of notions of what Campbell was talking about when Tim got going with his financial hocus-pocus.

Campbell usually won their arguments. He would reason that thanks to the depression there were acquisition opportunities all over the country: air terminals, airplane fleets, parts inventories, ground transport companies, instrument and engine manufacturers, and so on. If they didn't gobble up those buys, a competitor would. Campbell would remind Gold that he hadn't yet let the company down, and that he wouldn't in the future. Finally, Campbell would march upon Gold's crumbling defenses with an army of figures: projected revenues, compound interest calculations, income tax dodges. Reeling against the onslaught, Gold would give in, letting Tim do what he wanted. GAT and Skyworld became the holding companies for more than sixty separate operations.

In 1930 GAT's modified G-1 Yellowjacket won the United States Navy's competition for a new torpedo bomber. The navy contracted for an initial order of 150 airplanes, along with an extensive spare-parts order. This new cash infusion gave Gold the confidence to authorize Teddy Quinn to augment his staff with a dozen new, young aeronautical engineers who had been let go by those smaller companies that had gone under. Gold also authorized R&D on a new, all-metal, large-capacity passenger airliner, tentatively dubbed the Monarch, meant to steal a little thunder from Ford's "Tin Goose" Tri-Motor. The Ford was the premier passenger plane in the world—Skyworld owned nine of them   but the "Tin Goose" had its problems. It was noisy and slow, giving it little advantage over travel by rail for long trips. GAT, Ford, Boeing, Northrop, Lockheed, Douglas, and others, were looking to the future with new concepts as they raced to come up with a large, fast, comfortable airliner.

That same year, widespread reports of corruption in the

ways that the scores of smaller air transport companies were billing the postal service for carrying the mail led Congress to pass the McNary-Watres Act. The act was designed to rid the country of shoestring carrier operations, and to promote passenger air travel. The act's first key provision was that U.S. airmail carriers would no longer be paid by the pound. Carriers would be paid a sliding-scale flat rate, based on the amount of interior space its airplanes could offer, regardless of whether that space was used to carry mail. A large carrier like Skyworld had the big passenger airplanes to receive the maximum flat rate, thereby reaping grand profits. The marginal carriers with their little airplanes received the minimum rate, which was purposely fixed so low as to force them out of business. This dovetailed with the second key provision of the Watres Act, which gave the postmaster general the right to consolidate those routes abandoned by the marginal carriers, and award the territory to the lowest *responsible* bidder.

Thanks to the Watres Act, only the largest, most established carrier companies would henceforth be eligible to fly the mail. All others need not apply.

A meeting was held in Washington to divvy up the nation's newly consolidated routes among the aviation giants. Tim Campbell represented Skyworld, and went to Washington vowing to come back with a grand prize: a coveted transcontinental route. The conference lasted twelve days. Campbell came home without his coast-to-coast plum, but with a decent consolation prize: all the territory Skyworld currently held, plus a profitable route between Kansas City and Chicago. Skyworld's scarlet and turquoise fleet was now authorized to fly over the western two-thirds of the nation.

The Watres Act cut the legs from the civilian market for the G-1 Yellowjacket and G-1a Dragonfly. They were just too small. Fortunately, Gold still had his navy contract for torpedo bombers. He shut down the Dragonfly assembly line, stockpiled the six unsold passenger airliners on his airfields, and poured money into the Monarch project.

In 1931 the crash of a TWA Fokker tri-motor in Kansas took the life of Knute Rockne, the famed football coach, among others. An investigation revealed that the cause of the crash was rotted wood in the Fokker's all-spruce, internal wing assembly. The Fokker tri-motors were the workhorses of the airlines, and when they all had to be grounded for inspections it created havoc. Virtually all the major airlines, Skyworld excluded, flew them. The only reason Gold had stayed away from them was his unpleasant experience in the aftermath of the crash of his German-built Spatz, back in 1925. He was now a naturalized citizen, but because of his German origins he'd vowed to play it safe in the future and avoid all controversy by only buying American—until he could build a plane of his own to fulfill a specific need.

With the Fokkers out of service, the airlines looked around at what was available in a large-capacity transport, all-metal design, and found not very much. Gold's surplus of all-metal Dragonfly airliners was quickly sold out, but the G-1a was a stopgap solution. The Dragonfly was too small, while the larger, all-metal tri-motor offered by Ford was too uncomfortable and slow. Something better had always been needed, but now that need was crucial, and the potential rewards for the firm that satisfied that need had become far greater. The race to build a state-of-the-art airliner was heating up.

The Monarch project became GAT's top priority. Gold spent most of his time working with Teddy Quinn and the expanded pool of engineers. Long gone were the good old days back in Santa Monica, when the group could sit around one table, chewing the fat and brainstorming as they gazed out the windows at the sparkling blue bay. Today, Gold had engineers working for him whose names he didn't know.

The new airliner had started out as a tri-motor, but Rogers and Simpson had told Gold about their latest design for a powerful radial engine that made him think the Monarch could be a twin-engined craft. In the months since the project had gone into high gear, Teddy Quinn and his gang of boy geniuses had worked out a fuselage design that would allow the Monarch to carry twelve passengers plus a three-man crew in swift, quiet comfort. A prototype model of a twin-engined Monarch—designated the Gold Commercial One (GC-1)—had been built. Wind tunnel tests had proved that the aircraft could effortlessly cruise with only one working engine at any practical altitude. Unfortunately, wind tunnel tests also showed unsatisfactory rudder control flying on only one engine.

GAT could start on a full-scale prototype as soon as the damned rudder control problem was licked. Gold worked late nights at his own drafting table, laboriously struggling with the Monarch's engineering problems; dreaming about them during fitful sleep. He knew that he was obsessing on the Monarch at the expense of other important matters, but he couldn't help it. He did his best creative work when he was obsessed. Anyway, he'd always believed that Campbell could take care of routine business matters concerning Skyworld well enough without him.

The intercom snarled. Gold pressed the button. "Mister Campbell is here," his secretary said.

"Send him in." Gold took the anonymous note accusing Campbell of treachery out of its envelope. He folded the sheet of stationery into a paper airplane, meanwhile brooding that perhaps Campbell had been taking care of things without him *too well* . . .

"What's this about, Herman?" Campbell complained as he came into the office.

Gold watched him approach. It was fifty paces from the double doors to Gold's marble-topped, oak desk. The journey took Campbell past sideboards lining the paneled walls, the burgundy leather sofas and armchairs grouped together like campsites on the vast moss green plain of wall-to-wall carpeting. The walls above the sideboards were taken up with ornately framed, murky oil paintings of hunting scenes and seascapes. Gold did not know any of the artists. Erica had furnished and decorated the office for him. Banished to one corner of the cavernous room, looking somewhat forlorn, like country cousins come to the big city, were Gold's battered, old drafting table and glass-fronted bookcases filled with technical manuals. Erica had given him a hard time about that table, but Gold had stood his ground, insisting to her that he still spent more time at his drafting table than he did at his desk. He wished he were at his table right now, instead of desperately trying to come up with an idea of how to resolve this confrontation without losing Campbell's friendship.

"I've got a ton of crap to take care of before lunch," Campbell was saying. "And I get this goddamned summons from your secretary like I'm some kind of goddamned errand boy—"

Gold gestured toward a leather armchair in front of his desk. "Sit down. I've got something serious to discuss with you."

Campbell settled into the chair. He took a gold cigarette case from out of the breast pocket of his gray flannel, double-breasted suit jacket, extracted a cigarette, and then lit it with a matching gold lighter. His eyes flicked desultorily over the two envelopes lying on the burgundy leather desk blotter, and then at the paper airplane in Gold's hand. "Well?" He exhaled a stream of smoke. "I trust that gizmo in your hand isn't another new design you want me to finance for you?—"

Gold sailed the paper airplane into Campbell's lap. "Read it."

Campbell unfolded the note and skimmed its contents. When he was finished he looked up at Gold, his expression contemptuous. "You believe this?" he asked.

Gold shrugged. "Not if you tell me it's a lie."

Campbell didn't say anything for a moment; then he smiled. "Why the fuck should I bother lying? You were going to find out sooner or later." He crumpled the sheet into a ball.

"You want to tell me why?" Gold asked.

Campbell stared at him. "You don't know? Could your self-absorption—*your fucking ego*—be that big? You mean to try and tell me that you've been so focused on that goddamned Monarch project that you don't remember what happened?"

Gold frowned. "You mean that flap we had over Cargo Air Transport?"

"That *flap,* as you put it, was the final straw as far as I was concerned," Campbell said.

Gold leaned back in his chair. At present Skyworld was authorized to fly as far east as Chicago. A small airline,

Cargo Air Transport, had managed to survive the Watres Act, holding on to its single, lucrative Chicago/New York route, but now the company—in other words, its route—was up for sale. Campbell had wanted to go after Cargo Transport, calling it the last piece in the puzzle to make Skyworld a coast-to-coast airline. Gold had balked. There were other transport companies with the same idea; the bidding for Cargo Air had hugely inflated the price of its stock. Campbell was willing to overpay, believing that Cargo Air would turn out to be a worthy buy in the long-term, but Gold had refused to let Campbell sink Skyworld that deeply into debt.

"Cargo Air has made me realize that for the longest while we've been like two mules straining to go in opposite directions, but tied together by a piece of rope," Campbell said. "I figured it was time to cut the rope."

"That rope you're talking about cutting belongs to *me*," Gold said sharply.

"A public company belongs to its stockholders," Campbell said evenly. "I believe that when the truth comes out, Skyworld's stockholders will not react kindly to your argument against the Cargo Air acquisition: that buying up all that inflated stock would rob Skyworld of its liquidity at a time when GAT might want to borrow on those cash reserves to fund the Monarch project. The thing of it is, I'm sick of Skyworld always getting the short end of the stick. I'm willing to wager that most stockholders will agree with me."

"You know my philosophy—"

Campbell nodded. "That as far as you're concerned, GAT will always come first. Well, one thing I have to say for you, Herman, you've stuck to your guns on that. But a lot of us have worked damn hard to make Skyworld what it is today, and we don't see why we should have to take a backseat."

"Tim, listen to me," Gold began. "For once, I think it's you who's losing sight of the big picture."

"This I've got to hear." Campbell scowled, stubbing out the remains of his cigarette in the smoking stand beside his chair, and immediately lighting another.

"I've been thinking about history," Gold began. Campbell opened his mouth to say something, but Gold help up his hand. "Just hear me out. The Watres Act that gives the postmaster general the right to decree who can fly where is a product of the Hoover administration."

"So?" Campbell demanded.

"So now there's a new president. A Democrat. I think Roosevelt will move to rescind everything Hoover's done."

"You think FDR's going to try and repeal the Watres Act?"

"I'm saying he might." Gold nodded. "And with it, the postmaster's authority to parcel out routes. If that happened we could fly anywhere we want, with or without the postmaster's blessings, and without taking ourselves to the poorhouse to do it."

Campbell nodded. "Okay, that's an opinion." He smiled thinly. "It doesn't happen to be mine."

"Right, we disagree, and time will tell who's right." Gold acknowledged. "But what's the point of starting this civil war? Even if you could manage to take over Skyworld—"

"Oh, I'll manage it, all right." Campbell smiled. "I've been busy while you've been preoccupied with the Monarch project," Campbell replied. "I've put together a group of shareholders who, like me, disagree with your leadership. The group has authorized me to vote their shares by proxy."

Gold was startled. He hadn't realized until now just how out of touch he'd become concerning what was going on at Skyworld. "Is Hull with you in all this?" he asked softly.

"Yes, Hull's with me."

So now it's two old friends I'm losing, Gold thought wearily. "I take it you intend to wage a proxy battle for the company at this month's annual shareholders' meeting?"

"I do. With full-page newspaper advertisments, press conferences, the works. It's going to be messy, Herman, I can promise you that. And in the meantime I'll be buying up as much stock as I can."

"I could match you on that strategy," Gold threatened.

"You could," Campbell said. "But what good would it do you? You can't buy it *all*, Herman. But each share I grab will add to my credibility. And I still expect to be able to beat you in the proxy fight."

"The meeting isn't until the nineteenth," Gold said. "Cargo Air Transport will be long off the market by then."

"Cargo Air Transport is off the market now," Campbell said. "Because Skyworld has bought it. Or *will* have bought it, I should say, come April nineteenth, when I take over as chairman, and as soon as I can get to a telephone. I've made Cargo Air Transport an offer it is quite happy with. They've agreed to wait. I've also gotten from Cargo's board the privilege to top by ten percent any better offer they might get between now and the nineteenth."

"You haven't the authority to commit Skyworld to such a transaction," Gold protested.

"It's a touch illegal at present," Campbell admitted. "But it won't be after the nineteenth, when I control a majority share, and when I'm chairman."

"Why are you telling me this?" Gold asked. "Don't you realize that I could pick up the telephone and take legal steps against you?"

"I don't believe you're capable of ratting on a friend, not even one who's about to take your company away from you." Campbell grinned. "After all, I didn't rat on *you* concerning a certain incident in which a fire got started and a fellow burned to death."

"That was seven years ago," Gold said.

"There's no statute of limitations on murder, Herman, but let's not dwell on the past," Campbell said, dismissing the matter with a wave of his hand. "I brought that ancient history up merely to make the point that both of us have experience bending the rules when it suits us."

"Then I have your word that 'the certain incident' will not rear its ugly head during this present conflict?" Gold asked.

"You do, and I trust that I have your word that our conversation today will remain confidential?"

Gold nodded. "But if you don't succeed with this takeover you'll still be finished," Gold said. "I won't have to rat on you. Cargo Air Transport will sue you for everything you own, and you will go to jail."

Campbell nodded. "That's my problem, not yours. I know that I've put everything—including my freedom—on the line. So you see, Herman, there really is no turning back for me concerning this."

"You must have agreed to pay Cargo Air Transport a fortune for them to go along with this scheme . . ."

Campbell lit a third cigarette off the butt of the last. "Let's just say that I'm paying generously for something they have, that I want."

"Will you have to borrow money?" Gold asked. When Campbell nodded, Gold laughed. "I don't pretend to be the money master that you are, but even I know that it's bad business to overpay, and go into hock to do it. What good will Skyworld be to you if you bury your precious company in debt?"

"It gets a little complicated, Herman," Campbell patronized. "Let's just say that my long-term strategy is to wait for the economic climate to improve and then sell some of Skyworld's subsidiaries to help pay off the debt. During the short-term, I believe that while there will be an initial slump, once Skyworld has settled into its new coast-to-coast route, business and profits will resume their upward course."

"Good cash flow to debt ratio, eh?" Gold asked sardonically. Campbell's smile was faint. Gold picked up the envelope containing Campbell's resignation. "Know what this is?"

"I can guess. But it's no longer relevant, is it? I mean, I'm not resigning from anything, except, I guess, our friendship." Campbell hesitated. "Unless, of course, you're firing me from my position as president of Skyworld? As chairman, you do have the authority to do that," he seemed to encourage.

"Thanks, but no thanks," Gold muttered. "If I *did* fire you, you own enough stock to fight me on it, but suddenly you're being obliging. Now why is that?" Gold smiled. "Probably it's because without you—and Hull, who no doubt would loyally follow you out—Skyworld would grind to a halt, and revenues would plummet. Wall Street would get wind of it, and the price of the stock would drop. That would look just swell for me at the stockholders' meeting, wouldn't it?"

"Herman, you do learn." Campbell grinned.

"There'll be time enough for me to throw you out on your ass, *after* the nineteenth." Gold crumpled the envelope containing the resignation and tossed it into his wastepaper basket. "It's ironic. When you gave me this seven years ago, you said that it would be my insurance in case I ever thought that I could do better without you than with you—"

Campbell, nodding, finished it for him. "But as it turned out, that's the way *I* feel about *you*." He stood up. "Look, from now on it's going to be too awkward for me to work out of Burbank. I'll be running things out of the L.A. airport offices. Hull's made room for me and my staff . . ."

Gold watched Campbell walk to the door. "Tim," he called out. "I intend to fight back—"

Campbell, in the doorway, turned and smiled. "Happy April Fool's Day, Herman."

(Two)
GAT
Burbank
11 April 1933

Gold was frustrated. The morning newspapers were carrying Campbell's promised full-page advertisements soliciting Skyworld stock, and asking all stockholders to back him in the upcoming proxy battle. There were copies of the papers carrying the ads on every desk in every department in the Burbank complex. Wherever Gold went, his employees would stop talking when they saw him coming, and offer him a weak-tea smile with a kind of baleful, fisheye look in their eyes.

All morning he was being treated as if he were suffering from a terminal illness. Gold supposed he couldn't blame his employees. He was definitely the underdog. He'd made a few calls around town this morning to knowledgeable business associates, just to see how the ads were being received . . . Most people had three words for him: *Rest in peace*. The wags wanted to know where to send the flowers . . .

Gold retreated to the design studio, thinking to lose his troubles in a couple of hours' work on the Monarch Project.

But there was no work getting done down there, either. The atmosphere was morgue-like. Everybody, including Teddy Quinn, was tiptoeing around and talking in whispers, so as not to upset Gold, which, of course, upset him no end. Gold cornered Teddy and asked him to step outside the studio so that they could talk in private. They stood close together in the hallway, speaking in whispers, both men in their shirtsleeves, with their ties loosened and their shirt pockets bulging with pencils.

Gold gestured with his thumb toward the door to the design studio. "Why is everybody in there so concerned with Campbell's goddamned ad?"

"They don't give two shits about the ad, or Campbell," Teddy said. "Those guys care about *you*. They don't want to upset you, Herm."

"I don't need to be handled with kid gloves," Gold said. "And I don't pay my R&D people to be preoccupied with my corporate problems. I pay them to design airplanes; like the Monarch, for instance."

"You want people to get back to work, then go home," Teddy said. "You know the saying: 'Out of sight, out of mind.'"

"I don't get it." Gold frowned.

"These kids look up to you, believe it or not," Teddy said. "The Great Depression put them out of the work they loved, but then, thanks to you, they got another chance. There's not one of them wouldn't give you his right arm in gratitude."

"They can show their gratitude by concentrating on the task on hand," Gold said.

"How are they supposed to concentrate when they see you moping?"

"Who's moping?" Gold challenged. "I'm not moping."

Teddy's green eyes were mirthful behind his tortoiseshell eyeglasses. "Why don't you take a good look at yourself in the mirror? You've been skulking around here like soaked cat."

Gold scowled. "That was a damned good ad Campbell wrote, wasn't it? . . ."

"It was okay." Teddy shrugged.

"Come on!" Gold demanded ruefully. "By the time I was

done reading it, *I* was ready to join Tim's parade." He sighed. "Well, he always was a clever writer. That's why he handles all of our advertising for Gold Transport."

"Handled," Teddy quietly corrected. "And it's Skyworld, not Gold Transport anymore."

"Slip of the tongue," Gold said, flustered. "And *anyway*," he added defiantly, "in my *heart* it'll always be Gold Transport!" He noticed Teddy looking at him with concern. "What?"

"You're not crumbling, are you?" Teddy asked.

"Of course, not," Gold scoffed. "I'm just pissed. I feel hurt, and frustrated. I'm not used to feeling that way..."

"Okay, Herm, whatever you say..." Teddy hesitated. "Can I give you a little advice?"

"Always."

"If you're going to beat Tim, you've got to do it your way. You'll never win trying to play his complicated financial games ... Now you go home, and let me get the brain pool get back to work."

"I've got work to do upstairs in my office," Gold said.

"Whatever, just as long as you're out of sight. I can get a lot more out of those kids if they aren't being distracted watching you out of the corners of their eyes. Every time you sneeze they start wondering if they're going to be back on a streetcorner peddling apples."

That evening, Gold mulled over what Teddy had said as he made his way down to the parking lot. Whatever happened, if he wanted his people to concentrate all of their energy on the Monarch project, he had to conceal the emotional turmoil he was experiencing due to Tim Campbell's betrayal. He had to maintain an unflappable and confident image. That way his junior engineers could return to their drafting tables unencumbered by worries about him and their own futures.

Gold got into his British racing-green Marmon and started it up. The Stutz Bulldog tourer had been giving him trouble, so last year, when the '32s arrived in the dealers' showrooms, he'd retired the Stutz in favor of this V-16, 9.1-liter, convertible sedan. While he was shopping for a new car he'd looked at a Duesenberg, a supercharged SJ, but decided against it. The SJ was faster, and almost as long as the Marmon, but not nearly as roomy inside. Gold liked to be able to spread out in his car. Anyway, the Marmon had cost only six grand. They wanted ten thousand for the Duesenberg. Gold figured six thousand dollars was quite enough to pay for a car at a time when the average man, assuming he was lucky enough to have a job, was only making, say, two or three thousand dollars a year . . .

The traffic going into Los Angeles was heavy. Gold concentrated on his driving, expertly weaving the majestic Marmon through the logjams, but it still took him twice as long as usual to get from the Burbank complex to Bel-Air.

He'd sold the Pasadena house back in '28, and paid a hundred and fifty thousand cash for the English colonial sheltered behind stone walls in Bel-Air. The house had been previously owned by a doyen of the silver screen who found himself yesterday's news with the advent of talkies. It was a grand house, perhaps too grand for Gold's taste. He missed the manageable scale and bright cheerfulness of the Pasadena hacienda. The new house was four stories tall, with grapevines crawling over its stone exterior, and a mansard roof you could land a plane on. Inside it was dark, and cool, with high, gilded ceilings, lots of fireplaces, mahogany paneling, and long, meandering hallways sprouting suites of rooms. The house looked as if it had been standing for centuries, but it was only ten years old. Erica loved the place, and the kids were happy. The rolling lawns on which croquet and badminton could be played were far more suitable for children than the fussy, tropical landscaping of the house in Pasadena. There was a pool, and a four-car garage. Hidden by trees at the edge of the property was a stone storage building that had been converted into a stable for the kids' Shetland ponies.

Gold guided the Marmon through the wrought-iron gates. The full-time handyman gardener who lived above the garage was pruning the hedges that lined the crushed gravel drive. He tipped his hat as Gold drove by.

Gold parked in front of the house, next to Erica's lemon-yellow Bugatti roadster. As he trudged up the front steps the oak double-doors swung open, spilling soft warm light against the gathering twilight.

"Daddy's home!" Susan called out as she swung on the doorknob. His eleven-year-old daughter was dressed in blue jeans and a dirty sweatshirt. Her shoulder-length blond hair was in pigtails.

"Pop! Look what I can do—" Nine-year-old Steven, wearing chino shorts and a red and black striped polo shirt, was sliding down the polished wooden banister that lined the broad curved staircase.

Gold watched as his fireplug of a son rocketed off the end of the banister. Gold made a lunging dive and caught the kid before he cracked his skull on the hallway's polished stone floor.

"I taught him how, Daddy," Suzy self-importantly announced.

His kids had inherited Erica's features and coloring. Susan was tall for her age. She was boisterous and sassy, long-legged and lean, a tomboy just like her mother. Like Erica, lately Suzie had been showing hints of the femme fatale she was destined to become. Steven was built short and wide. He was an earnest and steady boy, but no match for his older, bossy, athletic sister. Just about anything poor Arnie tried to do, Suzy did better.

Steve liked airplanes, so Gold often took the boy flying. Gold would let his son sit on his lap. Once they were aloft, he would let Steve work the stick. Gold had promised to teach his son how to fly as soon as Steve's feet could reach the rudder pedals. Flying was something Steve could eventually claim for his own. Suzy would not step foot in an airplane. Somehow, somewhere, before she was barely beyond her toddler stage, she had developed a fear of heights.

Erica came into the hall. She was wearing pleated, gray wool trousers, and a man-tailored, white blouse, the sleeves rolled up to her elbows. She was smiling, but her eyes were grim.

"I guess you saw today's papers, right?" Gold asked. When she nodded, he said, "We'll talk after dinner."

Whenever possible, Gold liked to have the family together for the evening meal, even if it meant that the kids had to have a snack to tide them over. Gold didn't mind the kids' tumult at the table. He felt that he had endured his share of dining alone in his life. He was glad that Erica didn't mind the admittedly unfashionable arrangement, but then she'd grown up in a close-knit farm family.

The family had dinner in the big dining room. Gold got a kick out of the fact that Erica had begun collecting china, lining the walls with her collection so that the room began to resemble her mother's dining room back in Doreen. As usual, the conversation was commandeered by the kids as the servants served the meal. Ramona was still with them, but now there was also another Mexican girl to help with the cooking and cleaning. Ramona bossed her around like a drill sergeant.

After dinner the kids went into the solarium to listen to the radio. Gold and Erica went out to the patio beside the swimming pool. The submerged pool lights transformed the water into a shimmering, turquoise rectangle. Snowy moths fluttered around the glowing Chinese lanterns strung through the branches of the eucalyptus trees arching above.

Gold put his arm around Erica, who leaned against him. "The pool is beautiful tonight," he said.

"Yes." Erica sounded amused. "Strange thing for you to notice . . ."

"We've got so much. We have a luxurious home. We travel, we have all the money we'll ever need . . ." He paused. "I feel—satisfied." He looked at Erica. "Do you understand what I'm saying?"

"I think so," Erica replied.

"Good! Would you explain it to me, because I'm pretty confused . . ."

Erica laughed. "For starters, has this got to do with Tim Campbell?"

Gold nodded. "I guess."

"Care to elaborate?"

"I've been trying to get riled up over what he's doing. I mean, I *should* feel indignant, but mostly what I feel is hurt. You know what's been really getting me down? The fact that no matter what happens, it appears that I've lost both Hull Stiles and Tim as friends."

"Have you tried to talk to Hull?" Erica asked.

Gold nodded. "I tried telephoning, but he wouldn't take the call, so I drove over to the airport to confront him. We talked; I told him that there were no hard feelings on my part. That he was his own man, and had to do what he had to do." Gold grimaced. "It was like talking to a stranger."

"He's ashamed, that's what it is," Erica said confidently.

"Hull's just doing what Tim tells him to do. And I don't think Tim means to do me harm. He merely wants to do well for himself. It somehow seems petty to me to try and stop him. It goes back to what I was saying before. If Campbell wins, I'll still have GAT. If I win, Tim and Hull will be ruined. They've both sunk everything into this. For them it's do or die. I don't want to win that way . . . On the other hand, I don't want Tim to get away with this scott-free," Gold added. "It's a competition, and I don't want to be seen as a loser." He smiled. "Does that sound petty?"

"I think you *are* feeling indignation," Erica said. "You just don't know it. I can tell you that for as long as I've known you, you have never been a petty man. The question becomes, can you beat Tim at what we both know is his game?"

"Campbell seems pretty confident that I can't," Gold replied. He looked at his wife. "If I didn't win, how would you feel about it? I mean, you wouldn't look down at me on account of it? . . ."

Erica groaned, hugging him. "You are *so* dumb, sometimes. Why do you have to keep learning the same lesson? I'm proud of your accomplishments, but I *love* you. You've made it possible for me and the children to enjoy a wonderful life—"

"You've made your own life wonderful," Gold interrupted. "You're the racer in the family, not me—"

"Herman, I'm under no illusions about my racing career. I'm good, but I'm not the best."

"Hey, come on . . ." Gold chided her. "You do very well."

"But I'm not the best," Erica firmly repeated. "And by now I think we both know that I'm not going to be. It's the fact that GAT donates money and equipment to the racers that gets me invitations to participate in the more exclusive events, like the Schneider Trophy seaplane competitions, or the National Air Races. Anyway, do *you* love *me* any less because I don't bring home first-place trophies?"

"Of course not," Gold said. "It doesn't even occur to me to think that way."

"Well, that's how I feel about you. I've told you that before."

Gold hugged her. "I guess your reassurance is the only thing I can't get enough of."

"I know," Erica said. "But have no worries about that, darling. I'll never get tired of telling you."

Gold smiled. "Why don't we go upstairs, and you can explain all this to me at length, and in intricate detail?"

"Actions do speak louder than words, darling. Shall we go?"

As they walked back to the house, Erica said, "It's too bad there isn't a way for everyone to win."

Gold stopped. "Maybe there is," he said slowly. "You know, Teddy said the same thing to me today that you just said: that I can't hope to compete with Tim at his own game. I guess I have been trying to do that. I've been so busy reacting to what Tim's been doing that I haven't really thought about what I might want out of this, and how I should go about getting it."

"Does this mean we're not going to bed?" Erica sighed good-naturedly.

Gold glanced at his watch. "I have to make a few telephone calls first."

"Telephone calls, hmmm?" Erica nibbled at his ear. "My, aren't we a big man..."

"You wait for me in bed. When I'm done telephoning, I'll come up and tell you what I'm planning, and then I'll show you just how big."

(Three)
Campbell Household
Pacific Palisades

Tim Campbell, in pajamas and robe, was in his study. The walls were lined with hand-tooled leather volumes that

Campbell had purchased for their luxurious bindings rather than their precious contents. On his mahogany desk a brass lamp with a green glass shade cast a golden pool of light. Campbell had his cigarettes and a tall scotch on the rocks to keep him company. He was going over his personal brokerage accounts when the telephone rang, startling him.

As he lifted the receiver he glanced at the antique, black marble clock on the fireplace mantel. It was almost midnight. The house had been quiet. The kids were asleep and Aggie had long since gone to bed. Even the servants had retired for the night.

"Tim? It's Layton Saunders. Sorry to disturb you at this hour."

"No problem, Layton," Campbell said jovially. Saunders had a large holding of Skyworld, and sat on the board of directors as chairman of finance. Campbell wasn't sure which way Saunders was going to vote come next week's stockholders' meeting. "What can I do for you?"

"I received a call from Herman. I guess he asked me to contact you because I'm still a neutral party in all this. Anyway, he asked me to inform you that as chairman he's invoking his authority under the company's by-laws to call an unscheduled meeting of the board."

"A meeting?" Campbell repeated sharply. "When?"

"On the fifteenth, at ten A.M."

"Four days before the stockholders' meeting!" Campbell exclaimed. "What kind of rabbit does he think he can pull out of his hat at that late date! I won't attend, Layton, and I tell you now, Hull won't attend either. And there's a few other board members backing me who'll boycott that meeting when I tell them to—"

"Perhaps there are, Tim," Saunders replied evenly. "But I beg you to reconsider. I've made some other calls this evening. I can assure you there are enough board members who will attend for Herman to have a quorum."

"Well, I guess *now* I know whose side you're on," Campbell said stiffly.

"You do not," Saunders said. "Because I don't yet know. This much I *do* know. Herman has the right to call this meeting, considering all he's done for the company—"

"All *he's* done?" Campbell blurted in disbelief.

"—I think the least we can do is pay him the courtesy of hearing what he's got to say."

Saunders had a point, Campbell realized. And the more he thought about it, the more it seemed as if Saunders were sounding as if he too believed that Herman was licked. If everybody believed that Tim Campbell was a winner, why not act like one?

"You're absolutely right, Layton. I hold a winning hand. I can afford to be magnanimous to the *outgoing* chairman. I'll be at the meeting. But I insist that it be held someplace neutral."

"Herman anticipated your feelings," Saunders said. "He asked me if the meeting might be held in my downtown offices. I agreed. I assume that is acceptable to you?"

"That will be fine."

"See you at the meeting," Saunders said.

"Good-bye, Layton." Campbell hung up the telephone. An instant later it rang again. He snatched at the receiver. "Yes?"

"I've been trying to call, but the line was busy," Hull said.

"I was talking to Saunders."

"So you know about the meeting," Hull said nervously. "What are we going to do?"

"Nothing!" Campbell heard the latent panic in his tone, and forced himself to calm down. "There's nothing we have to do, because we've got it made. All that's going to happen on the fifteenth is that Herman is going to humiliate himself in front of the board by making some sort of last-ditch plea to be allowed to keep his company. The board isn't going to buy it. Even if they wanted to, they can't. I went over the stock tallies you gave me this afternoon. Are your figures accurate?"

"Of course they're accurate," Hull said, sounding offended. "When you put me in charge of keeping our Skyworld stock accounts I promised you I'd do the job right . . ."

"Yeah, you did," Campbell said. "I'm sorry, Hull. I'm tired, and I guess I'm a little high-strung these days."

"We both are," Hull muttered. "Don't forget that you're

not the only one in this. I've got every dime of my own locked up in this scheme."

"I know that," Campbell said. "And I know I couldn't pull this off without your help," he added truthfully. "And I promise you, we will pull this off."

"I hope you're right. Just don't underestimate Herman," Hull warned. "We *both* know what he's capable of when his back is up against the wall."

Campbell laughed uneasily. "A shotgun and a can of gasoline won't do him any good this time around."

"Just don't underestimate him," Hull repeated firmly. "Tim, we've both been poor, and we've been rich, and we know rich is a lot better." He hung up.

Campbell downed what remained of his scotch, and went to the drink tray on the sideboard. He picked up the decanter in which he kept his scotch, intending to pour himself another drink, but he paused. The decanter was crystal and gold. It was about 150 years old. It had been manufactured by a guy named Johann Mildner, who specialized in creating two layers of glass and fitting them together with engraved gold leaf sandwiched in between.

Mildner had been Austrian. Was that the same as a German, like Herman? Campbell decided that it was close enough—

To all clever Germans, he thought, taking a long swig of scotch straight from the decanter.

His ranch house was perched on a cliff above the Pacific. He took the decanter with him as he stepped out through the French doors of his study, onto one of the house's terraces overlooking the ocean. The warm wind blowing off the sea carried a tang of salt. The breeze rippled his robe. It was a cloudy, moonless night, but Campbell could make out the white spume as the waves raged against the rocks.

It was better to be rich than poor, Hull had said. Campbell couldn't argue with that. He and Herman had made themselves rich, and brought Hull Stiles and Teddy Quinn along for the ride. Both Hull and Teddy were good men, but Campbell and Gold had been the partners who'd made it all happen—

But now the partners were on opposite sides, Campbell thought, sipping from the decanter.

Campbell knew that money wasn't enough, that a man needed a challenge to make life worthwhile. He'd worked hard to become rich, and now he was risking it all in order to take control of the company he loved. Once Skyworld was in his hands he would run with it; take it all the way. He would forge it into the biggest and best airline in the country, and maybe even the world—

He hadn't been lying when he'd once told Herman Gold that he wanted the turquoise and scarlet fleet to dominate the skies, but now it was going to be *his* fleet. Skyworld was going to belong to him. He was gambling his and his family's future on being able to pull this off, and he knew he could do it. He was positive he could—

But why was Herman calling this meeting? What the hell did he have in mind?

"Don't underestimate Herman . . . ," Hull had said. "Remember what Herman can be like when his back is up against the wall . . ."

Campbell remembered, and shuddered.

He looked at the crystal and gold decanter in his hand. A hundred and fifty years old. Austrian. One of a kind, the shopkeeper had said. Campbell had a photographic memory when it came to remembering how much things cost. The price tag on this baby had been sixteen hundred bucks.

Campbell went to the terrace balustrade, drew back his arm, and hurled the decanter as far as he could. As it went spinning away in the darkness, trailing a liquid plume of golden scotch, Campbell prayed to whatever gods paid attention to such matters that he *win*.

He listened hard. He wasn't sure, but he thought he heard the decanter shatter against the rocks. The black and restless ocean's crash suddenly sounded like the sustained roar of a distant, cheering crowd.

"Fuck it," Campbell told the amused night sea. "Money isn't everything."

Chapter 13

(One)
Downtown Los Angeles
15 April 1933

Gold paused as he walked by the Horatio Building, on the corner of South Olive and Sixth Streets. Saunders's offices were up on the tenth floor. Gold knew that in a very little while he was going to have to do some pretty fancy fast-talking up there . . .

He looked at his watch. It was nine thirty in the morning, a half hour before the board meeting Gold had called.

"First things first," Gold muttered to himself as he continued past the Horatio Building and then turned right onto Sixth. As he walked he looked at his reflection in the storefront plate-glass windows. He was wearing an ivory linen, snap-brim fedora and a very conservative, dark blue, pinstriped suit. Double-breasted. If ever there was a day to look youthful and vigorous, this was it.

He turned left on Broadway and walked a couple of blocks to Berry's Cafeteria. He went inside. The breakfast rush was over. The place was fairly empty except for upstairs, where a few fellows down on their luck were smoking cigarettes and lingering over their "bottomless" cups of coffee at the tables along the balcony. Behind the food service area the attendants in their white coats were clearing the remains of the hotcakes and scrambled eggs from the steam tables. One of the employees was up on a stepladder, chalking the lunchtime specials onto the big hanging blackboard: *Chicken Noodle Soup with Crackers 15¢/ Macaroni & Cheese 35¢/Chipped Beef on Toast 55¢*

Gold finally spotted Hull Stiles. He was slouched at a table against the back wall, beneath a sweeping mural of California landscapes: the coastline, an oil field, a desert scene, a redwood forest.

Gold went over to the counter, ordered a cup of coffee, paid a bored-looking cashier in her booth, and then took it over to Hull's table. Hull was wearing a tan three-piece suit. Gold never could get used to Hull wearing a suit and tie, or anything other than flying clothes. Hull's square-jawed, leathery face, weathered by his years spent in open cockpits, looked drawn and haggard. Gold noticed that Hull's blond hair, slicked back and as thick as ever, had begun to show gray at the temples. Time was taking its toll on everyone, Gold mused.

Hull had a tray in front of him. On it was a cup of coffee and a barely touched slice of apple pie. Next to the tray was a crimson pack of Pall Malls, and an ashtray overflowing with cigarette butts. The pie looked good, but Gold, thinking about his ever-expanding waistline, decided against going back to get some.

"Thanks for agreeing to meet," Gold said, taking a seat.

Hull nodded, fidgeting. "If Tim finds out . . ."

"He won't." Gold sipped at his coffee.

"The reason I agreed is I'd like there to be no bad blood between us," Hull blurted. "Do you think that's possible? We could be friends again? . . ."

"You'll always be my friend," Gold said. "Christ, do you think I've forgotten how you saved my life? I'll always owe you for that, and for taking care of me again when you sent me that note tipping me off to what Tim was up to."

Hull stared at him. "How the hell did you know it was me who sent the note?" Hull finally asked, lighting a Pall Mall.

"Actually I didn't *know*, until just now." Gold smiled. "But two things made me suspect it was you. The note was typed. The lowercase 't' in the note had a broken crossbar that seemed familiar. It reminded me of the broken 'little t' on that banged-up, secondhand Underwood we bought for the Mines Field office, back when we first started Gold Express."

Hull chuckled. "You got a good memory, buddy. That was the typewriter I used, all right."

"I can't believe you still have it," Gold marveled.

"I got it up on a shelf in my office," Hull said. "I got a lot of stuff from the old days."

"Sentimental," Gold said.

"Nah," Hull said gruffly. He stared down at the ashtray as he ground out his cigarette. "Not about most things, anyway, but I think I do miss our old days, Herm. I'm glad I got money, and all, but I almost wish we could go back to that time. We might have been living hand to mouth, but we were happy, you know?"

"Yeah, I know," Herman said.

"Maybe it was that things were simple," Hull said, his voice full of longing. "I knew what I was doing. Now Tim's got me acting as his purchasing agent to accumulate Skyworld stock. I'm spending my days hunting down stray shares and keeping ledgers, like I was a goddamned bookkeeper."

"I heard that he had you doing that," Gold said.

"Sometimes I got to remind myself that I'm still in the airline business..."

"You're still in it, all right," Gold said. "No one knows the ins and outs of the airline business better than you."

"I can't wait until I can forget all this stock business and get back to doing what I know..." Hull trailed off, shaking his head. "You said there were two things that tipped you off about the note?" he asked briskly. "What was the second?"

Gold smiled. "You're the only person involved who cares enough about me to give me a warning about the takeover."

Hull looked miserable. "I do care," he whispered.

"Then help me, now," Gold said quickly.

"What are you talking about?"

"I can make it so that no one person gets hurt in this," Gold said. "But I need your help to do it. You've got to trust me, and do what I ask."

"Has this got to do with this morning's board meeting?"

Hull looked hopeful, but the expression faded. "You want me to betray Tim, right?"

"No," Gold said firmly. "If you care about everyone involved, it's not a betrayal to help put through a compromise solution that will be to everyone's benefit."

"Why do I have to come into it at all?" Hull asked uneasily. "If your plan is so goddamned clever why not just do it and leave me out of it?"

"I thought about trying to pull off what I have in mind without your help. It could work that way, but the chances of success are a lot better if you'll play along."

Hull nodded in resignation. "You give me your word that nobody will get hurt?"

"No, I didn't say that," Gold replied. "We're all going to be hurt. I can promise you that with my plan all three of us will get something we want, but all three of us are also going to have to pay a price."

Hull glanced at his watch. "It's almost time for the meeting. We ought to leave here separately." He laughed nervously. "It wouldn't do for us to be seen arriving at Saunders's office together—"

He's not going to help, Gold thought. He'd been counting on Hull's cooperation. Without it, his entire strategy was in jeopardy.

Hull gathered his cigarettes and stood up. "You call me, tonight, at my home. You tell me what you want me to do, and I'll do it. All right?"

"Yeah . . . Sure." Gold grinned with relief. "Thanks, Hull. But you don't yet know what I have in mind—"

"Don't have to," Hull said firmly. "I know *you*. Whatever it is, it's the right thing."

Gold watched Hull leave the cafeteria. He figured to wait a minute to give him a head start.

A busboy wheeling his cart paused at the table. He eyed Hull's tray. "Finished here?" the kid asked.

"All except the pie," Gold sighed, lifting the plate from the tray. He polished it off in three bites.

Tim Campbell was waiting in the doorway to Layton Saunders's conference room when Gold arrived. Campbell made a big show of smiling and shaking hands with Gold for the benefit of the other directors who were already seated. He stood aside to let Gold enter the room first.

"Get ready for world war two," Campbell whispered as Gold passed him by.

All ten directors were present as Gold took his place at the head of the rectangular mahogany table. Campbell, as president, sat at the opposite end. Beside him was Hull, the C.E.O. of the company. Next to Hull sat Layton Saunders, who was chairman of finance. Saunders was a burly, bearded gent, partial to Irish country tweeds, gaudy satin waistcoats, and smelly cigars. He had more money than anybody Gold knew. Saunders's grandfather had been one of the original California forty-niners. The old boy had struck gold in the rugged Sierra Nevada Mountains. The Saunders family had parlayed that stake into a West Coast real estate empire.

Gold avoided making eye contact with any of the directors. On the wall was an antique Wells Fargo banjo clock, bracketed by the dour portraits of Saunders's father and grandfather. The clock chimed the hour.

"Well, I suppose we can begin," Gold said, standing up.

He realized that he was sweating. He was having a hard time catching his breath. He stared down at the blank yellow legal pad in front of him. He had to get hold of himself. Hell, back when he and Campbell were traveling around peddling stock he'd faced far more hostile audiences. He could do this. He had to do it.

"Gentlemen," Gold began. "I called this emergency board meeting for a specific reason. If Mister Campbell wins his proxy fight and becomes chairman, he will acquire Cargo Air Transport, and with it, a Chicago to New York route that will make Skyworld a coast-to-coast airline. I applaud Mister Campbell's devotion to *my* company—"

Gold paused. He stared around the table, daring the others to contest his choice of words. The gazes of several of the directors could not meet his. Gold suddenly felt comfortable. For the first time since this mess began he felt in charge.

"Yes, I do applaud Mister Campbell's loyalty to Sky-world, but he is gravely mistaken in his intended course of action. I called this admittedly unprecedented, emergency meeting because I intend to rescue my airline from the brink of disaster."

Gold noticed that Campbell, leaning back in his chair, was smiling. Campbell winked, as if to say, *Have your fun while you can, Herman . . .*

And you smile while you can, Tim, Gold thought, but resisted the urge to wink back.

"The proposed Cargo Air acquisition is a disaster because of its cost, and because of the evolving political climate in this country. These two negative aspects are fundamentally related. Cargo Air's stock price has been artificially inflated by the unnatural conditions imposed upon the free market by the Watres Act."

Gold paused for a beat; the way he'd learned to do in order to recapture an audience's flagging attention back when he and Tim were scouring the countryside in search of initial investors.

"The skies above this great nation are vast, gentlemen," he continued, his tone reverent, impassioned. "There is more than enough room for the various airlines to compete with one another for passengers." Gold suddenly brought his fist crashing down against the tabletop. A couple of the directors flinched. "All that's stopping us is the Watres Act!" he declared fiercely. "I believe that part of our *new* president's *New* Deal may be a *new* look at this ill-conceived conspiracy by the postal service to barricade the heavens."

Several directors, Saunders included, were frowning in disapproval. Gold had expected that: these men had come out early and loud on behalf of Hoover's reelection bid. They'd long ago petrified each other by exchanging rumors about how that "socialist" FDR was going to "redistribute the wealth." Ironically, these so-called capitalists supported government intervention in their affairs through the Watres Act because it closed the door on new competition in their airlines industry. Gold hadn't intended to convince the Board to accept his antiregulatory point of view. He just wanted to plant an uncomfortable seed of doubt in their minds concerning the uncertain future.

"If the chairman will excuse the interruption," Campbell said. "We all know that in the recent presidential election Mister Gold was a Roosevelt man." Campbell made a show of looking at his watch. "If the chairman would get to his point, assuming he has one, it would be appreciated. I do have a rather important luncheon date . . ."

The directors who had already announced themselves behind Campbell did not try to hide their smiles. Gold ignored them.

"My point is that a conservative long-term corporate strategy is sound business practice during uncertain times. Skyworld should not be looking to expand, but to retrench. It should be looking to weather what you all must admit is a possible—and I would say *probable*—industrywide hurricane of reform. When that hurricane hits—not *if* it hits, gentlemen, but *when*—not everyone will survive. For those who do, transcontinental routes will be the least of their spoils."

Gold looked around. All eyes were upon him. There was nothing like a forecast of gloom and doom to rivet an audience's attention. Now was the time to make his move—

"As chairman it is my duty to do all I can on behalf of the stockholders to see to it that my company survives. Accordingly, I move that this board authorize a new issue of Skyworld stock—"

"Wait a minute!" Campbell shouted, jumping to his feet. "There's no call for a new issue of stock—"

"—A new issue of a quarter of a million shares," Gold pressed on, ignoring Campbell's outburst, "which is, according to my calculations, the amount necessary to recapitalize a weakened Skyworld—"

"What you really want to do is erase the numerical advantage of the shares I now hold!" Campbell yelled in accusation. "What by-law gives you the right to pull this hornswoggle!"

"Page fifty-two, paragraph four, clause D—" Gold began innocently.

"Don't quote me the goddamned rules," Campbell bellowed. "I wrote the goddamned rules! Paragraph four states there's got to be an emergency. There's no emergency—"

"Tim, calm down," Saunders interjected. "The chairman still has the floor."

Gold waited a moment, to let it sink in that Campbell had lost his control. Hopefully, with any further displays of temper, Gold could bait Campbell into showing the others just what sort of chairman Tim would *be* under pressure . . .

"Thank you, Mister Saunders," Gold politely said. "Now, then, to address Mister Campbell's objection: The emergency is the threat poised by Mister Campbell's proxy fight, and the disastrous course on which he means to take Skyworld should he win."

"A question, if I may, Mister Chairman?" Campbell asked. He was back in his chair, and had regained his poise. "Isn't it true that if we suddenly flood the market with a new issue of stock the price per share will drop, further weakening the company during your so-called time of peril?"

"I never said anything about putting those shares on the market," Gold replied. "What I propose is an exchange: two hundred and fifty thousand shares of Skyworld to be exchanged for three hundred and seventy-five thousand shares of GAT. For every one share of its stock, Skyworld would receive one and a half shares of GAT. Since I am chairman of GAT's board, and control fifty-one percent of its stock, I can assure you that GAT will look favorably on the transaction."

"This is absurd!" Campbell sputtered.

"Is it?" Gold shrugged. "Since 1925 Skyworld has steadfastly stood behind GAT, the former ready to lend its financial strength to the latter in its endeavors to bring new and advanced aeronautical designs into reality. I'm sure you gentlemen have been following the stock market recently. You all know that Mister Campbell's takeover threat has brought a measure of instability to the price of Skyworld. There have been troubling rumors swirling on Wall Street, rumors that there may have been some unethical windfalls being enjoyed by certain participants in this takeover battle."

Gold pretended not to see Campbell's glare. "On the other hand, GAT's stock price has steadily risen. This is because the public knows that GAT made aviation history with the G-1 Yellowjacket and G-1a Dragonfly. This is because the public witnessed the United States Navy select GAT to supply that branch of the service with its new torpedo bomber, and because the public, like the rest of the world, anticipates the debut of GAT's greatest triumph: the fabulous GC-1 Monarch, the commercial airliner of the future."

Gold paused. "Skyworld has been a faithful friend to GAT in its times of trouble and strife. Now GAT stands ready to rescue Skyworld."

"It won't wash, Herman," Campbell growled. His livid gaze swept the table. "I warn all of you, it won't wash! The stockholders' meeting is in four days. I'll use the votes vested in me by proxy to throw the lot of you out—"

"That is no way to talk to fellow board members," Saunders growled.

Gold was elated. "Excuse me, Mister Campbell," he said coolly, "but proxy authorizations can be rescinded. Four days is enough time for the board to get the word out to the stockholders via press conferences, radio announcements, and newspaper ads. Our argument will be that a substantial interest in GAT will raise Skyworld's stock price. Surely our stockholders will approve of that. Not to mention that GAT's profits from the sale of the Monarch will prove to be just the sort of fallback resource Skyworld will need in the chaos following the rescinding of the Watres Act."

"*What* rescission?" Campbell shouted in frustration. "*What* airplane? You haven't even got a goddamned prototype yet!"

That much was true, Gold thought. But actually, the Monarch project was further along than Campbell knew. Since he'd moved his office out of the Burbank complex, Teddy's team had solved the Monarch's rudder-control problem when flying with one engine out. Work had immediately begun on a prototype. The completion date was less than five weeks away.

"Gentlemen, I'm sure you understand that I'm reluctant to go into the specifics," Gold said. "This much I will say: Mister Campbell has been so immersed in his takeover campaign that he has been out of touch with what's been going on at GAT." Gold looked around. "Well, gentlemen, if there's no more discussion, I suggest we take a vote on my proposal."

Saunders looked at Campbell. "Any objection?"

"Hell, no. Let's vote." Campbell scowled. "And look, to save time concerning this nonsense, why not just go around the table with a voice vote?"

"That's highly irregular," Saunders worried, chewing on his cigar stub.

"*That*'s highly irregular?" Campbell burst out laughing.

"I certainly have no objection," Gold said. "Considering my personal interest in the outcome, I defer to Mister Saunders, who has remained neutral during this conflict, to carry out the procedure."

Gold sat down. Now it was out of his hands. He knew that of the eleven men on the board, three besides Hull Stiles belonged to Campbell's takeover group. Gold knew how he himself would vote, which meant that he needed all five of the remaining votes to win. Campbell needed only one vote from the five in order to defeat Gold's plan.

"A voice vote, then, on Mister Gold's proposal," Saunders said. "I will vote last. Mister Campbell, will you begin?"

"I vote no," Campbell declared.

"Mister Stiles?"

Hull, pale, his eyes downcast, whispered, "No."

That's all right, old friend, Gold thought.

"No." "Yes." "No." "No." "Yes."

The vote was moving quickly around the room: five to two in Campbell's favor. Campbell's faction, predictably, had voted in a block. Gold knew that those who'd so far voted for *his* proposal were doing so out of self-interest, not loyalty or friendship. GAT's record on successfully marketing new planes was one of the best in the business. If the Monarch followed suit, the GAT holding that Gold was offering could easily triple in value.

"Yes." "Yes."

Five to four, Gold thought. He was careful to keep his hands, with his fingers crossed, hidden under the table.

Saunders looked at him. "Mister Gold?"

"Yes," Gold said, making it five all. Saunders would break the tie.

"I vote aye, as well," Saunders said. "The vote is six to five in favor of the proposal."

Gold stood up. "Gentlemen, thank you for your support. I will at once set in motion—"

Campbell got to his feet. "It's only fair to warn all of you I will challenge this in the courts." He paused significantly. "*And* in the press."

"I'm disappointed, Tim." Gold shrugged. "But I can't say that I'm surprised. You always did like to wash your dirty laundry in public."

"And I'm going to crucify you at the stockholders' meeting!" Campbell vowed.

"Maybe not," Gold said calmly. "The new stock issue and subsequent exchange will muddy the waters for a lot of investors. The fact that the board has endorsed it will carry a lot of weight. The stockholders may decide to, for the time being, stick with the status quo, just to see what might be shaking down. They might decide that there's always time to make a change . . . Like during *next* year's stockholders' meeting."

Gold paused. "But, of course, you don't really have until next year, do you, Tim?"

Gold struggled to keep from grinning as Campbell stormed out.

(Two)
Gold Household
19 April 1933

Gold awoke at five-thirty in the morning; as usual, a few moments before the alarm clock on the night table was set to go off. He reset the clock for seven, when Erica, who was sound asleep and softly snoring beside him, wanted to wake up, and carefully got out of bed so as not to disturb her.

Gold showered and shaved, thinking all the while about the Skyworld stockholders' meeting scheduled to begin at nine o'clock in the grand ballroom at the Swadsworth Hotel in downtown Los Angeles. He wrapped himself in a terry-cloth robe and went downstairs, where Ramona fetched him a cup of coffee. He took it into his study. He stared at the telephone on his desk for a moment. He took a deep breath and let it out, to calm himself, and then telephoned Tim Campbell.

A servant answered, and protested that Mister Campbell was sleeping. Gold identified himself and insisted that the servant wake Campbell up. It took a couple of minutes for Campbell to come on the line.

"My God, Herman! What do you want at this hour!"

"That was pretty fast work the way you got that judge to issue a court injunction against the new stock issue," Gold said.

"That's what you called to tell me?" Campbell complained, yawning. "Anyway, it was easy," he said. "I didn't even have to bribe the judge to get it done. Nobody can pull that kind of stunt in the market anymore, and you can thank your buddy Roosevelt for that. You heard the talk that he's got some kind of permanent commission in mind to be a watchdog on Wall Street?"

"Yeah, I heard that," Gold said.

"I pity a guy starting out today," Campbell muttered. "There's going to be too many rules getting in the way of things . . ."

"You've got to admit, I whipped your ass at that board meeting."

Campbell was silent for a moment, but then he chuckled. "Yeah, you did, Herm. But you always did know how to work a crowd. God, you were good! You got balls, Herman. That's what I love about you. I always will. Anyway, we'll see whose ass gets whipped today."

"Meaning mine? We'll see . . ."

"Herman, please!" Campbell scoffed. "You're beat and you don't know it! The part I like is that you screwed yourself! That injunction I got against you made you look bad in the newspapers. The public hasn't forgotten how they got fleeced by fast-talkers back in '29, you know. My getting a judge to come out against you evidently scared quite a few investors out of your fold. Skyworld stock has had a lot of activity the past couple of days, and guess who bought all he needed?"

"I bet you paid top dollar."

"Who cares?" Campbell said. "There's no doubt in my mind that at today's meeting I'll get enough votes to put me over the top. Skyworld is mine."

"It sounds bad for me, Tim," Gold admitted. "Listen, there's some things I'd like to talk over with you, face-to-face. Why don't we meet? Say, at eight? In the coffee shop at the Swadsworth?"

"You want to talk surrender, is that it?" Campbell chuckled.

"Maybe we could work something out between us before the meeting," Gold said meekly. "Come on, for old times, what do you say?"

"Sure, Herman. See you at eight in the coffee shop," Campbell said, and hung up. Gold broke the connection and immediately dialed Teddy Quinn's number. Teddy answered on the first ring.

"He went for it," Gold said.

"What time?" Teddy asked.

"Eight o'clock. When I'm done with him I'll call you at Burbank."

Gold hung up, and left the study. He bumped into Ramona, the housekeeper, on his way upstairs to get dressed.

"*Señor* Gold, you must eat! I'll make you bacon and eggs—"

Gold gathered up the surprised maid and waltzed her around before continuing on his way upstairs. "No, thanks, Ramona. Today I'm going to have the new chairman of Skyworld for breakfast."

Gold got to the coffee shop in the Swadsworth Hotel precisely at eight. Campbell wasn't there, and Gold spent a few anxious minutes in a corner booth staring into his coffee as if it were a crystal ball in which he could portend the future. He worried that he'd misjudged Campbell's desire to gloat ... What if Campbell had decided not to show?

Campbell appeared at eight-fifteen. "Sorry, Herm," he said nonchalantly as he slid into the booth, opposite Gold.

"A couple of stockholders collared me in the lobby . . . to congratulate me," he pointedly added.

"Hey, you won. You deserve to be congratulated."

"Then you do admit that you're beat," Campbell pounced.

Gold sighed. "I've been thinking it over since we talked this morning." He nodded in resignation. "Yeah, I'm beat, Tim." He extended his hand across the table. "No hard feelings?"

Campbell shook hands. "None on my side, but hell, why would there be? I'm not the loser." He smiled.

The waiter came, and Campbell ordered coffee. When they were alone Campbell lit a cigarette and said, "Surely you didn't want to meet just to concede my victory?"

"No, I've come to make a deal with you. I know I can't stop you, so why not let me get out of this with something left of my pride, just for old times' sake?"

"What have you got in mind?" Campbell asked as the waiter appeared with his coffee.

"I've got twenty percent of Skyworld. Why don't you buy me out?"

"Too late, Herman. I don't need your stock," Campbell said. "Maybe if you'd come to me all nice and polite like this a week ago I might have obliged you. But now . . ." He shook his head.

"You certainly don't need me around cramping your style."

"On the contrary," Campbell replied. "I like the idea of having you around, witnessing everything I do, but helpless to stop me." He laughed. "You want to sell, put your stock on the market. Otherwise, you can get in the backseat, keep your mouth shut, and come along for the ride."

"Oh, sure." Gold scowled. "You know it's too late. The stock is dead in the water as of today. I'll take a beating if I try and sell now."

"You should have thought of that before you tried to take me on," Campbell said.

Gold nodded sadly. "There is one other idea I had . . . I mean, I really wanted you to buy my stock," Gold said dejectedly. "But beggars can't be choosers, I guess . . ."

"You've got that right, pal."

"You've won, no matter what, but wouldn't it be worth your while not to have me making trouble that will weaken the airline further after this nasty public fight?"

"Get to the point, Herman. What do you want?"

"All right, here it is. You're going to need new airplanes now that you're a transcontinental airline. Why not contract for say, twenty of my new GC-1s?"

Campbell shrugged. "I don't know, Herm. I was thinking of going with Boeing's 247 airliner..."

"Come on, Tim," Gold said. "We both know that there's a couple of years' waiting list for Boeing's 247. They've got to fill their order for United before they can begin to build airplanes for anyone else. You really want to wait that long?"

"Well, no... But Lockheed has an interesting design..."

"Sure, the Electra, right?" Gold dismissed it with a wave. "It's got only ten-passenger capacity, where my Monarch will carry twelve." Gold shook his head. "It's up to you, pal, if you want to cut off your own nose to spite your face."

"I hear you," Campbell said. "Let's say I went along with you on this. Are you willing to give me a price break?"

Gold shook his head. "Exactly the opposite, Tim. I'm going to charge you a premium—"

"I think this defeat has been too much for you," Campbell said. "You've lost your mind."

"Hear me out. We can work out the nuts and bolts later, but the gist of my idea is that Skyworld would contract for twenty GC-1s at a hiked price that would subsidize my manufacturing costs, enabling me to undersell the competition, getting orders for my new airplane from all the other airlines. My planes will be everywhere. That's what *I* want. In exchange, *I'll* subsidize Skyworld by sitting tight on the stock I own. In the long run, it could come out cheaper for Skyworld to play things my way."

"That's all I get out of this?" Campbell scowled.

"We both get good publicity out of it," Gold said. "You're the man who taught me the importance of a good public image. What better endorsement could a man have than having his former enemy buying his product? It's got to mean that I've got the best airplane on the market!"

"And me?" Campbell demanded.

"Think of it. You and me together up on that stage; shaking hands, embracing, in front of all the stockholders."

"That would play beautifully with the press," Campbell admitted, slowly starting to smile. "But you'd have to do more. Like, say, graciously concede victory..." Campbell snapped his fingers. "I've got it! I want you to make a motion at the meeting that I be unanimously elected chairman!"

"You've got a deal," Gold said, reaching across the table to shake hands.

The Swardsworth's lobby had a marble floor, walls painted red and black, and a forest of potted palms beneath a high, gilded ceiling starry with crystal chandeliers. The lobby was crowded with stockholders on their way to the ballroom for the meeting. Gold made a detour to the public telephones and found a vacant booth. He dialed his Burbank switchboard, and asked to be put through to Teddy Quinn. Teddy's secretary answered and said that Teddy was down on the factory floor, supervising the work on the Monarch prototype. Gold waited a few minutes until Teddy was located and came on the line.

"Herman? Did it work?" Teddy demanded.

"Like a fucking charm," Gold said.

Both men were quiet for a split-second, and then both burst out laughing.

"Oh, Lord, I'd give anything to be a fly on the wall in the room when Tim finds out he already *owns* most of your Skyworld stock. He will be shit-faced!"

"It may be a while before what I did comes to light," Gold said. "And that's fine with me."

There had been a renewed flurry of trading in Skyworld following the publicity surrounding Campbell's court injunction against Gold's stock-issue ploy. Gold had used the increased market activity to camouflage his selling off all but a fraction of his Skyworld holdings. His investment broker cooperated by disposing of Gold's stock through certain brokerage houses and other friendly outlets.

"Now that you mentioned it, I hope Tim doesn't find out, for Hull's sake," Teddy said. "And for the sake of the deal."

Gold had done all he could to remain anonymous, but it was Hull's cooperation that had been crucial. Campbell had delegated to Hull the authority to buy as much Skyworld as he could, no matter the price, as long as the buy was made prior to the stockholders' meeting. Despite all of Gold's precautions in disposing of his Skyworld holdings, Hull could have found out who was putting up such large blocks of stock if he'd asked the right questions. It was Hull's promise not to ask those questions that assured Gold that he could make good on his own, earlier promise to his old friend: everyone had gotten something they wanted, but everyone had paid a price.

"Don't worry. Hull's got a defense when the truth comes to light," Gold replied. "Tim's Achilles' heel is that he thinks he's so much damned smarter than everyone else. All Hull has to do is say that I tricked him, like I tricked Campbell. Tim will buy that. He has to. He needs Hull to handle the day-to-day running of his airline. And don't worry about Tim's promise to buy our airplanes. You know him as well as I do. He'll stick to his word, even if he was tricked into giving it."

"So how do you feel about it all?" Campbell asked.

"Tim and Hull have their company. I've lost Skyworld, but I've made a lot of money in the last couple of days, and the GC-1 Monarch is getting the leg-up on the competition that will help it to dominate the industry. What's most important to me, personally, is that it looks like we can all remain friends."

"Not bad," Teddy said. "Considering that during the past couple of years you've become only marginally interested in the airline business, anyway."

"I owe it all to Tim." Gold laughed. "I've never forgotten the lesson he taught me years ago: 'Never give anything away.'"

BOOK V:
1933–1943

AMERICA TOASTS TO PROHIBITION'S REPEAL—
"The Drink's on Us," Lawmakers Tell a Thirsty Nation—
Philadelphia Bulletin–Journal

HITLER ELECTED TO BE NEW HEAD OF STATE—
Germans Swear Allegiance to their Führer—
New York Gazette

GOLD AVIATION AND TRANSPORT WINS 1934
ROSS TROPHY—
GC-2 Monarch Airliner Takes Aviation's Top Award—
FDR Congratulates GAT Founder Herman Gold at White
House Fete—
Baltimore Globe

LUFT HANSA COMMERCIAL AIRLINE SPANS
GLOBE—
Goering Named German Air Minister—
RAF Calls Luft Hansa a Smokescreen for Secret War
Buildup—
London Post

U.S. WAR DEPT. HOLDS AVIATION CONFERENCE—
Aviation Industry Vows to Answer Call for a New Heavy
Bomber—
Herman Gold Rebuffed on Fighters—
GAT Founder Told the Future of Air Power Belongs to
the Bomber—
Aviation Trade magazine

JAPANESE FLEET INVADES CHINESE PORT OF
SWATOW—
Both Sides Shell Each Other at Yunting River—

Chinese Leader Chiang Kai-shek Warns That War Is
Imminent—

Boston Times

GERMANY ENTERS INTO PACTS WITH ITALY,
JAPAN—
Mussolini Describes "Axis" Around Which Powers May
Work Together—

San Francisco Post

FRANCE, ENGLAND DECLARE WAR ON
GERMANY—

Los Angeles Banner

U.S. ENTERS WAR AFTER JAPS BOMB PEARL
HARBOR—

Washington Star Reporter

Chapter 14

(One)
Hotel Regina
Venice, Italy
10 June 1938

Gold was awakened by the low rumble of a motor launch cruising past the hotel. He was all alone in the big, canopied bed. Erica, wide awake and dressed, was finishing putting on her makeup at the mirrored vanity table.

She saw him looking at her in the mirror, and threw him a kiss. "It's close to nine, sleepyhead. I'm on my way out."

"Where are you off to?" Gold mumbled, stretching under the covers.

"Suzy and I had breakfast sent up. We want to get an early start sightseeing so we can catch the first of the races before lunch."

"What about Steven?"

"He's a sleepyhead, like his father," Erica said. "He thinks sightseeing is sissy stuff, so I told him he could come along with you, later."

"Fine." Gold yawned, and sat up in bed. Erica was donning a plum-colored hat. Gold watched, amused, as she intently experimented with the rake of its wide brim in the mirror. She caught him looking, and stuck out her tongue at him as she stood up. "Well, do you approve?" she demanded, pirouetting.

Gold smiled. She had on a long-sleeved, tan silk dress, cinched snugly at the waist with a braided leather belt. Her white anklets were turned down over sand-colored, suede bucks with red crepe soles.

"Like a dewy young school girl," he said. "He patted the bed. Care to come over here and fool around with a dirty old man?"

"You sleep late, you miss out. See you at the races, to coin a phrase," she said gaily, grabbing her purse as she swept out of the bedroom. Gold heard her out in the sitting room, rapping on Suzy's bedroom door and telling her to hurry up.

He got out of bed and wrapped himself in his robe. He heard his wife and daughter leaving the hotel suite as he padded barefoot across the Persian carpet to throw open the French doors and step out onto the bedroom's balcony. It was a magnificent morning, clear and warm, with no humidity, thanks to the spicy sea breeze blowing in from the lagoon. Sunlight dappled the opalescent waters of the Grand Canal. The play of light and shadow embellished the unbroken line of stately, pastel-hued, quay-side palaces, their stone bulwarks etched by the centuries, grown dark and mossy down near the waterline. A gondolier, as timeless as Venice in his striped jersey, was poling his sleek, black, cigar-shaped craft toward the grand, baroque domes of the Church of Santa Maria della Salute, on the opposite side of the canal. A motor launch, a green and black, steam-powered vaporetto, passed by, churning up a frothy wake that set the spidery gondola rocking. The gondolier protested the indignity with a baleful shout as he shook his fist at the fast-departing launch.

Gold went back inside, through the bedroom, and into the parlor. Their hotel suite had three bedrooms and two baths, arranged off of this sitting room. The suite was furnished with antiques and hung with tapestries. One entire wall of the parlor was glass, opening up onto a waterside terrace that stretched the length of the room.

Gold knocked on Steven's bedroom door, telling his son to get up and get dressed. As he returned to his own bedroom, to shower and shave, and select the day's wardrobe from the armoire, its lacquered doors inlaid with mother-of-pearl, he found himself whistling in happy anticipation.

Venice held fond memories for him. The last time he had been here was back in 1936, a purely frivolous detour during a business trip that was in itself both a great pleasure and a triumphant vindication.

GAT's prototype, twin-engine, Monarch GC-1 airliner debuted in the summer of 1933, to a resoundingly positive industrywide reception. The airplane was everything that Gold had hoped, but the GC-1 never saw mass production. While GAT was tooling up its production lines, Teddy Quinn and his people worked out a way to stretch the Monarch's fuselage to allow for two more passengers. It was this "stretched" version, dubbed the GC-2, that was put into production and delivered to Tim Campbell's Skyworld Airline. Soon after, Tim Campbell would say that the smartest move he'd ever made was to let Herman Gold con him into buying the Monarch.

In 1934 the GC-2 won the coveted Ross Trophy, one of the aviation industry's highest honors. Gold would never forget the award presentation ceremony, held in the Rose Garden of the White House, and that sublime moment when President Roosevelt shook his hand in congratulations, while Erica and the kids looked on . . .

Nineteen thirty-four also saw FDR charge that the airlines were operating as an illegal cartel, and cancel all the route assignments awarded under the Watres Act. Gold took no pleasure in being proved right. He wanted things to go well for Tim Campbell and Hull Stiles. The government invited new bids on the routes, but in order to "punish" those who had participated in the cartel, no airline that had previously held a route could participate. The airlines got around that by simply changing their names: Campbell's Skyworld Airlines became Skyworld, Incorporated on its new papers. A potentially more serious restriction was that no contract would be awarded to any airline that still employed anybody who had attended the original conference in Washington to divvy up the routes, held just after the Watres Act had been passed, in 1930.

Gold was worried for Campbell; it looked as if the government was going to force Campbell's exile from his beloved Skyworld. It turned out that Gold needn't have been concerned about his old friend, who was a master of manipulating technicalities. Campbell merely resigned his position as president, put Hull Stiles in charge, and stayed on, taking no salary, as chairman emeritus. Campbell was already a very rich man, so the lack of a salary did not hurt him. Technically, he was no longer employed by the airline, he was merely an "investor"; nevertheless, no decision concerning Skyworld was made without the prior approval of the "retired president."

Gold and Campbell had become better friends now that they no longer had to argue about business. They got together once a month or so, for cocktails and dinner. They'd talk about recent happenings in the aviation industry, and reminisce about their old times. The one thing they never talked about was what Campbell's reaction had been when he'd found out how Gold had unloaded his Skyworld stock on the sly. That entire episode seemed to be closed, and Gold was content to leave well enough alone.

In 1936 the firm of Rogers and Simpson perfected a more powerful radial engine, which GAT utilized to make possible the Monarch GC-3, a deluxe, larger version of the GC-2. The "3" could sleep fourteen or seat twenty-one, in addition to a three-man crew. It was faster, sturdier, more comfortable than its predecessor, and even easier to fly. It came equipped with the latest radio aids, an autopilot, and a hydraulic system for raising and lowering the landing gear. Its large seating capacity meant that for the first time an airline could run profitably just hauling passengers and not worry about supplementing income with cargo shipments. The GC-3 sold for one hundred thousand dollars, and Gold couldn't build them fast enough. The influx of orders enabled Gold to complete phase-two construction at the Burbank complex, effectively doubling his production output. Gold also established a training school to which the airlines could send their mechanics tuition-free in order to learn how to maintain the Monarch GC series. Pretty soon, the GC was the only airplane that most airline mechanics knew how to fix, and that suited GAT just fine.

When virtually every airline in America was either flying or waiting delivery of his airplane, and the United States

Army and Navy had put in their orders for modified cargo carrier versions, Gold decided it was time to widen GAT's territory. That was when he and Erica made their grand tour of Europe, mixing business with pleasure as Gold sold the GC-3 to foreign airlines.

"I'm ready, Pop," Steven said, poking his head through the doorway of the bedroom.

"I'll be right out," Gold called, as his son disappeared back into the parlor. He patted the pockets of his silk tweed sports jacket to make sure he had everything he needed. He grabbed his white linen fedora and went out into the sitting room. Steven was out on the terrace, leaning over the balcony, his silky blond hair lifting in the breeze. Gold's son was wearing chino slacks and an open-necked white shirt like his own, and a dark-blue, summer-weight wool blazer with gold buttons. As Steven came back inside, Gold noticed that the blazer looked tight across his son's shoulders, and short in the sleeves. The blazer was only a few months old, but Steven, who was already big for his age, was growing like a weed.

They went downstairs, and had breakfast in the hotel dining room. Steven chattered madly throughout the meal, excited about the races. Gold shared his enthusiasm. The Moden Seaplane Trophy International Competition, like the Schneider Race, was a series of closed-circuit elimination races over water, restricted to flying boats or airplanes equipped with pontoons. The competition was open to any government organization or private individual. There were more than two dozen airplanes entered, but by the time the final race took place, a few days from now, weather permitting, the field would have been narrowed to the top five airplanes. The races would be taking place off the Lido's wide, flat, seaside bathing beach. It was going to be lovely in the family's private viewing box, high atop the official grandstand, enjoying the sun and the ocean breeze, looking down at the lollypop-colored beach umbrellas and sipping lemonade as the sleek race planes went buzzing like gaudy bees around and around the pylons erected offshore . . .

Gold and his son left the restaurant, and were cutting through the hotel's ornate lobby, a baroque fantasy of pink marble, silk-flocked walls, and stained glass, when they were intercepted by a bellhop who led them over to the concierge's desk.

The concierge handed Gold a sealed envelope. Gold tore it open, then checked his pockets for his reading glasses. He realized that he'd left them upstairs. Hell, he always forgot something. By squinting, and holding the note at arm's length, he managed to read it. He was surprised to see that it was in German.

"I don't believe it!" Gold exclaimed. "It's from Heiner Froehlig, of all people!"

"Who's that?" Steven asked.

"A friend . . . At least, he was, once." Gold shrugged. "I told you about him . . . Froehlig was my chief mechanic back during the war. Remember? I told you how he and I used to work together on my Fokker tri-plane?"

"Oh yeah," Steven said.

Gold smiled, lost in memories. "God, Heiner and I were the best of friends in those days . . ."

"You never told me what happened between you," Steven said. "Why aren't you friends now?"

"Well, the fact that I'm a Jew complicated things . . ."

"Why?"

Gold smiled. "I'm glad you don't know. I'll tell you about it, someday."

Steven nodded. "Pop, we've got to get to the races!"

Gold hesitated. "I haven't seen this man in almost twenty years. Now he's here in Venice, and wants to see me."

"You mean right now?"

Gold nodded. "He's invited me for coffee at a cafe in Saint Mark's Square."

"And I guess you want to see him?"

"I'm very curious about all this, Steven."

"What about the races?" his son asked, looking crestfallen.

"Saint Mark's Square is right on the way to where we catch the motor launch to the Lido," Gold promised. "Don't worry, I'll just have a quick cup of coffee. We won't be delayed long."

They left the hotel, walking up to the Calle Larga 22

Marzo, where they turned left. They passed the midmorning shoppers frequenting the stalls as they walked toward the Piazza di San Marco.

Thankfully, Venice seemed relatively untouched by the political turmoil in Rome, and in the rest of Europe. During Gold's first visit, back in '36, Mussolini had just been embarking on his Ethiopian campaign, and loudly pledging to keep Austria independent. The Italian dictator's successes in Africa, coupled with his defiance of Hitler's intended *Anschluss*—the union of Germany with Austria—had made Mussolini a hero among his people. The cafes of Venice had rung with laughter and joyous talk about how Rome would once again take its place as a great power.

Since then the future had darkened, beginning when the Italians and Germans had joined together to aid Franco's revolution in Spain. The Spanish Civil War had begun to wind down, but in March of this year, Hitler, despite his assurances to the Italians, had sent his troops into Austria. The Germans had advanced as far as the Brenner Pass, the Alpine gateway to Italy. Mussolini had been humiliated in the eyes of the world by Hitler's action, but if the Italian dictator had been upset by Hitler's breach of faith, he was doing a good job of hiding it. Gold had followed with regret and anger Germany's persecution of its Jews. Now, Mussolini, emulating Hitler, had begun issuing anti-Semitic proclamations.

The powder-keg international situation, along with the Italian government's officially sanctioned hostility toward Jews, had originally made Gold reluctantly decide to not come to the races, but then a number of factors led him to change his mind. He did adore Venice, and now that his two kids were old enough to travel abroad, Gold wanted them to experience the city's magic. There were also sound business reasons to make the visit. While GAT did not have an official entry in the races, Gold's company did have an interest in the competition's outcome. GAT had lent its technical expertise, and substantial financial sponsorship, to the race team fielded by an English firm, the Stoat-Black Aircraft Company. Gold had met the executives of Stoat-Black in 1936, while trying to sell the British on the GC-3, with little initial success. The British Airline executives, to their discomfort but out of national pride, were wedded to their home-built, lumbering, De Havilland and Handley Page airliners, despite the fact that they were far slower and more expensive to operate than GAT's GC series. The British had *wanted* to buy, they just didn't know how to climb down off of their jingoistic high horse in order to do so. Gold solved the problem by subcontracting to Stoat-Black the assembly of his airliners destined for England and the Continent. The solution worked out well for everyone: Gold was able to make a profitable sale, and take some of the pressure off of his overtaxed Burbank facility; the English were able to keep a stiff upper lip, and still buy the airplanes they wanted. Since then, GAT and Stoat-Black had worked together on a seaplane project for the RAF's Coastal Command, in addition to the prototype fighter/race plane entered in the Moden Competition.

The people at Stoat-Black wanted Gold to come to Venice for the Moden races in order for him to witness the performance of their joint venture. Since Stoat-Black was also currently representing GAT in talks with the RAF concerning a large purchase of modified G-3 military cargo transports, and since the negotiations were at a critical stage, Gold wanted to oblige his British counterparts. He'd talked it over with their European sales representatives, who'd assured Gold that Italy was safe, but it was only when Gold received an invitation from the Italian government, inviting him and his family to Venice for the races as official guests of honor, that he'd felt secure with the notion of bringing over his family.

Gold and his son entered Saint Mark's Square, passing between the Campanile and the Clock Tower crowned with its winged lion. The sun-drenched Piazza was crowded. Almost every outdoor table was occupied at the cafes ringing the square. Gold and his son headed for the Cafe Quadri, where Froehlig had written that he would be waiting.

Gold scanned the Quadri's rows of al fresco tables, wondering if he would recognize Froehlig after so many years. As he searched he noticed a couple of Mussolini's Fascist militiamen strutting in the direction of the magnificent, golden domes of the Basilica. The dour Fascists, self-important in their modernistic uniforms complete with berets and neckerchiefs, looked very out of place amidst the flamboyant, Old World, stage-set scenery of the Piazza: the flocks of pigeons and passersby; the amiable citizenry at the cafes, reading their newspapers or chatting as they sipped their expresso; and the *carabinieri*, wearing their goofy cocked hats and gleaming swords, leisurely strolling on police patrol.

Gold watched as the uniformed Fascists crossed the path of an old woman dressed in black, lugging a pair of stringnet shopping bags loaded with groceries. The old woman carefully studied the marble pavement as the soldiers passed, but then turned, to scowl at their backs.

When Gold finally spotted Froehlig, at a table toward the back of the crowded Quadri's patio, he recognized him instantly. Gold would have known Froehlig's bottle-brush moustache anywhere, even if it had gone salt-and-pepper gray. Froehlig saw him, and stood up and waved. Gold guided his son toward Froehlig's table.

Froehlig was a little over sixty now, Gold guessed. He was wearing a monocle, and dressed in a dark blue, linen suit. Froehlig had a black derby beside him on the table, which he should have been wearing. The morning sun had already painted a blush of sunburn onto his scalp. Gold was surprised to see that Froehlig was now totally bald. As Gold got closer to Froehlig he realized that the German had taken to shaving clean in the Prussian manner what little hair he had left.

"*Hermann! Wie geht est Ihnen?*" Froehlig smiled, letting his monocle drop from his eye. It swung, suspended by a black ribbon, across his broad chest. "Thank you for coming!" he continued in German.

"*Gleichfalls,*" Gold said. He shook hands with Froehlig, and then proudly put his arm around Steven's shoulder. "*Darf ich Ihnen mien Sohn vorstellen?*"

"This young man belongs to you?" Froehlig exclaimed in German. "Such fine blond hair! A splendid lad! How old is he?"

"Fourteen," Gold said, continuing in his native tongue. "But he's big for his age, yes?"

"Ach! I would say." Froehlig laughed. "He seems scarcely younger than were you when first we met!" He extended his hand to Steven. "How are you, young Herr Gold?" he asked in German.

Steven shook hands with Froehlig, but stared blankly in response to the question.

"He doesn't speak German, Heiner," Gold explained, and thought he caught a spark of something—amused contempt? —in Froehlig's eyes.

"Well, time enough to teach him the language of his Fatherland." Froehlig laughed.

Gold smiled uneasily. He himself was feeling oddly uncomfortable speaking German with Froehlig.

"So tell me, young man," Froehlig addressed Steven in English. "Are you going to be an aviator, like your father?"

"I can already fly a single-engine," Steven boasted. "When I'm older I'm going to be Pop's chief test pilot."

Gold laughed, patting his son's shoulder.

Steven was pointing at a gelatiere pushing his cart through the square. "Pop, there's an ice cream man over there. Can I go get one?"

"Sure," Gold said. He gave his son some money. "Then take a look around the square. Just don't wander too far."

"*Bitte, sitzen Sie!*" Froehlig said, taking his seat. "We will have a coffee, and a fine chat, yes?"

"*Sehr gut, danke schön,*" Gold said, lapsing back into German as his son ran off. Gold pulled out the spindly, wrought-iron chair opposite Froehlig's at the round, marble-topped table, and sat down.

"Hermann, how have you stayed so young when I have gotten so old?" Froehlig sighed.

"You have a poor memory, Heiner. I'm older, fatter, and balder, but you *really* don't look so different."

"*Danke, gut. Ich bin einverstanden.*" Froehlig laughed. "Yes, I do agree that I haven't changed, but then, I was already bald and old when you knew me . . ." A waiter came by. "*Gefällt Ihnen* espresso?" Froehlig asked Gold. When he nodded, Froehlig ordered espresso for both of them. "I hope you don't mind that I chose the Quadri, as opposed to the Cafe Florian, across the way," Froehlig said. "You see, back in the mid-1800s when Austria occupied Venice, this was the cafe that the Austrian officers frequented. I thought it would be an appropriate rendezvous for us, seeing as how our führer has at long last reunited Austria and Germany."

"Your führer, maybe, but not mine," Gold said, but Froehlig seemed to wave his objection aside. "What are you doing in Venice, Heiner?" Gold asked in order to change the subject. "And how did you know that I was here?"

"I am here for the same reason as you," Froehlig explained. "To enjoy the fruits of my labor. Germany has several entries in the Moden races, you know, and I am Air Minister Goering's deputy in charge of aviation research and development."

Gold nodded. "I'd read in the papers that you were a high-up in the Nazi party."

The waiter served them their espresso. Gold rubbed a curl of lemon peel around the rim of his cup and took a sip of the black, bitter brew. "So you and our old Oberleutnant from Richthofen's Jadgeschwader are now working together . . . You'd better not let Goering know you're having a coffee with me. He probably still holds a grudge concerning that little tussle we had . . ."

"Not in the least, Hermann," Froehlig said. "As a matter of fact, the Herr Reich Marshal specifically asked me to look you up."

"Really?" Gold asked, surprised. "Why?"

Froehlig leaned back in his chair. "We at the Air Ministry have been following the career of our native son Hermann Goldstein for quite some time. We commend you on the development of the GC series, and we are especially impressed by the GAT/Stoat-Black Sea Dragon. We think the Sea Dragon will be quite an asset to RAF Coastal Command."

"Yes . . . I suppose it will," Gold said evasively. He looked around, then remembered that they were speaking German, and, as such, unlikely to be eavesdropped upon by the surrounding tables. Gold didn't like the idea of talking to Froehlig about the GAT-SB Sea Dragon, a combination long-range flying boat/rescue craft and torpedo bomber U-boat killer. The Sea Dragon was huge: she had four engines and carried a crew of thirteen. Her extra-capacity fuel tanks made it possible for her to patrol for hundreds of miles while armed to the teeth with turret machine guns and a ton of bombs. If need be, even fully loaded with weapons, she could land in almost any sea, to airlift up to eighty people.

"I see it upsets you to talk about the Sea Dragon," Froehlig said approvingly. "That is good. We respect a man who knows how to get things done while keeping his business to himself." He paused. "Not only do we respect that sort of man, we would also welcome him in our great endeavor..."

Gold stared. "What are you talking about, Heiner?"

Froehlig took a vellum envelope embossed with a red wax seal from the breast pocket of his suitcoat. "Inside is a handwritten note from the Herr Reich Marshal himself." Froehlig reverently handed the envelope to Gold. "It is Goering's heartfelt invitation to you and your family to come home to Germany."

"I don't believe this conversation," Gold said, setting aside the envelope without opening it.

"You would enjoy the rank of general in the Reichsluftwaffe," Froehlig persisted. "It is a secret air force as of now, but soon, the world will know that name."

"You want me as a military commander?" Gold asked, perplexed.

"Oh, no, Hermann." Froehlig laughed. "You are much too valuable a talent to risk in combat. You would do exactly what you do now, use your genius to design and oversee the production of aircraft, but in German factories. You would report directly to Goering at the Air Ministry."

"This is all very flattering, but quite impossible—" Gold began.

"But why?" Froehlig asked. "Don't you miss the Fatherland, Hermann? Can you deny that the Fatherland is your home, that Germany is in your blood? Think about your children's futures. I know that you have a daughter as well as a son. How old is she?"

"Suzy is seventeen."

"Ach, a young woman!" Froehlig smiled. "Surely now is the time for her to begin socializing with fine young German boys, not the riffraff you have loitering on every streetcorner in America! And both of your children would benefit from an unparalleled education in Germany's finest schools," Froehlig added. "And what about your wife? She is from fine Aryan stock. You must be very proud! Your wife would thrive in the Fatherland, Hermann. Germany has cultivated and encouraged the careers of the finest female pilots. Your wife could be one of them, flying into the annals of history alongside Thea Rasche and Hannah Reitsch."

Gold laughed. "Heiner, you're forgetting something. I'm a Jew."

Froehlig shrugged. "These things can be managed, Hermann. Consider the case of Erhard Milch. He was an executive at Junkers before becoming a director at Luft Hansa, the predominant German commercial airline. Now he holds the military rank of general and the title of state-secretary in the Air Ministry, conferred upon him for the work he has done in airplane production for the Fatherland. And shall I tell you something else?" Froehlig chuckled, a gleam in his eye. "Milch is also a Jew . . ."

"A Jew holding the rank of general?" Gold asked in disbelief. "How can Hitler reconcile that in view of his well-known anti-Semitic stance?"

"As I said, Hermann, these things can be arranged," Froehlig said. "In Milch's case, it was his father who was Jewish. When Milch's value to the Reich became evident, certain new evidence was suddenly found, revealing that Milch's mother had long ago had an illicit affair with an Aryan. It turned out that this man was actually Milch's father, not the Jew . . ."

"I see," Gold said wryly. "And in my case new papers could also be found to miraculously cleanse me of the stain of my Jewish blood, is that it? I, too, could be an honorary Aryan?"

Froehlig shrugged philosophically. "You are an orphan, Hermann. In your case the transformation could take place even more easily. For instance, could there not have been a mistake made in your paperwork at the orphanage? Perhaps your unfortunate designation as a Jew was the result of some hideous clerical error?"

Gold shook his head. "Thanks, but no thanks, Heiner."

"There *is* something else," Froehlig said. He reached into his side pocket and came out with a small, rectangular, black leather box.

Gold stared as Froehlig opened the leather case and set it on the table. Nestled in crimson velvet was a blue and gold Maltese Cross strung on a black ribbon.

"The Blue Max," Gold breathed, unable to take his eyes off the lovely thing.

"The *Pour le Mérite*; Germany's highest military aviation award during the First World War," Froehlig quietly agreed. "This one is yours."

Gold glanced up at Froehlig. "What are you saying?"

"Take your medal, Hermann. Hang it around your neck right now. See how it feels to at long last wear the Blue Max. You earned it years ago, Hermann, but it was unjustly kept from you on account of that foolish clerical error back at the orphange. Goering recognizes the error now; the führer recognizes it as well. The error will be set right. The German people—your people—are eager to welcome you with open arms. Come home and be the hero you were destined to be."

Gold's fingers were itching to touch the medal as Steven returned to the table. His son glanced at the Blue Max. "What's that, Pop?"

"A medal," Froehlig said in English. "A medal for your father. It is the highest commendation from his homeland. The medal has belonged to him for all these years."

"That's my dad," Steven said proudly. "Did you know he shook President Roosevelt's hand?"

Gold looked at his son, and smiled. He turned to Froehlig and shook his head. "You can tell Goering that the recognition has come far too late. I'm an American now."

"*Ich verstehe*," Froehlig said stiffly. He snapped shut the lid on the Blue Max and put the box back into his pocket.

"Pop, can we go to the races, now?"

"Right now." Gold nodded.

"You're making the wrong choice," Froehlig warned in German. "One that you will live to regret."

"Thank you for the coffee, Heiner," Gold said in English, standing up.

"At least take the letter from Goering," Froehlig said.

Gold shook his head. "There's no point."

"Hermann, for old times' sake," Froehlig implored. "Consider it a favor for your old comrade-in-arms. Take the letter. Read it at your leisure. If you should change your mind concerning our offer I can be reached, worldwide, through our embassies."

Gold hesitated. "For old times' sake, then." He slipped the envelope into his coat pocket. "Perhaps I'll see you on the Lido."

"Perhaps, Hermann," Froehlig nodded. "*Auf Weidersehen.*"

They left the cafe and hurried past the Doge's Palace, anxious to catch the next vaporetto leaving the landing stage on the Riva degli Schiavoni for the fifteen-minute ride across the lagoon to the Lido. The motor launch was crowded with other latecomers to the races, but Gold and his son managed to find seats in the stern, near the engines. Once they were out on open water, with the wind in their faces carrying away the stink of the clattering diesels, Gold took the sealed envelope out of his pocket to stare at it.

"What's that, Pop?" Steven asked.

"That's a good question," Gold muttered, more to himself than his son, his words lost in the diesels' rattle. There was a lump in his throat. Gold's eyes felt wet, and not from the salty breeze. Home was home, and they wanted him back, and his feelings about it were all mixed up, as murky and roiled as the windswept lagoon.

"Pop? You okay?"

Gold put his arm around Steven's shoulders and hugged him close. "I'm fine," he said loudly. "And this—" he held the envelope so that it fluttered in his hand in the breeze, "—is nothing worth talking about. It's trash. Just trash is what it is."

Gold scrunched up his face, as if the envelope smelled bad. As Steven laughed, Gold opened his hand. The wind snatched away the envelope, wafting it aloft.

"Whatever it was hit the water and sank!" Steven exclaimed.

Gold nodded, but he never looked back.

(Two)
The Lido, Venice

Erica was in the family's private viewing box, high atop the grandstand, when Herman and Steven finally arrived.

"Where have you two been?" Erica scolded. "You've missed the best part of the race—"

"You hear that, Pop?" Steven complained. "Mom, can I go down to the beach to watch?"

"Yes, but be back here at one o'clock."

"Look at that kid move," Herman sighed, watching Steven dash down the stairs. "Coming up, he wasn't even breathing hard. I used to be able to take stairs like that."

Erica didn't reply, but she *had* noticed that her husband was huffing and puffing. Granted that it was a steep climb up to the grandstand's top tier, but she was still going to have to do something to get him to lose some weight.

"How have today's eliminations been going?" Herman asked, thumbing back his fedora to mop his brow with a white silk handkerchief.

"The Italian, and one of the French machines, were flying neck and neck for three circuits," Erica explained. "But then the French plane had to drop out. I heard there was an engine malfunction."

"How is the Supershark doing?" Herman asked.

"It's running smoothly," Erica said. The Supershark sea racer was the GAT/Stoat-Black entry into the race. The airplane had combined Herman's concept for a prototype single-engine military fighter with Stoat-Black's expertise in seaplane technology. "The problem with the Supershark is that it's relatively slow—"

She paused as the massed snarl of high-powered engines filled the air. The flock of rainbow-colored, mono-wing seaplane racers, their pontoons jutting out from their undercarriages, streaked past, a few hundred feet above the cheering spectators crowding the beach. The noise died away as the race planes headed south, flying parallel to the shore, toward their turning point at the island town of Chioggia, a few kilometers away.

"I thought I saw the Supershark about in the middle of the pack," Herman said as the race planes swiftly dwindled to dots.

Erica nodded, lowering a set of binoculars. "That's where we've been from the start of the race, I'd say. I suspect we'll be eliminated eventually. If not during today's race, or tomorrow's, the day after."

Herman shrugged. "I did warn Stoat-Black that my prototype design was nowhere near as fast as the purebred racing machines the French and Italians were expected to field."

"Are you disappointed?" Erica asked.

"Not really," Herman said. "Stoat-Black accepts and agrees that our ultimate goal is to refine the Supershark into a fighter plane, and a fighter needs to be more than fast. It needs to be sturdy, and reliable. I happen to know that one of the top Italian teams expects to fully replace their airplane's engine after every race. Can you imagine doing that with a fighter plane after every sortie?"

"Then I guess no matter where the Supershark places in the competition, as far as you're concerned, we've won," Erica said.

She knew Herman had struggled hard to convince the United States government that it should be contracting for fighter planes, but Washington was putting its money into bombers. When Herman found out that Stoat-Black had a contract with the RAF to build fighters, he was eager to put money and GAT design input into the project. Someday, hopefully, the experience designing and building British fighters that GAT was getting today could be put to use back in America. If the American military establishment ever wised up.

"Who's flying the Supershark?" Herman asked.

"A young Englishman named Blaize Greene. Suzy and I met him this morning, before the start of the race. He seemed very nice."

"Charm doesn't win air races," Herman grumbled. "We

designed into the Supershark a great deal of maneuverability to compensate for her lack of speed. I hope the pilot has the guts to put her through the tight scrapes for which she's been born and bred . . ."

"I was told that that young Mister Greene is an accomplished pilot," Erica said. "I was told that he trained and received his pilot's license at the London Aerodome Club, and has a certificate from the Aero Club of France."

"Really?" Herman said. "Well, I am impressed. I'd like to meet this fellow."

"You'll get your chance," Erica told her husband. "The Stoat-Black executives have invited us to a lunch at the Hotel Venezia, to meet the race team."

Erica remembered with pleasure the veranda dining room at the Hotel Venezia. On their previous visit to Venice she and Herman had enjoyed a romantic, midnight supper here. They'd been shown to an intimate corner table with a view of the beach in the charming dining room, with its pink stucco walls and seashell candle sconces. The service had been wonderful and the food delicious. They'd dined on shrimp grilled in the shell, tortellini tossed in a sauce made of sweet red peppers, and icy cold champagne. Even now Erica could close her eyes and vividly recall the wine's bouquet, so like ripe, sweet strawberries. After their supper she and Herman had gone for a walk on the deserted, moonlit beach. It had been a cool night, but Herman had insisted upon removing his shoes and socks, rolling up his trousers, and wading into the sea. He'd found her a pretty shell. She still had it, hidden away, somewhere . . .

With such fond memories attached to the Hotel Venezia, Erica supposed that it was hardly any wonder that today's lunch would turn out so harshly disappointing. Today, for example, the service was barely adequate. The annoyingly supercilious waiters took their time sauntering around the long table for fifteen, knocking into the backs of chairs, and rudely interrupting conversations as they served the nondescript meal. The antipasto was soggy, the pasta was gummy and served barely tepid, and the fish, well, Erica thought, the less said about the fish, the better. To be fair, the food was no worse than at any other large-scale business function that she and Herman had been forced to attend. At least here in Venice the bread was magnificent, and the Isonzo, a semi-dry white from the nearby Friuli-Venezia Giulia wine growing region, was well chilled and in generous supply.

Erica and Suzy were the only women at the lunch. The only interesting-looking man from the Stoat-Black contingent was Blaize Greene, the first-string pilot of the race team. Erica had not had the chance to form an impression of the young man during their brief morning meeting. He'd been swaddled in flying gear, and his manner, while exceedingly polite, had been very business-like; he'd been understandably preoccupied with the upcoming race.

Now Blaize Greene was seated at the far end of the table. Suzy had been placed on his left, a man Erica didn't know was on Greene's right. Erica was too far away to hear their conversation, but Suzy seemed to be hanging on Greene's every word...

That was understandable, Erica thought, amused. Suzy had her bedroom back home plastered with photographs of various leading men, torn from the pages of movie magazines, and Greene had matinee-idol looks: a thick head of black hair slicked back from his high forehead, a strong jaw, high cheekbones, and devilish, emerald-green eyes. He was tall and slender, but broad-shouldered, and impeccably dressed in a pearl grey, double-breasted silk tweed.

With nothing to distract her—certainly not the food, Erica thought with a shudder—she had ample time to study Greene over the rim of her wineglass. He drank sparingly; showed his good taste by glancing with polite, but unmistakable, distaste at the awful food in front of him; and chain-smoked cigarettes taken from a black onyx case.

As Erica watched, Suzy said something to the men surrounding her that made them laugh. Erica smiled proudly. Her daughter was well-educated, and had enjoyed a childhood that had fully exposed her to the finer things in life. At seventeen years of age, Susan Alice Gold was a very sophisticated young lady.

Blaize Greene offered Suzy a cigarette. Erica watched as

her daughter shot a glance her way before politely refusing the offer.

Sometimes Suzy was almost *too* precocious, Erica thought. Her daughter's physical charms had also blossomed at an early age, so that Suzy looked, as well as acted, much older than she was. Interested single men in the Golds' social circles who had imagined that Suzy was safely into her twenties were invariably shocked when they found out her true age.

But pretty, confident young debutantes were not all that unusual in Bel-Air. It was Blaize Greene's aura of masculine elegance that most intrigued Erica. He, too, had poise far beyond his years, but in his case, it was something that Greene had been born with, Erica instinctively knew. Herman, for all of his sophistication, and the respect he commanded from others due to his achievements, didn't have it, and neither did any of the other rich and powerful American men she knew. Her son, Steven, certainly never would, Erica thought, as she felt something inside her responding to Greene's remarkable aplomb.

And she was not the only one to fall under Blaize Greene's personal charm. Her daughter was working very hard to capture the attention of this young man, who had merely to raise an eyebrow, and instantly the waiters who were so blatantly contemptuous of everyone else at the table were fawning over him in the most maddening and delightful manner.

Erica finally managed to capture a waiter's attention, without resorting to firing off a signal flare. As he grudgingly filled her wineglass she turned to the man on her right, whom she knew fairly well: Hugh Luddy, the bearded chief engineer for Stoat-Black. "Hugh, what can you tell me about your Mister Greene?" she asked quietly.

"You mean *Lord* Greene . . ."

"My God, you mean he's titled?"

Luddy nodded. "He's only twenty-two, but he's been our chief test pilot for two years," Luddy said in his thick Scottish brogue. "He's got a bit of university-level engineering in his background to go with his flying ability. None of us knows the Supershark like he does."

"It's unusual for a test pilot to fly in a race," Erica said.

"We felt Blaize's familiarity with the Supershark would compensate for his lack of race experience."

"Enough about this flying expertise." Erica patted Luddy's hand. "Hugh, darling, be a dear and give me something terribly juicy and personal about him, won't you?"

Luddy looked blank. "You mean gossip?" He thought it over. "I seem to remember his mother died early, and there was a bad bit about his father, who's also passed away . . . Now there's nothing left of his family but his elder brother, the Earl of Weltingham."

Erica waited. "That's it? That's all?"

"I've never been much to gossip," Luddy said apologetically. "Usually it goes in one ear and out the other . . ."

"Oh, Hugh," Erica sighed. "You're absolutely hopeless." She looked down the table at Blaize Greene. "He must be fabulously wealthy," Erica mused. "Considering that he's landed gentry and all that."

"You Yanks." Luddy smiled, shaking his head. "In England one's personal finances are not the sort of thing gentlemen chat about."

After lunch, Erica found Herman and Blaize Greene deep in conversation together out on the patio adjoining the hotel veranda. She felt a little lightheaded and tipsy as she headed toward them. She hadn't eaten very much, and the wine had been so exquisite that perhaps she'd overdone it just a teensy amount . . .

"Blaize, may I present my wife, Erica," Herman said. "Erica, this is Blaize Greene."

The boy has an absolutely blinding smile, Erica thought as Greene turned toward her.

"Sir, I had the privilege of briefly meeting your lovely wife this morning," Greene said. "Mrs. Gold, a pleasure to see you again."

"How do you do, Lord Greene."

"What's that?" Herman asked.

"I'll explain later, dear," Erica said.

"Please, Mrs. Gold, I'd prefer it if you simply addressed me by my Christian name," Blaize said. "We were discussing your husband's experiences in the last war," he continued. "The German Imperial Air Service's prowess remains legendary. I'm quite awed to be in the presence of an ace who flew with none other than the Red Baron. I was hoping to coax him into sharing with me some of his more memorable conquests in the air."

"Actually, his most memorable conquest took place in Nebraska," Erica murmured innocently, taking hold of Herman's arm, in order to lean against him.

Herman laughed. "You see, Blaize, I met my wife while touring the Midwest in a barnstorming troupe." He smiled. "And I think she's had a bit too much wine at lunch."

"Quite the sensible course of action, considering the quality of the cuisine," Blaize smiled. "I would have done the same, but I *am* flying again tomorrow morning." He turned toward Herman. "Getting back to our original subject, sir, someday I really would like to hear about your combat experiences . . . I'm really quite certain that others would, as well. You really should consider publishing your memoirs . . ."

"I'm flattered," Herman said. "And more than a little surprised. Most young fliers share the establishment point of view that fighter planes are obsolete weapons, and that the lessons the fighter pilots of the past war have to teach will prove to be irrelevant in future wars."

"I don't have that view, Mister Gold," Blaize said earnestly. "Oh, I am familiar with the current, popular consensus of educated opinion against fighters. I have, for example, read General Douhet's work."

"Who?" Erica asked.

"Douhet's an Italian military man," Herman explained. "He's written a book in which he describes how swarms of bombers will darken the skies over enemy cities during the next war."

"I also believe that bombers flying in protective formations will be awesomely destructive weapons in future wars," Blaize said. "But I disagree with those who assert that fighter aircraft will be helpless against them. Mister Gold, I've read *your* articles on the subject published in the trade journals. I wholeheartedly agree with your viewpoint that a strong fighter arm will be essential to defend against bomber attacks. And I also totally agree with you that if fighters are to be effective against the new generation of bombers that you Yanks are working on— What do you call the latest? 'The Flying Fortress'?"

Herman nodded. "The B-17, built by Boeing."

"Anyway, I agree with what you wrote in your article published in the spring '37 issue of *Aeronautical Military Engineering:* that if fighters are to be effective against bombers like the Flying Fortress, the contemporary military air arm must adopt and incorporate into their strategies the German defensive air pursuit tactics formulated during the last war."

"Now I *am* quite flattered," Herman said. "All that sounds to me suspiciously like a quote. Either you have a phenomenal memory, or you've read that musty old article fairly recently?..."

Blaize smiled. "I admit, Sir, that I did re-read your writings when I found out that you'd be attending the races. Speaking of which, during the competitions I intend to incorporate into my strategy some of your theories regarding the *rotte* and *schwarme.*"

"The pair and the swarm?" Erica asked, mystified. "Of what?"

"Fighter planes, dear," Herman said. "The *rotte*, or pair, of fighters fly to cover one another's tail while attacking enemy fighters. The *schwarme*, or swarm, of fighters attacks en masse to bring down enemy bombers."

"As I remember it, Sir, you have in the past proposed a triad defensive strategy against bomber attacks," Blaize said. "You advocate the implementation of an early warning system, much like the one the German Imperial Air Service so effectively employed during the last war; then anti-aircraft batteries, and, lastly, *schwarme* fighter tactics."

Herman nodded. "I do believe that given enough warning to get into the air, the combined firepower of a swarm of fighters attacking in close formation would prove effective against the most heavily armed and largest of bombers that manage to survive the gauntlet of flak."

"If the fighters can't stop them coming in, they could most certainly inflict heavy losses on the bombers on their way out." Blaize nodded. "I heartily agree with your theories, Sir."

Herman smiled. "If you've recently reviewed my articles, you ought to remember that I clearly stated that these theories are not original with me; that I used the German terms *rotte* and *schwarme* to honor the memory of the great Oswald Boeleck, the man who did originate the theories, and who taught them to Richthofen." He shook his head. "Back during the war, I discounted Boeleck, believing that —assuming one had an experienced pilot and a sound flying machine—the one-on-one dogfight was a preferable attack strategy. It still may be, in combat between fighters. The Germans, for instance, have used the one-on-one tactic quite effectively in the Spanish Civil War. But when fighters go up against bombers, the *schwarme* tactic will be necessary for success, just as members of a wolfpack join forces to bring down prey too large or too powerful for the individual predator."

"Boeleck was a genius," Blaize said, as Hugh Luddy came over to join them. "But so are you, Mister Gold, for so brilliantly adapting the late master's theories to meet future contingencies."

"Young man, you make me blush," Herman said quietly. "Unfortunately, your opinion of my theories seems to be a minority viewpoint."

"Ah, there you are, Greene," Luddy interrupted, taking hold of the young pilot's arm and leading him away. "Come along, now. You mustn't monopolize Mister Gold, you know. Anyway, I need to talk to you concerning the Supershark. Now, what was this you were telling the chief mechanic about excessive torque? . . ."

Erica, watching, thought Blaize looked quite reluctant to go. "He's a nice enough young man, don't you think, Herman?" she asked once the young man was out of earshot.

"Yeah." Herman looked at her. "Now what's all this Lord stuff about?"

Erica filled him in on what she'd learned about Blaize Greene. When she was done, Herman smiled. "Why do you think our young peer was so intent upon buttering me up?"

"I wasn't going to say anything, darling, if you hadn't

picked up on it." Erica laughed, giving his arm an affectionate squeeze. "Whatever do you think he wants?"

"I'm sure we'll find out, sooner or later," Herman muttered, as Suzy appeared in the archway separating the patio
area from the veranda dining room, and came racing toward
them.

"Mother, Daddy, I've been looking all over for you!" she
said. "Did you know that Blaize is—"

"We know all about it." Erica laughed.

"During lunch Blaize offered to take me sightseeing
around Venice this afternoon!" Suzy continued. "Please,
may I go?"

Erica and her husband exchanged looks.

"Do you suppose *this* is what all that buttering up business
just now was about?" Herman wondered out loud.

"I suppose there's no harm in it," she fretted. "I mean, he
has to be a gentleman . . ."

"His Lordship had better *stay* one, too," Herman muttered, but softly, so that only Erica could hear him.

"You be back at our hotel suite for dinner," Erica said.

"Yes, Mother." Suzy kissed her cheek. "Thank you!" She
gave Herman a kiss. "Thank you, too, Daddy."

Herman was smiling as she ran off. "Know who she reminded me of just now?"

"Who?" Erica asked absently, watching her daughter disappear inside the veranda.

"You," Herman said.

"Not really!" Erica said, startled. "For one thing, she has
a much better figure than I do. More on top and on the
bottom." She laughed.

"I guess what I meant was the way she came running
toward us," Herman explained. "With her blonde hair flying
behind her, her bright brown eyes, her excited smile." He
paused. "I guess I can understand why you wouldn't see it."
He smiled. "Because to me she looked just the way you used
to look when I was courting you, back in Nebraska. Remember how you'd come flying down off the farmhouse
porch to greet me? And you weren't much older than our
daughter is now, as I recall . . ."

Erica, forcing a smile, nodded vaguely. She suddenly

wished that she knew a great deal more about Blaize Greene, and not out of idle curiosity, or admiration for his charm . . .

What Herman was remembering was how she'd looked when she'd been in the first throes of an infatuation for a certain young man—who happened to be a rakish young pilot . . .

(Three)

Suzy spent twenty fretful minutes in the powder room. She was frantic to hurry back to Blaize, who was cooling his heels in the hotel lobby. What if at this very instant he was changing his mind about taking her sightseeing?

On the other hand, she had to make sure that she looked perfect. At least, as perfect as possible, given what she had at hand to work with . . .

She took her comb from out of her alligator shoulder bag and did the best she could with it, all the while cursing the sea breeze that had put a frizzy curl into her shoulder-length hair. She tugged at her dress, trying to smooth it out. It was pale blue linen, and had wrinkled in the back. She felt like crying. She looked terrible! She wished that she had known to wear something more glamorous, but who dressed glamorously for a day of sightseeing and going to the beach to watch races?

She quickly freshened her makeup, and decided that the dark blue, silk scarf she had knotted around her neck could be used as a turban to both hide her frizzy hair and keep it out of her eyes during the windy boat ride back to Venice.

As she put her hair up, exposing her neck, she smiled to herself. A friend had read in a dirty book she'd discovered in her parents' bedroom that discriminating gentlemen found the nape of a lady's neck to be scintillating . . . Her friend had said that the book had photographs in it of men and women *doing it*. Suzy theoretically knew all about how *it* was done, but she'd never been able to imagine actually going about *it*. Especially not with the awkward, silly schoolboys she knew . . . Of course, a dashing man like

Blaize—an aristocrat—had probably done *it* hundreds of times . . .

Erica took a last look at herself in the mirror. She wished she had some jewelry with her, but all she was wearing was her gold, Cartier tank watch on its alligator strap. The watch had been a gift from her father. She'd found it in the glovebox of the bright red Jaguar runabout her parents had given her for her sixteenth birthday.

She experimented with buttoning and unbuttoning the top of her dress to expose a bit of cleavage. She better not, she decided, she might still run into her mother . . . Anyway, her sort of ripe, hourglass figure—her father like to tease her by calling her "*saftig*"—was supposed to be out of fashion . . .

She wondered if Blaize was thinking that very thing at this very moment . . . She hurried out to the lobby, and felt like pinching herself to make sure that she wasn't dreaming when she saw that he was still there.

At first Suzy was amused and put at ease by Blaize's charm, but as the afternoon of sightseeing wore on, she grew disappointed by his behavior toward her. He'd been so debonair and romantically attentive at lunch. He'd made her feel like a woman: the most special, only woman in the world! Now, as they trudged from palace, to museum, to church, he became more and more removed and aloof. He was still very kind, but the quality of his attentiveness had changed. She sensed that in his eyes she'd become less a woman, and more a kid sister.

Early on Blaize had promised her a gondola ride along the Grand Canal. At the time, it had sounded wonderful, but if Blaize insisted on continuing in his role of combination tour guide/distant uncle, Suzy thought that the gondola ride would be about as romantic as an excursion with her father.

In fact, Blaize was beginning to bore her. Her feet were aching, and if she had to look at one more painting while he dryly recounted some obscure anecdote about the artist, she was going to scream.

They were quayside at the Grand Canal, near the Grassi Palace, not far from the hotel where her family was staying. Suzy was thinking about cutting the afternoon short and going back to the hotel for a nap, when a curious thing happened while Blaize was negotiating in Italian with a gondolier concerning their ride.

"I'm afraid this fellow is booked for the immediate present," Blaize told her as he attempted to lead her away.

"No, he isn't," Suzy said, standing her ground. "That's not what he said, or even what you two were talking about. You two were arguing about money."

"W-what? What do you mean?"

He was actually stammering, Suzy realized. Like a flesh-and-blood person, not a movie star reciting lines, or a tour guide drearily recounting historical trivia. His eyes were piercing: bright green and glinting beneath the snap brim of his grey felt fedora. At first Suzy thought he was angry, but then she realized that he was smarting from embarrassment over being caught in his lie.

"I didn't know you could speak Italian," he said softly.

"I don't speak it nearly as well as you, but I do understand it pretty well. And French, and German, needless to say."

"Are all American schoolgirls so well educated?" he asked gruffly.

"Don't try to change the subject. Why did you lie to me just now?"

"I just— Well . . . I just thought it would be easier to explain it that way, I suppose," Blaize said.

To his credit he managed to rally a confident smile, but Suzy wasn't going to buy it.

"Come now, we'll find another fellow to take us for a ride—" He once again took her arm, trying to lead her away, but she resisted.

"That gondolier didn't ask for very much money," she observed.

"Suzy—" He sounded very much like he was going to lose his temper.

"Don't you take that sharp tone with me!" she warned. "I'm the one who was lied to!"

"And how would you know what the going rate is for a gondola ride?" he challenged.

Suzy stared at him, trying to figure it out. When the realization hit, she had to struggle not to laugh or even smile.

Ironic or not, any hint of amusement on her part would be far more than Blaize could possibly bear. "You don't have the money, do you?" she asked quietly.

"What are you talking about!" Blaize began to bluster. "That's just the most absurd thing . . ."

"*Do* you?" She waited for him to say something, but her answer came when he looked away, blushing bright crimson. She turned to the gondolier and in halting Italian politely requested his services at the rate he had just quoted.

"What do you think you're doing?" Blaize demanded.

"Taking *you* for a gondola ride," Suzy said. "And don't get all huffy about it!"

"I won't have it!"

"Why?"

"I *can't* let you to pay! I think we can find a gondolier who will charge us less. I have *some* money. . ."

"If you only have a little I wouldn't dream of letting you spend it on me," Suzy said firmly. "Especially not when my purse is literally stuffed with lira. Also, we don't have much time. I have to be back at my hotel to have dinner with my family. Now, then, you promised me a ride, and I mean to have it. Unless you intend to go back on your word, and surely a gentlemen such as yourself would never do that?"

Blaize sighed. "My dear girl, it's just that . . ." He hesitated, looking anguished. "You're right, of course . . ."

"Is it that you find yourself a little short of cash just now?" Suzy asked sympathetically.

Blaize offered her a whimsical smile. "I mean that apart from the salary I receive from Stoat-Black—and somehow that gets spent even before I actually receive it—I don't have any money at all. Never ever. I'm quite absolutely broke." He sighed. "Oh, Suze, what you must think of me? . . ."

"*Suze?* . . ." She smiled. "Suze—I like that!" She stood up on tiptoe to give him a chaste kiss on the cheek. "Shall I tell you what I think? Until this moment I was thinking that you were turning out to be an awful stuffed shirt, but now I think you're delightful, all over again."

* * *

Suzy worked hard to get Blaize to talk about himself as they drifted along the Grand Canal, past wondrous mansions and palaces fronted by mooring posts striped like barbers' poles. She felt regal; like Cleopatra on her barge as she basked in the warm sunshine, listening to the water gently lapping against the gondola's gleaming black prow. Meanwhile, in response to her gentle prodding, Blaize haltingly revealed his past to her.

"My family did have a fair amount of money once," he confided as their gondola slid lazily into the cool, dim shadows beneath the elaborately arched, white marble, Ponte di Rialto. "But then my father put everything into the British film industry. This was just after the war, you understand."

"I didn't know there was a substantial film industry in your country," Suzy said. They were sitting with their shoulders touching, sunk deep into comfortable velvet cushions.

"There isn't," Blaize laughed ruefully. "Oh, there were high hopes for one, but it was all put to rest by your Hollywood. My father was wiped out."

The gondola slowly made its way out from beneath the bridge, and rounded the bend, passing the ancient, German-built warehouse that was now used as the post office.

"Anyway, it was rather a dreadful time after father found out the extent of his losses," Blaize continued. "I was just a little boy, but somehow I remember it all quite well. Perhaps it was because it was just around that time as well that my mother died. My father inherited her estate, which for a period afforded us a small but tidy income. My father left the principal untouched for as long as he could, but postwar prices were high, my father was accustomed to a certain lifestyle, and finances were never His Lordship's forte, in any event. We eventually lost the house in Belgravia, and were forced to retreat to Weltingham."

"Where's that?"

"Oh, I'm sorry." Blaize smiled at her. "That's our holding in Yorkshire."

"A castle?" Suzy asked eagerly, her head full of fanciful images of moats, and stables, and oh-so-proper servants in formal attire serving high teas beneath candy-striped awnings erected on vast green lawns.

"Perhaps once I might have said Weltingham was a castle," Blaize told her, sounding wistful. "But no more. It became rather run-down, and there was no money for repairs. Anyway, my elder brother, the Earl of Weltingham, and I lived there with my father, until we were sent off to school. My brother and I both went to Eaton. Don't ask how my father managed to pay the tuition. Actually, I don't think he did. Some of his chums with money probably helped out. Eventually, my brother went to Oxford, and I to Cambridge University, both of us on scholarships. My brother successfully read for the Bar. I studied engineering, but after a couple of years I got impatient being cooped up in a classroom. I wanted some hands-on experience with airplanes, so I left school and learned how to fly."

"Was your father upset?" Erica asked. "About leaving school, I mean?"

Blaize didn't say anything for the length of time it took him to dig out his black onyx case and light a cigarette. "My father died in a hunting accident during my last year at Eaton," he said, exhaling the words in a steady hiss along with a stream of smoke.

"I'm very sorry." She saw Blaize offer her a thin smile, and immediately knew that his father's death was far too painful a topic to dwell on. "So, then you got yourself a job with Stoat-Black?" she asked brightly, and thought that Blaize looked grateful to her for changing the subject.

"Stoat-Black pays me a small salary," Blaize said. "It's not much, but, then, there's no shortage of young men who would gladly take my place. Not that I'm in any danger of losing my position. I do have my engineering background, which comes in handy when talking airplane performance with the people in research and design." He laughed, exhaling cigarette smoke. "For all that, I suspect that Stoat-Black favors me more for the cachet my title lends the company than for my technical expertise."

"I'm sure that's not true," Suzy said.

"I can't blame Stoat-Black, however. I've been living off my title for years."

Suzy, listening, recoiled at the cool disdain she heard in his voice as he talked about himself.

"I'm always overdrawn on my salary, you see. Like my father, I happen to fancy the finer things in life, but they don't come cheap, and I don't come with the ability to pay for them. In England, however, a peerage is often as useful as money in the bank. I use my title to get credit at restaurants and hotels. With it I manage to placate my tailor and my jeweler. My title also allows me to be something of a professional houseguest," he added dryly. "Those with money, but no social position, seem to enjoy having someone like me lounging about in tennis whites during the day, and in black tie in the evening. I suppose that for my hosts I fulfill rather the same need as their purebred spaniels in front of the fire."

"You're too hard on yourself," Suzy said. At least, she *hoped* he was.

Blaize studied her, and then smiled. "You're very kind to say so, Suze."

She smiled. "That nickname does make me want to giggle. It makes me think of champagne."

Blaize smiled back. "Do you like champagne?" he asked softly.

Suzy shrugged. "I've only had it a couple of times."

"Of course!" he chuckled. "You're only seventeen... Forgive me for forgetting..."

"Oh, that's okay!" Suzy said happily.

"And do forgive me for rambling on," he added, looking adorably earnest. "Please understand that I'm not used to talking about myself... I certainly haven't talked about my father to anyone in years."

She nodded. "Blaize, why did you invite me out for this afternoon?"

"Because you're a beautiful and charming young lady and I wished the pleasure of your company—" he began, smoothly.

"Oh, sure," Suzy interrupted. "I bet you escort seventeen-year-old girls all the time." She gazed at him. "Could I hear the truth, please?"

He looked glum. "You're certainly not a girl who misses

much. The truth, Suze, may be hard for you to hear. I'm certainly ashamed of myself concerning it, but you must understand that I didn't think you were as . . ." He trailed off, looking very uncomfortable. "As mature—as *knowing* and *wise*—as you seem to be . . ."

"Would you get to the point?" Suzy chuckled.

"Very well." He spoke quickly, as if he wanted to get the confession out all in one breath. "I invited you because I was hoping to get into your father's good graces. You see, I hope to convince him to give me a job as one of his test pilots."

"You mean in America?" Her heart was pounding wildly at the thought, but she kept a straight face, figuring that he expected her to show a little outrage. And anyway, he deserved to be on the hotseat just a little, for his presumption. "So you only wanted to use me," she said, trying to sound angry.

"Please forgive me," he said, sounding very ashamed. "As I said, I thought you were merely a child, so I didn't consider your feelings."

Something told Suzy that she didn't have to pretend with Blaize. That he liked her fine when she was just being herself. "You're forgiven."

"There's nothing for me in England, you see," Blaize continued. "I was thinking that perhaps I could make a fresh start of it in your country. I do intend to make the crossing, one way or the other. I just thought that things would be that much easier if I had a job doing what I love already lined up when I got there."

"I see," Suzy said thoughtfully. She patted his hand. "Maybe I can put in a good word for you with my father."

She expected him to be wildly grateful, but he remained silent, a pained expression on his face. For a moment she was confused, but then she understood, and felt very bad for him. She hadn't ever had to think about it until now; she guessed that it was no fun always having to ask people for things . . .

"You know, I do love these gondolas," he said. "The brass fittings, the varnished wood. They remind me somewhat of vintage airplanes. The kind of airplane your father flew during the war . . ."

"I wouldn't know," Suzy shuddered. "I've never flown in an airplane."

"What?" Blaize asked, clearly astounded.

"The whole idea of being up in the air petrifies me," Suzy said. "It alway has . . . I mean, I understand why airplanes don't fall out of the sky, but when it comes to actually going up in one . . . And don't you dare laugh at me!" she said hotly.

Blaize quickly muffled his smile. "You have to admit, it's rather rich," he said. "I mean, considering who your father and mother are? . . ."

"Tell me about it," Suzy said miserably. "I've endured ribbing about it all my life. My brother *never* lets up . . ."

"An impoverished nobleman, and the scion of one of the world's foremost aviation families, who is afraid to fly," Blaize mused. "What a pair we make."

Suzy resisted the urge to enthusiastically, wildly agree. She was going to show His Lordship Blaize Greene, at every opportunity, that she was a full-grown lady. "Do we?" she asked coolly.

(Four)
Hotel Reginia

Suzy waited until late that night to talk to her father about Blaize Greene. She was lying wide awake in her bed listening for her mother to tell her father good night. Her brother was already sound asleep in the room next door. She knew that her father would be up for a while. He liked to read and have a brandy just before bed, and mother couldn't abide having a light on in their bedroom while she slept.

Suzy waited an extra few minutes, to give the brandy time to do its work, and to make sure mother really had retired for the night. Something told Suzy that if she wanted to get Blaize a job as a GAT test pilot, and in the process keep him close at hand, she had best leave her mother out of this. Suzy knew that her mother loved her, but she certainly wasn't the pushover that Daddy was. When she was certain the time was ripe, she slipped out of bed, put on her robe, and went out into the parlor. Her father was sitting on a sofa. His reading glasses were perched on the tip of his nose, and a brandy snifter was within easy reach, just as she'd imagined, but he wasn't reading a book. He had several folders full of papers on the sofa beside him, and an unfolded blueprint blanketing his lap.

Her father looked up at her and smiled. "What are you doing up?" he asked mildly.

"Daddy, can I talk to you about something very important?"

"You're sounding very serious." He put aside the papers, to make room for her beside him on the sofa. "Come sit, and tell me what this is all about."

Suzy sat down, and began to idly flip through the folders. "What are you working on?"

"Those are the specs on the Supershark. I got them from Stoat-Black. We're going to build our own prototype version of that plane back in Burbank, and run some tests on her."

"That's interesting," she fibbed.

Daddy put his arm around her. "Quit stalling. You hate airplanes. Tell me what's on your mind."

"I want to ask you a favor, but not for me . . . For someone else . . ."

"And who would that be?"

"Blaize Greene," Suzy said. "He'd like to come work for you in California."

Her father merely nodded, not seeming at all surprised. But then, she'd never ever seen her father act truly surprised about anything.

"I see . . . Did Blaize ask you to come to me on his behalf?"

She thought about it. "No," she decided. "I mean, he said that he wants to come work for you, but he never asked me to talk to you about it."

"Then how did it come up?"

"When I found out he didn't have any money—"

"He doesn't have any money?"

"And I had to pay for our gondola ride—" She stopped,

and smiled. Her father was shaking his head, but he was laughing.

"Maybe you'd better start from the beginning," he said.

(Five)
Near the Porto Di Malamocco
Lido, Venice
11 June 1938

Blaize Greene ran along the beach. The sun was just coming up, glinting red fire against the Hotel Venezia's top-floor windows, visible above the trees. The sun washed the sky with orange light, and set to life the placid waters of the Adriatic. The soft dawn brought awake the seabirds. They stretched their wings and sprang aloft, cawing loudly, as Greene padded past.

He was wearing white canvas lace-up shoes with cork soles, white tennis shorts, and a crimson, cotton tennis sweater with a thin yellow stripe running along its V-neck and around the cuffs. Greene's hair was touseled and damp; sweat trickled down his spine; his breath came easily as his legs pumped rhythmically. The salt air was invigorating. As he ran he mentally visualized how he wanted this morning's race to proceed. Periodically he checked his wristwatch. He'd been up for the past hour and a half, running for the past forty-five minutes. Another fifteen minutes, and then he'd call it quits.

He waved to his race team as he ran past the three wooden launch ramps shared by all the Moden Competition entrants. His team was just rolling the Supershark on its dolly out of its tent hangar, onto the ramp apron. Greene kept on running, to the Porto Di Malamocco, a narrow channel that separated the southern tip of the Lido from the island town of Chioggia. As he turned to run back, he glanced at the stone breakwater jutting out into the sea. On its far end was erected a tall, red and white checkered pylon: one of the turning points in the race. Just for the hell of it Greene ran the length of the breakwater, skipping nimbly along the slippery, barnacle-encrusted jumble of rocks. He touched the pylon, then ran back to the beach, and continued on his way.

Greene's society friends in London had accused him of having a split personality. When he wasn't flying he was a late-night, heavy-drinking sybarite; an infamous partygoer who never failed to get his name into the society pages or the more crass gossip columns run by the Fleet Street rags. But when he was flying he became more spartan than a monk; no drinking, and no late-night carousing. He just ran, got lots of sleep, and concentrated on the job at hand.

He went along with the jokes his London friends made about his grueling, self-imposed—or self-inflicted, depending on one's point of view—regimen. He pretended to need their commiserations. It wouldn't do to expect them to understand, but he did want to oblige them. He needed the company of his friends in order to survive the interminable periods when Stoat-Black had nothing for him to fly.

He was happy when he was flying, and miserable when he wasn't. It was as simple as that, or as psychologically complex. He was not particularly fond of himself as a human being, but at least he was a tolerable test pilot: he knew how to fly, and he wasn't afraid to take a risk during the course of a day's work. People thought he was brave. He encouraged the perception. The truth was that he really didn't give much of a damn what happened to him. He suspected that the best of what life had to offer was already behind him. He wasn't going to be in his twenties forever, and it was going to be rather difficult to freeload off his title and his charm once the lines set in around his eyes. He'd be a rather pathetic kind of sort of bloke, then, wouldn't he? . . .

Rather as pathetic as his father was, the day he tramped off into the woods in order to undergo his "hunting accident," during which he evidently, "accidentally," put both barrels of his custom-engraved shotgun into his mouth and blew his head off . . .

Greene had only been eleven years old at the time. He'd been away at school. The headmaster had come to wake him in the middle of the night, saying only that something awful had happened, and that he and his brother must hurry in order to take the next train. And so they had, sitting alone, sleepy-eyed and staring at their own reflections in the rocking, brightly lit compartment's plate glass, sick to their stomachs with apprehension...

Greene stumbled on a piece of driftwood on the beach, almost turning his ankle. He realized that his steady pace had increased to a sprint. He forced himself to slow down, to calm down...

Everyone had been awfully good about the circumstances surrounding the death of his father, Greene remembered. Hence the "hunting accident" nonsense. Greene had been grateful to one and all at the time, and he still was, on his father's behalf. It was nice that they had let his father go off into eternity with at least his dignity intact. The old boy had been left with precious little else.

Greene hoped that they would be as kind toward him when the time for his "accident" came around.

He again passed the launch ramps. The other race teams were bringing their seaplanes out, and parking them on the aprons. Meanwhile, the Stoat-Black mechanics had the Supershark's engine cowling off. Greene knew that they would perform a maintenance check, then lightly mist the engine with oil and coat the seaplane's moving parts with thick grease, to protect against the salt spray. All of that would take a couple of hours. By ten this morning the Supershark would be rigged up to the crane and hoisted off her dolly, onto the ramp. She was scheduled to launch at ten-fifteen. She would be one of the last to hit the water. Today's eliminations competition was scheduled to begin at ten-thirty.

He had only a few more minutes left of running. He forced himself to increase his pace. He'd been at it for exactly an hour when he reached the Hotel Venezia, where the Stoat-Black contingent was staying.

He went down to the waterline, kicked off his shoes, took off his sweater, and hurled himself into the sea to wash away the sweat. He splashed about for a few minutes, then came out, gathered up his things, and trudged up the beach toward the hotel.

He was thinking about a hot shower, and a big breakfast, and the fact that he'd dreamt about his father last night. He hadn't dreamt about the old boy in years, but then, he also hadn't talked about his father in years, until yesterday... with the girl. She had been so very easy to talk to. He couldn't remember the last time he had talked to someone, *really* talked, not just exchanged inanities.

But she was a child, he told himself, suddenly embarrassed about the way he had opened up to her. He wondered if he had revealed too much about himself? If there was something unmanly in unburdening himself in such an unseemly manner?

He supposed that it didn't matter, one way or the other. She'd probably forgotten everything he'd said. And anyway, Greene didn't expect to see her again.

At the hotel Greene showered and shaved, and had breakfast sent up to his room. He dressed in a pair of wheat-colored linen slacks; woven, tan leather slip-ons; a light blue cotton shirt; and a loden-green corduroy sport jacket with tan leather patches on the elbows. At nine-thirty he checked his onyx case to make sure that he had an ample supply of his custom-blended Dunhill cigarettes, grabbed the battered leather valise that contained his flying gear, and went downstairs, where a water taxi was waiting to take him to the launch ramps.

The Supershark was ready and waiting for Greene when he arrived. She was a nasty-looking beastie, Green thought, grinning. Her gleaming, black and red striped aluminum fuselage was slender as a dagger, and tipped with a twin-blade prop that was also striped black and red. Her bright red wings were stubby and elliptical. Beneath the fuselage were the floats, like twin cigars, painted black, and almost as long as the airplane itself. The open cockpit was positioned well behind the humped cowling, which hid the big, in-line V-12 engine.

But for all her sleek beauty the Supershark was a tortoise among the hares, Greene knew as he went inside the tent hangar to change into his flying gear. Her top speed of four hundred miles per hour was at least fifty miles per hour slower than the fastest of the purebred racers entered in the race. Greene knew that she wasn't destined to win the Moden Cup. As a matter of fact, he suspected that the Supershark would be eliminated during tomorrow's competition. But that was tomorrow. She should make it through today.

He pulled on his cover-alls and his leather jacket, grabbed his leather helmet, gloves, and goggles, and went out to the launch ramp, where the race team was throwing buckets of water onto the planking in order to grease the Supershark's slide into the sea. Greene used a stepladder to get into the seaplane's snug cockpit. As always, the fact that the Supershark was raised up on floats made him feel as if the airplane were on stilts. He strapped himself in, performed a preflight check, and started the engine. The mechanics released the straps holding the Supershark's pontoons to the ramp, and rocked her tail up and down to get her sliding. As she began to move, Greene throttled back, to control the descent. The Supershark's churning prop seemed destined for a dunking as the seaplane dipped nose-first toward the sea, but, as always, she bobbed level as the pontoons entered the water.

While the Supershark's engine warmed up, Greene gauged the wind direction by watching the flags flapping on shore. He cranked the handle under the instrument panel, lowering the water rudders hinged into his pontoons, and felt his rudder pedals come to life. He opened up the throttle and taxied out into open water, heading north, toward the start/ finish pylon on the barge anchored offshore, parallel to the grandstand. The other seaplanes were taxiing along with him, rising and falling on the waves.

By now the grandstand was filled, and the beach was crowded with spectators. Out on the water the air was filled with the combined dronings of idling aircraft engines. Greene wiped the sea spray from his goggles and waited for the signal to take off. He happened to glance to his right, looked away, and then did a double-take. About thirty feet away was one of the German entries, looking vaguely insectile, thanks to its narrow fuselage; bulbous, enclosed canopy; spindly undercarriage; and olive green paint job, highlighted with yellow stripes. Perhaps it was his imagination, but Greene had the oddest feeling that the pilot was fixedly staring at him . . .

At ten-fifteen the signal for takeoff was given. At once the combined dronings rose to an urgent whine, splitting the sky as a baker's dozen of racing throttles were opened.

Greene blasted his own engine, and the Supershark surged forward. He retracted his water rudders, allowing his vertical fin tail rudder to take over now that the Supershark was creating a slipstream. The spray on the windscreen glistened like diamonds as the Supershark skimmed along. Greene could hear and feel the waves coursing against the raven-black floats. The controls abruptly felt light as the floats lifted out of the water, and the Supershark began planing like a speedboat. The water seemed to cling, but then slipped away with a final gentle caress, like a lover reluctant to part, as the Supershark rose up into the clear blue sky.

Greene, feeling warm in the sunshine, despite the brisk wind tugging at his cheeks, banked around to take his place at the end of the ragtag pack of seaplanes circling the start/finish pylon. The airplanes continued circling until everyone was aloft. A red smoke bomb was set off on the start/finish pylon barge. Then the tentative formation streaked past the pylon. The race—seven 32-mile laps of the triangular course—had begun.

The pack was fairly bunched together on the first leg of the course, from the start/finish pylon to the turning point on the breakwater at the Porto Di Malamocco. From here it was roughly eight miles to the second turning point, an offshore pylon at the southern tip of Chioggia. The pack next began a sixteen-mile straightaway returning the way they'd come, but well offshore. The straight allowed the purebred racers to surge ahead to the third turn, at the checkered pylon erected on the breakwater guarding the entrance to the Port of Venice. From there it was a seven-mile straightaway back along the Lido, past the grandstand, and again past the start/finish pylon.

Greene completed the first lap in under six minutes, averaging three hundred and fifty miles per hour. The furious roar of his engine deafened him, and the sea was a blur beyond his pontoons. By the end of the second lap, the entrants had all pretty much found their places. The Supershark was positioned in the bottom third of the pack. She'd been steadfastly in the middle the day before, but the slower planes flying yesterday had been eliminated for today's race.

From his position, Greene was more confident than ever that the Supershark would survive today's elimination to fly another day—one more day, to be exact, he guessed. Nevertheless, the Supershark had more than proven herself a reliable and relatively fast airplane. Once she was back in England, her floats would be replaced by conventional landing gear. Work would then proceed on transforming her into a fighter.

Greene glanced behind him and was surprised to see that the olive and yellow German plane was pacing him, flying on his tail. That was very odd, Greene thought. From the race the previous day he was sure that the German plane was somewhat faster than the Supershark. The German had to be purposely hanging back to remain on the Supershark's tail.

As Greene streaked low over the grandstand at the end of his third lap he wondered if Suzy was down there watching. That he found himself hoping she was amused him. He abruptly remembered that he'd also dreamt about Suze last night. He wondered why he'd blocked that out. He tried hard to remember the dream's details, but they continued to elude him. How very odd; he always remembered his dreams . . .

The fifth and sixth laps passed uneventfully, but then Greene had expected as much, considering his modest but safe position in the pack. The true struggles took place among the front-runners for first place, and those bringing up the rear, battling to squeak past elimination. By now he'd gotten used to the German on his tail.

Greene rounded the pylon at the Port of Venice breakwater. He was over the beach, approaching the grandstand, anticipating the final lap of the race, when the German put on a burst of speed, leapfrogging over the Supershark. Greene involuntarily hunched into his cockpit as the German's pontoons passed less than a yard over his head. The German dropped like a stone directly in front of him, forcing Greene to throttle back, so abruptly that the Supershark was put into a stall.

The German flew on, beginning his final lap, as the Supershark fell toward the beach. Greene, struggling with his controls, kept her from going into a spin, but he was already too low to go into a dive to break out of the stall.

The first order of business was to get the hell away from the crowded beach. He banked out over the water. The maneuver cost him further precious altitude, but Greene knew that he was going down one way or another, and he didn't want to kill anyone. The frothing blue sea was reaching at him as he managed to get the Supershark's nose up, an instant before his pontoons touched the waves. What he did next was the result of training and instinct rather than thought. He kept the Supershark skipping across the surface in a series of hops, controlling the pitch angle of the floats to avert a capsizing. He opened up the throttle, hauled back on the stick, and somehow, miraculously, regained the sky.

He'd survived, but he was out of the race. Saving his own and the Supershark's skin had cost time. The rest of the pack was already rounding the Chioggia pylon. The Supershark didn't have the speed to catch up and regain its prior position. What was worse, Greene was keenly aware that the German had made him look like a fool in front of everyone.

The German was a distant speck to the south, but he still had not reached the Chioggia turning point. To hell with the race, Greene thought, as he poured on the power. He no longer cared about the race; he wanted the German.

Greene had no inkling why the German had done this to him, but that didn't matter. Greene took pride in conducting himself like a gentleman, but the German had inexplicably chosen to rob him of his professional honor in front of his employer, and thousands of others. Greene would have his satisfaction.

The German seaplane was faster than the Supershark, but the latter had a smaller turning radius. Greene drew a bit closer to his quarry after each pylon. Both airplanes had reached the tail end of the pack as they approached the pylon at the breakwater marking the Port of Venice. Coming up was the final straightaway, to the grandstands and the start/finish pylon. The Supershark did not have the speed to take advantage of the straightaway and survive the eliminations.

Greene knew that the German did have the speed, but Greene was not about to allow the German to use it.

Greene banked steeply, veering inland, taking an illegal, diagonal shortcut across the triangular course in order to come around the Port of Venice pylon the wrong way, head-on toward the rear of the pack just rounding the turn. He imagined that he'd scared the hell out of the other pilots from the way that they scattered like a flock of frightened pigeons. Greene knew that what he had just done had been visible to all those in the grandstand who had binoculars, and that he had just disqualified himself. He didn't care, since he knew that he was going to be eliminated in any event. Far more troubling was the realization that Stoat-Black, likely embarrassed and outraged at his unsportsman-like conduct, would probably dismiss him.

It was all spilled milk, so Greene put it out of his mind. He concentrated on flying his head-on collision course toward the German, who, to his credit, was showing commendable courage by holding to his own flight course. Greene intended to force the German into an evasive maneuver that would cost him speed and time, and keep him from finishing the race.

Within seconds the two planes had closed to within a hundred yards of each other. The olive and yellow seaplane loomed, its whirling prop looking like a buzz saw through Greene's windscreen—

Greene gritted his teeth and held to his course. Sooner or later the German would lose his nerve, he grimly thought, or else there was going to be a pretty explosion in the sky. Either way, Greene would have his satisfaction—

The German abruptly fell over on his wings, banking steeply. "Got you!" Greene laughed. He could almost count the rivets in the olive and yellow fuselage as it slid sideways beneath his floats. Greene was tempted to try an Immelman loop in order to pursue, but rejected the idea as too risky for a seaplane. The stress force on the spars might tear off his floats.

Anyway, there was no hurry, he thought as he banked hard and came around, diving on the German's tail. He had the German where he wanted him.

They were approaching the grandstand as the German—evidently and sensibly frightened—tried to shake Greene, who stayed with his quarry. The German's evasive maneuvers cost him speed, allowing the Supershark to catch up. Greene pulled back on his stick, bringing the Supershark up and over the German, and then gently dropped down, so that his floats were bracketing the German's canopy.

The German dived. Greene, riding piggyback, stayed with him, letting the Supershark's pontoons almost but never quite touch the German seaplane. The German tried to get away, circling the start/finish pylon barge several times. Greene didn't let him, but kept forcing the German toward the sea in a leisurely spiral. He let up only at the last instant, allowing the olive and yellow seaplane an ignominious, but safe, belly flop of a splashdown, well away from the rest of the pack, which had since landed.

With the German vanquished, Greene pulled back on his stick to soar into the sky. He did a victory roll, enjoying the fact that he was now the only airplane flying, and the center of attention. He came around, waggling his wings as he passed over the downed German, and then began his own landing approach. He brought the Supershark down, throttling her back to her minimum flying speed, and then gently dropped her into the drink with nary a bounce.

He lowered his water rudders and taxied in, toward the launch ramps, cutting his engine as his race crew waded out to attach lines to the Supershark and haul her in. Greene thought the boys were all being rather poker-faced about his exploit as he hopped down out of the cockpit. He guessed that the word had already come down from on high that he was now an ex-employee of Stoat-Black. Well, if that were the case, he would have no regrets. Honor was the only luxury an impoverished gentleman could call his own.

He was pulling off his goggles and helmet when he saw Herman Gold, looking debonair in a cream-colored linen suit and matching fedora; wearing round, tortoiseshell sunglasses with green lenses. Gold was standing on the beach, a few yards from the ramp.

"Mister Gold." Greene nodded, approaching him. "I wonder, have I been disqualified as well as eliminated?"

Gold smiled. He took off his sunglasses and began polishing the lenses with the end of his tie. "You have caused, if I may use an English expression, 'a bit of a flap.' From what I hear, the race committee is taking the unprecedented step of fining Stoat-Black for your behavior."

Wonderful, Greene thought. *I'm out of work now, for certain.* "And the German?" Greene angrily demanded.

"The German's been disqualified, as well, but they're far more angry with you." Gold shrugged philosophically. "You had to expect that, kid, right? I mean, think about it; the race committee is dominated by the Italians, and considering the international political situation they're going to want to kiss the Germans' asses. The committee is taking the position that two wrongs don't make a right. . . ."

"Well, they do in my book, Mister Gold," Greene declared firmly. "I wasn't going to let that pilot humiliate me and get away with it."

"I realize that, kid," Gold said softly. "However, as much as I admire what you did, I can't say that I blame the race committee for the action they're taking. A seaplane race is no place to engage in a dogfight."

Greene shrugged. "I suppose Stoat-Black has dismissed me?"

"Yep," Gold said.

"Well, I did expect that as a consequence," Greene said sadly.

"Buck up, kid," Gold said. "Stoat-Black was obliged to fire you, otherwise it would look as if they were endorsing your actions, but Hugh Luddy informed me that you'll receive a sizable bonus in your separation pay."

"That is very kind of them," Greene said politely. His heart was breaking as the realization of his dismissal—his grounding—hit home, but he wasn't about to let Gold catch an inkling of his despair. Greene had already committed a *faux pas* in burdening this man's daughter with his problems. A gentleman did not wear his heart on his shirtsleeves. . . .

"Hugh also confided that everyone at Stoat-Black completely understands why you did what you did," Gold was continuing. "What's more, they're thrilled with your demonstration of the Supershark's combat potential. Thanks to you we now know what we had previously only suspected: that the Supershark has the makings of a superb fighter. We can't wait to get rid of those floats, and see what she can do with conventional, retractable landing gear.

But she'll be doing it with some other pilot in the cockpit, Greene wistfully thought. He forced a smile. "The one thing *I'd* like to know is *why* the German did that to me. . . ."

"That's a long story," Gold said.

"What?" Greene blurted. "*You* know why?"

"For now, let me just say that early this morning I received a note from a German government official I'd had coffee with yesterday morning. His note said that the Supershark was going to be humiliated during today's race due to my company's business relationship with Stoat-Black."

"I don't understand," Greene said, perplexed.

Gold shook his head. "I'm not sure I do, either, but it seems that you were blindsided in retaliation for my refusing a certain invitation from the German government. I guess that what the Nazis wanted to do was point out to me the error of my decision by demonstrating the superiority of German pilots and airplanes." He smiled. "Of course, thanks to you, things didn't work out quite the way the Nazis had planned. Don't worry about it now. I'll tell you all the details over dinner, tonight."

"Excuse me?"

"Dinner. Tonight," Gold repeated. "During which we can also discuss the terms of your employment as a test pilot for GAT."

Suze remembered after all, Greene thought, and smiled thinly. "Sir, your daughter promised that she would speak to you on my behalf, and obviously she has been brought up to keep her word. I appreciate her kindness toward me . . . and your own generosity," he quickly added. "But I'm not proud of the way that I took advantage of an impressionable young girl's sympathy. Although this may be hard for you to believe, considering the way that I've manipulated your daughter to speak on my behalf, my honor is very important to me—"

"Just a minute," Gold interrupted, impatiently. "First of

all, if you really knew my daughter, you'd know that no one has ever manipulated her in her life. Second, I didn't get where I am today by hiring people just because my kids told me to."

"Sir, are you saying that your daughter didn't?—"

Gold held up his hand to silence Greene. "Sure, Suzy talked to me about you. But even before she did, I'd begun to consider making you an offer. GAT will be continuing to work in tandem with Stoat-Black on the Supershark fighter project. Accordingly, I can use a test pilot who knows this particular airplane inside and out. Like I was saying, I was seriously considering hiring you, but what convinced me was seeing you fly today. When I saw how you recovered out of that stall, and the way you put that German pilot in his place, I said to myself, this kid is one of the finest pilots I've ever had the pleasure to know, and I've got to have him in my employ."

"Am I really, Sir?" Greene laughed. "I mean, I *knew* I was rather good, but am I really one of the finest? . . ."

Gold grimaced. "You want the job or not, Your Lordship?"

"Yes, I certainly do want it." Greene laughed, extending his hand.

Gold, smiling back, shook hands with him, and then turned away. "Dinner, tonight," he said over his shoulder as he trudged up the beach. "For now, rest up."

"Yes, Sir!" Greene called after him. "Thank you, Sir!"

Greene, preoccupied with bright dreams of his future in America, hurried up toward the tent hangar to change out of his flying gear. He stopped short when he saw Suze—a big smile on her face—waiting by the hangar entrance. Her hair was up, held in place by a sun visor. She was wearing a halter top that left her midriff exposed, and pleated linen trousers that fit snugly at her hips, then flared into wide cuffs that ended at the knee. She did not in the least resemble a child. Greene felt his pulse quicken, and a certain flutter of apprehension in the pit of his stomach.

She saw him and waved excitedly. "You're going to love California!" she shouted, laughing.

Without thinking about it, Greene felt quite wonderfully happy to see her.

Chapter 15

(One)
GAT
Burbank, California
9 November 1939

Gold was in the design studio conference room, attending a meeting. He had just heard the reports on the work to date on the BearClaw fighter, and was now listening to a report on the fledgling BuzzSaw light bomber project.

"The dilemma we're facing is a classic one," concluded the young engineer in charge of the twelve-man design cell working on the BuzzSaw. "Do we stand still, satisfied that we have something successful, knowing all the while that it's in danger of becoming outmoded? Or do we take a chance on something new, painfully aware that it could resoundingly flop?—"

The telephone on the sideboard rang. One of the engineers closest to the phone got up and answered it, and then said, "It's your secretary, Mister Gold."

Gold got up and went over to the telephone. "Roz, I asked that I not be disturbed—"

"I'm sorry, but Blaize Greene is up here. He wants to see you. He says it's very important."

"Well, send him down." Gold looked at Teddy Quinn. "Is

it all right if I use your office for a few minutes?" When Teddy nodded, Gold told his secretary, "Tell Blaize to meet me in Teddy's office." Gold hung up. "Blaize Greene needs to see me about something," he explained to the engineers in the room. "I'll see him and come right back."

"Tell Blaize I went over his preliminary specs for the turbine," Teddy said. "I think they're solid. And while you're gone, think about what you want to do about the BuzzSaw, Herman. We can't afford to waste any more time on it if it's not a go-project."

Gold, nodding, left the conference room. That young engineer in charge of the BuzzSaw R&D cell was right, Gold thought as he walked the short distance down the corridor to Teddy's office. GAT was faced with a classic dilemma.

The Pursuit Plane 6 BearClaw was GAT's improved version of the GAT/Stoat-Black Supershark. The Supershark, little changed except for redesigned wings to allow for her machine guns, and to house conventional, retractable, landing gear, had been wholeheartedly adopted by the RAF. Thanks to GAT's cooperation with Stoat-Black on the Supershark, Gold had been first in line with a viable fighter concept when the United States Congress, alarmed by the situation in Europe, and Japanese aggression in the Pacific, voted to appropriate three hundred million dollars to rebuild the Army Air Corps. The Army had looked at GAT's proposal, and liked what they'd seen. GAT had been awarded a generous preliminary contract. Gold had his design staff and his best factory people working to build some P-6 BearClaw prototypes for the Army to test.

Recently, Teddy and his R&D staff had presented Gold with a new design proposal for a twin-engined, combination fighter/bomber, tentatively designated the Combat Support 1 BuzzSaw.

Gold thought that the CS-1 was a splendid idea. In size it would fall somewhere between medium bombers and single-engine fighters rigged with bomb racks beneath their wings. The CS-1 reminded him of the armor-plated, low-flying, troop-support gunships that had made up the *Schlastas*, the ground patrol air squads that had been so successfully utilized by the Germans during the last war. Gold also agreed with his design staff that GAT needed an ace up its sleeve, something to count on beyond the BearClaw. Gold had no doubt that the P-6 would be well received, and that GAT would be awarded a large initial order, but would reorders come? The rest of the aircraft industry wasn't standing still, after all. There were other fighters being developed, and these newer designs would likely incorporate and surpass the BearClaw's innovations. Sooner or later, Gold would have to divert money, research talent, and production-line time to some new project, or else lose out on the lucrative military buildup contracts that were sure to come... But was now the time? And was the BuzzSaw Combat Support bomber the project?

"Blaize Greene is on his way down, Sir—"

Gold nodded to the secretary as he went into Teddy Quinn's office. The office was large, with windows overlooking the newly constructed, phase-three factory complex. Teddy's desk and drafting table were both blanketed with blueprints and thick folders. The carpeting around the wastebasket next to the drafting table was littered with balled-up pieces of graph paper. Gold smiled sadly at that. He envied the fact that Teddy still managed to find the time to be creative, despite his mounting administrative duties. Gold couldn't remember the last time he'd sat down at his drafting table...

Gold wandered over to the glass display case that held scale models of the entire GAT family of aircraft, starting with the G-1 Yellowjacket. There was a space reserved for a model of the P-6 BearClaw, when the time came. A new glass case would be needed to house the model of whatever airplane came after the P-6, Gold thought proudly.

"Thank you for seeing me, Herman."

Gold turned away from the display case as Blaize came into the room. He was dressed in a sport coat and slacks instead of his usual flying gear. "Teddy says your stuff on the turbine is up to snuff."

"Good... Look, I know how busy you are, but could we sit down and talk for a minute?"

Gold resisted the urge to glance at his watch, and pushed aside his concerns about the conference room full of engineers waiting for him. He led Blaize over to the sofa in the corner of Teddy's office. "Now, then, what's on your mind?"

"Well, Herman, first of all let me remind you of the conversation we had some time ago, concerning my own plans," Blaize said, lighting a cigarette.

Gold nodded. Like most British pilots, Blaize was a member of the RAF civilian reserve. Back in the beginning of the year—when Hitler began making threatening noises toward Poland, and the British Prime Minister Chamberlain was warning that if Poland were attacked, Britain and France would honor their defense agreements with that country—Blaize had come to talk with Gold about returning to England to begin active service with the RAF. Gold had argued that Blaize was being too hasty; that there was no certainty that England would go to war. In the meantime, Blaize was doing important work here at GAT.

Gold had managed to talk Blaize out of leaving at the time, but throughout the spring, summer, and fall the situation in Europe had steadily deteriorated. On September 1, the German *blitzkrieg* had sliced into Poland. Two days later, a weary and disillusioned Chamberlain had sadly issued a declaration of war against Germany, joined by the governments of Australia, New Zealand, and France.

"I've been thinking long and hard about this the past couple of months, Herman," Blaize began. "I've come to the conclusion that my place is back in Britain, defending my country."

"Can we discuss this?" Gold asked.

"If you'd like, but I warn you, my mind is made up. I should think that you, of all people, would understand . . . In the last war you did not hesitate to act on Germany's behalf."

Gold smiled. "I do understand—or at least, *remember*—a young man's passions, but young men don't always make the wisest decisions."

"Perhaps." Blaize shrugged. "But with all due respect, it is, nonetheless, *my* decision to make."

Gold didn't answer. "Speaking of passions, have you told my daughter of your decision? It seems you two have become pretty inseparable the past seventeen months you've been a part of GAT."

"Well, yes, I have discussed my decision with her," Blaize said, looking uncomfortable. "I mean, as friends might . . ."

"And what did she have to say about it?" Gold asked, watching Blaize closely.

"She's unhappy about it, but . . ." Blaize looked him in the eye. "If I may be perfectly frank, Suzy and I have a very close, but platonic, relationship . . ."

"Then she isn't your sweetheart?"

"I don't have a sweetheart," Blaize said gruffly.

Gold wasn't surprised by the tart reply. He knew that Erica had tried on several occasions to match Blaize with some of the eligible and attractive women they knew. Nothing had ever come of those matches, and not for the women's lack of trying, Erica had subsequently discovered. Gold and his wife had since concluded that Blaize simply was not interested in the opposite sex, per se. Erica had thought it very eccentric, even for an Englishman, but long ago in Germany Gold had known men like Blaize: chaste men, who sublimated their physical needs in strenuous exercise and demanding work. He respected such men, even if he could not personally comprehend what made them tick.

"Herman, I do hope that you won't try to manipulate my fond feelings for Suzy in order to get me to stay . . ."

"Actually, I'm prepared to do *anything* to get you to stay," Gold replied, only half jokingly. "Your work here is vital, and I'm *not* talking about your test piloting."

Blaize smiled faintly. "You're referring to that gas turbine notion I've been toying with?"

Gold nodded. "If you know anything at all about fighter tactics, you know that superior speed is paramount. A jet engine that would allow a fighter to fly rings around an enemy plane equipped with a piston engine just might make the difference for your country in its war with Germany."

"There are other people working on airplane gas-turbines," Blaize said. "Most notably, Frank Whittle. Actually, it was Whittle who first introduced me to the notion. He was doing graduate work at Cambridge University when I was there."

"I'm familiar with Whittle's work, and I agree with you that right now he's the front-runner," Gold replied. "But it's very possible that if you put your mind to it you could leap-frog him."

"Herman." Blaize smiled. "I do appreciate your confidence in me, but I'd need a lab, and technicians to assist me."

"Now that the new construction here has been completed, I can supply you with a state-of-the-art lab."

"Assuming I didn't blow myself up, we'd eventually have to bring a full-fledged engine-design firm into it."

"Rogers and Simpson have been supplying GAT with engine designs right from the beginning," Gold said. "I can assure you that there's no better outfit. You'll like working with them," he added confidently.

Blaize laughed. "And you're quite a salesman, Herman, but you haven't sold me. I'd like to stay. I really would, but I feel my country needs my skills as a pilot."

"I think you should be asking yourself how you can be of greater service to England. Is it through shooting down a few Nazi airplanes, and perhaps getting yourself shot down and killed? Or is it through using your brains to present England with the means to bring down the entire Luftwaffe?"

"Herman, it's all very enticing." Blaize smiled. "I wish I could accept. But I believe in action. I'm not the backroom type. Now then, will you please accept my resignation?"

"There's no way I can persuade you to reconsider?" When Blaize shook his head, Gold nodded, sighing. "Okay, then let me offer you a deal. With the war on, you're going to have a hell of a time getting yourself passage home to England, right?"

Blaize frowned. "I—I really hadn't thought about that . . ."

"I know." Gold chuckled. "It's the kind of detail usually forgotten by passionate young men. The deal is this: you give me one more full month, during which you forget about test flying. You just spend the time working with Teddy Quinn and his people, bringing us up to speed on your turbine design so that we can continue working on it while you're off patrolling the English sky in your RAF Supershark. In exchange, I'll pull a few strings to arrange your transatlantic passage on a United States diplomatic flight."

"A full month?" Blaize asked doubtfully.

"Don't worry, the war isn't going to end so fast," Gold replied. "And it'd probably take you longer than a month to get home on your own."

"I suppose you're right about that," Blaize said slowly.

"Then we have a deal?"

"We do," Blaize said. "Thank you."

"All right." Gold stood up. "Now I've got a meeting waiting for me, and you've work of your own to do."

"I'll start immediately," Blaize said.

Gold waited for Blaize to leave the office. Young men were all very much alike, he thought. It seemed the less they knew about life, the stronger were their certainties about the paths they wished to take. Gold had never had anyone looking out for him when he was young. Nobody to keep him from making mistakes. His son, and Blaize, were more fortunate . . . Gold would look out for them.

He went over to Teddy's desk to use the telephone, dialing his secretary. "Roz, it's me . . . what time is it in England? . . . They're what? Nine hours ahead of us?" He glanced at his watch. "Hell, then it's too late over there to catch anybody in their offices with an overseas call . . . Tell you what, let's send a wire . . . yeah, I'll dictate it to you right now. It's to Sir Alfred . . . yeah, the President of Stoat-Black . . ."

(Two)
Gold Household
Bel-Air
22 November 1939

Gold was working at his desk in his study when his son, Steven, came in. Steven was wearing tan corduroy slacks, leather slip-ons, and a striped, short-sleeved polo shirt with a soft knit collar. Gold smiled proudly. The boy was just fifteen, but he was already six feet tall, and weighed in at one eighty, and all of that was muscle. His son had taken to brushing his thick blond hair straight back, the way Hull Stiles had used to comb his hair. Back when old Hull still had hair...

"What are you doing hanging around the house on a beautiful Saturday afternoon like this?" Gold asked, smiling. His son was staring down at his shoes, looking ill-at-ease. "Is anything wrong, son?"

"Pop, I got an idea a while back, while listening to Suzy blubbering about Blaize leaving for England—"

"I hope you haven't been teasing your sister," Gold said sternly.

"Honest, Pop, I haven't been ragging Suzy about Blaize," Steven said, and then shrugged. "Well, not much, anyway," he continued sheepishly. "I mean, I just couldn't take listening to all of that female blubbering. It's not like she was Blaize's girlfriend or anything, right?"

"They're good friends, Steven. You know how it can be when you have to say good-bye to a friend..." Gold had made good on his promise to Blaize, securing him a place on a U.S. diplomatic flight to London, departing from Washington D.C. on the fifteenth of December.

"Anyway, Pop, listening to Suzy complain about Blaize leaving gave me this idea," Steven said. "I've been thinking about it for a while. With Blaize gone you're going to be needing a new test pilot. You always said that someday I could be one of your pilots—"

"Hold it." Gold laughed. "*You* always said that, not *me*."

"I could do the job!" Steven said eagerly. "I got my pilot's license!"

"What about school?"

"I could quit school, Pop!" Steven replied. "What do I need to finish high school for? I know what I'm going to do for the rest of my life. I'm going to work at GAT."

"You can't quit high school, Steven. You're only fifteen," Gold said impatiently, struggling to control his temper. He had work to do, and here he was talking nonsense with his son. "Not only that, I expect you to go to college—"

"What for? You don't learn how to fly planes in college! Blaize didn't finish college—"

"But at least he gave it a try, Steven," Gold pointed out. "He had a few years at Cambridge University. He studied engineering—"

"But you value him for being a test pilot."

Gold shook his head. He glanced at the folder spread open on his desk, and turned it around so that his son could see it. "Look at that," Gold commanded. "Tell me what it is."

Steven leaned over the desk and idly flipped through the pages covered with notes and drawings. He shrugged. "Teddy's chicken scratches concerning some new project, I guess."

"You guess wrong," Gold said. "Those notes belong to Blaize."

"About the BearClaw project?"

"Wrong again! What you're looking at are Blaize's notes for a new kind of engine: a gas turbine engine—"

"No kidding?" Steven nodded. "So what?" he asked innocently.

Gold shook his head in disgust. "You haven't the slightest idea what I'm talking about, and yet you want to quit school!"

"Pop—"

"Be quiet! Don't interrupt!" Gold snapped. "Blaize came upon the idea of an airplane jet engine back at Cambridge University. Now he's working on the idea for GAT. Sure, Blaize's abilities as a pilot are helpful, but it's what's inside this folder that makes Blaize invaluable!" He pounded the folder with his fist. "*This* is what will one day make him a *winner*! Without his time at Cambridge it wouldn't have happened!"

Steven frowned. "But what if I don't turn out to be some kind of inventor like you, or Blaize? What if *that* isn't who *I* am?"

"Of course that's who you are," Gold insisted. "I know my son."

"Pop, I want to be a flier—"

Gold, studying his son, forced himself to let the anger and frustration drain out of him. He wanted to avoid a direct confrontation with Steven—if possible. "Look, I'll tell you what . . . If you want, you can start work at GAT—"

"Thanks, Pop!"

"But *after* school, and on weekends," Gold cautioned. "You can work upstairs, with me. Or hang around with Teddy and the designers . . . We'll find something for you to do. You could file papers, run errands—"

"In other words, be an office boy," Steven sulked.

"In other words, get a feeling for how GAT operates!" Gold glared at his son.

"Yeah, and everybody will look at me and whisper behind my back, there goes the boss's son. When are they going to know *my* name, Pop? When am I going to stop being your son and become my own man—"

"When you do something worthwhile," Gold shot back.

"That's exactly what I was thinking," Steven replied softly. "The problem is we have different ideas about what that 'worthwhile something' should be."

"Look, I don't want to discuss this nonsense any longer," Gold said firmly.

"Right. It's always what *you* want," Steven said, clearly angry now. "And what *I* want for *myself* you call nonsense."

"Get out of here," Gold ordered, shocked at his son's tone. He felt like he was confronting a stranger.

"Sorry," Steven said sarcastically. "You've been very generous with your time." He stalked toward the door. "Next time I'll remember to make an appointment."

"I've been very generous, period!" Gold shouted.

"Right!" Steven yelled back as he left the study. "The only thing you won't give me is the chance to prove myself!"

(Three)
GAT
Burbank
12 December 1939

Blaize Greene was at his drafting table in the little office he'd been assigned for the duration of his stay at GAT. He'd been working on his turbine blade drawings for the last six hours. He was exhausted, but he was determined to press on. He didn't have much time left. The few weeks he had promised Herman had zoomed by. Tomorrow he was leaving on a flight to Washington D.C., and on the fifteenth he would depart from Washington to London, on the diplomatic flight that Herman had arranged for him.

Greene stood up, to stretch away the ache in his back from the time spent hunched over his drawings. He'd already decided to work straight through the rest of the day, and all night, up until it was time to stop by the Santa Monica apartment he was vacating to pick up his bags and head over to the airport. Herman had held to his part of the deal, and Blaize intended to do the same. He would do all he could to bring Teddy Quinn up to speed concerning his ideas for the turbine. After that, Teddy could have a bang at it on his own, Greene thought. He himself was fervently looking forward to getting into the cockpit of an RAF Supershark, where he could take far more direct action against the bloody Nazis—

"Knock, knock," Suze said, standing in the doorway.

Greene looked up, and smiled. "What are you doing here?"

"What kind of greeting is that?" she pretended to scold. "Haven't you missed me?"

"Since last night, you mean?" Greene chuckled. For over a year now now he and Suze had been spending most of their free time together. Suze had taught him his way around the city, and together they'd enjoyed museums, the theater, concerts, and films. Most every night the two would become involved in long, and deeply intricate, conversations about life and art and a host of subjects. The talk would go on for hours, often while they were parked outside her family's Bel-Air residence. Those were the times that Greene most loved: when he was staring up at the moon and stars, with the scent of bougainvillea perfuming the evening, listening to Suze's soft voice . . .

"Well, then, now that you mention it, I suppose I have missed you," he said.

"Oh! You mean I had to remind you!" She laughed. "Now I am insulted!"

"Don't be." He came around the drafting table to give her an affectionate hug. "You know how it can be . . . Say you're whiling away an afternoon reading, and gradually the light fades, but then somebody comes into the room and switches on a lamp?"

"And you didn't know how much you needed the light until it was there?"

Suze was smiling up at him, her arms warm and comforting around his waist. Greene could feel the rise and fall of her breasts as she breathed. At times like this the age difference between them seemed needle-thin, but then Greene had to remind himself that time had passed since they'd first met. Suze was almost nineteen.

He kissed her on the forehead, and then gently extricated himself from her embrace. He pretended not to see her subtle frown as he stepped away.

"You look like you're on your way to the shore," he said. She was wearing a tan skirt and matching top, both of which buttoned up the front, but he could discern the outline of her dark-colored swimsuit beneath the light cotton fabric.

"I am, and I've come to kidnap you for the afternoon," she announced firmly.

"I can't!" Greene sighed. "I've got so much work to do here! I was planning on working straight through the night."

"Why worry about it? No matter what you do, you won't be able to finish it before you leave tomorrow!" she said, her tone artificially bright.

"Suze, we're not going to get into the matter of my leaving again, are we?" Greene cautioned. "We've been all through it so many times . . ."

"I know, I know!" Suze said cheerfully. "And I promised you I wouldn't cry anymore, and I won't. I keep my promises."

"I know that you do," Greene said fondly, gazing at her.

"But it's a beautiful afternoon, just perfect for the beach," she said. "Since it's a weekday it won't be crowded. I brought you a pair of Steven's swim trunks to wear, and I have a picnic lunch and a bottle of chilled wine in the trunk of my car."

"It sounds wonderful," he said longingly.

"Oh, please, come! It'll be our farewell time together," she said. "After, I'll bring you back here and you can spend all night working on your notes if you want... And then tomorrow, you can leave..."

Greene enjoyed watching Suze expertly weave the nimble Jaguar through the Hollywood traffic. Before he knew it she'd spirited them to the sun-drenched coast road, and they were motoring past Los Tunas. The breeze rolling off the Pacific smelled of seaweed. The light sparkling on the white sand and blue water dazzled, and pleasured, the eye.

Greene took the opportunity to study Suze's profile as she concentrated on her driving. She was wearing red-framed sunglasses. Her skin was tanned, and her blond hair was whipping behind her in the slipstream. She looked absolutely lovely, and he thought that it was a damned good thing he was leaving, because at some point during the year and a half he had been in California he had fallen in love with her. Friendships were one of life's great pleasures, but the entanglements of love were so messy...

She abruptly glanced his way, and smiled. Greene imagined that she'd sensed his eyes upon him, or perhaps she'd even sensed his thoughts. That had happened between them on occasion, when they'd been deeply, passionately engaged in conversation about music or books, and one had managed to finish the other's thought...

"This is wonderful!" Greene shouted above the wind's warm whistling, and the Jag's buzz. "Thank you for kidnapping me!"

Suze blew him a kiss, almost shyly, and then quickly turned her attention back to the road. Greene, settling back against the burnished leather of the bucket seat, was supremely happy. He felt quite free to love Suze with all his heart, considering it was the eve of his departure...

They'd reached a deserted stretch of shore, with no other cars in sight, when Suze turned off the road and parked. Greene took the blanket and towels and picnic basket out of the Jag's boot, kicked off his shoes, and followed Suze across the hot, squeaky sand. They spread their blanket in a secluded spot that was close to the water, but sheltered between high dunes.

The white wine had warmed during its stay in the Jag's boot, so Greene took the bottle down to the water line and buried it up to its neck in the cool mud to regain its chill. He went behind a sand dune to change into the swim trunks that Suze had brought him, and then they went swimming, laughing, and playing in the waves together like children. Greene adored watching Suze at play. She was a big girl, but she was strong and supple, and her body was as tight as it was blessed with abundant curves. God had clearly intended Suze to be larger than life, and she had fulfilled that promise.

Greene retreived the wine and they drank some with the lunch that Suze had packed for them. They went swimming again, and then came back to their blanket, to bask in the sun and finish the last of the wine.

Greene was lying on his back, quite close to Suze, almost touching. He was feeling sleepy in his damp suit, staring into the ruddy crimson that was the sun against his closed eyelids, feeling the gentle breeze eddying feather-light against his salty skin.

His breath quickened as he felt Suze's thigh pressing against his. Her toes began tickling the sand from his own foot.

He felt her breath, wine-scented, on his face, and opened his eyes. She was up on one elbow, gazing down at him. Her sea-damp hair, limply hanging in curls and tendrils, formed a tawny curtain around her face. She had a slight blush of pink sunburn across the bridge of her nose. Her long eyelashes were encrusted with salt. Keeping her sable eyes locked with his, she took his hand and pressed his fingers against her breast. He could feel her nipple, raised and hard, beneath the moist, taut fabric of her swimsuit. Her front teeth seemed startlingly white; they glistened, pearl-like, as her lips parted and she lowered her mouth to his.

The taste of her overwhelmed him. He thought, oddly, that he'd known all along what her taste would be, and yet, that was quite impossible. They had never before kissed. Not like this. Thinking about it in retrospect, Greene would realize that it was after this first kiss that he was lost . . .

Suze drew away. Her eyes again searched his. He said

nothing as she studied him, but from the merry glint in her bewitching, dark eyes, he guessed that she'd learned whatever it was she needed to know.

She kissed him again. Then, slowly, watching him all the while, she slid the straps of her suit off her shoulders, peeling down the bodice to expose her breasts. Feeling as if he were in a dream, Greene reached for her. He pressed his face into her deep cleavage. She shivered and moaned, as goose bumps puckered the large, tan aureoles of her lush breasts. He licked and sucked the salty ocean from her pink, swollen nipples. Gradually she relaxed, becoming warm and fluid in his arms.

Her hands glided over his bare chest, and then skated down the hard, flat planes of his belly. Her fingers deftly unplucked the knot in the drawstring of his swim trunks, and then her hands were everywhere, and he was the one doing the moaning. He peeled her swimsuit down past her flaring hips, kissing her everywhere: her soft belly, her navel, and the briny, blond fur curling up from below; the silken mounds of her high, sassy bottom, so startlingly white where the sun had never touched. They nestled, facing each other, on the blanket. Suze's spreading thighs were cool and damp. Her center drew him like a magnet. She was warm and syrupy when he penetrated her. They fit together perfectly, and rocked and kissed, limbs entwined for a long, sweet time, and stayed locked together afterward, until the sound of voices coming up the beach startled them out of their blissful laziness. They pulled apart and hurriedly dressed.

Only then did the spell that had been cast on Greene vanish. It seemed to disappear the way the glistening, early-morning dew lifts from a spider's web.

"Look at me," Suze said softly. There was lightness in her tone, but also a tinge of panic. "Look at me and tell me what's wrong?"

He didn't know where to start. The guilt and depression were so cold and hard in the pit of his stomach, and inexorably swelling. "I shouldn't have taken advantage of you . . ." he said hoarsely.

"Are you joking?" Suze asked, sounding astounded. "I

seduced you! You're just confused because I was the virgin and you're experienced."

He glanced at her. "Well, no . . . I'm not really so awfully experienced, actually. . ." He sighed. "Actually, I've never really done this before."

"You . . . You've never? . . ." Suze abruptly grinned; but just as quickly, her smile vanished. "You're kidding me, right?"

"No, I'm not kidding you, if you must know . . . I mean, I suppose that in the past I *have* been presented with what one might refer to as *opportunities,* but somehow the idea just never seemed . . ." he paused, pursing his lips, ". . . *apropos* . . ."

Suze was laughing.

"Well, what I mean to say is that this sexual business is not really the sort of thing one can easily picture oneself doing," Greene quickly added.

The girl was laughing so damnably hard she was in tears.

"Now, what have I done with my cigarettes?" he muttered, blushing, trying to hide his confusion by patting the blanket, shaking out the towels, and searching beneath the picnic basket.

"S-stop!" she begged, gasping and holding her belly. "Don't make me laugh anymore! I c-can't catch my breath!"

"You know, I really fail to see the bloody humor . . ." he began, feeling quite stung.

She quickly put her hand over his mouth, and then, still chuckling, cuddled against him. "Well, for your first time out, I think you were just wonderful," she told him. "But then, that's the sort of performance I'd expect from a test pilot."

"Ah, yes, I do see that." He smiled, hugging her.

She looked up at him, her dark gaze intent and purposeful. "And, of course, I'm biased because I love you, and you do love me, right?" When he didn't immediately reply, she pinched him. "Right?"

Greene laughed, but then his smile turned sad. "Of course you're right," he sighed. "I do love you. But what happens next, Suze? I'm leaving, remember?"

"You'll come back," she declared bravely. "I'll wait."

"Who says that I'll be coming back?" he asked sharply. "I'm going to be a fighter pilot, love. Do you have any inkling of the life expectancy for fighter pilots?"

"Don't talk like that!"

"And there's something else," he muttered. "I gave my word to your father—and to myself—that I wouldn't take advantage of you."

"But *I* was the one that seduced *you*, remember?"

He shook his head, frowning. "But I acquiesced, you see. No, it was an unforgivable breach of conduct on my part."

"Well..." Suze began, for once in her life seeming at a loss for words. "We don't have to tell anyone," she suggested hopefully.

"My dear girl, I can lie to everyone, but I can't delude myself. My honor meant everything to me, Suze. It was the only thing I could truly call my own, but now it's gone."

"Now you *are* making me angry," Suze warned. "You're just a person, Blaize. You're not some knight from King Arthur's court."

He realized that for what was probably the first time since they'd met, she had absolutely no idea what he was trying to tell her. "You can laugh at me if you like," he said, getting to his feet, "but I think one's honor is like one's virginity. You can lose it only once, and then it is gone forever." He began to walk away, toward the water.

"Where are you going?" she called after him.

"For a stroll... By myself," he added, as she rose to follow. "I—I need to think... Suze... I need to come to terms with what's happened."

(Four)

Suzy found Blaize withdrawn and distant after he'd returned from his walk. The conversation was painfully polite as they got dressed, packed up their belongings, and trudged back to the car.

The drive back to Burbank passed in awkward silence. Suzy felt trickling wetness between her legs, and a bothersome throbbing. She wasn't in any pain, so she guessed that what she was feeling was normal. She glanced at Blaize. He was slumped down, cupping a cigarette to protect it from the wind. His mouth was twisted into a scowl, and his gleaming black hair was in his eyes, which were half-closed, like hooded bits of dull jade.

He looked as if he'd just killed someone, not gotten laid, Suze thought. Oh! She couldn't bear to look at him, she was so angry!

She had no regrets about seducing him. She knew all along that she was going to have to be the one to make the first move; that Blaize was just too caught up in his fairy tale moral code. At times like these she felt that the things he worried about were outdated and silly, but she'd fallen in love with him a long time ago. When she learned that he was leaving to go to war, she'd decided that she wanted him to be her first lover. She wasn't the romantic that Blaize was. She was pragmatic enough to know that someday she would fall in love with someone else, get married, and have a family, but she also knew that she was always going to be at least a little in love with Blaize. She looked forward to that. It was going to be nice to have his sensitive, brooding presence now and again haunting her dreams down through the years . . .

It would be nicer still if some miracle occurred to keep him right here in California with her, but Suzy knew that wasn't going to happen. She certainly wouldn't do any more weeping over his leaving. She'd promised him she wouldn't, and, anyway, if she wept now, who knew how he'd take it? Poor Blaize thought he was so sophisticated and mature, but in reality he perceived things with a child's emotional literalness. If she let him see her tears now he'd probably assume that they were due to her remorse over becoming a fallen woman, and probably throw himself off a cliff . . .

"What are you smiling about?" Blaize grumbled.

"Can't a girl smile?"

"Hmph," he said, and went back to sulking.

It was close to seven o'clock by the time they got back. The plant's parking lots were empty, and the night guards were on duty at the main gate. They recognized Suzy's car, and waved her through. She drove to the main building. Blaize had the door of the car open before she'd come to a full stop.

"Suze, I—I guess, this is good-bye, then," he mumbled, not looking at her.

She watched, dumbstruck, as he got out of the car and walked quickly—almost ran, it seemed—through the entranceway of the building.

"Dammit!" Suzy swore. "He never even looked back! Dammit!" She put the Jaguar into reverse, backed around in a tire-screeching turn, and then rocketed forward down the drive, toward the main gates.

He never even looked back! She wasn't going to let him get away with that!

"Dammit!" She stepped hard on the brakes, geared down into second, and wrenched the Jag hard left. Her smoking back tires sprayed gravel as she made a U-turn and roared back to the entrance where she'd dropped off Blaize. She skidded to a stop, shut the engine, kicked open the Jag's door, swung herself out of the car, slammed the door shut, and strode into the building. She took the elevator to the design floor. It was quiet here. Everyone had quit for the day. She hurried down the corridor to Blaize's office. His door was closed; she opened it without knocking.

Blaize was seated at his drafting table, his head in his hands. He looked up at her with a bleak expression as she came in.

"Please, go," he began.

"Shut up, and listen to me!" Suzy said, furious. "I'm not going to let you martyr yourself over what happened this afternoon! Or maybe I will let you! I haven't decided yet! But you're definitely not going to be rid of me until I've given you a good piece of my mind!—"

"Excuse me . . ." she heard her father say. He was standing in the doorway behind her. He looked at her, and then at Blaize. "Forgive me for interrupting . . . Blaize, I could come back? . . ."

"No, Herman," Blaize sighed. "That's quite all right. Suze was just leaving . . . Weren't you, Suze?"

"You don't have to go, honey," Herman quickly told her,

coming into the office. "This will take only a minute." He laughed uneasily. "Actually, Blaize, I think it would be better if my daughter stayed. That way maybe you'll keep your lid on when you read this."

Suzy looked on as her father handed Blaize an envelope. She watched Blaize open it, unfold the official-looking sheet of stationery, and skim its contents.

Blaize turned white.

"What is it?" she asked fearfully.

"It's from the office of the RAF Air Chief Marshal," Blaize whispered before her father could reply. "It seems that I've been commissioned into RAF active service, as a captain . . ."

"Congratulations," Suzy said dryly.

"But that's not all the letter says, Suze," Blaize continued, glaring at her father as he spoke. "It goes on to say that per the request of Herman Gold, relayed to British Air Staff through Sir Alfred Black, president of Stoat-Black Air Works, I've been assigned until further notice to GAT, in order to continue scientific experimental work herewith deemed essential to Britain's national interest." He crumbled the letter in his fist. "Goddamn you, Herman! You lied to me!"

"I did no such thing. I kept the deal I made with you. In exchange for one month's work I did secure you passage on a diplomatic flight."

"But it was all a charade!" Blaize accused. "You tricked me into staying, and used the extra month to push through this nonsense!"

"That nonsense, as you put it, are your official orders," Herman replied. "As an officer and a gentlemen you are expected to obey them."

"Damn you! You know I have no choice in that matter!" Blaize muttered.

Suzy turned her face away from Blaize, afraid that she was unable to hide the joy she was feeling over the fact that now they would have more time together. If Blaize saw her expression he might misunderstand, and think that she was taking pleasure in Daddy's having outmaneuvered him.

"As for tricking you," Daddy was saying, "I did what I

felt I had to do, for the greater good. I happen to feel that your work here on the turbine takes precedence over your desire to see combat. That letter proves that your RAF superiors agree with me. Now, if you'll excuse me, I'll leave you two to whatever it was you were discussing."

"So I'm trapped, is that it, Herman?" Blaize demanded.

Her father paused in the doorway. "I took the liberty of having my secretary cancel your flight for tomorrow," he said evenly, no hint of triumph on his face, or in his voice. "She also called your landlord, to inform him that you've had a change in plans and that you'll be keeping your apartment. I'll expect to see you here, bright and early, tomorrow morning. Good night, Blaize."

"I guess Herman Gold lets nothing stop him from getting what he wants," Blaize growled as her father's footsteps faded down the corridor.

That goes double for his daughter, Suzy thought, but she didn't say a word. She didn't have to. She had time.

Chapter 16

(One)
GAT
Burbank, California
22 September 1940

Gold was meeting with Teddy Quinn, in Teddy's office. Between them was a coffee table littered with production sheets and folders containing the paperwork on old and new projects.

The P-6 BearClaw had passed all of the U.S. Army Air Corps tests and was in production. Meanwhile, GAT's proposal for the Combat Support One BuzzSaw light attack bomber was in Washington. The dual-engine BuzzSaw would be powered by Rogers and Simpson's 2000-horsepower radials. Teddy's people felt confident that she would have a top speed of approximately three hundred and twenty-five miles per hour, and a maximum range of twelve hundred miles, while hauling a ton and a half of high explosives in her bomb bay. The BuzzSaw would have a gun turret up top the fuselage, a tail gun compartment, and a half-dozen ports etched into her nose for forward-firing machine guns.

Officially, no decision had yet been reached by the government concerning the CS-1 BuzzSaw, but Gold's sources at the Defense Department had informed him that General Henry H. "Hap" Arnold, the Air Corps chief, looked favorably on the CS-1, which meant that she was a sure thing to be approved.

"On to new business," Gold said. "I've received a lengthy correspondence from Stoat-Black. It seems they've been given the go-ahead to construct a prototype aircraft for the jet engine being developed by Layten-Reese Motor Works."

"No shit." Teddy's eyebrows went up. "They get good funding?"

"For England." Gold nodded.

"What else do we know about it?"

"Quite a bit," Gold replied. "The letter was transported via diplomatic pouch, so they felt they could be explicit about the details. They say they're about a year from a prototype. You can read the letter for yourself. The bottom line is they want to know what we've come up with so far . . ."

"If by that you mean what has Blaize come up with, the answer is not very much," Teddy said, taking off his glasses and rubbing the bridge of his nose. "It's hard for a fellow to come up with bright ideas when he's expending most of his energy sulking."

"Come on!" Gold scowled. "It's been seven months since I had him assigned here. He can't *still* be angry about it . . ."

Teddy shrugged. "Maybe it's not so much anger as bitterness. You know as well as I do what's been going on overseas . . ."

Gold nodded. In May, the routed British Expeditionary

Force had been more or less successfully evacuated from Dunkirk, thanks to the protective cover flown by the RAF. Less than a month later, France fell to the Germans, who then quickly turned their attention to Britain. German bombers sporadically flew raids over London, and RAF Bomber Command had retaliated with a night raid over Berlin, but the air battle began in earnest on September 7, when the Germans launched a devastating daytime air attack on London. The city burnt for days. Since then, the Luftwaffe had been rolling in on Britain like the fog. Formations of hundreds of German bombers and fighters filled the English sky day after day, while RAF Fighter Command valiantly struggled to defend the country.

The *Luftflotten*, those awesome German air fleets, had the RAF outmanned and outgunned, but the British did enjoy several advantages. RAF Fighter Command was defending home territory, which meant its planes could remain in combat longer in terms of fuel expenditure. Also, British pilots forced to bail out could be rescued by their own side, and be back in the battle almost immediately. The German attackers had to expend fuel crossing the Channel and then had to leave a fuel reserve in order to get home, and if they bailed out during combat the chances were that they'd end up as P.O.W.s.

Most important, the British enjoyed the added edge given them by a state-of-the-art early warning system, the heart of which was an electronics miracle called radar.

Gold couldn't help feeling some pleasure in the fact that the air battle for Britain was proving right his own air combat theories, which had been discounted by so many so-called authorities. Fighters were proving to be indispensable for air defense and massive formations of marauding bombers were proving to be vulnerable. An efficient early warning system was proving to be as essential to the British against the Germans in this war as it had been for the Germans against the Allies in the war previous.

"You know as well as I do that Britain is at risk," Teddy was saying. He paused to light a Pall Mall. "Their aircraft industry is straining to rebuild the RAF's fleet of Spitfires and Hurricanes and Supersharks, and hundreds of their pilots have been killed or wounded. I read the other day that the British have recruited a couple hundred Polish and Czech fighter pilots. How do you think that's going to make a guy like Blaize feel, knowing his country is that desperate for pilots, and that he could be an ace, but here he is stuck behind a desk in California?"

"I don't know and I don't care," Gold said flatly. "So he's a little upset. He's going to have to deal with it, and then get on with his job."

"There's another alternative," Teddy said. "You know as well as I do that if you gave the word, the RAF would pull him home and then he could get reassigned to Fighter Command."

"But I don't want him in combat," Gold said. "I want him safe and sound and at his drafting table, being very bright for GAT."

"Even if he's miserable? If he's not getting any worthwhile work done?"

"He'll snap out of it," Gold said confidently.

"On a couple of occasions I've caught him drinking in his office."

Gold shook his head. "There must be some flaw in that boy . . . Here I've tried to do what was best for him—"

"How do you know what's best for him?" Teddy challenged.

"What do you mean?"

"You heard me, so answer my question." Teddy took a last drag of his cigarette and then ground it out in the ashtray on the coffee table. "Wait a minute," he added, his voice rising. "Instead of answering that one, answer *this*: What gives you the fucking right to play God?"

"I don't get it?"

"You know what I'm talking about. There's this bullshit concerning Blaize, and what you were trying to do to your son, forcing him to be an engineer."

"And Steven's going to be one—"

"Bullshit," Teddy said. "You had him working for me for two months, remember? I can tell you that the kid hasn't the slightest aptitude for it. He's a competent mechanic, sure. He's inherited that much from you, but that's not enough.

Trying to turn him into an engineer is like trying to force a square peg into a round hole."

"You hammer it hard enough, and it'll happen," Gold said.

"And cause a lot of damage in the process," Teddy replied.

"Look! Don't tell me what my kid can or can't do!" Gold jumped to his feet. "He'll do what I tell him! And who the fuck do you think you're talking to, anyway?"

"*S'cuze me, massa.*" Teddy looked up at him and smiled.

"Fuck you, Teddy," Gold said, and stormed out.

Gold strode angrily down the corridor to the elevators, wondering where Teddy Quinn got off talking to him that way. He slammed the elevator call button with his fist, waited a second, then slammed it again.

Nobody talked to Herman Gold that way. Nobody! Not even old friends—

"Hi, Pop."

Gold turned. His son, wearing a mailroom smock, was coming toward him, wheeling a cart filled with interoffice correspondence.

Steven had taken up Gold's offer to work at GAT after school and on weekends. When his stint in Teddy's R&D department hadn't worked out, Steven had transferred to the mailroom.

"Pop, can I talk to you for a minute?"

"Yeah, sure," Gold muttered.

"I took some mail over to Brian Thomsen, the chief test pilot," Steven began.

"I know who Thomsen is," Gold grumbled. He was only half-listening to his son. He was still brooding over his exchange with Teddy. The more he thought about it, the madder he got . . .

"Well, I was talking to him about flying, and he offered to let me try out one of the new BearClaws, if it was okay with you—"

"Godammit!" Gold exploded.

Steven flinched. "Hey, Pop, calm down—"

"I'm so fucking sick of talking about the same things over and over!"

"Why can't I do a little test flying? I've been working here almost nine months, just like I said I would."

"But you showed absolutely no interest in engineering!" Gold accused. "Probably because you wanted to spite me!" He savagely jabbed the button: Where was the fucking elevator?

"Come on, Pop!"

"Don't raise your voice to me!"

"It's just that I haven't worked for Teddy for two months now," Steven complained. "It's old news!"

"So is this entire conversation," Gold coldly replied. "But you still insist on having it. Well, let's see if I can get this through your thick skull: That stuff about you being a test pilot, that was kid talk, you get it?"

"Kid talk?" Steven repeated, looked baffled, but then his eyes narrowed. "What do you mean?"

"Just what I said! It was funny at the time, but it's not funny to hear you talking that way now."

"So no matter how I try to compromise with you it doesn't matter, is that it? My life is going to go the way you want, and that's it?"

"You finally figured it out, Steven."

The elevator arrived. Gold stepped inside and pushed the button for his floor. As the doors slid closed they framed his son. The look in Steven's eyes made Gold think his son was on the verge of tears. The kid was pale and trembling. He had a white-knuckle grip on the mail cart.

The elevator reached the top floor, and Gold got out. As he walked along the corridor, he began to think that maybe the glint in Steven's eyes came not from tears, but from anger. By the time he got to his office Gold was sure of it.

The thought haunted Gold all the rest of the day. A couple of times he thought about calling down to the mailroom and having Steven come up, so that they could make peace, but his own telephone kept ringing with lengthy, important calls; there were letters to read and revise and sign; and people in and out to see him. Before he knew where the afternoon had gone, it was five-thirty. He tried the mailroom, but there was no answer.

Steven had evidently left for the day. Gold would see him at home. No harm done.

(Two)

That night Gold decided to unwind by going for a drive instead of going straight home. It was a nice night, so he put the top down on the Cadillac convertible coupe and headed out along the coast, letting the sea breeze, and the steady purr of the Caddy's big V-8, lull him into relaxation.

The more he thought about his arguments with Teddy Quinn, and his son, the more Gold felt that he'd been in the right. Sure he understood how Blaize Greene or Steven might have their own ideas about what they wanted to do, but it was the obligation of those older and wiser to set kids straight. By keeping Blaize out of combat, and his own son out of the cockpits of experimental aircraft, he was saving their lives. Blaize and Steven might resent his actions now, but someday they would thank him, just as Gold could imagine how he might have thanked his own father for looking out for him—if he'd had a father.

He stopped at a seafood shack near Newport Beach for some dinner, and to telephone home that he'd eaten and would be late. He got the maid, and asked her to relay the message to his wife.

After dinner he went for a walk along the beach, so by the time he got home it was around midnight. The house was quiet and dark. At first he thought that everyone had gone to bed, but he noticed that a light was on in the kitchen. He went in and found Erica, in her robe and slippers, sitting at the table in the soft light, having a cup of tea.

"I'm sorry I'm so late," Gold said. "I did telephone; did you get my message?"

Erica nodded. "I got it."

He thought she sounded funny, but decided she was probably just tired. "I went for a drive after work. I wanted to unwind." He yawned. "It's been one hell of an awful day."

"And it's not over yet," Erica said.

"You're right about that," Gold sighed, not really paying attention. "I have to talk to Steven. We had a little argument today. I was already in a foul mood when it began. Maybe I was a little too rough on him. I think I should apologize—"

"He's gone," Erica said.

She looked up at him, and when he saw that her eyes were red-rimmed from crying he suddenly got very scared. "What do you mean?' he asked urgently. "What are you talking about?"

"He's gone away. He left a note on his bed, asking us not to try and find him. He's taken a dufflebag and some clothes."

"That's ridiculous!" Gold fumed. "Is Suzy all right?"

"She doesn't know yet. She's been out with Blaize."

"We'll call the police," Gold said. "We'll give them a description and the license plate of his car."

"He didn't take the car."

"Why wouldn't he take his car?" Gold demanded.

"Because it's not his," Erica said wearily. "It's yours."

"Of course it's his car! I just bought it for him when he turned sixteen!"

"*You* bought it *for* him."

"Our son is missing and you're sitting here playing word games with me—"

"Herman, sit down."

He nodded. "After I call the police."

"Sit down, now," Erica insisted. "Right now!" she added sharply.

Gold stared at her, and then nodded. He took the chair directly across from Erica, who reached across the table to take his hand.

"I've been thinking about this for hours. I've come to some conclusions. They may be hard for you to accept, but I want you to try to understand." She sighed. "First of all, he's a big boy, and he's smart, even if he is only sixteen. I doubt very much that anybody is going to pick on him, or that he's in any immediate danger."

"But why didn't he take his car? That's what I want to know..." Gold was muttering.

Erica seemed not to hear the question. "Listen to me," she repeated. "I'm as much to blame as you, but these past few months the two of us have been pretending everything was all right concerning Steven, and everything wasn't all right."

"The kid was acting a little nuts about his future is all," Gold shrugged, but he stared down at the table, unwilling to meet Erica's gaze. "He's a little confused. That's what happens with kids these days."

"I know that you love Steven, and I know that he loves you, but you're a very strong man, Herman. It's hard for Steven to try and live up to your standards. He wants to make you happy, and, someday to fill your shoes, but he's got to do it his own way."

"So far, he's on the wrong track," Herman grumbled. He looked up accusingly. "So what are you saying to me? That my success is suffocating my son? That it would have been better for him if I'd been a failure, and that way he wouldn't have so much to live up to?"

Erica laughed. "No, darling, I'm not saying that. I'm saying that if you think about it, you'll realize that he has been trying to talk to us, but we've been so busy talking *at* him that we couldn't listen."

"When you say 'we,' you mean 'me,' right?" Gold asked gruffly.

Erica nodded, smiling. The dim light was softening the lines that time had put in her face. Gold always thought she looked beautiful, but just now, for a few moments at least, he found he could pretend he was talking to Erica as she'd looked when Steven was little enough to sit on his lap, and when Gold could do no wrong in his son's eyes.

"You asked why he didn't take his car. I think it's because you gave it to him. He didn't earn it, you *gave* it. It's easy to feel inadequate when you're existing off of others' generosity."

"That's an interesting notion. I'd like to experience that sort of inadequacy someday," Gold said dryly. "Of course, no one has ever given me anything—"

"That's my point!" Erica quickly replied. "You earned everything you have, so you're secure about who you are.

Now, think about your son. Where does he lay claim to *his* manhood?"

Gold leaned back in his chair and did think about it. He slowly nodded. "I . . . I never looked at it that way. Erica, you must know that all I wanted was to be a good father to him! Honestly, all I ever wanted was to do everything I could for him, like my father might have done for me, if I'd had one . . ."

"I do know that, my love," Erica said softly. "But now listen, and I'll tell you how you *can* be a good father. The kind of father he needs, right now."

"Anything," Gold said. "Anything at all to bring him home."

"You *don't* bring him home," Erica said. "You don't call the police. You let him go."

"What are you saying? What about school?"

"He can always go back to school."

"What if he gets into trouble, or . . ." Gold trailed off, helplessly. "Or something dangerous?" he moaned.

"Here's what I think we should do," Erica said. "We hire private detectives—"

"Now you're talking!" Gold said, feeling relieved. "That's better than the police! Detectives can work for us twenty-four hours a day."

"It shouldn't be all that hard to find him," Erica said. "After all, he is *your* son. No matter where he wanders, chances are he'll always wind up near airplanes."

"And that means airports!" Gold exclaimed. "Sure! Assuming he can't find a job flying—and he won't because he's too young—he'll get a job as an airplane mechanic."

"Once the detectives find him, we have them keep an eye on Steven to make sure he doesn't get into trouble," Erica said. "But otherwise they're to leave him alone."

"They're not to bring him home?" Gold asked weakly.

"If they did, what do you imagine would happen?" Erica demanded.

"You're saying he'd run away again?"

"Unless you kept him under lock and key. Let your son have his adventures," she said. "Let him get a taste of the world on his own terms; a taste as Steven Gold, not as Herman Gold's son. Let him try his wings. Believe me, that will be the quickest and surest way to bring him home, and *keep* him home." She paused, and smiled. "And who knows? Maybe it'll end up that someday *you'll* be known as Steven Gold's father..."

"That's fine with me," Gold said. "As long as he stays out of trouble, and as long as he stays out of danger! I don't want my son risking his life."

(Three)
Donovan Air Charter
Wilterboro Airport
Wilterboro, New Jersey
16 April 1941

Steven Gold was up on the stepladder, working on the Beechcraft's engine when the guy came in. At first Steven thought the guy was a gangster here to see Ernie Donovan, the proprietor of Donovan Air Charter. Ernie mostly did cropdusting, and made a little dough in summer by fitting floats on the Beechcraft and taking tourists for rides along the Jersey shore, but sometimes he did fly gangsters here and there. Not that Ernie liked to talk about that too much.

On closer inspection, however, Steven realized the guy who had just come in was too cheap-looking and shabby to be a gangster, who were all real sharp dressers. This guy's purple mohair suit looked worn, his collar looked grimy, and his tie had spots on it. He had white whiskers stubbling his cheeks, like he hadn't had a shave in maybe two days. Being up on the stepladder, Steven could see that the guy's hat brim was frayed. And he had no overcoat, despite the brisk April weather.

Also, the gansters who came around tended to act edgy. They would always be looking over their shoulder and complaining that they were anxious to get going. This guy just looked down on his luck, and kind of tired.

"The boss around, kid?" the guy asked. He was coming over to the Beechcraft when he suddenly skidded on the greasy concrete slab floor and began windmilling his arms to keep from landing flat on his ass. Steven wanted to smile, but he didn't dare. The guy didn't look like a gangster, but you could never tell.

"Back here, Red," Ernie called, standing up, so that the guy could see him over the stacked cardboard boxes filled with used airplane parts and odds and ends.

The guy checked the bottom of his shoes and made a face. He gave the the grease buckets and tools littering the floor a wide berth as he meandered over to the office area of the hangar. It was kind of dark back where he was heading— Ernie liked to save on electricity—but Steven figured the guy could make his way all right. There was as much light coming in through the chinks in the hangar walls as from the bare bulbs strung from the roof rafters above his work area.

"What brings you around here, Red?" Ernie asked the guy. "I thought you got yourself a job working for Bradley Aviation Export?"

"I am working for Gil. That's why I'm here. We heard a couple of truckloads of mint altimeters got lost coming out of Norton Instrument's Brooklyn warehouse. I thought maybe you could give me a lead on them. By the way, you got a drink here, Ernie?"

Steven smiled to himself. Ernie was known to fence hot airplane parts and supplies on occasion. He went back to working on the Beechcraft.

It was an old D-17 biplane with an enclosed cabin. It was painted tan, except where the dings and rust spots had been touched up with gray primer. The Beechcraft may have looked like hell, but it flew okay. It wasn't as good an airplane as the GAT Yellowjacket or Dragonfly had been, but the Beechcraft hadn't been bad, in its day.

Steven guessed he could say the same thing about Ernie, who reminded him of Popeye the Sailor from the funny papers. Like Popeye, Ernie was little and wiry, with gnarled forearms and a lantern jaw. He looked about a hundred years old. He had a granite-gray brushcut, and watery blue eyes. He claimed that he'd flown with Rickenbacker's Hat in the Ring Squadron during the war. Steven was respectful, but he didn't much believe Ernie's war stories. Nevertheless, he knew that his father had been somewhere around that area of

France during the war, and would have liked to have asked Ernie if he'd ever crossed swords with a scarlet and turquoise Fokker with a centaur painted on its side. Of course, Steven didn't ask. He was using a phony name and struggling to grow a moustache to disguise himself; the last thing he wanted was to call attention to his real identity.

"Steve! Quit daydreaming and get that fuckin' plane back together!"

"Sorry, Mister D!" Steven called, and went back to work.

The Beechcraft was the only airplane Ernie had. Whenever Steven worked on it, Ernie would fret that somebody might come in and want to charter a flight.

Whenever Ernie wasn't around he would sit in the Beechcraft and fool around with the controls. A couple of times he'd even started her up and taxied her around the field. Steven sure wished he could take her up for an hour or so ... He hadn't flown anything for a long time, not since leaving home, almost seven months ago. At least back home he got the chance to fly some of the old Yellowjackets his dad kept around the GAT airfield ...

He sure missed home, and his parents, and his sister, but he didn't see how he could go back now. He couldn't go back until he did something ... something *big*. If he went back now, they'd just laugh at him.

Steven had been on the road for about five months before ending up here. Traveling around hadn't been too bad. He'd found that truckers would almost always stop and give him a lift, and when he ran low on money, he had no trouble getting a couple of days' work at gas stations and garages, changing tires or oil, or spark plugs. When the weather was good, he slept outside, in a sleeping bag he'd bought in Cody, Wyoming. When it was cold or rainy, he'd keep on traveling until he reached a decent-sized town, and then he'd rent a bed at the local YMCA. He had no trouble with the police. It helped that he didn't yet have much of a beard. Being clean-shaven seemed to make a good impression on people. He was always careful to wear clean clothes, and to have some money in his pocket, so the cops were no bother at all.

Taking care of himself might have been easy, but finding

work that had to do with airplanes was another story. He knew that nobody would let him fly, but he figured that he could at least find something as a mechanic. It hadn't worked out that way, however. He'd made the rounds at the big and small airports all across the country, but nobody would even talk to him about a job unless he was willing to fill out forms that always asked the same damned things: where was he born; who were his closest living relatives; where had he gone to school; where had he learned his trade; where had he worked last, and did he have references. Of course, he couldn't truthfully answer any of those questions, and worried that any employer who went to the trouble of having people fill out the forms might also go to the trouble of having the information checked. Steven couldn't take a chance on that. He was a minor, after all. If the cops ever did give him a second look, they'd call his folks and he'd get shipped home just like that.

He'd about given up hope, when a trucker he was riding with made a delivery to Wilterboro. It was a pretty crummy excuse for an airport. Just a chain-link fence wrapped around a mangy crab-grass field that looked like it would turn into mud-soup when it rained. There were a couple of moth-eaten wind socks flapping from a pole, a handful of run-down buildings, and a graveyard of obsolete or banged-up airplanes.

It was pretty dismal, all right, but then Steven saw the hand-scrawled MEKANIC WANTED sign that was taped in the cracked front window of a run-down barn that had DONO-VAN AIR CHARTER painted over its double doors.

Back then Steven had guessed—correctly—that this was the sort of place that wouldn't much care if you didn't fill out a form, as long as you could demonstrate that you knew your way around an airplane's innards. He'd been working here for two months. Ernie asked no prying questions and in exchange paid him squat, but he let Steven sleep on the cot in the office area, and let him use one of the junk cars he kept out back. Steven hadn't yet gotten up the nerve to tell Ernie that he knew how to fly. Ernie would surely ask questions then. *One of these days, though,* Steven thought, and patted the Beechcraft's cowling.

"So I guess if the price was right I could maybe get you those altimeters," Ernie was saying.

"I'd need 'em soon," Red cautioned.

"What's the rush?"

"It's like this. My boss got called by some other guy, who's putting together a big deal for the Chinese government," Red explained. "The Chinese talked the United States into selling them a bunch of P-40 Tomahawks. The fighters are sailing on a freighter leaving New York Harbor at the end of the month. This guy who's handling the logistics of the sale for the Chinese called my boss to ask if he knew of any pilots who might be willing to go over there and fly those planes against the Japs."

"Guys like me?" Ernie asked.

"Nah." Red chuckled. "No offense, but they want young guys."

Steven, intrigued, set down his socket wrench and wiped his greasy hands on the backside of his overalls. He knew that things were heating up in the Pacific. China and Japan had been at war for years, and lately all the newspaper editorials were making a big thing about how America had to help China if it wanted to avoid getting involved in the actual fighting. Steven had agreed with what he'd read: that the Japs had to be stopped from getting Malaysia's rubber, or the oil in the Dutch East Indies.

"I don't get why the Chinks would want them altimeters," Ernie was saying. "They ain't gonna fit in no Tomahawk fighters . . ."

Steven wanted to hear more. He climbed down off the stepladder and wandered over to the cardboard boxes, where he pretended to be scrounging around for a part. He had a good view of the two men sitting at the folding card table that served as Ernie's desk. They were passing a pint of rye back and forth between them as they talked.

"The Chinese won't know they're getting no altimeters, until it's too late," Red said. "You see, when my boss got that call asking if he knew of any guys who might be willing to volunteer as mercenaries to fly them P-40s, he remembered the altimeters were floating around, and sent me across the river to see you. He figures why not put the altimeters on the freighter along with them airplanes and bill the Chinks for them? They're so gung-ho for shit to throw at the Japs, they'll buy anything."

"Well, I'll see what I can do," Ernie nodded, taking a long swallow off the pint.

"Just remember, I need 'em by the end of the month," Red said, standing up. "And remember, if you should hear of any pilots who're looking for work, put 'em in touch with me . . ."

"What's in it for me?" Ernie asked as he handed him the pint.

"Fifty bucks a head," Red said. He took the stogie out of his mouth, took a swig from the bottle, and quickly popped the stogie back between his lips, like it was a cork.

"What's in it for you?"

"Fifty bucks as well. My boss makes another fifty. I don't know what the guy who called gets. Probably more than that put together. This operation is half-assed in some respects, but there's a lot of money floating around. For instance, the pilot gets a three-hundred-dollar bonus for signing on, and at least six hundred a month, with a bonus for any Japs he might shoot down. And then there's insurance, and disability pay, and so on. It's a good deal." He smirked. "If you don't mind getting shot at."

"Jeez, I'd think they'd want military guys to fly fighters," Ernie said.

"They do. The Feds gave the okay for them to recruit military fliers—"

That was good, Steven thought. It had to be jake if the government had given the okay for army fliers to get involved.

"—but they's so desperate they'll take anybody who fits the minimum requirements," Red was saying. He ticked them off on his fingers. "They's got to have good health and good character; be at least twenty years old, and have at least three hundred hours flight time."

"I'll go," Steven said, coming around the boxes.

Red looked at him, and then back at Ernie. "What's this guy about?"

Ernie shrugged. "Name's Steve Smith. Started work here

a couple months ago. Can tear down and build back an engine okay, at least the small stuff."

"And I'm a pilot," Steven said. "The kind of pilot you're looking for."

"Sure, kid," Red humored him. "Look, I know you mean well. You want to have yourself an adventure, kick-ass against the Japs; all that good stuff," He shook his head. "But they want accomplished pilots over in China. Guys capable of flying fighters to defend against Jap bombers."

"You said the minimum requirements were to be in good health and twenty years old."

Red chuckled. "You're forgetting the little matter of a minimum of three hundred hours in the air."

Steven hesitated. He knew there was a risk in showing his pilot's license. It was legitimate, all right. *Too* legitimate. It had his real name, and, more important, his real age on it . . . But what choice did he have if he wanted to convince this guy that he was a pilot?

"I've got my license," he said.

"I guess you mean driver's license." Red grinned around his stogie, winking at Ernie. "Look, kid, flying an airplane ain't like driving a car up in the sky."

"I *meant* pilot's license."

Red exchanged another look with Ernie, who shrugged. "Fork it over," he demanded, snapping his fingers impatiently.

Steven extracted the license from his wallet and handed it over. Red slowly rolled his stogie from one side of his mouth to the other as he studied it.

"Says here his name's Steven Gold," Red told Ernie.

"He told me Smith," Ernie stubbornly said.

"It says here you was born in 1924, kid." Red scowled. "That would make you only barely seventeen."

"Holy shit, he told me he was twenty," Ernie complained.

"He looks twenty, I'll give him that," Red mused. He handed back the license. "It takes dough to get one of those, kid. Your folks loaded?"

Steven shrugged. "This isn't about my folks."

"Why you using a phony name?" Red asked. "You on the lam from the law?"

"I'm on the lam, period," Steven said.

"It's tempting to me, kid. I could use a quick fifty bucks . . ." Red shook his head. "But I got to pass—"

"But—"

"And you should count yourself lucky that I am. You volunteer for something like this, it ain't no day at the beach, kid. You'd be living in the jungle. Risking your life flying every damned day."

Fucking sounds great, Steven thought, and then pondered how his father might negotiate to turn this around the way he would want it to go.

"Red." Steven grinned. "You said that there's a three-hundred-dollar bonus due any man who signs up, right? Well, you take me on, and I'll kick back to you a hundred bucks of that . . ."

Red stared at him. "What about your age?"

"You said yourself that I look twenty," Steven said quickly.

Red was nodding, then he frowned. "But what about the three hundred hours?—"

"What the hell?" Steven said jovially. "Maybe I *don't* have three hundred hours, *exactly* . . ."

"Maybe you don't even have half of that," Red sourly agreed.

"But the two of us could work up a phony history for me," Steven enthused. "We could say I've been flying for years! For . . ." He glanced at Ernie. "For Donovan Air Charter!"

"I need a drink," Ernie said, reaching for the pint.

"You'll go along with this, won't you, Ernie?" Steven pleaded.

"For another fifty bucks I would," Ernie solemnly said.

"There you go, Red!" Steven beamed. "I'll give you a hundred, and I'll give Ernie fifty out of my own sign-up money. That's added to the money you both get just for recruiting me."

"It might work, if you could pull it off, kid," Ed mused.

"Sure I can pull it off! We can make up my record right here and now. Both you guys know airplanes. You'll know in a few minutes that I've got the patter to back myself up."

"Fuck, kid, you're seventeen years old," Red complained. "You really want to get yourself into this?"

"Yeah, I do," Steven said earnestly. "You can't imagine how much I want to get myself into this."

Red nodded. "And I get the one hundred from you?"

"As soon as I get my bonus I'll fork it over. You can't lose."

"Okay, on one condition, kid. You use a phony name, and we all agree to keep our mouths shut about this. That goes for you, too, Ernie," he warned.

"No problem with me," Ernie said.

"If the shit ever hits the fan, I'm going to claim you lied to me, kid, just like you lied to everyone else. But what we got to do is keep our traps shut so that the shit never does hit. The guy in command over there in China ain't like me. He's got scruples."

"No problem." Steven grinned. "What's this guy's name, anyway?"

"An ex-army Air Corps captain. Expert flier. A guy named Chennault. Clair Lee Chennault."

"Never heard of him," Steven said.

"Hah!" Ernie shook his head, laughing. "Now I need *another* drink."

Red sighed. "Kid, I do hope you know what you're getting yourself into."

(Four)
Santa Monica, California
11 October 1941

"You say he's disappeared?" Blaize laughed.

Suzy nodded. It was early evening. They were in the front room of Blaize's apartment on Colorado Boulevard, near the pier. It was a warm night, and the windows were open. They could hear the merry-go-round's jolly calliope melodies, the shouts and laughter coming off the boardwalk, and over it all, the ever-present murmur of the Pacific.

"It turns out that my parents have had private detectives keeping an eye on Steven ever since he ran off."

"How typical of your father," Blaize said. He reached for the bottle of gin next to the overflowing ashtray on the glass-topped, bamboo coffee table.

"Blaize, don't you think you've had enough of that for tonight?" Suzy asked gently, but he pretended not to have heard. She thought he looked terrible. He hadn't shaved in a couple of days, and looked like he was losing weight. His face was gaunt, and his eyes were dark hollows: green fires burning in deep caves. When they made love, which these days they did infrequently, Suzy could feel his bones, cold through his thin skin, as if he were a skeleton masquerading as a man.

"Blaize, I said haven't you had enough—"

"Never enough . . ." Blaize laughed joylessly.

"Daddy says you haven't come to work for three days."

"Doesn't matter." His voice was slightly slurred. As he poured the gin into his glass he slopped some of it onto the coffee table. "I am blessed with a job from which I cannot be fired. Now tell me more! Tell me everything about how your brother has fucked over your fuck of a father."

Suzy hated it when he talked about Daddy like that, but she'd learned not to say anything, or else Blaize would accuse her of being disloyal, and she didn't have the strength to deal with that scene again, not tonight.

"Well, it turns out that ever since Steven took off, my parents have had detectives regularly reporting in on his whereabouts. The detectives tracked him to some horrid place in New Jersey where he was working as an airplane mechanic. I guess it looked to them like he was settling in, so the detectives got lazy. They kept taking my dad's retainer money, but they checked on Steven only once every couple of weeks, instead of every couple of days, like they said they were."

"Marvelous," Blaize murmured. He gestured toward her with his glass, sloshing gin onto the carpet. "Do go on—"

"Well, one day they went to check, and he was gone. Poof! Just like that he'd disappeared. The guy he was working for claimed not to know anything . . ."

"A friend in need is a friend, indeed," Blaize mumbled.

"Well, the detectives called my folks, who panicked.

They must have hired every gumshoe on the East Coast, and brought the police into it, but so far, nobody has any idea where Steven could be."

"Marvelous," Blaize repeated. He downed his drink and poured himself another. "You say this all took place months ago?"

Suzy nodded. "He disappeared from New Jersey the beginning of May, but I didn't know about any of this detective stuff until today. You see, all along my parents have been feeding me this song and dance about how worried they were; that they were martyring themselves to allow him his freedom."

"Some freedom!" Blaize snarled. "With detectives watching his every move. He was merely on the world's longest leash. What a hypocrite your father is . . ."

Suzy gritted her teeth and ignored the dig. "But for the entire summer, and into the fall, my parents have been *really* moping around, you know? Finally, I managed to get my mother to tell me the whole story."

"A toast to Steven," Blaize said, raising his glass. "At last he has accomplished what I have failed to do. He is free of your father."

He turned his bleary eyes toward Suzy. She knew that look. He was drunk. Again.

"And a toast to you, my pretty," he murmured, saluting her with his glass. "A toast to my pretty jailer."

"Don't say that to me!" Suzy jumped to her feet, livid with rage. "Don't you ever say anything like that to me—"

"Aren't you my jailer?" he asked, bemused. "My Circe, keeping me bewitched and a prisoner—"

She snatched up the gin bottle and hurled it against the wall, where it shattered. "You keep yourself a prisoner!"

She turned on her heel and ran through the apartment.

"Where are you going?" Blaize called out, and the raw panic in his voice almost stopped her.

"Home!" she yelled, pausing in the kitchen to grab her purse, and then out the door, and down the steps, out onto the street, where she stood transfixed.

Down the block, where the boardwalk began, the fairy lights and music of a happy world beckoned. How she wished that she could venture forth and lose herself in that promised gaiety; meet a happy young man, and never look back . . .

How she wished she didn't love Blaize so much, or that she could at least find the strength to deny herself that love . . .

His hand upon her shoulder did not startle her. She knew that he would appear to draw her away from the lights and laughter. There were tears in her eyes as she turned to face him. "It's not fair that you can make me so happy, *and so sad*—"

Blaize nodded, and gently embraced her. "I can be a fool," he whispered. "I am sorry."

"Damn you! How could you talk to me that way?" she demanded.

Blaize continued to hold her tight. "I get angry . . . and I get drunk, and I say hurtful, foolish things to you. Things I don't mean." He tilted up her chin. "This much I do mean. I need you, Suze. I love you and I need you. If you ever left me, I'd walk out to the end of that pier and jump—"

"I don't want to hear that kind of talk, either—"

"I swear that I would, Suze."

She pulled away from him. "This feud between you and my father is destroying you."

"Do you have any idea how much I detest myself for being *here*, when my country needs me?" Blaize said.

"But your RAF superiors assigned you here!" she argued. "You have your orders! Why can't you just accept that?"

Blaize nodded. "It appears that I must . . . But I will never forgive your father for orchestrating my predicament!"

"Very well, hate my father!" Suzy shouted.

"I will! He's spoiled everything!"

"But must he spoil our love, as well?" Suzy challenged.

Blaize stared at her a moment, and then he smiled. "No," he whispered. "He needn't . . . Do you really love me, Suze?"

She resisted the urge to smack his face. "Would I be hanging around here if I didn't?" she asked wryly.

He smiled, nodding in acquiescence. "Then let me try to explain. When I think of you as your father's daughter, I see him in you—there *is* plenty of him in you, you know—and that makes me hate you a little."

"But what can I do about that?" Suzy demanded.

Blaize took a step toward her and kissed her lightly on the lips. "You could marry me," he said.

"W-what are you saying?" she asked, shocked.

"Actually, I'm not saying, I'm proposing." Blaize smiled. "You see, my love, if you married me, you would no longer be Herman Gold's daughter. You'd be Mrs. Blaize Greene." He laughed. "Actually, seeing as I'm Lord Greene, you'd be Lady Susan . . ." He winked. "Lady *Suze*, to me."

"But . . . married . . . How could we?"

"We could elope! To Nevada! We could leave now! By this time tomorrow we could be man and wife."

"Blaize, I do love you . . ." She stared at him. "You *are* sober? You know what you're saying?"

"Absolutely."

"And you do want to marry me for *me*, right?" Her eyes narrowed. "You're not trying to get even with my father?"

He looked angry for an instant, but then he relaxed. "I deserved that, for having behaved so abominably toward you these past few months. If you will do me the honor of accepting my proposal, I swear to you that I will never again give you cause to hold me in such low esteem."

"Good answer." Suzy chuckled, slipping her arms around his waist and giving him a kiss. "But why do we have to elope? It'll come as such a shock to my parents."

"I want this to belong to us, alone. I don't want your father tainting it for me. *Can* you understand?"

"Yes, I suppose I can. But I can't—I *won't*—choose between you two," she warned. "I'll love my father just as much as I always have."

"I understand that," Blaize said. "And perhaps I'll be able to come to terms with him." He smiled, shyly. "If you're by my side."

Suzy needed to ponder it for only an instant to know what was right. She did love him, and wanted to marry him. "I'll accept, on a few conditions. Number one, no more drinking."

"Done."

"And you'll take a shower, and shave, before we leave for Nevada."

"Agreed." He laughed.

"You'll put on some weight—"

"I'll blow up like a balloon!"

"And we don't fly to Nevada," Suzy said, between kisses. "We drive!"

Chapter 17

(One)
Downtown Los Angeles
15 December 1941

At noon Herman Gold told his secretary he was leaving for lunch, and never went back. He was just too depressed to face the office. He ended up driving to downtown L.A., where he decided to escape his own, and the world's, troubles by going to the movies.

On December 8, the day after the attack on Pearl Harbor, President Roosevelt had declared war upon Japan. Three days later, Hilter had declared war on the United States, and the day after that Herman Gold had declared war on the Axis, by presenting himself at his local army recruiting center to volunteer for the U.S. Air Corps. The army's doctors had looked him over and then rejected him for any sort of duty, never mind being a pilot, telling him that he was too fat, and that he'd failed the eye test.

Granted, it had been a dumb idea for Gold to have gone down there in the first place, he now thought as he wandered past the Broadway movie houses. No doubt he was doing far greater service for America by overseeing GAT's production of war birds. It still irked him that he had been found unfit to defend his country.

He hadn't told anyone about his misadventure, and he never would tell about it. He knew he'd never be able to endure the ribbing if word of it ever got out, especially considering what he'd done to keep Blaize Greene out of the war. Gold shuddered at the thought of the humiliation he'd have to endure if Teddy Quinn ever got wind of it...

But being stamped 4-F was only the final straw upon Gold's backbreaking burden of disappointments, beginning with the news that Blaize and his daughter were now man and wife.

Blaize and Suzy had run off to Nevada to get married, without telling anyone of their plans. Surprisingly, Erica hadn't been all that upset upon hearing the news. She'd seemed to think that eloping was romantic, and that Blaize wasn't a bad catch for their daughter, but Gold didn't trust Greene's motives. He'd been keeping his mouth shut for fear of being branded paranoid, but Gold couldn't shake the notion that Blaize Greene's marrying Suzy was the young Englishman's way of getting even...

But what was done was done, Gold now thought. At least Suzy was safe and sound, even if it was in some shabby apartment near the Santa Monica pier, and as the wife of a man who professed to hate him. Gold could only hope that his son was also safe and sound—

Somewhere...

Steven was still missing. Gold had hired more detectives, but they could find no trace of his son. He'd brought the police into the search, but the New Jersey authorities had been no help at all. As far as they were concerned, a boy approaching his eighteenth birthday was no kid, and had the right to go where he wanted. Gold supposed that was the point that Steven had been trying to make all along, before giving up and taking off.

If only he hadn't been too stubborn to listen, Gold brooded. Given the chance now, Gold would be too happy to swear that he'd learned his lesson.

He paused to study the marquee outside the Century Grand Theater. *The Maltese Falcon* was playing. Gold had heard good things about the movie, but hadn't gotten around to seeing it. He did like Humphrey Bogart . . .

Too bad he couldn't hire a guy like Bogart to find his son for him, Gold thought as he bought a ticket and went inside. He paused to buy a sack of popcorn in the mirrored lobby, and then he followed a uniformed usher's bobbing flashlight to a seat in the darkened auditorium. The theater was crowded, and Gold had to sit fairly close to the screen. He crossly wondered what all these people were doing spending their afternoons hiding away in the dark. You'd think these able bodies would be able to find work . . .

A newsreel was just beginning as Gold settled in. Up on the screen an intrepid fellow in a turtle-neck sweater, his trousers tucked into high boots, was peering through a movie camera mounted on a tripod.

Kaleidoscope Productions presents your news picture magazine of the world— the narrator exclaimed, as trumpets blared in the background.

The newsreel led off with pictures of the smoking devastation that was Pearl Harbor. There were airplanes burning on the tarmac, and crumpled battleships going belly-up as they slid silently beneath the sea.

December seventh, a day that will live forever in infamy! the narrator intoned, his voice quivering with indignation as he quoted Roosevelt.

Next came a shot of President Roosevelt himself, standing before a huge American flag backdrop as he addressed Congress, asking for a declaration of war.

Watch out, Tojo! the narrator warned. *Pearl Harbor is going to be the mistake you won't live long enough to regret!*

We take you now to Russia, where the German blitzkreig advances!

There was an aerial view of the vast, snowy tundra that was Russia in winter. Russian peasants—men, women, and children—were shown building a barricade across the road that led into their village.

Yes, they'll die in defense of Mother Russia, every last one of them! And they swear to Stalin that they'll take a Nazi with them! Watch out, Huns! Your "lightning strike" just might end up frozen dead in its tracks by Russia's secret weapon: Ol' Man Winter!

Gold sighed. All this war stuff was only further depressing him. He'd come here to forget reality, not have the awful state of the world thrust at him in images thirty feet tall. He was about to head out to the men's lounge until it was time for *The Maltese Falcon*, when the screen was filled with a pair of fighter planes—Curtiss P-40s, Gold thought they were—banking across a clear sky.

The P-40s had the twelve-pointed Chinese Nationalist stars on their wings, and bizarre, toothy shark profiles painted on their noses just aft their props.

Hi-ho, Tojo! the voiceover chortled. *Before you yellow-bellied sons of the rising sun lay claim to China, you'll have to deal with these fellows! Don't let those Chinese stars painted on the wings fool you. These pilots are Yanks! And this time they're ready for you, Tojo, and spoiling for a fight!*

Gold settled back in his seat. Anything to do with fighter planes interested him.

We take you now to the exotic mountain jungles of Asia—

The movie screen showed a map of Southern China and Burma, and then a bird's-eye view of a narrow road, zigzagging between rugged mountain passes thickly blanketed with vegetation.

And slithering like a serpent for seven hundred miles through these vast jungles is the Burma Road. With the Japs controlling China's sea-lanes, the Burma Road is China's last supply link to the outside world!

The picture dissolved to an indoor scene: a rugged-looking American in military uniform was seated at a table beside a Chinese woman and man in civilian clothes. All three were smiling into the camera.

The camera zoomed in for a close-up of the Chinese couple. *Meet Generalissimo and Madame Chiang Kai-shek, rulers of China. They've appealed to FDR for American air power to keep the Burma Road open, so that China can keep fighting the Japs.*

Next came a close-up of the American in uniform. *And here's the man FDR has sent to do the job. He's Captain*

Claire Lee Chennault, recently of the United States Army Air Corps, and now in China per FDR's mandate. Chennault's leading a special fighter-pilot volunteer group of broad-shouldered American boys. This American Volunteer Group vows to wrest control of the China sky from the Japs, before Tojo can do to the Burma Road what he's done to Pearl Harbor!

The screen flickered with footage of an airdrome staked out in a jungle clearing. There were a number of P-40s parked beneath the trees. Some of the fighters were draped under camouflage netting, and some looked ready to fly, but all had their engine cowlings festooned with those fierce-looking shark-snout paint jobs. In the background were thatch-roofed huts, fuel-barrel stockpiles, and men hurrying about in baggy, khaki shorts and leather flying jackets.

From bases like these hidden away on high jungle plateaus—

The scene shifted to show a number of men bending over the hood of a Jeep, studying maps.

—Chennault and the boys of the A.V.G. are ready to give Tojo's gnat swarm a shellacking they won't ever forget!

There was another scene of two P-40s in flight, performing loops against the clouds . . .

Isn't that right, fellows?

The sky scene faded into a close-up of a half-dozen of the volunteer pilots in their khaki and leather garb, wearing pistols around their waists, or in shoulder rigs. They were laughing and joking with one another as they looked shyly into the camera, and then put their arms upon each other's shoulders to improvise a ragged, kicking, conga line. The line broke apart as the young men grinned and waved into the cameras one last time.

No wonder the Chinese call them "Fei Hu"— the narrator said jovially, as the background music began to soar.

Gold was staring at the screen. There was something about the pilot second from the left . . . Something familiar, even if his light hair was close-cropped, and despite his hollow-looking face, and the dark shadows under his eyes . . .

"Oh my God, is that Steven? . . ." Gold murmured to himself.

Fei Hu, in Chinese, that means Flying Tigers!

"That's Steven!" Gold bellowed, jumping up from his seat in the darkened movie house.

"Hey, buddy!" somebody behind Gold yelled. "Down in front!"

Gold ignored him. He pointed at the screen, as Steven, thirty feet tall, waved back at him. "That's my son!"

(Two)
Madame Marie's
Rangoon, Burma
25 December 1941

Steven Gold was awakened by a distant rooster, crowing to greet the dawn. The room was bathed in silvery half-light. He stared up, sleepy-eyed, through the cloud of gauzy mosquito netting enveloping the double bed. The slowly revolving ceiling fan was gently wafting the currents of incense-scented air, barely stirring the brightly colored Chinese tapestries hung from brass stretchers on the walls.

Christmas day, he thought to himself, stretching beneath the satin coverlet. Beside him, Monique stirred. Steven kicked off the coverlet. Monique was lying on her belly. Her feet were beside his head on the pillows. Her magnificently rounded ass, the color of toffee, was within easy reach. He patted it, and then reached between her legs to tickle where she was shaved as smooth as a baby's bottom. She made a sleepy squeak of complaint, but pressed her strong thighs together to lock his fingers inside her.

"Merry Christmas," he told her.

She released his hand, curling around to take hold of his penis as Steven lightly stroked her long, sculpted back. Monique had straight black hair, shiny as patent leather. Her eyes were black as well, and shaped like almonds. A slight smile began to play at the corners of her pink rosebud mouth as she began tickling his balls with her long, crimson-enameled fingernails. Then she began to suck him. Steven lay back and watched the ceiling fan go round and round.

Madame Marie's was a four-story building located in the anthill-like labyrinth of alleyways behind Rangoon's terribly British, terribly proper, Silver Grill. The girls at Marie's came in three basic flavors: kimono girls, girls spiced with leather, or girls swathed in lace. The kimono girls were okay, with their intricate hairdos, and geisha giggling, but Steven preferred the lace girls, with their black-satin garter belts and peek-a-boo bras, and their silk stockings with the seams up the back. Steven didn't at all understand the appeal of the leather girls, but Sam "Cappy" Fitzpatrick had once explained to him that they were an acquired taste, like scotch malt whiskey. Cappy was an ex-Army Air Corps aviator, and Steven's fighter squadron leader, so Arnie looked up to him. And Cappy had sure been right about the scotch.

Monique was a lace girl. Just now her garter belt and bra were missing in action, but her stockings were still in the battle; one flying high up on her slender thigh, the other bunched around her ankle. Her black lace panties had seen a lot of dogfighting during last night's tussles. Just now the sheer, lacy material was bunched in the crack of her ass, and no wonder. Monique was just average in the chest department, but her rear end cleavage was positively inspirational.

Steven had been spending his nights with Monique for a couple of weeks, ever since Chennault had assigned the squadron to Rangoon. He was fond of Monique, and liked to think that she cared for him. Not that he was born yesterday. Hell, he was young, but not so young that he didn't know better than to fall in love with a whore. After all, every morning that he left Madame Marie's, a guy was waiting at the door to collect the rent . . .

Nah, it wasn't love. Steven just looked forward to seeing her. Every night he'd bring her chocolates, cigarettes, and whatever else he could swipe from base camp that he thought she might like. Each night she'd be waiting for him, eager to give the gift of herself. She didn't have much English, but she managed to tell him stories about growing up in her village, where there were rice paddies, and forests full of gaudy parrots and chattering monkeys. Madame Marie had recruited Monique when she was just eleven, during a trip to French Indochina—a place called Viet Nam.

Monique wasn't her real name of course, but Madame Marie gave all her girls French names. Monique had claimed that she didn't remember what her real name had been. He accepted that. Madame Marie's pleasure rooms were designed for such sweet little lies.

Monique was still busy inhaling him, but he didn't think he had much left to give her from last night. Anyway, the sun was full up, even if he wasn't.

"You leave so soon?" she pouted as he eased himself free of her multiple delicious embraces.

"My heart's just not in it this mornin', li'l darl'n," Steven said, emulating the lazy drawl of the veteran pilots in his squadron.

"You no bloody like me no more?" Monique demanded, sitting up in bed.

Steven had to smile. Rangoon *was* a British post. "I like you fine, honey," he said. "But we got a feeling over at the base that it might start raining Japs today."

A few days ago the Japanese had made their first bombing assault against Rangoon. The squad had gone up to meet them, and the ensuing dogfight had painted fire and smoke and blood across the sky above the city's timeless pagodas. When it was over, Rangoon's waterfront was ablaze from Jap bombs, but sixteen of their planes had been downed, as had four of the squadron's P-40s. One of the squad's pilots had been killed, but the other three were okay, despite the Japs' attempts to strafe them while they were helplessly suspended beneath their parachutes.

Steven grabbed his baggy khaki trousers off the floor and shook them out before stepping into them. Scorpions and centipedes were uncommon above the ground floor in city buildings, but Arnie had gotten into the habit of checking his duds since last summer at Toungoo training camp, where there'd been all types of creepy-crawlies. He checked his ankle-high, rubber-soled work shoes and laced them on. He retrieved and donned his sleeveless gray sweatshirt, then shook out his New York Yankees baseball cap before putting it on his head.

He felt himself lucky to have been assigned to Rangoon, away from Chennault, who was pretty much a stickler for rules and regs. If the old man had been around, there was no way that Steven would have been out of uniform, never mind spending his nights with Monique. But Chennault was at the A.V.G. headquarters camp, in Kunming, China, and that was almost seven hundred miles away, at the opposite end of the Burma Road. Cappy Fitzpatrick, Steven's base camp commander, didn't give a flying fuck about rules and regs, as long as a guy had his shit together up in the air, where it counted.

"You kill lots of Japs for Monique today, okay, honey?" Monique smiled.

"I sure hope so." Steven muttered, more to himself than to her. He gave her a kiss for good luck as he reached past her to unwrap his holstered Colt .45 from the teak bedpost. He shrugged into the shoulder rig, fastening its strap across his chest.

That dogfight a couple of days ago had been the squad's first taste of combat, and Steven had been a part of it for only a short while. He'd managed to lock on to the tail of a Jap Ki-27 fighter, and let loose a burst, but his guns had jammed before he'd done much, if any, damage. Defenseless, he'd had to drop out of the fight and return to base. It had been a frustrating and worrisome experience. Cappy had said that every guy has reason to doubt himself before he's experienced combat; that no one could know for sure how brave he was until he'd experienced his baptism by fire . . . Steven wanted to get his personal baptism over and done with, so that he could begin enjoying himself.

He had another worry that nagged at him constantly. He hadn't yet stopped kicking himself in the ass for letting himself be filmed by that newsreel crew a couple of months back. He'd been drunk at the time, but that was no excuse for such stupidity. Here he'd gone to all this trouble to create a new identity for himself, and now his mug was being flashed on movie screens all over America. He could only hope that anyone back home who knew him would not see the damned thing and alert his parents.

He shook out his leather jacket and slung it over his shoulder. The sun had just come up, but already the temperature felt close to ninety.

On the jacket's back was sewn a large silk patch emblazoned with the Chinese flag, and a message in Chinese characters identifying him as an ally aviator fighting on behalf of China. Somebody had come up with the patches after one of the guys had suffered a close-call crash landing. The poor guy had been in trouble for a while, trying to convince some hostile Chinese peasants that he wasn't some new kind of Jap.

He kissed Monique good-bye a final time, and then tramped downstairs. A couple of the other guys from the squad who were shacking up here were waiting for him in the front lobby. One of them had the distributor cap to their Jeep; taking the cap with you when you parked was the surest way of making sure the vehicle would be there when you returned.

Steven cheerfully paid the doorman ten bucks on the way out. By Steven's way of thinking, ten bucks a night was cheap as hell just to get to sleep in a soft bed with clean sheets, and with indoor plumbing just a short walk down the hall. Monique was the icing on the cake.

Outside in the alleyway, away from the bordello's perfumed air, the stench hit him like a slap in the face. Back to reality, Steven thought as he and the others piled into the Jeep and rolled out of the alleyway.

Rangoon was a British bastion. From what he had learned so far, he guessed that meant that it was a good place for foreigners to do business. But the places of light and pleasure, like the Silver Grill, or Madame Marie's, were few. Mostly, Rangoon was a dark and crowded place, teeming with filth. The acrid stink of excrement and unwashed bodies mixed with the diesel fumes and the bluish haze of thousands of charcoal cookfires to hang like a mist in the stagnant air.

They drove through a food market, already open for business and busy, even at this hour. The produce venders had their boxes out on display; fruits and vegetables with warts and hairs, colored so impossibly scarlet or green that they made you shudder. There were the fishmongers with their piles of glistening gun-metal-gray squid, and baskets of writhing eels. The butchers were open. Some of them were hacking portions off their rusty slabs and glistening limbs of beef and pork, hanging from hastily erected bamboo scaffoldings. The meat shimmered with flies that rose and fell with each swipe of the cleaver. Another kind of butcher sold things that were alive in cages: white ducks with orange beaks and feet; trembling rabbits; crying puppies.

Steven and the others kept their hands on their automatics as the driver slowly made his way through the crowded market street, honking his horn to cut a path for the Jeep. They didn't let down their guard until they were on the relatively open road at the outskirts of the city. They hated themselves for their fear and suspicion, but they all felt it, just the same. It was just too strange here in Rangoon. The poverty and misery were too overwhelming. The only possible response, firsthand, was fear and loathing.

He thought about his father, who donated so much money to charity. Steven had never really understood what that meant, until he'd come here. Nothing, not even his travels across America, during which he'd seen some pretty bad things, could have prepared him for Rangoon. If what his father contributed to charity helped even a little bit in places like this, well, then his father was doing something important. He hoped he would remember to tell Pop that, next time he saw him . . .

It was roughly fifteen miles to base camp from the outskirts of Rangoon. Steven tilted his cap down over his eyes and slouched in the back seat of the Jeep. He would have liked to doze away the slow ride—along a narrow road that tunneled through jungle greenery—but sleep was impossible. He was too keyed up wondering if today he might finally enjoy his first victory. He sure had come a long way in the months since he'd left his job at Donovan Air Charter.

Back around the middle of May, Steven had used what was left of his sign-up money to buy himself a railway ticket to San Francisco. Once he was in Frisco he'd made contact with Cappy Fitzpatrick, who was in charge of the group of volunteers setting sail via freighter for the voyage to the Far East. They'd arrived in Rangoon in August, and had enjoyed a couple of weeks of free time in which to explore the city until the rest of the A.V.G. had arrived. Soon after, Chennault had showed up, to take all two hundred and ten of them—pilots and ground support personnel combined—on an uncomfortable railway trip to the training camp he'd set up in Toungoo, about a hundred miles to the north.

The Toungoo camp was an abandoned RAF base. Once Steven and the others had set foot in it, they'd understood why the Brits had left. The heat and bugs would have been bad enough, but steamy Toungoo, which was in the process of being reclaimed by the jungle, was also home for rats and snakes and bloodsucking bats . . . Well, he hadn't exactly seen the bats suck blood, but other guys had said they had, and he believed them.

There had also been disease. Steven had suffered a nightmare bout of dysentery, but he managed to get over it and hang in. A lot of guys hadn't been as lucky, and had left the A.V.G.'s employ on stretchers.

Toungoo had been bad news, but the A.V.G. fleet of P-40 Tomahawk fighters had been just as unfriendly to the men. A lot of the guys had gained their experience flying multi-engined aircraft. For them, getting acquainted with a single-engine fighter had been like learning how to fly all over again. There'd been a lot of crashes, especially during landings. Steven remembered how Chennault got progressively angrier and more frustrated as the accidents ate away at his precious fleet, and his sparse inventory of spare parts.

It had been sometime in the fall that one of the pilots, remembering how the Japs, who were an island people, were supposed to be afraid of sharks, received permission from Chennault to have the P-40s' noses painted up like ferocious man-eaters. Meanwhile, the old man's stateside contacts had asked the Walt Disney Studios for their help in coming up with an insignia for the A.V.G. The Disney people had devised a tiger wearing a pair of little wings, leaping though a V for victory. Chennault loved it. From then on, the A.V.G. were The Flying Tigers.

Now, bouncing along in the Jeep on his way back to base, Steven couldn't help smiling, remembering how the old man had been so contemptuous of him after reviewing his "career" at Donovan Air Charter, and after having laid eyes on him. As it turned out, Steven had been one of the A.V.G.'s better pilots, right from the start. While he hadn't the shooting expertise of the veteran fighter pilots, Steven had cut his teeth flying his pop's single-engine jobs, so he at least hadn't needed to unlearn a lifetime's worth of experience, unlike those poor multi-engine veterans . . .

The news delivered via radio of the Japanese attack on Pearl Harbor had cut short Chennault's "kindergarten." Thinking back on it, Steven figured that had been just as well. School had already cost the Tigers a dozen planes, lots of ammo, and the life of one man. If they'd kept on training, pretty soon there would have been none of them left for the Japs to pick on. As it was, they could put up only some fifty airplanes at one time, and they had to split their numbers to try to protect hundreds of miles of territory against the Jap air force, one of the best in the world.

That second week in December, the A.V.G. squadrons went their separate ways. Chennault took the majority of the A.V.G. to Kunming. Cappy Fitzgerald led twenty-one airplanes to Rangoon.

It was just a little after 6 A.M. when the Jeep pulled into base camp. The grounds, and the packed dirt airstrip, had been hacked out of the banyon trees and jungle creeper. There were several hangar tents for the airplanes, a supply tent that also housed the squadron's radio equipment, a mess tent, and a tent that served as operations room and bar. The motor pool—a couple of Jeeps, and three lorries laden with oil and fuel drums—was hidden under camouflage netting. Several orderly rows of smaller tents where the men slept were staked out under the shelter of the tall palms.

"Cappy wants all pilots in operations," one of the motor pool guys said as the Jeep came to a halt.

Steven made a quick detour to the mess tent for a mug of coffee, and headed over to operations, where he found himself a folding chair in the back. Cappy was up on the raised platform at the front of the tent.

Cappy was in his thirties, Steven guessed. He was only about five feet, nine inches tall, but he was broad-shouldered, and Steven knew from personal experience that Cappy was very strong: the guy could whip Steven in arm wrestling anytime. Cappy had a thick black moustache, and curly black hair. He was dressed for flying in high boots, khaki pants, and an olive green T-shirt. He had a holstered .45 cinched around his waist, and his leather jacket draped over a chair.

Cappy was joking with some of the guys seated up front. "Tell us your secret for success!" the guys were demanding. In the previous battle, Cappy had singlehandedly accounted for two Jap bombers and two fighters. That meant an extra two grand, so far, in Cappy's pay envelope this month. The A.V.G. was paying its pilots a bonus of five hundred bucks per confirmed kill.

"All right, listen up," Cappy shouted. "I want to go over the mistakes we made last time. First off, I've been told those radios the old man managed to scrounge up have finally been installed in our planes, so we should be able to communicate with each other, and the base.

"Okay, about the battle a couple of days ago. I guess we now all know that the old man was right when he warned us against one-on-one dogfights. The Jap fighters can outmaneuver us every time in individual duels, so what we've got to do with them is just what Chennault taught us to do against bombers: get above the enemy, and power dive on him. Bounce the suckers with all six machine guns blazing, and then haul ass away from them, circling and climbing to repeat the maneuver. Everybody got that?

"Second, it's a safe bet that there's gonna be one fuck of a lot more of them than us. Fortunately, they like to fly in tight formations. What we do is pick out the thickest concentration of the enemy for our dives. That way we're likely to hit something on each pass. Finally, I want you to concentrate on bombers. Don't let yourselves be decoyed by Jap pursuits looking like they're turning tail and running away. Stay with the bombers! They're easier targets, they've got bigger crews, and they're the real danger to the city and our base—"

"Hey, Cappy! What's going to keep the fighters off our

tails?" Stan Jenkins called out. Jenkins, close to forty, had been a captain in the U.S. Army Air Corps. Word had it that the corps had offered to promote him to bird colonel to get him to stay. Jenkins would have been base commander, but he'd turned down the job, explaining to Chennault that he didn't want to deal with the paperwork.

Before Cappy could reply to Jenkins' question, one of the radio men entered the tent and made his way to the front. He whispered something to Cappy, who nodded.

"All right!" Cappy announced to the group. "We've received word from one of our coastal spotters that a large force of bombers accompanied by fighter escort is heading this way. For a change, we've got all our planes on the ready line.

"Now, getting back to Stan's question," Cappy continued. "We'll work it this way. We'll split up into two flights. Ross will lead Flight One against the fighters. It'll be their job to keep the fighters occupied. I'll lead Flight Two against the bombers." Cappy quickly divvied up the pilots.

"Any questions?" he demanded, looking around. There were none. "Then let's saddle up, cowboys! We've got about fifteen minutes to get our asses in the air to meet 'em!"

Steven was first out of the tent. He shrugged on his jacket and zipped it up while he was running to the airstrip, where the ground crews were busy preparing the planes. He stopped short when he saw that his own P-40 was not on the ready line. He looked around, and saw his plane—with its engine cowling off—parked just inside the hangar tent.

Steven saw the chief mechanic pacing up and down the ready line, directing his men, and hurried to intercept him. The chief saw him coming and shook his head. "Sorry, Steve. She's just sprung a coolant problem. She ain't going nowhere." He hurried away.

Steven just stood there, too angry to say anything, or even to curse.

"Tough break, kid."

He turned. Cappy was standing behind him. "Your first time out, your guns jam." Cappy shook his head. "And now this . . ."

Steven nodded. "Now I'm *still* not going to know if I've got the guts to make it as a fighter pilot. I'm worried about what you said. That the longer a guy waits, the worse it'll be for him . . ."

"What *I* said?" Cappy looked mystified, but then he smiled wearily. "You talking about that baptism of fire shit?" He rolled his eyes. "Kid, I was drunk . . ."

"You're just saying that now."

Cappy sighed. "Ah shit, this serves me right for getting drunk and shooting my mouth off to impressionable young kids . . ." He tossed Steven his canvas flight helmet. "Go on, you can take my plane."

Steven stared at him. "You mean it?"

"Go on, move your ass! Before I change my mind—"

"I'm gone!" Steven laughed. "Thanks, Cappy!" he yelled over his shoulder as he dashed to the ready line.

The rest of the olive green and brown, camouflage-painted P-40s had been started up, and were taxiing out onto the runway. The ground crew stood clear as he climbed into the cockpit of Cappy's fighter and strapped himself in. He pulled on the canvas flight helmet and then murmured a prayer as he went through the complex start-up procedure, worried that now Cappy's airplane would malfunction.

She didn't. Her Allison V-12 engine wheezed to life coughing blue smoke, and gradually built to a confident roar. Grinning with excitement, Steven waited for the revs to climb, and when she was ready, he slid shut the Plexiglas canopy and taxied out onto the runway.

Everybody else was already in the air, so he had the runway to himself. He picked up speed and took off, raising his landing gear as he climbed to join the rest of the Tiger pack, heading toward the coast to intercept the Japs.

After his last experience, Steven was itching to test his guns, but he didn't dare. Ammo was precious. No plane carried more than a minute or so worth of firepower. His radio crackled and he heard Cappy inform the Tigers that Steven Smith was flying his plane, and that Jenkins was now the leader of Flight Two.

Clouds began to appear as they neared the coast. The

Tiger pack was about fifteen miles from the field, within sight of the Rangoon waterfront, when Steven spotted the Jap formation, a flock of dark-winged specks, closing fast. He keyed his radio. "I see them!"

"We all see them, kid, over," Jenkins said, his voice sounding calm over the static.

"Jesus, there's a lot of them, over," one of the other pilots said, his voice sounding tinny, his signal breaking up over the little speaker hanging by a twist of wire from Steven's instrument panel.

"I count sixty bombers, over," one of the others chimed in.

"I count twenty fighters, over," another Tiger said.

"Cut the chatter," Jenkins ordered. "Everybody stay off the radio, unless it's an emergency. Let's get some altitude on those suckers, over and out."

Steven pulled back on the stick of his P-40 and climbed. The Japs were pretty close now. He could see that the fighters were open-cockpit, fixed-landing-gear, Ki-27 monoplanes. The Ki-27 was armed with just a pair of light machine guns in her nose, which were not terribly effective against the P-40's armor-plating, and self-sealing fuel tanks, but the Jap fighter could turn on a dime, stick to your tail like glue, and eventually chew you up. In an individual duel, a Ki-27 against a P-40 was a lot like a judo expert up against a heavyweight boxer. The Ki-27 delivered lots of little stings that eventually added up, and, meanwhile, was itself hard to hit—but if the P-40 did connect, its four .30-caliber wing guns and the pair of fifty-calibers in her nose could literally explode the unarmored Ki-27 out of existence.

"All right," Jenkins radioed. "Split up into your flights. Ross, go after those fighters, keep them off our backs; over."

"Happy hunting." Ross chuckled. "Over and out."

Steven watched as the airplanes of Flight One banked away and then began to dive on the Jap fighters.

"Flight Two, follow me!" Jenkins radioed. "Let's kill some bombers! Over."

Steven pushed his stick forward and dived toward what looked liked an acre of Jap airplanes in the sky. Deep in concentration, feeling no fear at all, he flicked off the safety on his guns and picked out a target. The gray, twin-engine Mitsubishi bombers were heavily armed, but it was their turret cannons on top their fuselages, just behind the cockpit, that were especially dangerous to the Tigers. During training, the A.V.G. had been taught to use their .50-caliber, long-range guns to kill the turret gunners, and then open up with their close-range, .30-caliber wing guns.

As Steven dived, his target's turret cannon swung his way and began winking fire. He resisted the instinctive impulse to veer away. He took his time framing the cannon in his cross-hair sights and let loose a burst. The drumbeat pounding of his twin fifties vibrated through the cockpit. He saw his tracer rounds impact on the turret. Shards of plexiglass went spinning off, twinkling in the sunlight. The cannon stopped firing and began to swing lazily, aiming at nothing at all.

He sighted in on the red circle painted on the bomber's gray wing and cut loose with everything he had. Now the crackling of his quartet of wing guns almost drowned out the jackhammering fifties. Steven saw the bomber's wing begin to smoke, and then break off. The crippled bomber, spilling oily black smoke, fell out of formation, and began cartwheeling toward the ground.

"I got one! I got one!" Steven called out excitedly as he streaked through the hole he'd carved in the bomber formation.

"Great work, kid!" Jenkins laughed. "But look sharp! This duck shoot ain't over yet, over and out."

"Duck shoot is right." Steven laughed to himself as he came around in a wide sweep and began to regain altitude for another bounce. The five planes of Flight Two had knocked five bombers out of the sky on their initial pass. Steven dived on another bomber, this time concentrating all his firepower on the ball turret. He never did get the gunner, but some of his rounds must have hit a fuel tank, because the bomber erupted in an orange cloud of flame. One of its engines went spinning off, striking the starboard wing of another bomber, and *that* plane, leaking black smoke from its starboard engine, sunk out of the formation.

Steven unable to resist an easy kill, throttled down, to settle on the crippled bomber's tail. He traded shots with the Jap tail gunner for a bit, until the Jap gunner got a little too good and holes began appearing in Steven's canopy. He quickly dropped below the bomber and used his guns to stitch hits across the entire length of the Mitsubishi's fuselage. As he peeled away he had the satisfaction of seeing his third kill of the day fall out of the sky. He happened to glance overhead. High above, Flight One was still tangling with the Jap fighters, keeping them busy and out of Flight Two's hair.

By now, the battle had drifted over Rangoon. The ten bombers in the lead were beginning their runs, but the Jap bombardiers in those plexiglass nose compartments must have felt awfully naked, because they were too hasty. Most of their bombs fell harmlessly into the sea, sending up thunderous geisers of blue water.

Flight Two dropped five of those ten bombers as they were peeling away. That was his kill number-four. After that, the rest of the Jap formation didn't even try to drop their bombs. They just broke up into clumps of two and three and began hightailing it in retreat. Seeing what was happening, the Ki-27 fighters that were still in the air quit their dogfight with Flight One and hurried to give escort, but the Ki-27s were not as fast as the twin-engined Mitsubishi bombers, and the latter weren't sticking around to give the Ki-27s a chance to catch up.

Steven got on the tail of a retreating Jap fighter and blew it out of the sky with a three-second burst. *Five planes*, he thought to himself as the red warning light on his fuel indicator blinked on. *Five planes, in one fucking battle! I'm an ace!*

A Ki-27 suddenly appeared about five hundred yards directly in front of him, coming his way. Arnie simultaneously thought that the damned thing looked like a bird of prey with its fixed landing gear hanging down; that he didn't have enough fuel to execute evasive maneuvers and still get back to base, and he wasn't about to spoil the triumphant day by cracking up Cappy's P-40—

"Fuck you! Tojo!" Steven screamed as the Ki-27 loomed in his cross hairs. The Jap fighter began firing at him. Steven saw the almost pretty flames twinkling from from the twin guns mounted just above the Jap's prop. His own tracers licked out in fiery spurts, arcing above the Ki-27. He heard something that sounded like pebbles rattling against tin; he was taking hits. He flicked his stick forward, dropping the P-40's nose, and, in the process, hosing the Jap fighter with lead. The fighter exploded in flame an instant before Steven's guns, out of ammo, went dead. Groaning, he shut his eyes and gritted his teeth as he flew right through the oily smoke cloud that a second ago had been a very solid airplane.

Six planes, he realized as he came through the cloud in one piece.

"I guess you won't do that again, son, over," Jenkins' easy voice came over the panel speaker.

Steven jabbed the radio key. "Where are you?" he gasped. "Over."

"Right behind and above you, over."

Steven twisted his head around and looked up. Jenkins waggled his wings in salute.

"Why didn't you help?" Steven demanded. He waited a bit for an answer. "Over," he blurted.

"I would have, son, if I'd had any ammo left." Jenkins chuckled. "Congratulations. You've got six confirmed kills. See you at home, over and out."

Steven realized that he was laughing giddily, and that he was sweat-soaked, and that he had peed in his pants. His hands were shaking. He hoped he had the strength left to land.

Ah, he *knew* he had the strength...

Six planes. He was going to have a lot to tell Pop the next time they met, he thought as he headed back to base.

Steven landed to find that the British citizenry of Rangoon had delivered a truckload of groceries, cold beer, and scotch to the camp to show their appreciation to the Tigers for saving their city. The numbers were fantastic: the Japs had lost twenty-five planes, while only three P-40s had been shot down, and all three pilots had parachuted to safety and were now back at base.

That night there was a grand celebration in the mess tent. Steven, by now exhausted, and very drunk, sat at the head of the table in honor of his being the high-scorer.

"Here's to beginner's luck," Cappy announced as he poured a bottle of beer over Steven's head. "Since Stevie has today earned himself three grand in bonus money, I want him to know I intend to charge him for lending him my plane."

The rest of the squad was yelling, "Speech! Speech!" as one of the radiomen came into the tent and handed Cappy a sheet of paper.

Steven, laughing, clutching a tumbler of scotch in his fist, rose a bit unsteadily to his feet, and said, "Before I pay Cappy, I'll have to see how much Monique leaves me . . ."

There were whistles and catcalls. "Quiet down!" Cappy suddenly yelled. He waved the sheet of paper in the air. "This is just in, from the old man."

"Chennault want to congratulate me?" Steven laughed.

Cappy shook his head. "Not quite, son." Something very serious in Cappy's tone quieted the tent. "It seems you've been joshing us a bit, haven't you, Stevie? . . ."

"Huh?" Steven blinked.

"It seems your name isn't Steve Smith, at all. It's Steven Gold."

"Oh, shit," Steven muttered, shaking his head. "That fucking newsreel."

"And worse yet," Cappy said, tapping the page. "It says here you aren't even eighteen years old."

"It's true," Steven admitted.

"How's the old man taking it?" Jenkins broke in.

"Well, let's just say that Chennault is pissed," Cappy said. He looked around the tent. "You all know how he feels about anything reflecting poorly on the Tigers . . ." He turned back to Steven. "Evidently, *your* old man is somebody real important."

"Tell me about it," he said dully.

Cappy frowned. "Whoever your father is, he's got the muscle to threaten the existence of the A.V.G. by having the federal government cut off our supplies, and the British here in Rangoon withdraw their support, unless we get you home, pronto."

"*Stevieee, you got to go home*," one of the men taunted in a quivering falsetto. "*Your mama's calling youuu!*"

"Shut up!" Cappy growled. "It's not funny! This kid just broke the record for kills in a single day, and he's about to get a raw deal!"

"What do you mean, Cap?" Steven asked, worried.

"I'm sorry to have to tell you this, son, but the A.V.G. is wiping their personnel records clean of you. It'll be like you were never a part of the Tigers. There'll be no record of your kills, and no bonus money. And I've got orders to restrict you to camp, until I can put you on the first freighter sailing out of Rangoon for America." He glanced back at the paper in his hand. "According to base command, that's in five days."

Steven wanted to argue, to plead to be allowed to stay, but he knew there was no point. It wasn't even up to Cappy. It looked like his father had won again . . . "There'll be no record, but I still did it, right Cappy?" Steven smiled proudly. "I've got what it takes, right?"

"Yeah, we'll all know you're an ace," Cappy solemnly said. He shook hands with Steven. "I'd be proud to fly with you as my wingman, anytime."

"That goes for me, too." Jenkins smiled, coming over to pat Steven's shoulder.

Steven blushed. "Cap? If I give you my word that I'll come right back, could I at least go and say good-bye to Monique? I'd hate for her to think something happened to me, or that I'd leave without saying good-bye."

Cappy smiled. "Sure thing, son." He crumpled the radio message in his hand. "Hell, what the old man doesn't know won't hurt him. Since you're grounded, you might as well spend the entire five days with Monique." He winked. "See what other kinds of records you can break—"

Chapter 18

(One)
GAT
Burbank
17 February 1942

Herman Gold was in his office when his secretary buzzed to say that Blaize Greene was waiting to see him.

"Good morning, Herman," Blaize said, coming in a few moments later.

"Good morning." Gold smiled, thinking what a pleasure it was to be genuinely glad to see Blaize. "That's a nice tie you're wearing," Gold complimented him. "You look good, kid. You're looking healthy. I think you've even put on some weight. I guess travel agrees with you."

"I rather think that it's marriage that agrees with me," Blaize chuckled.

Gold nodded as Blaize took a chair in front of his desk. He had to admit it: he'd been against the marriage at first, and he'd been wrong. Not only was the relationship between his daughter and Blaize going strong, his own relationship with Blaize had improved considerably since the marriage. The kid was coming to work regularly, and was making progress on his gas-turbine project. Gold was even beginning to think that Blaize was ready to let bygones be bygones between them.

"You must be pleased over the fact that GAT has just received a large reorder on the BuzzSaw bomber..."

"Yeah," Gold said happily. "Things are going pretty well for us. All our assembly lines are operating at full capacity.

We're building military-transport version GC-3s, BuzzSaws, and I just got word this morning that we've got the go-ahead on a new long-range escort version of the BearClaw fighter. It's another joint project with Stoat-Black. We'll be sending the redesigned fighters, sans engines, to England, where S-B will fit them with Layten-Reese Stag II power plants, and underwing fuel drop tanks. We're predicting the modifications will allow a two-thousand-mile cruising range."

"That's marvelous, Herman," Blaize murmured.

Gold watched as Blaize settled back in his chair, taking out his cigarettes and making himself comfortable. Gold didn't want to be rude to his son-in-law, but he did have work to do . . .

"I understand your son will be home next week."

"Yeah." Gold beamed. "I thought I had him on an RAF seaplane flight departing Burma for Pearl Harbor, but there was some kind of foul-up."

"There is a war on, I believe." Blaize smiled.

"You mean to tell me the combined Allied air forces don't exist to ferry my kids around?" Gold laughed. "So anyway, Steven ended up taking a boat. Talk about your slow boats *from* China." He shook his head. "That freighter must have stopped at every two-bit atoll between Rangoon and here. But the wait's almost over."

Blaize nodded. There was a moment of silence.

"Blaize, was there something *specific* you wanted to talk to me about?" Gold coaxed gently.

"I'm afraid there is, Herman," Blaize sighed. "It's ironic. A few months ago I would have been eager to confront you with this, but now . . . Well, we have been getting along *so* well that I *do* want you to know, old man, that there's nothing personal in this, but I've managed to persuade some rather influential friends of my family to do some lobbying on my behalf with British Air Staff . . ."

Gold sighed. "I guess you've gone and gotten yourself new orders, is that it, Captain Greene?"

"Yes, Herman. I'm to return to Britain for eight weeks of fighter training, and then it looks as if I'll be assigned to the Mediterranean."

"So you'll be going up against Rommel's Afrika Corps."

Gold frowned. "The Luftwaffe has some fine—and deadly—pilots operating in that theater."

"The more combat I see the better," Blaize firmly said.

"I hope you don't see more action than you've bargained for."

Blaize shrugged. "Herman, I do want to reiterate that there's—"

"Nothing personal in it." Gold smiled. "Yeah, I understand that." He stood up and leaned across his desk to shake hands with Blaize. "I will miss you—"

But I'll really miss Suzy . . . Gold brooded, realizing that Blaize would rightly expect his wife to accompany him back home. It frightened Gold that this man would be taking his only daughter out of the United States to Britain, where she would be within reach of Nazi bombs, but he realized that there was nothing he could do to prevent Blaize taking her. To try would just reopen old wounds.

"When are you and Suzy leaving?" Gold asked sadly.

"Actually, that's something else I'd like to discuss with you," Blaize began. "I've tried my best to convince Suze to stay here—"

"You've tried to convince her to *stay?*" Gold echoed, surprised.

"Why, yes, Herman," Blaize said, sounding a bit miffed. "I love Suze very much. I would never willingly part from her, but at present my country is a relatively dangerous place . . ."

"I understand," Gold said, relieved. "Blaize, I must admit, I'd underestimated you! You have my highest respect—"

"Hold on, old man." Blaize laughed. "I said I've *tried* to talk her out of coming with me. I didn't say that I'd *succeeded*. You know your daughter. Once she sets her mind on something she usually gets it, and she seems to have set her mind on accompanying me to Britain. I was hoping that you'd have a go at trying to convince her to stay here in California?"

Gold telephoned Suzy as soon as Blaize left his office, told her that Blaize had given him the news, and asked her if she were free for lunch. She told him that she was busy packing up the apartment, but if he wanted to take a drive into Santa Monica, she could grab a bite with him at one of the lunch counters along the boardwalk.

Gold left his office at noon. By quarter to one he and his daughter were strolling arm in arm past the pier's huge, castle-like Ocean Park Bathhouse. Gold had left his suit jacket in his car. He had his sleeves rolled up, and had loosened his tie.

He thought that Suzy looked wonderful. Her golden hair sparkled in the sunshine. Marriage was definitely agreeing with her, Gold decided as they stopped for fish and chips. They took their paper sacks of food down to the end of the pier, where they found a bench overlooking the water.

"This is Blaize's favorite meal," Suzy confided as she nibbled at a french fry. "He says it reminds him of home. I think that's why he insisted we live near the boardwalk, so he can get his 'bleedn' fish-'n'-chips whenever he has a craving."

"The English never did know how to eat," Gold muttered, picking gloomily at his meal. "I think this fish has bones in it . . ."

"Blaize does complain about one thing, however: he says the fish doesn't taste right because it isn't wrapped in newspapers." She laughed. "He says the ink adds a certain *je ne sais quoi*. I suppose I'll have to try it when I get there."

Gold put aside his lunch and turned to regard his daughter. "Speaking of you going to Britain, I'm wondering if it's the right thing for you to do . . ."

"Now, Daddy . . ." Suzy began.

Gold held up his hand. "Just hear me out. Blaize and I both feel that you'd be so much better off staying here—"

"I can't stay here, Daddy," Suzy said firmly. "My place is with my husband. It'd be different if Blaize were immediately being posted to the Mediterranean Front. But he's going to be training at Croybridge for eight weeks, and that's just a few few miles outside of London. We can be together at least some nights . . ."

"Is that enough reason for you to put yourself in danger?" Gold asked. "Even Blaize wants you to reconsider."

"Daddy," she said shyly. "There's something else . . ." She looked away, blushing.

"Well? What?" Gold began. "What else?—" He stopped short. "My God, am I going to be a grandfather?"

She giggled. "No, not yet, anyway. But I'd like for you to be one. I've been trying to get pregnant for a while now, but it just hasn't happened yet."

"Why? I mean, why haven't you? There's nothing wrong, is there?"

"No, Daddy. We've both been to the doctor about it, and we're perfectly normal. Blaize and I just figure that it's going to take practice to make perfect," she said brightly.

"I see," Gold mumbled, looking away. Now it was his turn to blush.

"But we can't practice if Blaize is in Britain and I'm here, now can we?"

"No, I suppose not . . ."

"And you *do* want grandchildren, don't you?"

"Yes, of course . . ."

"There! Now that that's all settled," Suzy patted his hand, "tell me? What V.I.P. strings can you pull to arrange transportation for us overseas? . . ."

(Two)
Gold Household
Bel-Air
4 March 1942

It was a Sunday afternoon, a couple of weeks after Steven had come home, when Gold went looking for his son, and found him in the garage. Steven had the hood up on Suzy's Jag, and had most of the engine dismantled. The parts were on dropcloths spread across the cement floor.

"Hi, Pop," Steven said, wiping his greasy hands down the front of his white T-shirt. "I thought I'd give her a tune-up."

Gold laughed. "I hope there's something left to tune by the time you're finished."

"No problem, Pop. She's a snap to work on. But she's

been getting lousy gas mileage. And with gas being rationed, I figured—"

"Steven, I told you I can get as much gas as we need, no problem . . ."

"I know that, Pop," Steven sighed, turning away. "But I like to play by the same rules everybody else plays by . . ."

"Yeah, sure, son," Gold said quickly. He stared at Steven, feeling so distant from the boy, but not knowing how to bridge the gap. Gold had hoped that things would be all right between them once Steven was back at home, but his son was more of a stranger to him than ever. He'd let the days trickle by, hoping that somehow the problem would solve itself. It hadn't, and Gold had reluctantly come to the conclusion that it wasn't going to, unless he did something about it.

Steven was looking at him out of the corners of his eyes. "I do appreciate the offer about the gas, Pop," he said softly.

"You don't have to thank me, son . . ." Gold said quickly. "Anything you want you can have, just ask . . ."

"Anyway," his son grinned, "it's a matter of personal pride that this Jag run smooth, now that I've inherited it from Suzy."

Gold nodded. Suzy and Blaize had departed for England last week. "Steven, you've been home a while now. I thought we could talk a little bit . . ."

"We've talked, Pop," Steven said, sounding uncomfortable. "I told you all about the A.V.G., and Rangoon, and shooting down those Japs . . ."

Gold saw that he was smiling. It seemed to Gold that the only time his son did smile was when he was lost in memories of his time away from home.

"I guess I just keep wanting to make sure that you're not holding a grudge against me for pulling you home the way I did," Gold said.

"Pop, we've been all through that," he said. "I've admitted that I was upset when it happened. But I'm not mad anymore. Hey! I forgot to tell you! I received a letter from Cappy Fitzpatrick yesterday."

"Fitzpatrick . . . ," Gold repeated, frowning.

"My base commander at Rangoon," Steven reminded him patiently.

"Oh, sure!" Gold said brightly.

"Well, Cappy writes that things have been going sour for the A.V.G. The Japs have pushed into Burma, and Stan Jenkins was killed in the fighting . . ."

"A friend of yours?" Gold asked.

"Kinda." Steven shrugged, and turned away. He pretended to be engrossed with something beneath the Jag's hood.

"Well!" Gold said, trying to sound cheerful. "What else does Cappy have to say?"

"That he's planning on resigning from the A.V.G. He's going back into the Army, as a fighter pilot." Steven straightened up from beneath the hood to face Gold. "Cappy says he has some pull, and that if I enlist, he can pretty much see to it that I get a chance at flight school." He shrugged. "I figure I'm going to do that, Pop. That is, when I turn eighteen, in a couple of months."

"But why?" Gold asked, helplessly.

"Because I want to get back in the war!" he said passionately. "I want to do my part! I'm a good fighter pilot. At least I've got the makings of being a good one. I want to see what I'm capable of . . ."

Gold stared at his son. His first impulse was to forbid him to do any such thing as enlist. He wanted to tell his son that he had the pull to keep him out of the draft. That he could arrange it so that his precious only son would be assigned safe, comfortable defense work deemed essential to the national interest, right here in California, at GAT.

Steven was watching him closely, waiting to hear what else he had to say. Gold remembered how he used to promise to himself—promise God?—that if he ever did come home, he would treat his son like a man.

"Army Air Force, huh?"

"Yeah, Pop," Steven replied defiantly, sounding ready for a fight.

"Flight school . . . Well, if your buddy Cappy can't get you in, I could pull a few strings . . ."

Steven's eyes went wide. "You . . . you'd do that for me?"

"If that's what *you* want," Gold said hoarsely, his eyes filling with tears. He moved quickly to embrace his son. "I'm sorry for everything," he said. "I never meant to hurt you. It's just that I've always been so afraid of losing you—"

"It's okay, Pop . . . It's okay," Steven murmured. He seemed too embarrassed to hug back, but he was tentatively, awkwardly, pressing his cheek against Gold's.

"I love you very much, Steven."

"I know that, Pop. I love you too," Steven said quietly. He gingerly patted Gold's back. "But don't carry on so. Don't worry about me, I'm going to be fine."

"Sure, sure you will," Gold muttered fiercely, holding on to his son with everything he had.

"Pop!" Steven laughed in embarrassment, trying vainly to wrestle free. "Come on, now. Let go!"

Gold sadly chuckled. "It's hard for me to let you go, Steven. It always has been."

"But I've been working on the car. You're getting yourself all greasy."

"Nothing wrong with a little grease," Gold murmured. "I started out with grease on my hands."

(Three)
RAF Fighter Squadron 33
Desert Air Force
Near Buerat-el-Hsur, Libya
27 December 1942

Captain Blaize Greene was having his morning coffee in the mess tent when he overheard a couple of the other pilots swapping gossip.

"Excuse me," Greene called out, interrupting their conversation. "What do you mean we're going to be busting tanks from now on?"

One of the pilots shrugged. "That's what I just heard from the major. Day after tomorrow we're to take part in the

Yanks' air attack upon Rommel's forces, dug in at Buerat.
But we won't be flying fighter escort for their bombers.
We'll be busting tanks—"

Livid, Greene strode out of the mess, toward the operations tent which Major Bolten, the squadron's commander,
used as an office. On his way there he paused. Greene's
light-cotton khaki shorts and short-sleeved shirt was sweat-
soaked and caked with dust, and he hadn't yet shaved. He
briefly considered making a detour to his own tent, to clean
up a bit, before making an official call on his commanding
officer. To hell with that, he decided, he was was in too
much of a hurry, and he was too angry.

He'd arrived in Egypt at the end of June, in time to join
the Squadron and take part in the fighting that ended in the
Huns being stopped by the weary 8th Army at El Alamein. It
was over El Alamein that Greene scored his first kill: a
Stukka dive bomber.

In August, General Montgomery arrived to take command. Things were relatively quiet through September and
the first part of October as Monty reorganized his forces.
During a late-afternoon patrol over the desert, Greene and
his wingmate encountered a twin-engine Me-110 long-range
fighter. The Me-110 was a tough nut to crack. It was fast,
and had a fierce bite: the Me-110 carried four machine guns
and two cannons in her nose, and had a rear-facing machine
gunner. What Greene and his wingmate initially tried to
do on that October afternoon was get beneath the Me-110
and shoot up at its unprotected belly. What the Hun pilot
tried to do was skim the desert as he hightailed it for home.
Greene's wingmate gave up, but Greene, determined to get
his second kill, bounced the low-flying Me-110, braving
that rear machine gun's spray. Greene's Hurricane took a
few hits, but he managed a lucky shot, evidently hitting
the pilot. The Me-110 abruptly nosedived, to skid across
the sand. Greene and his wingmate circled high overhead
like vultures over the downed Hun fighter, until they saw
the Me-110 explode in a bright crimson fireball, sending
plumes of oily black smoke up from the sun-bleached yellow
sands.

Back at base that evening, Greene had his crew chief stencil a second tiny swastika on his Hurricane.

On October 23, Monty unleashed Operation Lightfoot against Rommel's Afrika Corps, intent upon driving the Germans out of El Alamein once and for all. The British Desert Air Force, along with a small United States Army Air Force contingent, flew air cover for the operation. On October 31, Greene shot down an Italian, Macchi 202 single-engine fighter over Kidney Ridge near Tell el Eisa.

In November, General Eisenhower's American forces invaded French Morocco and Algeria, and began moving against Rommel from the west, while Monty continued his eastward advance. The Huns, low on supplies, were now caught in a pincer, and began grudgingly retreating, scorching the earth as they went, laying mines and booby traps every foot of the way. The Huns dug in their heels at Fuka, sixty miles west of Alamein, were blasted out at great cost, and then fell back to Mersa Brega on the Gulf of Sirte, where the November rains bought them some time. In December, Monty's 8th Army pressed on, and the Germans fell back once again, this time to Buerat-el-Hsur, on the Libyan coast, a couple of hundred miles east of Tripoli.

By then Greene's Fighter Squadron had gone mobile, and was bringing up the rear as the army secured Libyan territory. On the twenty-second, Greene, flying patrol, bagged a big, three-engined, Junkers 52 transport carrying reinforcements and supplies to Rommel's beleaguered forces.

That had been his fourth kill. Since then, Greene had been volunteering for extra patrols, anxious to get his all-important fifth kill, and become an ace.

But he wasn't going to get any more kills if he and his squadron were turned into tank busters. You could shoot up a dozen tanks and it wouldn't make you an ace—

The operations tent was a barracks-sized canvas structure with a rough-planked floor. A petrol generator supplied power to the bare bulbs hanging from the tent's ridgepole, the light reflecting harshly off the drab-green canvas walls. Most of the tent was taken up with long, backless benches arranged before a raised platform. This was the operations area used for pilot briefings. Major Bolten's office area was in the tent's rear quarter, and was sparsely furnished with frayed throw rugs upon the raw planking, dark-green metal desks and file cabinets, and several folding tables loaded down with radio equipment.

Greene barged into the tent, past Corporal Leonard, the radioman, who was seated at his equipment, his Sten submachine gun slung across the back of his canvas folding chair. The corporal glanced up smiling. "Morning, Captain—" he began.

Greene ignored him, striding up to Major Bolten, who was seated behind his desk, reading a report. "What's all this about us becoming boar hunters?" Greene fiercely demanded.

Bolten looked up with a deadpan expression. He was in his fifties, tall and heavyset, and wore his thinning auburn hair slicked from his high, perpetually sunburned forehead. He had a pencil moustache, pale brown eyes, and exceedingly bad teeth. He also had an annoying habit of never seeming to sweat. Just now his long-sleeved, khaki shirt looked freshly pressed and dry as a bone.

"So you've heard the latest?" Bolten asked.

"Yes, I've heard! I'd like to know what the hell kind of nonsense—"

"Calm down," Bolten said sourly. He reached into his desk drawer and came out with a gun-metal gray cigarette case. He took a smoke for himself, and then offered the case to Greene, who declined. "Now, then, Blaize," Bolten began, as he fitted his cigarette into an ivory holder. "I'm no happier about these recent developments than you. For what it might be worth to you, when the orders came down to transform our fighters into tank busters, I argued against it." He paused to light his cigarette, and then exhaled a long, thin stream of blue smoke. "My arguing, needless to say, did absolutely no good. The day after tomorrow the Yanks' B-17s based at Benghazi will fly across the Gulf of Sidra to conduct a bombing raid over Buerat—"

"Major, those Flying Fortresses are going to need protection against Italian and German fighters—" Greene impatiently interrupted.

"The Yanks are supplying their own fighter escort," Bolten sharply replied, his eyes narrowing in response to Greene's disrespectful attitude. "They've got P-38 Lightnings and P-60 BearClaws equipped with long-range drop tanks. Those fighters can fly higher and faster than our Hurricanes."

"The Hurricane is a bloody fine airplane, Sir," Greene protested.

Bolten smiled faintly. "And you and the other lads have done well by her. But we've got to face facts: the Squadron is down to less than a dozen airworthy planes of an outmoded design. We're simply not needed as fighters any longer. We are needed as tank busters, and we both know that Hurricanes fitted with cannons are well suited for that job. A lorry load of cannons and armor-piercing shells is on its way to us, right now, and should be here by this afternoon. The armorer assures me that he can have the planes refitted by tomorrow night. I was going to have you lead the attack on the day after."

"Major, I need only one more kill to become an ace," Greene said, frustrated.

"That's enough," Bolten snapped, growing pale with anger. "I advise you to get hold of yourself, Captain! I've been rather easygoing concerning discipline, considering that we're a front-line outfit operating under adverse conditions. Perhaps I've been *too* easygoing. Do remember that you're speaking to a superior officer."

"Yes, sir," Greene said, coming to attention. "I beg the major's pardon."

Bolten nodded, seeming somewhat mollified. "You might also remember that this war isn't being conducted for your personal amusement. Now then, I've got work to do, Captain. You're dismissed."

Greene saluted, turned on his heel, and began to leave the tent. He felt Bolten's eyes upon him as he walked away.

"Captain—"

Greene turned. "Yes, Sir?"

"Captain . . ." Bolten repeated, and then hesitated. "Blaize." He smiled. "I've been meaning to ask, how is your missus?"

"Sir?" Greene had never been that friendly with Bolten,

and was a bit startled by the major's sudden interest in the state of Suze's health.

"Well, I heard from some of the other fellows that your wife is pregnant. It's your first child, isn't it?"

"Yes, Sir," Greene said. He realized that Bolten was waiting for him to say something more. "Her due date is sometime in the middle of January."

"Splendid, splendid," Bolten murmured. He looked uncomfortable. "I say, Blaize, I was wondering, with your wife due to deliver in just a couple of weeks, perhaps you'd rather I removed you from the flying roster for a while?"

"Whatever for, Major?"

"Well, some chaps get a bit . . ." Bolten hesitated. "Wobbly in the knees; superstitious, shall we say, at such times. I thought, perhaps, that was why you're acting so . . . peculiarly."

"Major, I do appreciate your concern," Greene said coolly, but there are plenty of RAF chaps with wives and kiddies to fret about just now flying in combat. Nobody's taking them off the flight roster, now, are they?"

Bolten seemed to flinch at Greene's tone. "Suit yourself, then, Captain," he muttered.

Greene, sensing that he'd hurt Bolten's feelings, realized that he was behaving like a cad. He'd been taking out his frustrations on a superior officer who was only relaying orders that had come down from on high. "Sir, I apologize for my behavior. I do appreciate your offer. It's just that I feel bad enough as it is, losing out on any opportunity of becoming an ace. I'd much rather be flying with the rest of the squadron, even if we have been reduced to tank busting."

"Which is risky enough," Bolten pointed out. "And taking into account our area of operations, even more valuable to the war effort than shooting enemy fighters."

"Maybe," Greene sighed.

Bolten rolled his eyes. "Off with you, then."

On December 29, the Squadron's ten airworthy Hawker Hurricanes sat like drab butterflies, drying their wings in the sun, as Greene and the other pilots made their way to the ready line. The Hurricanes wore desert camouflage colors: mottled brown and tan on top, sky blue on the bottom, with British roundels on the fuselages' rear quarters, and the wings. Normally, the Hurricanes were armed with eight Browning .30-caliber machine guns, but to equip the fighters for their tank-busting duties, six of those guns had been stripped away, replaced by a pair of 40-millimeter cannons. Each cannon, its long barrel jutting out like a bayonet from its pod nestled beneath the wing, was loaded with twelve armor-piercing shells.

The Hurricane was a big plane. Its cockpit was about ten feet off the ground. Greene, wearing his soft canvas helmet and goggles, burdened down with his parachute, and a Webley .38-caliber revolver in a canvas flap holster strapped around his waist, needed a stepladder, and the assistance of the ground crew, to climb into the cockpit. He strapped himself in and tested his radio.

"Your flight's cleared, Captain," Corporal Leonard's voice came in over the earpieces built into Greene's helmet. "Best of luck."

"Thank you, Corporal," Greene said into his throat mike. He slid forward the Hurricane's canopy and locked it into place, and then started his engine. As he began taxiing across the sandy airfield, he checked his watch. It was just noon. With any luck he and the boys could go Hun hog-bashing and be back in time for tea. Greene hoped that would be the case. He had a letter he wanted to finish writing to Suze.

(Four)
Hubert Place, near Russell Square
London
29 December 1942

It was a little after ten in the morning when Suzy Greene, peering out the bay windows of the parlor-floor flat, decided that it was now or never if she were going to go for a walk. The sky was a blustery gray, threatening rain, and it did look chilly from the way that people were hurrying by all bundled up. Still, her doctor had told her to get at least a little exercise each day.

She moved slowly through the flat to the hall closet. These days, slow was the only way she could move. Her stomach was hugely swollen. She couldn't believe that she still had a month to go until her due date. From the way the boy—she was certain that it was a boy—had been kicking all morning, she felt as if any moment he was going to punt his way through her belly.

She pulled on a couple of Blaize's sweaters, and his old tweed overcoat: his were the only garments she had that could make it around her middle. She'd gone shopping for maternity clothes a while ago, but with the war shortages there hadn't been much to choose from in the shops. She wrapped a scarf around her throat, pulled on her mittens and earmuffs, and left the flat.

She shivered, turning up her coat collar against the wind as she waddled as quickly as she could past the red-brick rowhouses that lined Hubert Place. Folklore had it that pregnant women weren't supposed to get cold, but she guessed that didn't hold true for pregnant women transplanted to gloomy Britain from balmy California. Growing up in Los Angeles must have thinned her blood, or else it had to do with the lack of central heating in England. Whatever it was, she hadn't been truly warm since she'd set foot here, she thought, as she passed by the British Museum.

The truth of it was that she'd never really felt all that comfortable here in Britain. It hadn't been that bad back in the spring, when the weather was balmy, the gardens freshly green and vibrant with flowers; and Blaize had been with her. Blaize had been so happy to be home, so anxious to show her London, that somehow she'd seen it all through his eyes, and never felt like a stranger.

But once Blaize had graduated from fighter training school—so handsome in his blue uniform, his white-silk pilot's wings stitched above the breast pocket—he had to go off to the front, and leave her all alone in the Hubert Place flat. His going seemed to take the light and life out of London for Suzy. The cold, damp, lonely nights seemed to last forever, and the shadowy, bombed-out buildings seemed to leer at her like skulls. Blaize's friends tried to make her feel comfortable, but Suzy couldn't shake the feeling that nobody here really knew her or cared about her. A few times she'd been on the verge of wiring her parents and asking them to arrange her transportation home. She hadn't, because her husband was an Englishman, and as his wife, she felt, she should loyally reside in the country he was risking his life to defend. It wasn't much, but it was *something* she could do to demonstrate her love.

For all of that, she was very thankful that Blaize had said that he was willing to move back to California once the war was over. Suzy couldn't wait to see palm trees, and to experience a day without rain, and to have something decent to eat again.

She also couldn't wait to have this baby. It hadn't been an easy pregnancy. Of course, she was grateful to *be* pregnant. God, it had seemed as if they'd been trying forever. Not that it hadn't been *fun* trying . . .

She just wanted her body back, thanks very much.

At the corner of Montague Street, she paused, wondering how far she should press on. She decided to stroll a bit through the manicured greenery of Russell Square. It turned out that her spirit was willing, but her ankles were weak. Halfway through the park she had to sit down on a bench to catch her breath.

An elderly man, wearing a derby and a velvet-collared gray chesterfield overcoat, carrying a newspaper tucked under his arm, came along and sat down beside her. He had pink cheeks and a white, walrus moustache, just like the English gents in the *Esquire* magazine cartoons. Suzy tried not to giggle. He nodded to her, and then hid his face behind his copy of his *London Times*.

She'd rest just a bit longer, she thought, and then head back to the flat for a nice hot cup of tea, and some cookies . . .

She shoved her mittened hands into the pockets of the overcoat and felt something hard that had slid through a hole in the left pocket, to become caught in the coat's lining. She carefully worked it free and pulled it out of the pocket. It was a slender, leather-bound volume; a book of poems, by

Yeats. She'd never seen it before. When she opened it she was delighted to see that many of the poems had been annotated by Blaize. She began to read—first a poem, and then Blaize's comments—and quickly lost track of the time. As she read his inked notations she could hear his voice in her mind. Discovering the book was like being treated to a visit with Blaize, and, a teeny bit, served to assuage her loneliness.

(Five)
Near Buerat-el-Hsur

Greene led his flight along the Via Balbia coast road. Off his starboard wing was the brilliant blue Mediterranean, the molten African sun casting glittering diamonds across the waves. To his left was the limitless desert, the ochre dunes stubbled with green and brown tangles of brush, and the purple hills shimmering in the heat. There was no substantial cover down there, no decent place for men and machines to hide. To the American bombers, the Huns infesting the dunes and ravines would look like military miniatures arranged on a yellow-tablecloth battlefield. The Germans would fight back with flak guns, tank fire, and heavy machine guns, but would mostly count on their fighters for protection.

"Look sharp, now, lads," Greene said into his throat mike. "We've left our lines behind."

The formation of ten planes broke apart, spreading out inland and flying low, hoping to flush out their armored quarry.

The objective was to destroy the Afrika Corps' tanks patrolling the perimeters of the Hun's Buerat position. Hopefully, any enemy fighters in the area would have been drawn off to intercept the Yanks' bombers and their fighter escort just now on their way across the Gulf. The refitted Hurricanes were not armed for dogfighting.

As Greene watched the desert terrain rushing by beneath him, he thought about what Major Bolten had said about the Hawker Hurricane being outmoded. The more he pondered how Bolten had maligned the Hurricane, the angrier he got. Part of his indignation stemmed from guilt, of course. He himself had been awfully disappointed when he found out that the 33rd was equipped with Hurricanes instead of Spitfires or Supersharks. He'd been even more upset when he learned that the filters fitted onto the Hurricanes' Rolls-Royce Merlin engines to protect against sand and dust further decreased the planes' performance capabilities. But after a few weeks spent flying his Hurricane, Greene had found himself grown quite fond of her. She was easy to land, easy to repair, and a stable gun platform. Most important, her rather old-fashioned metal and wood frame, covered over with fabric, allowed enemy fire to pass through her without doing the terrible damage that bullets did to the newer fighters of monocoque metal skin construction.

Anyway, a pilot had to have tender feelings toward an airplane that had safely seen him through four victorious dogfights. If only there could have been a fifth, Greene thought longingly.

The flight came up low over a high dune, roaring past a line of seven Panzers strung out single-file, rolling westward across the sand.

"Tally-ho, lads!" Greene told his flight as it split up. "Good hunting!"

Greene banked hard right, swinging out over the sea. The G-force braided his belly around his spine as he slid sideways into a rolling turn that put him into position for an attack dive an the Panzer column. Greene began an approach that positioned him to be third in line for a crack at the Huns.

The Panzers were kicking up clouds of dust, scuttling like mottled yellow and tan desert tortoises across the dunes as the first Hurricane went at them. Greene watched as the pilot used his machine guns to zero in on a tank, and then cut loose with his 40 millimeters. Orange fire spouted from the barrels of the cannons as the spent shell casings tumbled from ejection ports cut into the pod housings. The rounds impacted around the tank, sending up high pillars of sand. Meanwhile, the tank's turret was coming around, and its cannon barrel rising, like an angry scorpion's stinger. The first Hurricane peeled off as the second airplane came in toward its different target. The first tank fired its cannon and cut loose with machine gun bursts as the second Hurricane's Brownings stitched twin lines toward its tank. As its machine-gun rounds closed on its target, the Hurricane's cannons began firing, scoring two direct hits. The Panzer's turret lifted off in a geyser of flame. Thick black smoke began pouring out from the busted tank's innards, blowing across the desert, and obscuring the retreat of several other Panzers fortunate enough to be in the right place at the right time.

Greene picked out a target and began his own power dive. He used his two machine guns to guide his aim, and when the time was right he fired five rounds from each of his cannons. The guttural coughing of the heavy guns reverberated inside the Hurricane's cockpit. Greene could feel the vibrations numbing his fingers on the stick, and the cannons' heavy recoil measurably slowing the aircraft. His cannon spray was kicking up a cloud of dust around his target. One round struck the tank's tread, sending metal linkages flying. The Panzer was hamstrung, but still dangerous. As Greene flew by, its turret tracked him with cannon and machine-gun fire.

He was swinging around for a second pass when he saw one of the Panzers fire its cannon at a banking Hurricane and score a direct hit, swatting the plane out of the sky in a puff of fire and smoke. One of the other Hurricanes immediately attacked that tank, raining cannon fire on it until it exploded.

Greene finished off the Panzer he'd crippled in a six-round burst, and then climbed, to look for another target—he still had eight cannon rounds left. The rest of his flight was now scattered across the sky, Panzer hunting. It was understood that everybody would make their own ways home.

A sound like distant thunder was filtering into Greene's cockpit above the drone of his own engine. He looked to the west, and saw that the Yanks had arrived at Buerat. Greene saw clouds of gray smoke rolling inland, carried by the sea breeze, as the silvery B-17s scattered their bombs. Black carnations of anti-aircraft fire were spreading their petals within the stately bomber formations. Orange tracer fire was licking upward toward the B-17s as all around them fighters swirled like angry hornets.

Greene's attention was caught by a moving dust cloud beneath him. He banked and dived for a closer look: it was a Hun armored car darting on its eight tires like a centipede across the sand. As he dived on the car, its rear-mounted machine gun stuck out its orange tongue at him. Greene answered the insult with a burst from his own machine guns, and three rounds apiece from his cannons. A 40-millimeter shell clipped the rear-left fender of the armored car, and it went veering out of control, roaring up a dune and then flipping onto its side, spilling men as it rolled like a barrel into a bramble-choked ravine. It came to rest sitting upright on its eight tires. Greene came around to give it his remaining cannon rounds, and this time he managed to turn the damn thing into twisted, smoking metal.

As he climbed he saw several of the armored car's crew running across the sand, but he let them go. He still had some ammo left in his machine guns, but he wasn't the bloody sort to go strafing helpless men.

With his cannons empty, there was no point in hanging around. Anyway, he was running low on petrol. Greene climbed, to put himself out of range of small-arms ground fire, and headed back toward the sea, thinking that he would follow the coast road back to his own lines, and home base. He was about over the Via Balbia, when he saw a solitary Yank B-17, in some distress, flying low over the water, about a quarter mile offshore. He closed in slowly on the big four-engined bomber, giving its crew plenty of time to notice his British markings, and then made a slow circle around the faltering craft. The Flying Fortress had *Jazz-a-Bell* painted on her nose, just beneath the cockpit. The foot-high, light blue letters curved beneath a painting of a scantily clad blonde riding a saxophone in the manner of witch on her broomstick. The painting was the only good-looking thing about the bomber. Machine-gun fire had raised ugly pockmarks upon her skin. Her number-two starboard engine was half blown away, its prop slowly windmilling in the slipstream. Her tail and belly gun-turrets had been shot up, and she had a gaping hole in her starboard side, just forward the waist gunner's position.

Suddenly Greene's radio crackled to life. "—tle friend, this is Jazz-a-Bell. Come in, if you read me, over. Hello, little friend, this is Jazz-a-Bell. Come in if you read me, over."

Greene keyed his throat mike. "I didn't know you chaps had our frequency, over."

"We didn't. I've had my radio man hunting up and down the dial ever since we spotted you. This is Lieutenant Feldman, of the United States Army Air Force 301st Bombardment Group. Please identify yourself, over."

"Captain Greene, RAF 33rd Fighter Squadron. Can you chaps make it back to Benghazi? Over."

"That's a damned good question, Captain." Feldman dryly laughed. "We were doing fine blasting Jerry into little pieces, but then the fighters came at us. There turned out to be more enemy fighters than we expected. Sure as hell more than our escort could handle. Before we knew it, the bomber formation was all alone. We kept a tight box and managed to hold off the Italian bandits all right—a B-17 can take a hell of a lot of machine-gun fire—but then we got chewed up by one shit-storm of Messerschmitts armed with rapid-fire 20-millimeter cannons. The Huns took out my tail gun and my belly turret, hit my starboard engine, and put a real nice hole in my starboard side. We began losing altitude, and had to drop out of formation. We were hoping to come across some stray little friends once we reached the coast. We could use some fighter escort to cover our ass, which is feeling mighty naked with our tail and belly guns out of commission. Glad we found you—"

I'm sure you are, Greene thought. *But then, you don't know that all I've got to cover your ass with is a measly pair of .30-caliber Browning popguns that are just about out of ammo.*

"With your help, we should be able to make it home," the bomber pilot was continuing. "Leastways, we're going to try, but the plane is shaking so hard I can feel my teeth fillings about to fall out... Over."

"Why don't you get back over land, and parachute? Or

better yet, ditch into the sea? There's no threat of enemy ships around here. Just radio in your position, and wait it out in life rafts until the flying boats come for you. Over."

" 'Fraid I can't do either, Captain. You see, I've got hurt men here. Matter of fact, of the ten of us, six are in no condition to go parachuting or swimming." Feldman hesitated. "And I got to say, I'm not all that sure I know how to splash her down in one piece. Over."

"Just how much experience have you had, Lieutenant? How many bomb raids have you participated in? Over."

"Counting this one?" Feldman began. "One."

"Oh Christ," Greene muttered to himself. He'd *thought* the lieutenant had sounded young. It was one hell of a spot for a green pilot to be in. He keyed his throat mike. "Lieutenant, I'm running low on fuel. I suggest you follow me to my base camp. It's a hell of a lot closer than Benghazi."

"Sounds good, Captain. Lead the way. We sure 'preciate the hospitality. I guess our luck changed when we ran into you. Talk about a knight in shining armor . . . Over."

What a charming thing to say, Greene thought, smiling as he maneuvered his Hurricane into position just slightly ahead of the crippled bomber, on its port side. "If I may say so, Lieutenant, your accent sounds familiar. Might you be from California? Over."

"Hey, yeah—" Greene could hear the pleasure in the young lieutenant's voice. "I'm from Anaheim. How'd'cha know that, Captain? I mean, no offense, but you being English, and all. Over."

"I've spent some time in California. My wife's from Los Angeles. Over."

Feldman's laughter bubbled in Greene's earpieces. "California girls are somethin', aren't they? Bet your wife is blonde, right, Captain? Over."

"As a matter of fact, she is." Greene laughed. "Tell me, are you married, Lieutenant? Over."

Feldman sighed. "Sometimes I think I was born married, Captain. I got me a wife, all right, and two little kids waiting for me back in California. Sure do wish I was home. Over."

"So do I, Lieutenant. So do I." Greene realized that when he thought of home he didn't picture London, but that flat he'd had in Santa Monica, and Suze, tanned and lovely in a bathing suit, frolicking on a California Beach. "I'll be going back to California, after the war. Over."

"I'm relieved to think that *I* might make it back to California, and that my whole crew might live to see home, thanks to you. Over."

"I'm glad to be of service to you. Say, have you ever eaten at Donde's near Santa Monica Pier? Over."

"I love Donde's," Feldman exclaimed. "You ever have the abalone sautéed in oil and garlic? Over."

"That's all my wife and I have ever ordered there." Greene laughed. "Over."

"God, just talking about it makes my mouth water—" Feldman began, but then stopped abruptly. "My copilot thinks he saw the sun glinting off something coming up fast on the starboard side. He's not sure, but— Shit, yes! There it is. Oh, shit—"

Greene turned to look, in time to see an Me-109 swing past, and then seem to abruptly waver in the air as its surprised pilot evidently spotted the Hurricane.

"Captain, you've got to get that fucker!" Feldman cried out, panicked. "If he zeroes in on our tail with those 20-millimeter cannons, we're dead ducks! Over."

"I'm going after him, Lieutenant," Greene said calmly, banking to pursue the fighter. *Of course, I'm running on fumes as it is, about all I've got left to throw at him is spit*, Greene thought as he opened up the throttle to climb up onto the still dumbfounded Hun pilot's tail. He centered the Messerschmitt in his sights and fired. His rounds were striking home, but his two .30-caliber Brownings were just not enough to knock the fighter down. His guns clicked empty as the Me-109 rolled away.

"You had him, and you let him go, Captain! What happened? Over."

Greene watched ruefully as the Messerschmitt began circling around to take up an attack position on the bomber's tail. "I'm out of ammo. Over."

"Then we're out of luck," Feldman said softly. "Fuck it, Captain. You tried, now save your ass, while you still got the gas left to do it. Go on, get out of here. Over."

"I'm not going to leave ten men to that goddamned German bastard," Greene said angrily. "I'll go after him again. Maybe I can bluff him, or at the very least, decoy him away from you. Over."

Greene came around to make a passing dive at the Hun pilot, who totally ignored him. Evidently the German had realized that the Hurricane was out of ammo, and harmless. Nor was the German about to be decoyed into chasing after a skinny little fighter when he had a big, juicy, Yank bomber to chew on.

The Me-109 was just opening fire on the bomber when Greene swooped past again. This time he gritted his teeth, and came in so close that the Hun pilot had to break off his attack and take evasive maneuvers for fear of a collision. The German seemed to lose his temper and began to chase after Greene, but then he seemed to regain control of himself. The Me-109 broke off its pursuit, returning its attentions to the bomber.

Greene turned as well, locking onto the Messerschmitt's tail, hoping to once again distract the German—

Not a chance. The Hun pilot had clearly caught on. Greene angrily thumbed his useless triggers as he watched the silvery Messerschmitt insolently take its time rolling past his gun sights on its way back to the limping bomber. The bloody Hun! If only he had some ammo! But he didn't. All he had was his airplane . . .

He keyed his throat mike. "Listen to me, Lieutenant," he began evenly. "Here's the coordinates and radio frequency of my base." Greene quickly ran through the information. "Take it slow and easy and you'll make it okay. Over."

"What are you going to do?" the Yank pilot demanded. "Over."

"Do what I get paid to do," Greene said. "Knock down enemy fighters. Over." He pulled back on his stick to climb high above the Messerschmitt that was angling down onto the low-flying bomber's tail.

"You haven't got any ammo—"

"Tell you what, Lieutenant, when you get back to California, you go to Donde's and have some abalone for me—"

"*Goddammit*, Captain—"

Greene had to smile. The poor lad sounded close to tears. "And give my love to the wife and kiddies. Right, lad?" He thought about Suze. His heart began to pound and his mouth was suddenly bone dry. "All of your crew," he stammered hoarsely. "Tell all of them to give my love to their wives and kids . . ."

"Captain—"

"Over and out, Lieutenant," Greene said, and switched off his radio. Down below was the Me-109, locking onto the bomber's tail. As Greene watched, the Hun's cannons began to wink fire—

He pushed the stick forward and began to dive on the Messerschmitt, taking great care to line the enemy fighter up in his sights.

It was really quite simple, Greene told himself. It was a matter of mathematics. One man's life to save ten. His altimeter was unwinding so fast that it was hissing. The Me-109 was looming ever-larger in Greene's gun sight. The Hun pilot was flying steady as a rock. He wasn't going to go into evasive maneuvers. Why should he? He knew the Hurricane was out of ammo.

Greene realized that he was crying. No shame in that, he decided. Just good sense—

Suze, I love you very much, he thought, to take his mind off the fact that all he had to do was jerk the stick to fly away from this; fly home to Suze—

One life for ten, he reminded himself. Simple mathematics. Can't argue with the numbers.

The German had stopped firing at the bomber. Greene imagined the Hun glancing up at the diving Hurricane and wondering . . .

As the Hurricane fell like a flame-singed moth toward the Messerschmitt, Greene wondered if Suze was right, if his child inside her was indeed a boy. He decided it was.

An instant before his Hurricane slammed into the Messerschmitt, Greene realized that this was his fifth kill, and that he was going to be an ace after all. Just like him to have to do everything the hard way.

Suze—

(Six)
Russell Square

A shriek seemed to echo inside Suzy's skull. The book of poems fell out of her hands as thunder, followed by an orange ball of fiery pain, engulfed her. She slumped sideways, falling off the bench.

"I say, Miss—"

It was the gent in the derby speaking. As Suzy writhed on the cold, damp grass, her eyes were level with his polished black brogues. She managed to look up at him.

"I say—" He was looking around wildly. "Hello! Somebody! Over here! A pregnant woman!"

Suzy felt an agony, like drops of acid, in her belly. "My baby," Suzy groaned, and her eyes squeezed shut. "My baby—"

"Steady now, Miss, help's on the way," the gent soothed, stooping over her. "You there!" he shouted. "Do hurry!"

She felt gentle hands lifting her up. "My baby—" she moaned. Her eyes were still shut, but orange and black tendrils of fire and smoke were curling against her eyelids.

"Yes, luv. You're having your baby," a woman suddenly said. In the distance, a siren had begun to wail. "There's the ambulance for you now. You and your baby are going to be quite all right."

Suzy felt herself drifting off into a faint. *My baby,* she'd wanted to say, but the pain inside had never let her. *My baby is crying inside me.*

"I wonder where her husband is," somebody was asking.

"My husband is dead," Suzy heard herself murmur, before blacking out.

Chapter 19

(One)
United States Army Air Force 320th Fighter Squadron
Henderson Field
Guadalcanal
21 April 1943

Second Lieutenant Steven Gold received the letter from his father telling him about Blaize Greene's death only a few minutes before he was scheduled to take off on patrol. He was in the ready room, changing into his flight overalls, when one of the orderlies brought him the letter, apologizing for the snafu that had prevented it being delivered during the morning's mail call. Steven had torn the envelope open, figuring to quickly skim the letter and then reread it later, but he never got past the opening sentences concerning how Blaize had died.

"What's wrong, kid?" asked Cappy Fitzpatrick. Cappy's curly hair was cropped short, and he was clean-shaven, now that he was a major and squadron commander in the Air Force. "You get a Dear John letter?" He chuckled.

"It's about my brother-in-law. He was an RAF fighter pilot in North Africa. He was killed in action, saving an American bomber from a German fighter."

Cappy frowned. "Tough break, kid." He glanced at his wristwatch. "Hey, we've got to go. You all right to fly?"

"Huh?" Steven looked up, and then smiled weakly. "Yeah, sure. I'm fine." Just a few days ago fighters from the 339th had shot down the Mitsubishi bomber carrying Admiral Yamamoto, the Jap who'd planned the sneak attack on

Pearl Harbor. Because of that, rumor had it that today the Jap Zeros would be out in force, like pissed-off hornets from a busted nest, and Steven didn't want to miss this chance to rack up some kills. He stuffed the letter into the pocket of his khaki coveralls, grabbed the rest of his flight gear, and followed Cappy out of the ready room.

Steven squinted against the sunshine as they hurried through the palms, past the sandbag machine gun emplacements, to the hangars. As they reached the muddy ready line Steven saw that the rest of the patrol were already in their silver and green Lockheed P-38 Lightning fighters equipped with auxiliary fuel drop tanks.

His squadron had been one of the first to get the twin-engined, swallow-tailed Lightnings. Some of the guys didn't like them, claiming they weren't all that agile in a dogfight, but Steven was happy with the plane. Equipped with drop tanks, the P-38 had the extended range to take the fight to the northern end of the Solomon Islands chain, where the Japs were still dug in. The Lightning was fast and could outclimb and outdive anything the Japs had, and with its single twenty-millimeter cannon and four fifty-caliber machine guns clustered in its nose the Lightning packed one hell of a knockout punch. With it Steven had already racked up three victories against Jap Zeros in the two months he'd been here.

Steven hoisted himself up onto the Lightning's wing and then into the cockpit. He buckled in, called out "Clear!" to the ground crew, and started his liquid-cooled Allison engines. Steven lowered his canopy and began to roll forward, following Cappy onto the runway. Once all four airplanes were airborne, the patrol banked out over the immense, sparkling blue Pacific.

Steven had entered the Army last spring. Boot camp had been grueling, but once those initial six weeks of hell were behind him, things got considerably easier. The toughest thing about Aviation School was keeping himself from showing off. After all, he already was an experienced fighter pilot and combat veteran.

Upon receiving his wings and his second lieutenant's single gold bar, he'd requested duty with Cappy's squadron. Cappy had called in some old favors to get Steven assigned to the squadron. His father, who had made good on his promise to help get Steven into flight school, had also used his influence to get Steven his choice of duty assignment.

Steven smiled to himself as he looked down at the green dot in the blue and silver ocean that was Savo Island. His father still hadn't stopped grumbling over the fact that he was pulling strings to get his son *into* combat. Too bad he hadn't been willing to do the same for Blaize. Weird how the world worked: if his dad had been willing, Blaize would have entered combat months earlier, would have been assigned to a different unit, and might still be alive.

Steven, lost in brooding reveries concerning Blaize, was startled by Cappy's voice crackling over the radio.

"Rat-a-tat, kid. You're dead—"

Steven craned his neck to look behind him. Cappy was sitting on his tail.

"At least you'd be dead if I were a Jap," Cappy added. "What's your story, Steven? It's not like you to let anybody sneak up on you like this. You still thinking about that letter from home? Over."

"I guess I am. Over," Steven said.

"Kid, a man measures himself in combat not just by how he confronts the possibility of his own death, but also by how he deals with the deaths of other people. People he cares about. Over."

Steven thought about it as the patrol approached Russell Island's thick jungle coastline. He keyed his throat mike. "You know something, Cappy? War sucks, over."

"MacArthur will be so pleased to hear that you agree with him." Cappy chuckled.

"Hey, you guys, we've got company, heading east," one of the other pilots cut in.

Steven looked and saw sunlight glinting off a swarm of specks heading toward the Jap air base on Rabaul.

"I don't think they've seen us. All right, everyone. Drop your auxiliary tanks and let's get some altitude on those babies," Cappy said. "Let's go, cowboys! Steven, you're my wingman."

The patrol split into two pairs as Steven pulled back on his stick to follow Cappy. They leveled off and increased their speed, gradually overtaking the Japs.

They were Zekes: Mitsubishi-built Zero-Sen single-engine fighters. There were six of them, flying in two rows of three abreast. Their red rising sun insignia shimmered like blood blisters on their burnished silver wings.

"Steven and I go first," Cappy said, pushing his Lightning over into a whistling attack dive toward the rear trio of Zeros. Steven followed him down, picking out a target as the Jap formation spotted them and split apart. Cappy's guns caught one of the Zeros before he could decide which way to go.

That was always a bad mistake, Steven thought as he watched the enemy fighter leak smoke and fall toward the sea. It was better to just *go* when somebody bounced you. Decide which way later.

Steven went after his own Zero, which was twisting like a hooked trout, trying to get away. Steven stayed on the Jap's tail, and each time the enemy plane appeared in his sights Steven blipped his triggers. His fifty-caliber tracer rounds were raising sparks off the Zero's fuselage, and then his cannon shells caught the Zero's cockpit. Steven saw shards from the Plexiglas canopy go spinning away, sparkling in the sunlight. His target abruptly seemed to stand on its tail, and then slide sideways, going into a spin. There was no smoke and no fire. Watching the Zero splash down, Steven figured that he must have hit the pilot.

Four kills, Steven thought. *Just one more, and I'm an ace—*

He looked up and around and saw that the other two Lightnings were each accounting for an enemy plane. Steven was banking his own Lightning, prior to climbing for altitude to get back into the battle, when Cappy's voice filled his cockpit.

"Jesus Christ, Steven! Look alive! You've got one on your tail!"

Steven didn't look to see where the Jap was, he just wrenched his stick hard to the left, hoping like hell that he was making the right choice. As the Lightning slipped sideways he felt it being pelted and saw sparks like fireflies lifting off his own wings. His starboard engine began smoking. The Zero was chewing him up!

"Get him off me, someone!" Steven yelled as Jap tracers slid past his canopy like fiery worms. The Plexiglas splintered, and he felt white heat slicing into his left thigh. His leg went numb.

"I'm hit, I'm hit," he announced, feeling strangely calm as his lap began filling with blood.

He looked behind him and saw the Zero that had gotten him break off its attack. He watched the Jap veer past in a shallow dive, and then bank to the right in preparation for climbing to look for another target.

"You want to be an ace, too, is that it, buddy?" Steven murmured to the Jap. "You're in too much of a hurry, pal. You shouldn't let a little smoke fool you like that."

Steven grimaced with pain as he worked his rudder pedals. He wondered how bad his leg was. He sure didn't want to lose it. *Look on the bright side,* he thought to himself. *You probably aren't going to live long enough for them to amputate.*

The Lightning's controls were sluggish and his smoking engine was sputtering, but the blessing of a twin-engined fighter was that its second engine gave you a second chance. Steven managed to bring the plane around in a gradual banking turn that put him on an approach to the Zero's tail. Now if he could only close the gap before the Jap started to climb.

The Jap evidently spotted him and panicked. That was the break that Steven needed. The Jap tried to climb too steeply, almost stalling his airplane. He recovered, but that little bit was all Steven needed to close in.

The smoke spewing from the Lightning's shot-up engine was blowing across Steven's windscreen, making it hard to see, but when he caught a glimpse of the Zero less than a hundred yards in front of him he pressed his triggers and kept them pressed.

The smoke enveloping Steven's canopy lifted for an instant, and he saw his tracers and cannon rounds streaking past the Zero's port wing. He jerked his stick to the right.

The tracers drifted sideways with him, catching the Zero and chewing off its wing. An instant later the crippled fighter disappeared in a blossom of orange flame.

"I'm an ace!" Steven shouted happily, just as his starboard engine coughed and died and his port engine began to sputter. He quickly became preoccupied with his own troubles. The ocean was coming up fast. Steven leveled off, skimming the waves. If he didn't mash down just right, he was going to be a dead ace.

"Sorry we couldn't help you out," Cappy said in a burst of static. "But at the moment we were all a little busy."

"Did you see it?" Steven asked.

"Yeah, I saw both your kills go down. They're confirmed. Congrats, kid. For the second time in your life you've become an ace. But this time it's official. Steady now. Get your nose up. It's almost time for you to mash it."

The spray was glistening on his windscreen as Steven nudged the Lightning's nose up a trifle.

"We got all the other Zeros, so don't worry," he heard Cappy say. "Air rescue is on the way kid, so—" The radio went dead. Shorted out, Steven guessed.

He let the Lightning drop another few feet and then skipped her like a flat stone across the surface of the ocean, finally mashing her down. She was filling up with water as he shoved open his canopy and threw out his life raft. The yellow raft inflated and began bobbing in the white froth.

Steven, crying out in pain, used his arms to hoist himself out of the cockpit. He crumpled onto the Lightning's wing, and then rolled into the water. The cold salty ocean bit into his leg wounds, making him moan, but his life jacket kept his head above water. He used his hands to paddle himself over to the drifting raft and hoisted himself up and in. He lay on his back for a while, eyes closed, trying to regain his strength. He heard gurgling and managed to raise his head in time to see the Lightning slipping smoothly beneath the waves.

He guessed that he was losing a lot of blood, because he was feeling faint. He must have passed out, because the next thing he knew, hands were lifting him up out of the raft.

He opened his eyes. His raft was floating alongside a huge

flying boat. A couple of the airboat's crew were helping him into the rescue craft through the side door.

"Hey, this is a GAT/SB Sea Dragon, isn't it?" he managed to ask as the sailors hauled him aboard.

"It is, mate," one of the sailors replied.

"This is my father's airplane," Steven said proudly.

The two sailors exchanged looks.

"Well, you tell your daddy the Australian Navy will bring it right back to 'im, mate. As soon as you bloody flying blokes don't need it anymore."

Chapter 20

(One)
Gold Household
Bel-Air, California
3 July 1943

Home looked good to Steven Gold as the taxi slowly made its way through the gates. As the cab continued up the drive, Steven noticed that two flagpoles had been erected on the lawn next to the house. On one pole, the stars and stripes waved proudly. On the second pole, the British Union Jack fluttered at half-mast.

Good for you, Pop, for making the gesture, he thought, smiling.

While he'd been convalescing in the hospital he'd received a letter from Suzy telling him that Blaize had been posthumously awarded England's Victoria Cross, and the Distinguished Flying Cross from the United States, "... for extraordinary heroism while participating in aerial flight ..."

He guessed that Blaize would have been proud of those

medals, but that the Union Jack flying over the Gold house would have meant even more to him. He hoped that Blaize got the chance to realize how much a part of the Gold family he'd become, and would always be . . .

The cabbie stopped by the front door, then turned in his seat toward Steven. "You sure you don't need help with that bag, Lieutenant?"

"No, thanks. I can manage," Steven said. "Don't let my cane fool you. I won't be needing it in another week or so."

The Jap bullet that had wounded him had passed through his thigh muscle without hitting bone. He'd spent less than a week in the hospital, and the doctors had assured him that, given a little time, his leg would be as good as ever and he could return to active duty.

Steven opened the cab door, set his bag down on the driveway, and then slid himself out of the cab. He leaned on the cane in his left hand as he dug into his trouser pocket for his money.

"Hey, there's no charge, Lieutenant." The cabby smiled. "A free ride's the least I can do for a wounded airman. You home for long?"

"Three weeks R&R." Steven smiled. "And then I've got a squadron to get back to."

As the cab pulled away the front door opened, and his father and mother came rushing out to greet him.

"Son, welcome home!" His father grinned, giving him a hug. "But I thought you were going to call when you got in? I was going to come pick you up . . ."

"I wanted some time to get used to being back." Steven smiled. He embraced his father. "You look good, Pop. You losing weight?"

"I'm *making* your father lose weight!" his mother said. "Son, you look so handsome in your uniform!" She almost knocked his officer's cap to the ground as she threw her arms around his neck to give him a hug and a kiss.

Suzy appeared in the doorway. In her arms was a bundle swathed in a white blanket. Steven rushed up to his sister to give her a kiss.

"Oh, God, Herman," he heard his mother say. "Do you see that? He's limping—"

"It's nothing, Mom," Steven murmured over his shoulder. "It'll go away." He was shocked at how drawn and tired Suzy looked. At the sadness and pain in her eyes. *She has to be the bravest one of all of us*, Steven thought. *To lose her husband, but still stay strong for the sake of her child*

"Steven, meet your nephew, Robert Blaize Greene." Suzy smiled.

"Oh, Suzy, he's beautiful. And that's a beautiful name."

"I think so." Suzy nodded. "Robert was Blaize's father's name."

"How do you do, little Bob?" Steven asked his nephew. "You and I are going to be great pals. We'll be doing a whole lot of flying together." He glanced up at Suzy. "If it's okay with you?"

Suzy laughed. "It's a little early to strap him into a cockpit, I think, but of course it's okay with me. He's going to be a great flier. Like his father, and his grandfather, and now his uncle. Congratulations, Steven! First Blaize, and now you! It seems we've got nothing but aces in this family."

(Two)

Herman Gold, a drink in his hand, was standing just inside the French doors that led out to the pool. His house was crowded with people who'd come to pay their respects to his son the war hero. The ace.

Erica, drifting past Gold on her way out to the patio, paused to give him a kiss on the cheek. "What did I tell you?" she demanded, gesturing to where Steven, sitting in a chair at poolside, was telling war stories to a rapt audience. "I warned you that one day you'd be reduced to being Steven Gold's father!" she pretended to scold. "Now it's happened!"

"You're always right." Gold smiled. "That's why I love you."

"I think I've given you more reasons to love me than *that*, darling." She laughed, flitting away, as Teddy Quinn came over.

"You look like a happy man, Herman."

Gold smiled. "I am happy, and lucky. I've got a wonderful family. It's what money can't buy. It's what I've always wanted, and despite any stupid mistakes I might have made—"

"You said it, Herm. Not me." Teddy chuckled.

Gold nodded. "I admit it, despite the *very stupid* mistakes I've *definitely* made, my family is still together."

Gold saw Suzy, carrying her son in her arms, come up to Steven.

"Hey, Lieutenant!" she asked. "You want to hold your nephew?"

"Do I?" Steven laughed. "Hand him over."

Teddy, watching, frowned. "I'm just sorry about Blaize," he confided to Gold.

"Yes," Gold said softly. He looked at his daughter. "Thank God Suzy has the baby, or else . . ." He trailed off.

"I know Blaize died a hero," Teddy began. He shook his head. "It just seems like such a waste."

"You're wrong," Gold said, his eyes on the baby. "See there, Teddy? He's left a son."